I0821878

✦ NIGHTINGALE SONGS BOOK THREE ✦

'TIL THE LAST EMBER OF STARLIGHT

by

CHRISTINA MAI FONG

An Imprint of Acorn Publishing

This is a work of fiction. References to real people, events, establishments, organizations, or locales are intended only to provide a sense of authenticity and are used fictitiously. All other characters and all incidents and dialogue are drawn from the author's imagination and are not to be construed as real.

'Til the Last Ember of Starlight

Printed in the United States of America.

For information, address Oak Tree Press, 3943 Irvine Blvd. Ste. 218, Irvine, CA 92602.
An Imprint of Acorn Publishing.

Cover design by Damonza.

Book interior design and digital formatting by Debra Cranfield Kennedy.

ISBN—979-8-88528-085-3 (hardcover)
ISBN—979-8-88528-084-6 (paperback)

AUTHOR'S NOTE

I know maybe not everyone has had the same experiences as me, but the following note comes from observations I've made in my life. Take them as you will.

There are a lot of things I love about my culture. The food, dramas, fashion, history, etc. After all, the stories I write are heavily influenced by all of this. That being said, as with all cultures and belief systems, while there are pros, there are also cons.

Filial piety comes to mind. Respecting one's parents is a positive value. I think it's a great thing to be close with your family, and you should be respectful and show gratitude for the sacrifices your parents/the people who raised you made. But extreme filial piety can become a problem when you blindly obey at the expense of your own personal freedom and happiness. Like when they tell you to become a doctor, not an artist. When they tell you where you should live, how you should live, what you should wear, and what you should be. When they make you feel obligated to never leave them or guilt you into doing as they say, their excuse being that they raised you, and therefore they get to control your life. And in an effort to please them, you silence your own voice.

Another cultural belief is that we should just keep our heads down and not rock the boat, stay in our safe jobs and not follow our dreams, keep silent even when we're facing some kind of injustice. Rilla's mama had this belief, and it's sad that she died not using her tin-chai to help more people in her world. These self-limiting beliefs are what cause us to lose our voice and to never use the tin-chai that Old Grandfather Heaven gave us.

I feel the need to bring this up not because I'm trying to attack anyone personally, but because the pen is my personal scepter. Words are my superpower, my tin-chai. I hope to create helpful dialogue through my writing that might challenge some of the unhealthy ideas we grew up believing and inspire us to grow into healthier people. Because by doing so, maybe I can help some people reclaim the power in their voice.

And so, throughout the Nightingale Songs trilogy, it should come as no surprise that the recurring theme has been finding your voice. In *Under the Lavender Moon*, Rilla discovered the power in her voice, despite growing up with her mama's voice in her mind telling her it was too dangerous to use it. *Ballads of Shadow and Light* had Rilla overcoming her self-doubt and self-sabotage that threatened to stifle her voice. And in *'Til the Last Ember of Starlight*, both Aiden and Rilla needed to reclaim the voices they lost due to being drowned out by louder voices surrounding them.

In *Last Ember*, Rilla had to relearn the power of her voice when the battles got tougher and she didn't have Aiden to lean on for emotional support as she had for the first two books. For Aiden, on the other hand, I realized despite all his wittiness, he never seemed to have found his own voice, having had others tell him what to do his whole life. First, as a child with his parents, who did everything for him, then in the shadows as Carrick's bodyguard, unable to speak for himself, and finally back with his parents, who still spoke for him, despite him being a grown man. Even Rilla told him what to do as she was the planner, and he just went along for the ride. In writing Aiden's character development, I thought about the times we can lose our voice in relationships. With friends, co-workers, family, romantic partners.

Throughout writing this series, life imitates art imitates life. Book 3 was the hardest of the bunch to write. I was going through some tough times filled with grief, and as a result of this dark period, I'd lost the voice I thought I'd found in Book 1. But through the fog, I picked up my pen and I wrote, inserting my experiences and feelings into the lives of my characters. It was here that I was able to fall in love with writing again and learn how to sing again.

And so, with whatever power I have in these words I write, I want to encourage everyone else out there who feels like they've lost their voice. We all have people in our lives who try to stifle us. From well-meaning parents who never want to see us hurt or fail so they speak on our behalf and never let us make our own decisions (my friend calls them lawnmower parents, always clearing the way for their children, including all potential hardships), to the narcissistic boss who only knows how to criticize you but never gives any praise, to the friend who gives unsolicited advice on how to live your life and why everything you do is wrong in order to make him/her/themselves feel better. It's not your fault that your voice was drowned out by these louder voices. However, it's your responsibility to reclaim your voice and to use the tin-chai you have. It's your choice whether or not you become the hero/heroine and live out your purpose or simply remain the victim, blaming everyone around you for your circumstances and making excuses for why you can't take charge of your own story.

I may or may never become a best-selling author or a world-renowned person of the year on the cover of Time Magazine, but I will always still have a voice. I will always choose to use my voice to encourage each and every one of you to use your tin-chai. Because you never know who you might help heal by doing so. And at the end of the day, we all learn from each other.

Much love,

Christina Mai Fong

For Nate. I pray you'll find the courage to step out of the shadows and into the light so you can show the world your tin-chai and be a reflection of your name, a God-given gift to those around you. May Old Grandfather Heaven grant you the faith to choose to create your own happiness, the strength to find and use your own voice, and the desire to answer the call to living out your true passion and purpose. I believe in you. 'Til the last ember of starlight . . .

✦ ✦ ✦

✦ ✦ ✦

'TIL THE LAST EMBER OF STARLIGHT

✦ ✦ ✦

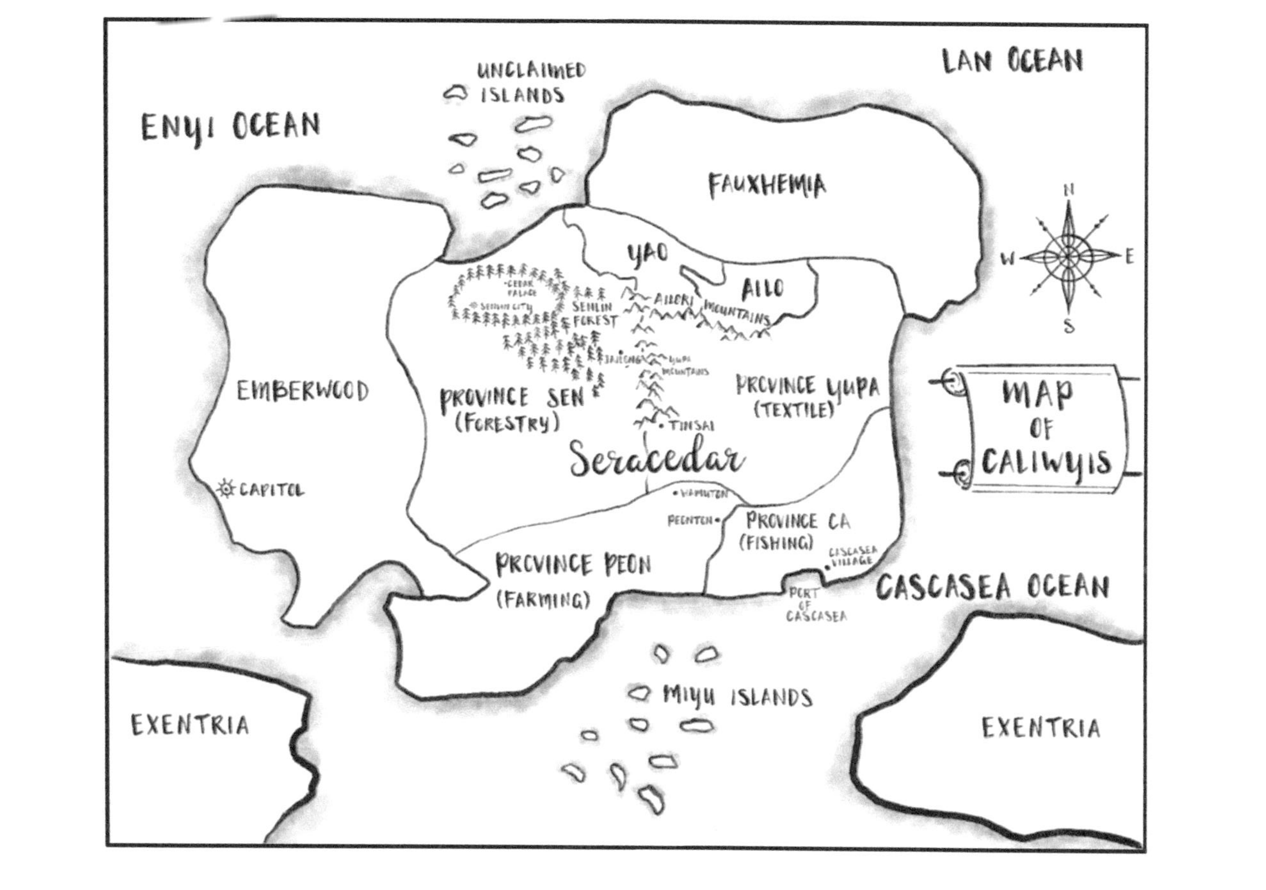

LAN OCEAN
UNCLAIMED ISLANDS
ENYI OCEAN
FAUXHEMIA
N
W
E
S
YAO
AILO
CEDAR PALACE
SENLIN FOREST
AILORI MOUNTAINS
EMBERWOOD
PROVINCE SEN
(FORESTRY)
PROVINCE YUPA
(TEXTILE)
MAP OF CALIWYIS
TINSAI
Seracedar
CAPITOL
PEENTON
PROVINCE CA
(FISHING)
CASCASEA VILLAGE
PROVINCE PEON
(FARMING)
CASCASEA OCEAN
PORT OF CASCASEA
MIYU ISLANDS
EXENTRIA
EXENTRIA

CHAPTER 1

✦ ✦ ✦ ✦ ✦ ✦ ✦ ✦ ✦ ✦

Across the courtyard from where I sat reading, the ivory birdcage hung on the bough of a newly planted cherry tree. I couldn't stop looking over at it. The pink clusters bloomed like fireworks around the cage. Its metal bars glinted under the light of the Lavender Moon that streamed through the glass windows of Linlang Palace and reflected off the frozen lake that ran throughout Water Crystal Courtyard.

Deciding to take a break from reading the three-hundred-page book, *Helping the Grieved and Distressed: A Guide to Counseling*, I set it down on the table. Then I walked across the courtyard to the birdcage. I watched the songbird inside. She'd been a gift from a distant relative for my upcoming marriage to Aiden. She hadn't sung a single tune since arriving here. It made me sad to think she might have lost her voice.

She gazed back at me, her expression wistful. Then she turned her head toward the window, looking longingly at the stars of the night sky. I took the cage off its perch and walked to an open window. Then I opened its door. "Goodbye, little songbird. Go live your life the way you wish. I hope you find your voice again."

I could have sworn she smiled at me. Then she flew out of the cage and soared outside the window. She finally whistled a beautiful song, flying higher until she disappeared among the stars.

"I hope my second cousin twice removed doesn't ask how the bird is doing." The voice of my future husband startled me. I whirled around. Aiden was so silent and light-footed, I hadn't heard him approach.

I winced. I should have thought about that earlier. "Do you think she'll be terribly offended? I can't stand seeing any animal in a cage."

Aiden gave me a reassuring glance. "Don't worry, that relative lives on the other side of the kingdom and can't come to the wedding. I doubt we'll see her anytime soon. And if she does ask, I'll say the bird was so smart, it figured out how to pick the lock."

"Can we also get rid of the cherry tree?" I wrinkled my nose. "I'm sorry. I know the gardener just planted it, but I can't stand the smell."

"Done," he said. "I'll have someone remove it tomorrow. It must have also been a wedding gift."

I stifled a yawn and stretched. "What time is it?"

"Almost midnight," Aiden said.

"That late already? Have you been working up until now?"

"Not sure it can be called work, but I've been sitting in on discussions between my father, Welder, and the royal council."

I worried my bottom lip. "Any word of activity from Seracedar?"

A dark look crossed his face, and I knew where his thoughts had strayed.

"So far, still no. Everything has been quiet. Too quiet. Welder wants us to attack first, but my father and I agree that unless we're provoked, we should try to maintain the peace for as long as possible."

"Carrick must have heard by now that our wedding ceremony is next week," I said. My stomach lurched with anxiety. "What if that's the day he starts an attack?"

"Let me worry about that. Besides, there's no reason to think he will. All our spies have been on the lookout, and Carrick hasn't made any moves since we left his borders. In fact, he—" Another dark look slipped on his face before he masked it. "Never mind him now. I don't want to talk about Carrick or any politics at all. I've already spent the whole day doing that."

Aiden's humorless tone was so unlike the man I had known during our journey from Cedar Palace to Emberwood. In fact, ever since we had returned to Emberwood from our last meeting with Carrick, I'd sensed this dark change in Aiden's mood. I didn't like it, but every time I tried to ask what was bothering him, he didn't want to talk about it.

"All right," I said. "I should be going to bed soon."

"I'll walk you back to your room." He took my hand, and I let him lead me across the courtyard. The eternally frozen lake beneath our feet sparkled under the moonlight. Under the water, koi fish swam in circles.

"How's work?" Aiden asked. It was obvious he was trying to lighten his tone by switching topics, so we wouldn't end the day on a dark note. "It's almost been a month at the clinic now."

"I love it," I said. "Doctor Flamyor is a great teacher, and I've been able to help so many patients."

Aiden grinned. "I'm excited for you. Your dream is finally coming true."

"I hope Doctor Flamyor actually wants me there and isn't just putting up with me because of my connection to you."

"No, of course not. I mean, I'm sure it had something to do with your connection to me, but it's not the only reason. She really did need an apprentice, and what doctor wouldn't feel lucky to have you by her side? Bet her job got a lot easier. Why use traditional treatments that take way longer to heal patients when you can sing their ailments away within seconds?"

I frowned. "But I can't heal everything. Missing limbs, for example. I can't recreate what's already gone. And there are other scars that aren't physical. Ailments of the mind and spirit. My tin-chai can't heal those. I'm ready to learn more, and I've been reading so many books on mind healing. I want to extend my healing abilities beyond treating common colds and bone fractures and be able to care for people whom my tin-chai can't help."

"Give it time," Aiden said. "You've only just started working there."

We reached the door of my bedroom. I slid open the door and stepped in, then turned, giving him a pout. "Can't you spend the night? We used to sleep next to each other all the time during our travels. I miss it."

"No. I told you before, we can't here. The servants might see and talk, and then my parents will find out."

"So what if they do?" I said. "Our relationship is our business. Besides, we're getting married next week."

"And after we get married, I promise to spend all my nights with you," he said. "Besides, you need to sleep, so you can focus on your work tomorrow. And my parents want to talk to me before I go to bed."

"Again? It's so late already," I said.

"I know. They have private thoughts they wish to share with me regarding something I said today. Then my ah-fu will probably make me do more research on our defense before our meeting with Welder in the morning."

"It seems like your parents have been scheduling these private meetings with you ever since we returned from Seracedar. Can't you tell them you're tired, or that you're spending time with me?"

"They'll just complain that I don't spend enough time with them and prefer your company over theirs."

"It's not a competition," I said. Although recently it felt like I *was* their rival for Aiden's time and attention. There was rarely a time that I could have Aiden alone to myself without an interruption asking Aiden to join them or help them with something.

"I can't refuse them. They're my parents. I've made them go through hell during my ten years away from home. I already feel like the worst son for that."

He sounded so stressed again. I didn't want to say anything rude, but I'd noticed he seemed less like the lighthearted Aiden I knew and more like this anxious stranger whenever he had these meetings with King Ashbel and Queen Leonora. I wondered what they were telling him. And also, why didn't they ever include me? They had always been nice to me, but I wondered if they still regarded me as an outsider.

I frowned. "If there's something bothering you, you know you can tell me about it. If your parents are giving you a hard time or guilting you into doing things you don't want—"

"Why would you say that?" A defensive look rose on his face. "They aren't making me do anything. They're nice people. They've shown you nothing but kindness, haven't they? Besides, parents have a right to tell children their expectations."

I sniffed, feeling hurt. "All right, sorry. They have been kind to me. I didn't mean to offend."

Aiden's gaze softened. "No, I'm sorry. I didn't mean to lash out. I don't know what's wrong with me lately. I don't feel like myself. I feel like I can't do anything right. These meetings with Welder and the royal council are stressful."

"You've been having meetings from dawn to dusk," I said. "It's bound to be stressful. If the situation between Seracedar and Emberwood has gotten worse, I want to know. I want to help."

"I promise Seracedar hasn't started anything yet. Even if they had, it would be impossible to keep it a secret from you or anyone else. But I do have work. I need to be prepared to address Welder and the council, or my ah-fu will think I have nothing useful to say."

"Are you sure you don't want me at these meetings? After all, the Sacred Cedar Scepter chose me, too. You shouldn't have to bear the responsibility alone."

"We all need to live as normally as we can for the time being, and for you, that means following your dream and focusing on your apprenticeship with Doctor Flamyor." He gave me a quick peck on the cheek. "I'll see you tomorrow. Good night."

I watched him leave. Between the upcoming wedding, the situation between Emberwood and Seracedar, and parental expectations, I knew Aiden wasn't coping well. Part of it was his need to please his parents.

I knew he felt guilty about disappearing on them for all those years. I still didn't know the real reason why he hadn't returned home when he could have. There was the reason he gave, which was that he wanted to support Carrick's cause and felt like he could help Emberwood better from the shadows. But something told me that wasn't the full story.

Besides that, I didn't believe that everything was as peaceful as he wanted me to think. There had been so many meetings with the royal advisors and Welder lately, discussing how Emberwood should deal with Carrick and Seracedar. No one outside of them, us, and Queen Leonora knew yet that the Sacred Cedar Scepter had amplified both Aiden's and my tin-chai, and therefore, given us the Will of Heaven. But we planned to reveal this to the kingdom and the rest of the world on our wedding day.

Which also meant we'd have to expose Carrick's lies and declare that we were the rightful rulers of Seracedar. I had a feeling that would not go over well with Carrick or his subjects.

Tensions were only rising between Seracedar and Emberwood, as well as internally between Welder and King Ashbel. Welder wanted us to instigate war on Carrick first. Force him to abdicate. But King Ashbel was of a different mind. There was no news of Seracedar acting aggressively toward Emberwood, and therefore, no reason to go to war. The king wanted to maintain peace for as long as possible, and he still had the hope that if we spoke to Carrick privately, we could all come to a resolution without resorting to violence. To Welder's horror, Ashbel had written to Carrick, asking him to concede before Aiden and I married. Ashbel told Carrick if he had any decency left in him, he'd leave Aiden alone after all the years Aiden had devoted to being Carrick's bodyguard, unable to return home to his grieving parents. Ashbel had asked Carrick how he'd feel if his daughter had been lost to him for a decade. The king truly believed he could guilt Carrick into surrendering.

Being in the middle of Welder and King Ashbel's arguments probably only added to Aiden's stress and anxiety. Though Aiden had never said so, I imagined even if he disagreed with some of his father's actions, he couldn't openly say this.

I'd gone to the meetings at first and sat with the royal council, but Welder and King Ashbel did most of the talking. The rest of the council interjected once or twice, with the majority remaining loyal to the king. This didn't stop Welder from speaking his mind.

After listening to Welder and King Ashbel argue with no resolution after hours of talking, I didn't care to listen to them anymore. I asked if I could stop attending, and Aiden agreed. He said he would make sure I was involved in important decisions, but unless something significant occurred, he'd just give me a summary of anything I missed.

"Why waste time listening to two old men argue when you could be working toward your dream of becoming a healer?" he'd said. "Eventually, you'll have to be involved since we both have the Sacred Cedar Scepter, but for now, there's no need."

Aiden was such a sweet man. He knew I would rather spend my time at the clinic and stay out of politics completely if I could have my way. It had been easy this past month to get used to this new life, where everything felt at peace for the first time. I could go to work and do what I loved, and nobody tried to stop me. My time in Cedar Palace and my adventures with Aiden seemed like they had happened in a past life. Sometimes I even forgot that the scepter was in my possession, still disguised as a pan flute until we were ready to reveal it to the public.

But I didn't know how long I could continue living this simple life. As much as King Ashbel wanted to maintain peace, Carrick wasn't likely to let his throne go without a fight. He wouldn't forgive Aiden and me so easily for what he believed was our betrayal.

And with the Sacred Cedar Scepter in my hands, Aiden was right that I wouldn't be able to stay out of politics forever. Old Grandfather Heaven had chosen both Aiden and me to lead the Shyan, and that meant uniting Emberwood and Seracedar. No, I wouldn't be able to ignore Old Grandfather Heaven's call for much longer.

CHAPTER 2

✦ ✦ ✦ ✦ ✦ ✦ ✦ ✦ ✦ ✦

Early the next morning, I took a short five-minute coach ride a mile down a winding street from Linlang Palace to Linlang Clinic of Healing. Doctor Flamyor was the head doctor at the clinic, and I'd been shadowing her. I admired the woman, who held so much knowledge despite not having a magical tin-chai. Doctor Flamyor had suggested that I apply to university to study medicine, but there was so much uncertainty lately. Aiden and I were about to be married, and not only were we trying to juggle our new responsibilities, but the possibility of war also made it difficult to plan anything. I couldn't think of furthering my education at a time like this.

Still, I could dream. It was enough knowing that it had become an achievable goal to attend university when the very notion had been inconceivable back in my hometown village.

I walked into Doctor Flamyor's office. She was busy writing something in a file but looked up at me.

"Always right on time," she said. "How would you like a different assignment today? Instead of shadowing me, I'd like to introduce you to Counselor Eliza Ponch, who works with female survivors of abuse and trauma."

Adrenaline shot into my veins, taking away any lingering sleepiness from waking up so early in the morning.

She smiled. "I know you've mentioned wanting to heal more than just physical ailments. Many of the patients in Counselor Ponch's group are fugitives from Cedar Palace and from the tribute nations, Ailo and Yao. A few are former baubles and novelties from the previous two Seracedarean emperors. Given your own past in Cedar Palace and with Terran, I think you'd have the empathy needed to be a good counselor. I've already told Counselor Ponch about you, and she agrees with me. What do you think?"

"I'd like to try it," I said.

"Good. Then follow me."

She took me down a corridor, and we went outside the building. I followed her down a garden path to another building with windows on every side.

Within the glass building was a garden of stone sculptures. The ground, consisting of evenly-raked pebbles, made a shuffling sound with each step I took. On one side of the garden was a stone archway that separated the sculptures from an open courtyard, where a group of fifteen or so women practiced martial arts movements in unison. Behind the courtyard was a corridor that led to another building.

"That building is the residence hall where the patients live," Doctor Flamyor said.

We came closer to the group of women in the courtyard but remained at a distance so as not to interrupt the martial arts session.

A woman stood pacing at the forefront of the group. She wore black slacks and a buttoned-up coat. Her hair was tied in a loose, messy bun.

"That is Counselor Eliza Ponch, but we all call her Ponch," Doctor Flamyor said. "She has a rather remarkable story. She's from Seracedar. Her family was poor, so they sold her to become an aristocrat's faela. Unfortunately, the man and his wife were cruel, but she managed to run away to Emberwood, where she trained to be a soldier in the king's army. She was named the best fighter, known for her abilities in hand-to-hand combat."

We watched as Ponch yelled commands, and the group of women answered back as they practiced punches and kicks.

"Woo! Hah!"

"Louder," the leader shouted. "Let out all your emotions. Don't hold back."

"Hah! Woo! Huh!"

Doctor Flamyor continued. "After becoming a lieutenant, she felt called to become a counselor here, so she went to university and graduated at the top of her class. She now helps women like her, who experienced abuse and trauma. But I should let her tell you more about what she does."

Ponch saw us watching. Without missing a beat, she commanded the group. "Counselor Trine, take the lead. I need to speak to Doctor Flamyor, but that doesn't mean any of you get to stop yet."

Another woman ran to the front and continued leading the group. Ponch strode toward us.

"Ponch," Doctor Flamyor said. "I didn't mean to interrupt your session, but I wanted to introduce you to Rilla. As I told you, she'll be working with you three days a week."

Ponch beamed at me. "It's such an honor to meet you, Miss Rilla. I've heard the stories of what you and Prince Langdon faced in Seracedar. How you defeated Terran and rid the world of the cruelest dictator in history. I've been dying to meet you."

"The honor is all mine," I said. "Doctor Flamyor told me your story, and it sounds far more inspirational than mine."

"Every story is powerful and can be used to inspire others," she said. "I'm excited that you're here."

"I'll leave Rilla in your hands," Doctor Flamyor said. "I should be getting back to my patients." She took her leave.

I gestured across the pathway to the stone courtyard, where the group of women still practiced punches and kicks. "Are those all patients?"

"A mix of patients and former patients training to become counselors," Ponch said.

"Former patients? They're all trauma survivors?"

Ponch smiled. "You sound surprised."

"They all look so strong and lively," I said. "Like they're warriors."

The counselor's gaze returned to the group of women in the distance. She watched them practicing their moves, and a look of pride crossed her face. "We *are* warriors. Some of us may have been baubles or novelties in the past. Others among us were beaten by our husbands or whipped by our mistresses. But we survived, and our trauma no longer defines us. That's why we choose to train and become stronger. We will never feel helpless again, and we can help others who face similar stories. Those who train with me are further along in their healing journey. There are many others who aren't at this stage yet."

I thought back to the baubles in cages back at Cedar Palace. Some of them had killed themselves. "I mean no offense when I say this, but I never thought it was possible. I knew a faela back at Cedar Palace who experienced such trauma that she couldn't even get out of bed most days. And another friend of mine tried to kill herself after she was rescued from her bauble cage. I wish they would have had the opportunity to come here. Maybe then they could heal."

Ponch's gaze swung from the women back to me. "I've had patients who escaped from Seracedar. Others suffered abuse from their own families. So many different stories, and everyone has a different healing journey."

The women had stopped training and were now in a circle, seated cross-legged as a counselor led them in meditation.

"Training in martial arts is a part of our trauma recovery program," Ponch continued to explain. "So is meditation. We encourage those who feel ready to join us, but we never force anyone. Some patients can't leave their rooms yet. Others need to talk out their experiences. And there are those who can't talk about anything yet. Even those who begin training with us have different reactions. Some cry. Some get angry. We allow them to have their feelings. We try to make everyone know they are in a safe place here and monitor them to make sure they don't inflict self-harm. Our goal is to help each individual reach the point where they can build a new life, a new identity."

She gestured for me to come with her. "I'll introduce you."

We walked across the way into the courtyard. As we approached the group, the women lifted their heads and opened their eyes, a signal that the meditation session was at its end.

Ponch cleared her throat, drawing the attention of the women. "I have someone I'd like you all to meet. I'm sure you all know her name by now. This is Miss Rilla Marseas, future consort to His Majesty, Prince Langdon. She is working at our clinic as a fellow healer."

"I'm glad to be here learning from all of you," I said.

"Very good," Ponch said. "Now is time for sharing. Everyone has a chance to speak whatever is on their mind or heart. Any anxieties or concerns they have. You can also tell your story if you wish, so Miss Rilla can get to know you."

Seconds passed, but no one spoke. Some of the women glanced at me, and I saw a glimmer of uncertainty in their faces.

Was it because of who I was?

"May I say something?" I said. "My role here is a healer in training, not future consort or any high title. Please don't give me any special treatment. You don't have to call me Miss Rilla. It's just Rilla. I want to learn how to be a counselor so I can help patients suffering from illnesses that I can't heal with my tin-chai. Illnesses of the mind like what I watched some of my friends suffer back at Cedar Palace. That's why I want to know how you were able to overcome your past experiences. I promise whatever is said or happens here will not leave the clinic. Don't feel the need to refrain from speaking your mind."

The other counselor who had taken over for Ponch addressed me. "Thank you, *Rilla*. I can share first. I'm Counselor Trine. Everyone here has heard about your incredible tin-chai and how you fought to bring down Terran and Limera. Personally, I'm inspired by your story, so I'd like to share mine with you, too. I am from Yao Kingdom. I escaped to Emberwood after witnessing my whole family get murdered by Terran's soldiers for refusing to send him tribute. I became a patient here four years ago to overcome the nightmares and depression that resulted. I still have days when the grief feels unbearable, but these women here have been my support. I wouldn't be here today if not for them, and that's why I became a counselor."

The group applauded her. In unison, they said, "We hear your story, and you are seen. May you continue to heal."

A middle-aged woman raised her hand. She had several scars on her face. But one of them, I realized, was a brand like my scar. The cursed number four.

"My name is Felicity. I was a faela to Emperor Yikan. Like you, Rilla, I have a unique voice and was chosen for my tin-chai to cause pain or pleasure whenever I sang. But my time at the palace brought me nothing but suffering. When Yikan died, all his faela were supposed to commit suicide and be buried with him. When we refused, Terran gave us another option. To be branded, then cast out on the street with nothing to our name. I took that option." She stared me in the eye and smiled. "I see we wear similar battle scars, little sister."

Another woman in her mid-twenties spoke up. "Name's Jun. Terran was a rotten piece of shit. Kept me as an assassin. I can turn invisible, which made it easy. I hated doing his dirty work, but my sister served a faela. They'd have her killed if I didn't obey." Her hands were clenched into fists, so tight her knuckles were white. "My sister killed herself to save me. I escaped after that. For the longest time, I couldn't hold a sword or any blade without shaking or passing out. Then I joined a group of lotuses who worked for Haming. I know you've got a history with that dead fool. But I don't give a shit if you judge me."

She flashed me a defiant look as though challenging me to say something against her choice.

I simply nodded. "Go on."

"Haming taught me to be strong again. To fight again. I wasn't afraid to kill again. But this time, I killed little shits like Nelan. Abusers, rapists, you name it. Once I realized Haming was a fraud, I came to Emberwood. Had a friend in this recovery program." She pointed at the woman next to her. "If not for Venn, I wouldn't have stayed in this stupid place for so long. I'd rather be out killing more bastards, but I've got no money and there's free food and lodging here." She gave me another challenging look. "So if you're here thinking you can heal me with your stupid songs and useless words, don't bother. You should go back to the palace and marry your pretty boy prince. You don't know half of what most of us have been through."

Her friend, Venn, slapped her shoulder. "Don't be rude."

"It's fine," I said. I thought back to the counseling books I'd been reading, and I tried to choose my words carefully. "Jun is entitled to her feelings about me, and she's right. I don't know what most of you have been through. I'm here to learn so I can be a counselor."

"So we've become your project now?" Jun crossed her arms and glared. "Using us to learn how to become a counselor just to accomplish your goals and dreams. Will it make you feel better about yourself?"

"Th-that's not what I meant," I stumbled. "I just—uhm . . ."

Reading the books in theory was much easier than practicing what I'd learned in person.

Thankfully, Ponch came to my rescue. "We're all here to learn from each other. Thank you, Jun, for sharing your personal story and your feelings. Rilla is a new counselor, so it's all right if you don't trust her today. Trust has to be earned."

"Yes," I echoed. "Thank you, Jun, for sharing. I hope we can talk more again if you decide I am trustworthy enough."

Jun sniffed. "We'll see."

Some of the other women opened up. I learned about two Fauxhemian women, Wray and Nena. Their blood gave them supernatural abilities like being able to communicate with nature or the dead. They had been used and abused for their blood by their own families and eventually ran away. Then there were the Shyan women, Venn, Yin, and Lina, each with strong tin-chai. Venn, who had been a serving trifle to a cruel faela, could transform a person's appearance into someone else entirely. Yin had been a caged novelty with the tin-chai to form electric sparks in her hands. And Lina, who had also been a novelty, could amplify sound to an earth-shattering degree. All three Shyan women had been freed after Carrick's ascent to the throne, and they had come to Emberwood to find a new life and to train to become warriors.

There were others, too. I could sense their strong wyis, but they were quiet and didn't volunteer to share their stories. Maybe one day they would.

Ponch cleared her throat. "Does anyone else want to share?"

There was a moment of silence.

Ponch's ears twitched. "Oh, wait. Someone's about to join us."

Seconds later, I heard footsteps approach behind me. Ponch had very good hearing.

I turned. A young lady was walking down the corridor from the residence hall.

Her familiar face had me doing a double take. It was Galai, my childhood friend, who had grown up with me in Cascasea Village, and who had been taken to Cedar Palace with me.

CHAPTER 3

✦ ✦ ✦ ✦ ✦ ✦ ✦ ✦ ✦ ✦

"Sorry I'm so late," Galai said. "May I still join?"

"Of course," Ponch said.

Galai stepped forward, and her gaze fell upon mine. She stopped, a look of surprise on her face. Back in Cascasea, we'd been good friends until Irica, my neighbor who hated me, pressured Galai to choose her over me. Though we hadn't been as close after that, we'd still enjoyed an amicable relationship, and Galai had talked to me in secret when she thought Irica wasn't looking.

My eyes teared up to see her. She was a reminder of home, and I never thought I'd see her again after escaping from Cedar Palace.

Ponch saw our eyes connect. "Do you know one another?"

Galai's eyes were shadowed and sadder than I remembered. "Yes. Rilla and I are from the same village."

"Oh. Then I'm sure the two of you want to catch up," Ponch said. "We're about done here, but I'd like to make sure everyone has had a chance to talk. Any other concerns or comments?"

A few other women spoke about some of their struggles recently. I forced myself to remain attentive. But all I wanted was to talk to Galai. That was, if she wanted to talk to me. Who knew what she had gone through and if she would want to confide in me at all? I might be too closely associated with some of her bad memories.

"All right, that's the end of sharing time for today," Ponch said. "We'll have an hour of free time before lunch."

Ponch came up to me. "I should have realized sooner that you and Galai were sent to Cedar Palace for the same showcase. Galai came here two months ago with another girl from the palace. Galai hasn't talked much to anyone, and the other girl hasn't even left her room. We haven't forced either of them to do anything they aren't ready for, but it's a big step for Galai to join us. Maybe she'll open up to you. I'll give you some privacy to reconnect."

She touched my shoulder briefly before walking away with the other ladies.

Two months. Where had she been before then? It had been four months since Carrick had become emperor and ordered all novelties and baubles to be free, and for Terran's faela to be given the choice of leaving the palace. Why hadn't Galai gone home to Cascasea Village?

Galai came up to me. "Hi Rilla. I've been keeping up with your whereabouts, so I know you're about to marry the crown prince. I didn't expect you to be here, though. It's kind of a nice surprise to see you." A smile flickered on her face.

We sat in a private corner of the garden on a stone bench. I stayed quiet, unsure how to proceed. Galai and I had always been friendly, but I had so many questions and wasn't sure what to ask first.

She gazed up at the trees. "I'm glad these aren't cherry trees."

"Yes, me too." I paused again, then asked, "What happened these past few months? How did you end up here? That is to say, I don't want to pry if it's difficult to talk about, but—"

Galai interrupted me. "Look, it's not as gruesome a story as you think. There's no need to pity me. I'm comfortable sharing. After Terran died, I became Nelan's novelty. He said I had to use my tin-chai to entertain him. Fortunately, I only had to spend one night in his bed, and he lost interest in me and my tin-chai."

"That's a lot to endure," I said. "I'm sorry that happened."

She shrugged. "Not as bad as what other women have been through. I've got no reason to complain. I just sat in that cage until he died, and Carrick became emperor and freed us all. I wanted to return home, but when I wrote to my family, I received a letter from the chief magistrate. My parents were killed days before Carrick granted my freedom. Pirates."

"I'm so sorry, Galai," I said.

"Yes, they pillaged several houses in the village. Killed Irica's baba, too."

"That's awful." I couldn't help but feel relieved that my brother and his family had moved to Fauxhemia. They might have been killed as well.

"There was nothing left for me, but the empress knew I was from your village."

"Empress? You mean, Radi." I still had yet to think of her as the empress, a role that had previously been filled by cruel Limera, who hated us all.

"Yes, Empress Radi," Galai said. "She said I could stay at the palace and serve as a trifle. But then I—" She paused and looked away. "I changed my mind soon after, and I decided to come to Emberwood. My companion and I met a doctor who told us about this clinic. And now here we are."

Galai rushed through the last part. Something told me that wasn't the whole story. Why would she come to Emberwood? Where had she gotten the money to book a passage here? Besides that, as children, we'd been taught that Emberwood was the enemy. Galai wouldn't have known otherwise unless someone had told her to come here.

"Did Radi treat you poorly?" My hands clenched at the thought that my friend could have become like Limera.

"No, no," Galai said quickly. "She was very kind. I wasn't even her trifle. I attended an Ailo princess who was to become Carrick's faela."

Faela? Carrick was already accumulating a harem. I wondered how

Radi felt about this. Not that she'd have any say in it. Carrick must want to solidify a political alliance with the Ailo.

Galai sniffled. "It wasn't anything the empress or my mistress did. It was—" A tear rolled down her cheek.

"You don't have to tell me anything further if you're not comfortable."

"I want to tell you, but I don't want to cause more antagonism. I've heard the rumors. How Seracedar and Emberwood are on the brink of war. Emberwood has become my sanctuary. I'm afraid."

"Emberwood is strong. We won't let Seracedar defeat us."

She paused, then sighed. "The servants gossip. They say Carrick gets drunk every night. He hasn't done anything to improve the kingdom, and the noblemen and androgies grumble about how they can't believe he was given the Will of Heaven."

She looked down. "Also . . . he didn't free all the novelties. I stumbled across some cages."

My stomach lurched. "What?" I shook my head in disbelief. "Has he gone mad? What happened after you found those poor girls?"

"I went to tell Radi and my mistress." She swallowed as though struggling to speak the words out loud. "But Carrick found me first. He was drunk."

She blinked quickly, trying to stop herself from crying. She stood from the bench and focused her gaze on the trees. "Maybe it was because we have a similar complexion and high cheekbones. And I have lost weight since the showcase. But Carrick mistook me for you. He overpowered me. The next morning, I told Radi what happened. She said she believed me, but she still had to send me away. Carrick found me desirable, and if I stayed, I'd become her competition. She was already angry that he had taken the Ailo princess as a faela. She put me on a carriage to the Emberwood border, along with . . . with another girl."

"Who is the other girl?"

"Her name is Miah. She's . . . I think she used to be a novelty. I'm not sure. We haven't really talked. Anyway, enough about her." A slight tremor came into her voice. I could tell she didn't want to talk about the other girl, so I didn't push.

"And what happened when you came here?" I asked.

"We both got sick. Miah fainted, and I found a doctor. Luckily, she knew of this clinic and told us we would find shelter here. We probably would have died if we hadn't come here."

"I'm so sorry, Galai," I said.

"Don't feel sorry for me," she said. "Feel sorry for those girls. Carrick abducted them from their homes. What if he starts a war with Emberwood and wins? What if he cages us all?"

I shook my head. "That won't happen."

"How do you know?"

I wished I could tell her that Aiden and I had received the Will of Heaven. It might offer her some comfort to know Old Grandfather Heaven was on our side. Even so, I had to remind myself that even with the scepter, there was no guarantee that we would triumph. If we couldn't prove ourselves to be worthy leaders or allowed the power to go to our heads, Old Grandfather Heaven could still take the scepter away. Let someone steal it from us.

Galai finally began to weep, unable to stop the tears from streaming down her face. "I don't want Carrick to win. I don't want to lose my freedom again."

I reached out, offering a hug, which she took.

Uncontrollable sobs shook her whole body. "My life has been filled with one tragedy after another. Will I ever feel peace again? What if I never find happiness?"

I had no answer for her. All I could do was continue embracing her and let her cry on my shoulder.

CHAPTER 4

✦ ✦ ✦ ✦ ✦ ✦ ✦ ✦ ✦ ✦

I marched to the meeting room on the Gold Song Courtyard level of the palace, where I knew Aiden was meeting with the royal advisory council, Ashbel, and Welder. Several royal advisors filed out of the room. Among them were a few middle-aged men I recognized. Captain Kang, Lord Pan, and Colonel Beyling, a highly decorated commander, second only to Welder. They acknowledged me with a nod but didn't stop, seeming to be in a hurry to get somewhere.

But behind them was a friendly nobleman, Lord Tu, who saw me and smiled.

He bowed. "Ah, Miss Rilla."

"Lord Tu," I said, bowing back. "Is the meeting over?"

The lord looked back into the room. "Well, it is for the advisors. We're all eager for a meal break after a long morning. But Welder and the king are still having a discussion. The crown prince is with them. If I were you, I wouldn't go in. They're bound to be in there for another hour, and it would only bore you."

"Thanks for the warning," I said. "But I have something to tell them that can't wait."

"Then I wish you luck." He bowed again and walked away.

As I walked into the room, I heard Welder's frustrated voice arguing with King Ashbel, who couldn't keep the heat out of his tone either.

I saw them standing on one side of the long meeting table. Welder and Ashbel glared at one another. Aiden stood between the two of them, not saying anything but looking uncomfortable. No one had noticed me yet.

"I don't understand your reasoning," Welder said. "It's the perfect time to strike."

"Seracedar hasn't provoked us yet," Ashbel said. "There's still a chance war can be avoided. We have one week before the wedding, and I gave Carrick until that day to agree to my terms of peace."

"You're kidding yourself if you think he'll concede. No man would be willing to give up his power."

Ashbel's voice rose another notch. "Don't speak to me as though I'm an idiot. I told Carrick we have no desire to take him off the throne. He can continue being emperor. All I want is for him to become a better ruler and stop antagonizing my son."

Aiden shifted on his feet, then looked up and finally saw me. "Rilla, what are you doing here?"

"I think it's about time I join one of your meetings," I said.

"There's no need for that," Ashbel said. "Nothing a young girl like you can do. It's my job to protect you and my son by stopping this war from happening, and that's what I intend to do."

"Actually, I want Rilla to be here," Welder said. "Aiden said you were too busy, and His Majesty said not to involve you, but I think it's important that both wielders of the scepter are present. They are, after all, destined to rule Seracedar one day."

"I agree," I said, maintaining my stance. "No disrespect, Your Majesty, but I'm staying whether you like it or not."

Ashbel sighed. "Do as you will. But remember, I have authority over all matters involving Emberwood. The scepter and the Will of Heaven only applies to Seracedar. Old Grandfather Heaven gave our family a separate right to rule over Emberwood when we seceded from Seracedar many years ago. Also, since Aiden is my son, I have authority over him even if he is a wielder of the scepter."

Welder frowned, looking like he wanted to argue again. "Even so, we have to do what's best to protect Emberwood. Carrick will never agree to your terms. We should have attacked two months ago and revealed the scepter to both Seracedar and Emberwood. Wait until the wedding day, and mark my word, that's the day Carrick strikes. You gave him fair warning when you wrote that letter to him. Do you really think he's not preparing for war? You basically told him our strategy is to wait until after the wedding day to attack him."

"I hate to admit it, but I think Welder's got you there, Ah-fu," Aiden said.

Ashbel turned to him. "Stay out of this, son. You are here to listen and learn how to rule as king one day, but right now, you're too young to make decisions for yourself or this kingdom. I don't need your opinions."

I frowned. I didn't like the way Ashbel was talking to Aiden. As if he didn't know what he was talking about and didn't deserve to be speaking.

"But it's not an opinion, Ah-fu," Aiden said. "I already told you. Carrick said in his letter he's not interested in peace."

"Exactly," Welder echoed. "How do you intend to respond to the letter, Your Majesty? It can't be ignored."

"What letter?" I asked.

Aiden turned to me. "This morning, an emissary delivered a letter to me from Carrick. He's made it clear he has no wish to talk of peace. He swears to attack us in a way we least expect."

"I'll write back to him," Ashbel said. "I'll ask what it will take to change his mind and maintain peace. No one has to know we have the scepter. I just want him to stay away from my son and future daughter-in-law."

"Are you insane?" Welder exclaimed.

Ashbel glared. "I don't like your tone. I am your king."

"Excuse me. Are you insane, *Your Majesty*?" Welder emphasized the title and bowed with dramatic flair.

Aiden frowned. "Welder, you've crossed a line. Show your king some respect."

"I can have you arrested for contempt," Ashbel said.

Welder didn't move. He maintained a calm stance. "I apologize if I've offended you, Your Majesty. But you know I'm not one to shy away from speaking my mind, especially when I believe your decision may be detrimental to the kingdom. Look, you appointed me to command your army and advise you on tactics of defense against our enemies. I don't believe it's wise to continue negotiating peace with Carrick when he's made it clear peace is not on the table for him. He's already told us he's going to attack."

Ashbel's expression softened. "I appreciate your apology. We can both get heated at times. That being said, I stand by decision. Carrick hasn't attacked yet. It could be all talk. Let's continue to monitor him. As long as he hasn't initiated, we won't start anything either. We'll pray and ask Old Grandfather Heaven to change Carrick's heart."

Welder gaped. "But—"

"No buts. That is my decis—" The king broke off.

"Ah-fu, what's wrong?" Aiden asked.

King Ashbel wore a confused look and suddenly cried out. "No. Don't take him. This is my fault."

His eyes glazed over, and he put his hands out as though catching his balance.

Welder reached out, stabilizing the king before he fell.

I crouched by the king's side and sang a short tune, letting my wyis flow out. At the same time, I checked his pulse. I'd suspected a blood clot preventing oxygen from getting to his heart, but that was not the case. Everything, including his physical wyis, felt normal. I couldn't pinpoint what was wrong with him at all.

Ashbel stopped babbling, so I stopped singing and waited to see if I'd done any good.

Aiden placed a hand on his father's shoulder, looking worried and uncertain. "Ah-fu, can you hear me? Are you okay?"

The king regained clarity in his eyes and looked around at us. "What happened? I blacked out for a moment."

"You were saying something strange," I said. "I used my tin-chai, and it seemed to have helped."

Whatever it was had passed, thankfully, but I hoped it wouldn't recur. I wasn't sure if I'd healed his ailment long-term or merely covered it up with a bandage.

I checked his pulse again in case I'd missed something. "How are you feeling?"

"Better now. Thank you, Rilla. Perhaps I'm overtired."

"We should send Doctor Flamyor to check on you," I said. "I didn't sense any physical ailment, but maybe she'll catch something I didn't."

"Yes, you should go rest, Your Majesty," Welder said. His tone was gentler than before, though I still noted the annoyance in his eyes. Was he angry that he couldn't continue debating the king? "We can't have you under the weather for the wedding. Let me worry about Carrick. My spies will continue to monitor his movements. I'll notify you if something changes, but I doubt he'll make a move before the wedding."

The king nodded. We summoned a servant, who escorted His Majesty out of the room.

Welder waited until the king was gone before he sent Aiden and me an incredulous stare. "I don't mean to be insensitive after what just happened, but we still need to discuss the king's delusional view that he can prevent a war. He's turned us into sitting ducks. I can't plan anything without his permission. And the way he's been talking to you, Aiden, like you're a child with no intelligent thoughts."

So I wasn't the only one who had caught onto that.

"Ah-fu just wants to protect us," Aiden said. "Go easy on him. He's stressed, and I'm worried about what just happened. I hope it's not a sign of a heart ailment. I don't want him to have another attack."

I folded my arms across my chest. "I understand, and I'm concerned for his well-being, too. We'll follow up with Doctor Flamyor later. But Aiden, if your father is unwell and can't make a decision, then you need to take responsibility and be the leader. I came to this meeting to tell you that Carrick has gone mad. He's been keeping novelties. Gets drunk every night. Hasn't done anything to improve the kingdom."

"Where did you hear that?" Aiden asked.

"A patient at the clinic told me she saw the novelties before she managed to escape to Emberwood," I said. "She's a reliable source. It proves Carrick hasn't changed for the better. He's getting worse. We need to take away his power before he ruins the kingdom further. We have the Will of Heaven, and it's our responsibility to help Seracedar."

"Yes, but my ah-fu thinks—"

"He's allowed to think what he wants, and you're allowed to disagree," I said. "He may be the king of Emberwood, but he's not the wielder of the scepter. We are. If he's not willing to provide the Emberwood army to help us, then we need to find another way to defeat Carrick. We need to take the lead in communicating with Carrick instead of letting your father lead us. This is our duty, and your father can't protect us by doing the work for us. The scepter may not apply to the rule of Emberwood, but your father and the Embers still believe in Old Grandfather Heaven and follow the tenets. If he doesn't at least take our opinion into consideration, he would be disobeying Old Grandfather Heaven."

"I agree," Welder said. "I'm so glad someone's finally speaking sense around here."

"Ah-fu isn't disobeying Old Grandfather Heaven," Aiden said, looking annoyed. "I'm sure he's listening to our opinions, but he said he just wants me to continue praying for guidance before stepping into a leadership role."

"You can pray all you want, but prayer without action doesn't lead anywhere," Welder said. "It just makes us victims, powerless to do anything. Old Grandfather Heaven calls us to action, too."

"I don't know what to do yet," Aiden said. "I can't think. What if I make the wrong decision? What if Ah-fu disapproves of my decision, and I end up making everything worse?"

He looked frustrated and unsure. I'd never seen him without confidence before coming to Emberwood. It worried me.

"Maybe we should postpone the wedding," I said.

Welder shook his head and sighed. "No. I still believe Carrick is planning something on the wedding day. I can't initiate an attack without King Ashbel's consent, so we have no choice but to see what Carrick does and go from there."

CHAPTER 5

✦ ✦ ✦ ✦ ✦ ✦ ✦ ✦ ✦ ✦

Two weeks passed, and I settled into a routine. I worked at the clinic in the mornings three days a week, counseling and talking to the women in the recovery group. The other mornings, I continued working with Doctor Flamyor to heal patients' physical ailments. Then every afternoon, I returned to the palace for meetings with Welder, Aiden, Ashbel, and the royal council.

Thankfully, the king hadn't gotten another strange attack. But he and Welder argued so much, I worried for his health. The majority of the council was still on the king's side, opposing war as long as Seracedar showed no signs of attacking first. Welder was a good talker, though, and he'd managed to sway a few more advisors to his side.

The meetings frustrated me. Especially the way Aiden kept quiet. And if I tried to assert my opinion, the king would tell me that kingdom matters were not my concern. According to him, it wasn't necessary for me to sit in on the meetings, and I should be focusing on wedding planning and whatever girls my age did.

Which led to my evenings, booked every night for wedding planning with Queen Leonora over supper. Aiden and Ashbel joined occasionally, offering input. Not that it mattered. Leonora was going to plan this wedding her way in every detail. Even if I had a different preference, she'd tell me why her way was better. For example, I wanted a modern wedding, something simple. An exchange of vows in front of friends and family, with a public announcement to the kingdom to follow. But she wanted a formal, traditional wedding, styled after the ancient Shyan weddings, with the entire kingdom bearing witness to the ceremony.

"I don't want too much pomp and circumstance," I had told Leonora. "It doesn't feel right when there's so much going on. War is looming, and I don't want to throw money away when the kingdom could use it."

"It won't cost that much," Leonora had said. "And Emberwood expects the pomp and circumstance. They are celebrating the wedding of their one and only crown prince. I am celebrating my one and only son's wedding. The son I thought was dead. You understand how much this means to me, don't you, Rilla?"

I nodded, forcing myself to smile. How could I argue with that?

"And, of course, we'll have the traditional banquet," she said.

"Do I get to help plan the menu?" I asked.

She blinked as though she didn't understand the question. "It's a traditional banquet. The courses are set. It's the same menu I had for my wedding banquet. Don't worry, dear. You don't have to plan anything."

Though I'd appreciated her kindness since the day we first met, I was starting to get annoyed. Out of politeness, I kept my mouth shut.

Aiden could see my frustration and tried placating me. "I'm sorry. I know you have your own ideas, but I don't have the heart to tell my ah-mu she doesn't get to make the decisions after all the years I made her grieve. Besides, you know she loves you and wants this day to be special. Can we just let her do as she pleases?"

"I understand where you're coming from, but this is my wedding," I said. "It's not that I'm ungrateful. I just want to make some decisions, too."

"I know. If you really want me to, I'll try talking to her."

I sighed. I didn't want to add to all the stress he'd been under lately. And Queen Leonora had been nothing but kind to me. This wedding ceremony was probably more important to her than to me. I tried to put myself in her place. If I thought I'd lost my son and found him again, I'd want to plan the best wedding for him and his bride, too. Maybe this was a battle I didn't need to win.

"Never mind," I said. "It's fine if she plans everything."

He looked relieved. "Thank you." He kissed my cheek. "We're already married as far as I'm concerned. To me, our wedding was the night we spent together in that dingy inn on the way home from Cedar Palace. The night before we were granted the Will of Heaven."

He was right. That was the night we'd exchanged our true vows and became one with each other. This wedding ceremony was merely a formality.

"I still don't feel good with such extravagance," I said.

Aiden rubbed my shoulder and gave me a comforting look. "Think about it this way. Our wedding day is also the day we announce that we have the scepter and the Will of Heaven. We need to make sure the whole kingdom bears witness to it and the news travels to Seracedar. Pomp and circumstance are all part of it."

He had a point there, too. But it didn't make me feel much better. I felt like my opinions didn't matter to Leonora just as Aiden's opinions didn't matter to his father. To them, we were children incapable of making decisions on our own.

One night, we all sat around the table together for supper. We were taste-testing the food that would be served at the banquet.

"I hired a new chef for the occasion," Leonora said. She bit into a fried prawn and chewed. "Delicious. The man knows what he's doing. What do you all think?"

I ate a prawn and said, "It's great." Not that it would matter even if I told her I hated it.

Both Ashbel and Aiden had their plates piled with food and ate like they hadn't eaten for days.

Leonora frowned at them. "Not so much fried food. Bad for your health." She used her chopsticks to take away several deep-fried prawns off Aiden's plate, then did the same for Ashbel. "I'm limiting you to two each."

"Compliments to the chef," Ashbel said. "Where is he from?"

Leonora took a sip of tea before answering. "He didn't say, but he looks Fauxhemian. Chef Clox can make soaps and ointments, too. Talented man. He made me an ointment to rub on my joints." She took a vial from her pocket, poured out a bit of ointment, and dabbed it on the pressure points on her neck. "See? Helps relieve stress, he said. I gave you some to try, remember?"

"Mm-hmm. Do you have a lot more to plan, dear?" Ashbel asked. "I don't want you to be too stressed."

"No. Everything's set." Leonora put the vial back in her pocket. "Except for the dress fitting, which I'll take care of with Rilla tomorrow."

"We should plan on when we're making the announcement about the scepter," Aiden said.

Ashbel set his chopsticks down and looked at us. "About that, we should talk. Your ah-mu and I have decided to take on the Will of Heaven for you children."

I jolted up. "Excuse me?" Had I heard him correctly?

Aiden gaped. "What do you mean, you decided to take on the Will of Heaven for us?"

Leonora chewed and swallowed, then answered. "It was my idea. Your ah-fu and I will announce to Emberwood that Old Grandfather Heaven gave us the scepter and the right to rule. We'll bear the responsibility for you."

"Welder's still convinced that war is inevitable," Ashbel said. "And as much as I wanted Carrick to concede, he's showing no signs of it. I'm starting to face reality. We'll have to use the scepter to defeat him and join Seracedar with Emberwood. Better that the people believe your ah-mu and I have the Will of Heaven and right to rule. You children have no experience running a kingdom on your own."

"You still don't understand the concept of the Will of Heaven," Aiden said. "Old Grandfather Heaven chose Rilla and me. The responsibility can't just be transferred to you."

"Why not?" Ashbel asked. "You are my son, and Rilla's about to become my daughter. You're our responsibility. Therefore, your responsibilities are ours."

Aiden shook his head. "It doesn't work that way." He looked at me. "Say something, Rilla."

I wasn't sure what to say. I couldn't believe we were having this conversation. Did Leonora and Ashbel really believe they could take on the Will of Heaven for us?

"The scepter didn't amplify your tin-chai," I said. "How will you prove you have the right to rule?"

"You can use the scepter to amplify our tin-chai," Ashbel said. "It's the same thing. You and Aiden still have the Will of Heaven, but the people will think we do. That way we can guide you through all the decisions you'll have to make with the war and with ruling the kingdom."

"We can't trick the people, Ah-fu," Aiden said. "The tradition of the scepter and the right to rule stopped being important to Emberwood once we separated from Seracedar, so that's probably why you don't understand. But what you're proposing is a serious offense. Old Grandfather Heaven gave the Will of Heaven to Rilla and me. It's our responsibility to take the throne away from Carrick and help to rebuild Seracedar."

"And we'll need to use the scepter during the war," I added. "The people will eventually find out we have the right to rule when we use the scepter's powers in battle."

"Your ah-mu and I also decided neither of you will be involved in the battles," Ashbel said. "I'll have Emberwood soldiers fight Carrick's men. We may be outnumbered, but we have better modern technology.

And Welder's a brilliant strategist. You're both staying here where it's safe."

"So you plan on making my decisions for me without listening to what I want, just like you did when I was a child," Aiden said.

Leonora sent him a warning look. "Don't speak to your ah-fu that way. And I don't appreciate you raising your voice at us. No respect."

Aiden took a deep breath. "I'm not raising my tone. I just want you to listen to what I have to say. You don't hold the Will of Heaven. This isn't your decision. Old Grandfather Heaven gave us the right to rule, and it's our responsibility, not yours."

"I'm protecting you, son," Ashbel said. "You and Rilla. Old Grandfather Heaven gave you to me. It's my job to help you make the right decisions and to keep you safe."

I bit my tongue. *Keep quiet.* This was between Aiden and his parents.

"No, you're stopping us from obeying Old Grandfather Heaven," Aiden said.

Ashbel sat back in his chair. He wore a hurt expression. "I don't appreciate your accusatory tone. Especially when I'm doing my best as a parent to lessen your burden and keep you safe. Also, since you're talking about Old Grandfather Heaven, as I remember, he also commands us to honor our parents. I want you to honestly reflect on yourself. As our child, don't you think you should be doing a better job of obeying me and your ah-mu? We've done nothing but try to protect you and make you comfortable when you were a child and since you've come back to us."

Honor your father and mother. Yes, this was one of Old Grandfather Heaven's tenets. But I wanted to quote another of Old Grandfather Heaven's commands back to Ashbel. *A boy must separate from his parents and become a man accountable to his own actions before he can cleave to a woman in marriage.*

I didn't think Ashbel and Leonora were allowing Aiden to separate from them if they were deciding everything for him. Protecting their son was just an excuse for keeping him under their control.

Should I say something? Come to Aiden's defense? I didn't want to interfere, and it felt so awkward to witness a family fight. I wasn't married to him yet. Better to keep quiet for now. But if this issue came up after we were married, I wasn't about to stay silent.

"All I'm asking is for some respect as an adult to make my own decisions," Aiden said. It sounded like he was struggling to maintain a calm voice. "I'm not a child anymore."

"After all the bad choices you've made in the past, can you blame me for not believing you can make wise decisions without my counsel?" Ashbel asked him. "If you had obeyed us when you were a kid and hadn't snuck out that night, you wouldn't have been taken to Cedar Palace. Your ah-mu and I grieved twelve years believing you were dead. You could have escaped and come home, but you didn't. You were loyal to that boy, Carrick, when you should have been here with us. If you had been at home, we wouldn't be in this situation. Carrick wouldn't have a vendetta against you and our kingdom. How can you be trusted to wield the Sacred Cedar Scepter and take the throne of Seracedar when you couldn't even come home to be the crown prince of Emberwood?"

Aiden's face turned white at his father's words. His normal confident demeanor crumpled like an autumn leaf. I wanted to attack Ashbel for his cruel words.

Leonora burst into tears. "Please stop fighting. Just listen to your ah-fu and me."

I was surprised by her reaction, especially when Leonora rarely cried. She was more likely to get angry. Her whole body was shaking with sobs.

Was there something wrong with her physically? I went to her and she cried into my shoulder, seeming unable to stop.

Leonora wheezed, struggling to breathe through sobs. "I . . . can't . . . stop."

Something definitely was not right with the queen.

CHAPTER 6

✦ ✦ ✦ ✦ ✦ ✦ ✦ ✦ ✦ ✦

I gestured to Ashbel and Aiden. "You two, stop fighting."

Ashbel rushed over to Leonora. "What's happening with her?"

"Why can't she stop crying?" Aiden asked.

I quickly checked her pulse and wyis, but nothing seemed to be off.

Still hugging me, Leonora sobbed louder. Uncontrollable weeping shook her entire body.

Between sobs, she choked out, "Why can't . . . I . . . stop?"

She wailed, the sound alarming. I stepped back to look at her. Her eyes were glazed over, and she began muttering something incoherent.

I handed Aiden's ah-mu over to him to hold her up. I assessed her pulse and her wyis again in case I'd missed something the first time. Everything was normal. This felt like what had happened to Ashbel a few weeks ago.

I sang, but again, I couldn't find any physical ailment to cure. Maybe these episodes were stress-related. Something I didn't think I could cure. But if it worked with Ashbel before, it might work now.

I finished a stanza, and Leonora's sobs subsided. Thank Old Grandfather Heaven.

She dabbed at her eyes. "I don't know what came over me. I was crying and couldn't stop, and then I blacked out for a minute."

"You need to rest," Ashbel said. "I think all this wedding planning has made you uptight. And the constant stress of the scepter and Seracedar certainly doesn't help."

"I'm sorry," Aiden whispered. He wore the guiltiest expression I'd ever seen.

"Your ah-mu and I are going to bed now," Ashbel said. "We'll continue this discussion another time."

"We should send for the doctor," Aiden said. "I don't like that these strange episodes have happened to both of you."

"I agree," I said. "I'll ask someone to check what you're eating and drinking as well. Make sure there's nothing poisonous. You can't be too careful."

"We're fine," Ashbel said. "We're probably just tired."

Ashbel strode off, tugging Leonora after him.

I summoned a servant to send for Doctor Flamyor. Then I turned to Aiden. He looked so crestfallen.

We sat back at the table. So much uneaten food remained, but Aiden didn't even look at it.

"I should have spoken more respectfully," he said. "Maybe I shouldn't have argued so much."

I sighed. "Look, I don't want to say something you might find offensive, but I have to tell you the truth. I respect your parents, and they have been kind to me. However, I don't like the way they speak to you. They aren't listening to your opinions, and if you disagree, they make it sound like you're disobeying them. They shouldn't be trying to take away the responsibility of the Will of Heaven from us."

"Yes, but they have good intent."

"Even so, it isn't right of them to use guilt to make you feel like you're in the wrong. And you don't have to keep making excuses for their behavior. I also don't understand why they treat you like a child who needs to be shielded from every danger in the world. Don't they realize you were a bodyguard in Cedar Palace?"

Aiden was silent, his gaze falling to the table. I thought I might have

offended him and braced myself. But then he looked at me. "My parents and I have a complicated relationship. When I was a kid, they always made my decisions for me. If I didn't agree, they said they knew what was best, and I just had to obey their orders. The way they're treating me now is the same as when I was a kid."

"Except you're not," I said. "And it sounds like they're using the fact that you stayed in Cedar Palace for so long to guilt you into doing things their way."

"They have every right to make me feel guilty about it," he said. "Because I could have come home but I didn't want to."

"What do you mean you didn't want to?" I asked. "I thought you stayed with Carrick for so long because you believed in his cause and thought you could work behind the scenes to keep peace between Seracedar and Emberwood."

"That was only part of the reason. Truthfully, it was more selfish. I didn't want to become the crown prince again. And I thought Emberwood and my parents were better off without me."

"That's a terrible thing to believe," I said. "You actually thought that?"

He picked up his chopsticks and absentmindedly poked at the cold food on his plate. "I thought Sito might be better as the crown prince. He could be the son my parents always wanted. Obedient and smart. He was studious and always got good marks at school. But I didn't like sitting still. I preferred being active and doing martial arts. Why couldn't I be more like Sito, my parents always asked. I always felt like they wanted me to become someone I wasn't."

I hated that they had compared Aiden to his cousin. It must have made him feel so unseen. "They should have celebrated your strengths. Not everyone is meant to be a scholar."

He shrugged, then continued. "The day I got kidnapped, I failed another test. My teachers had a meeting with my parents and me about how I needed to improve, or they'd have to hold me back from graduating to the next level. They suggested that I stop martial arts training to study until I improved my marks. I begged them not to make me stop martial arts. Promised I'd study harder. I'd work on extra assignments if I had to. My parents told me to leave the room while they talked privately to my teachers, but I hid and eavesdropped. I heard my ah-fu use his authority as the king to tell the teachers not to fail me. He said even if I stopped martial arts to study more, he wanted to guarantee that I would receive passing marks. He knew I wasn't bright like Sito, and it would be humiliating if the crown prince failed to graduate to the next level. My ah-mu didn't say a word, which I took to mean she agreed with him. I felt so horrible that I must have made a sound because then everyone turned around and realized I was in the hall spying."

"I'm so sorry that they interfered without letting you try to work hard on your own."

"I knew they had good intentions," he said. "They didn't want to see me fail. But it hurt to know they didn't believe I was smart enough or that I could work hard enough to improve my marks. After that meeting, I asked Ah-fu and Ah-mu if they really thought I was dumb and an embarrassment. I said I didn't want them using their power to make the teachers pass me. Ah-fu said he was trying to protect me, and Ah-mu said I just needed to work harder to get better grades like Sito. I insisted that they let me earn my marks on my own, but they said they knew what was best for me and it was already decided. I told them I'd prove I was smart. I was serious, but they just laughed it off."

I winced. "What a horrible thing to be dismissed like that."

"I don't think they meant to be cruel. It's just how they are." Aiden set down his chopsticks and stared at his hands. "Anyway, that night, I snuck past all of the guards after midnight. It was stupid. I thought when everyone came looking for me in the morning, I'd jump out of hiding and say, 'I just outwitted all your guards. That proves I'm smart.' Instead, I got kidnapped. Rino had been watching me all day after that teachers' meeting and knew I might be vulnerable."

I remembered Mr. Rino was the teacher who had kidnapped Aiden and sold him to slavers. When we'd come to Emberwood, Rino had tried to kill us. He also happened to be Sito's real father, but Aiden said Sito didn't know this and still had no idea.

"So I guess my ah-fu is right. I wasn't smart enough to make good choices on my own before. What makes me think I can lead Emberwood and take the responsibility of the scepter now?"

"You were a child," I said. "You didn't know what would happen. But it doesn't mean your parents should still be treating you like a ten-year-old. You're an adult now, and you've survived on your own."

"It doesn't make me feel less guilty for what happened," he said. "I stayed away so long on purpose, which makes the guilt worse. I'm not trying to make excuses for myself. It's just that in Emberwood, I always felt like I had to pretend to be someone else to please my parents. They decided everything for me. What I ate, what I wore, what time I went to bed. I was overprotected. But in Cedar Palace, I did the protecting. I felt like I was doing something worthy. I gained confidence I never knew I had. Carrick and I were thrown into danger, and we were forced to make life or death decisions. I may have been enslaved to Carrick, but he trusted me. With him, I felt smart and useful. I'd never felt that way with my parents."

He paused, looking down as though he felt ashamed. "When I finally returned to Emberwood, I saw how much I had hurt my parents by staying away. They couldn't have children after me. My ah-mu told me she thought she'd never be an ah-mu again. They said they didn't touch anything in my room, and even though they regarded Sito like another son, no one could replace me. It was the worst feeling to see how much they loved me and know I had caused them so much pain."

"Oh, Aiden," I said.

"They had become old, something I didn't expect either. Funny. I had a picture of them in my mind that they'd stay the same age they were when I left. Like time hadn't passed. But it had. And I'd let them sit in their pain for twelve years. I made a promise that I'd be a good son and make up for the last twelve years. Take care of them in their old age. I owe them for what I put them through. But it's so hard when my ah-fu has his own ideas and won't listen to any of mine. When my parents are talking to me, I feel like all the decisions I want to make are wrong. And if I make a decision that ends up being a mistake, he'll throw it back at me as proof that I'm not capable of leading the way he can."

He sighed. "Maybe I don't have what it takes to be a leader. I've made so many bad choices."

I shook my head. "You don't owe anyone anything. Parents are supposed to love their children without expecting them to return anything. You're allowed to disagree with them. It's a tricky balance, but you can respect them while also standing your ground. And you do have what it takes. You just need to find your voice again and own it."

He paused, appearing thoughtful. "My voice. What if it's not powerful enough to stand on its own? Old Grandfather Heaven was right in choosing you to hold the Will of Heaven, but without you, I'd never have been chosen. He could easily replace me. And my parents made it clear that they don't think I'm able to bear the responsibility."

"He chose both of us together," I said. "We're stronger when we're together. You can't let what your parents say make you doubt yourself. And they definitely don't get to decide to take the responsibility away from us."

"I know you're right," he said with a sigh. "But it still makes me feel horrible to have made my parents angry with me. Especially since Ah-fu is only trying to protect both of us. Anyway, I don't want to think about them anymore. It's getting late. We should get ready for bed."

Aiden walked me back to my chambers. We stopped outside the door.

"Stay with me tonight," I said.

He hesitated, though I could see the longing in his eyes. "I shouldn't. My parents wouldn't like it. Not before we're married."

"What we do is between us," I said. "Besides, we're as good as married."

He still didn't move. "Which isn't the same as married. If my parents find out—"

I was tired of him listening to his parents all the time. "So what if they find out? This is our relationship, not theirs."

"What if I get you pregnant?"

We hadn't talked about having children yet, but now that he'd brought it up, I realized the idea didn't scare me.

"We're expected to have children. I want your child. Don't you want to have children with me, too?"

"Yes, of course. But I'd be more comfortable if it happened after our wedding. We're lucky I didn't get you pregnant that night at the inn. My parents would have killed me. They wouldn't want to damage your reputation. Neither do I."

"We're going to be married next week. If it happens, it happens. No one's going to be counting days. They'll be excited to have a new prince or princess. And even if there are judgmental people, I'm not worried as long as you're here with me." I caressed his arm. "Please? I miss being with you."

I could feel him yielding. I leaned closer and whispered into his ear. "I promise to make you forget all about your obligations and duties tonight. Let me take care of you."

That did it. He picked me up, carried me into the room, and shut the door behind him. "If my parents find out about this, I'm blaming you."

"Stop talking about your parents already," I said and kissed him.

And there was no more talk for the rest of the night.

CHAPTER 7

✦ ✦ ✦ ✦ ✦ ✦ ✦ ✦ ✦ ✦

The next morning, I slept in later than usual. I didn't have to be at the clinic that day, so Aiden told me to rest and he'd join me for lunch.

A servant knocked. I opened the door, and she handed me an envelope. "A letter for you, miss."

"Thank you," I said.

Closing the door, I saw the letters "R.M." scrawled over "Fauxhemia" on the envelope.

My heart beat faster. It had to be from my brother. I broke open the seal, pulled out the letter, and sure enough, it was signed Rell and Nia Marseas. I'd written to them a month ago and had been expecting a reply. This was our first correspondence since I'd come to Emberwood.

Dear Sister,

Congratulations on your upcoming marriage to the crown prince of Emberwood. We received your wedding invitation. We wish we could attend, but unfortunately, your nephew is still too young for such a long journey. In a year or two, we hope to be able to visit Emberwood, but you and the prince are welcome to come stay with us much sooner. Perhaps after the wedding?

As for our own life happenings, my (Rell) practice is getting busier each day. I'm blessed to be able to serve so many patients. Apparently, I'm the first Shyan doctor in this town, and my Fauxhemian patients are impressed that my tin-chai can diagnose any disorder within seconds. Even disorders that other doctors haven't been able to figure out for years. I don't mean to brag, but I feel fulfilled here. Nia is enjoying being a mama to Tristan. Your nephew is a quick learner. He can say so many more words than other children his age, and I think many parents are jealous that we have such a clever boy. We hope he can meet his courageous and beautiful aunt soon.

Take care of yourself, and we look forward to the day our family may be reunited again. If Aiden doesn't treat you right, you must let me know at once. I'll take care of him, prince or not.

Love,

Your family—Rell, Nia, and Tristan

I held the letter to my chest and smiled. When I'd been taken from my home to Cedar Palace, I thought I'd never see my family again. But now, I had the chance to visit any time I pleased.

That was, if Seracedar and Emberwood avoided war.

My heart fell. I still couldn't see my family any time soon. Not until things were settled with Carrick and Seracedar.

At least my family was in Fauxhemia, a kingdom that had nothing to do with this war or with the scepter. They were safe, which was all that mattered to me.

Another knock sounded on my door, interrupting my thoughts.

"Enter," I said.

Aiden stepped in. "Ready for lunch?"

"Yes." My gaze went to his hands, which were nervously pulling at his clothes. "Are you worried about something?"

"My parents are still upset with me about last night. They won't be eating with us. I feel so guilty."

"Sorry to hear that," I said. "And I hope they feel better soon, but you didn't do anything wrong. Voicing your opinion, even though you disagreed with your parents' beliefs, isn't wrong."

He sighed. "I don't want to talk about them anymore. On to other exciting news. My cousin, Sito, is here. He'll be joining us. I knew he was coming to the wedding but didn't expect he'd arrive a week early. We haven't talked since he exiled himself. He was so ashamed about Mr. Rino being the one who kidnapped me even though it wasn't his fault. But I hope we can move past it."

I kissed his cheek. "It will be okay. Based on what you've told me about Sito, he sounds like a good person. I'm sure he wants to reconcile with you as much as you'd like to with him."

Aiden nodded and rubbed my shoulder, a gesture that seemed to offer him more comfort than it did me. "We used to be so close as kids. I'll be so disappointed if we never become friends and brothers again. You know people change over time, and sometimes nothing can repair a relationship." His gaze fell away to the ground.

He must be thinking of Carrick.

"If a relationship can't be repaired, then that person isn't meant to be kept in your life," I said. "You have a right to be nervous, but I'll be there with you. If it gets too awkward, I'll throw in a stupid joke, dangle chopsticks out my mouth, and start wailing like a sea wanpo. Sito will be too flabbergasted wondering what you see in me to remember that any tension exists between the two of you."

Aiden smiled at me. "Thank you. Even if it does go well, I still want to see you imitate a sea wanpo. It'll be the best entertainment I've had all year."

He took my hand, and we made our way through the corridors of

Water Crystal Courtyard and up the glass lift to Gold Song Courtyard. The fire flowers were illuminating their bursts of colorful light. It always made me smile when I passed them.

We cut across the courtyard and headed for the main dining room where we usually had family suppers. As we entered the room, Sito was already seated at the end of the table. I remembered his face from the last time I'd seen him. I calculated him to be about my age.

He saw us and stood from the table. He looked unsure and awkward. "Cousin, it's been awhile."

"Indeed," Aiden said. He didn't let go of my hand.

The two of them stared at each other. Aiden's grip tightened on my hand. "Um, yes. Welcome back to Linlang, Sito. I've been wanting to—"

Sito spoke at the same time. "I'm so happy to see you again and to meet your future bride. I've been going through this moment a thousand times in my head." He exhaled deeply, and the next words out of his mouth were said so quickly and jumbled that I couldn't catch everything.

". . . expect you to hate me . . . no idea about Teacher . . . and . . . and . . . I don't want the throne."

Sito spoke faster than I could think. And he was still going. "I want you to know that I can't forgive myself and don't expect you to forgive me, and if you want to banish me forever, I understand."

"Hold on there," Aiden said. "I never once thought you had anything to do with your teacher's actions. There's nothing to forgive, and no one's going to banish you."

"Really?" Sito's face was flushed. "I've been so embarrassed by what happened."

"There's no reason to be," Aiden said. "Anyway, it's all in the past, and I'm glad we're together again. Let's sit down and eat, shall we?"

Aiden finally loosened his hold on my hand, and the tension in his shoulders lifted. He flashed me a quick smile of relief and mouthed so only I could see, "Glad that's over."

We sat on one side of the table, opposite Sito.

Aiden eyed the food on the table. He piled some onto Sito's plate. "Guest of honor first." Then he did the same to my plate. "Now for my love."

I put food on his plate. "And for you."

Aiden grinned and dug in as though he hadn't eaten in days.

I regarded Sito and smiled. "I've seen you once before, but you probably don't remember."

"Of course, I do," he said. "You were eating noodles, and my cousin pretended not to know me. But I was so sure it was him. If I had known my teacher wanted him dead, I wouldn't have said anything. I was the one who led him to you." His expression filled with guilt.

Aiden stopped chewing and frowned. "What did I just say? We're not going to talk about your teacher anymore. Fill your mouth with food and start eating, cousin."

Sito nodded and took a bite. He slowly chewed as though pondering a deep thought, which was the exact opposite of how Aiden ate. He looked up at me. "I've heard a lot about you from other people, so it's nice to finally talk to you."

"Oh?" I said. "What have you heard?"

"That you're a healer, and you have an incredible tin-chai," he said. "It must feel so good to heal people with your voice. I wish I could heal people, too, but first, I've got to study the books and pass the tests." He made a face.

"Are you studying medicine?" I asked.

He nodded. "I'm taking classes at university. It's been my dream for years to become a doctor. More specifically, a mind doctor. I've even traveled to Fauxhemia to study there for half a year, and the prince of Fauxhemia came to our university to learn about mind diseases from our teachers. You see, we've discovered that using their blood, specifically from emerald-bloods, can lead to cures for mind diseases. The emerald-blooded can manipulate and poison minds, so they can also create powerful antidotes for people driven to madness."

"Fascinating," I said. "I'm so glad to hear that their blood is leading to advances in medicine. You know, I used to work for a faela at Cedar Palace who was half Shyan and half Fauxhemian. She said her mother was a seer, and she told me of the different colors of blood that Fauxhemians have, and how each color has a different kind of magic."

"She was Shyan and Fauxhemian?" Sito dropped his chopsticks, his gaze flying to me in excitement. "Did she have any blood magic or tin-chai?"

"She was an exceptional artist, but she was a koong. No tin-chai. She wasn't a Faux-blood either as far as I know. Why?"

"There was a recent study about cases of people with both Shyan and Fauxhemian blood who possess magic from both races. These people had a tin-chai and Faux-blood magic, or even had one type of magic blended with the other. One woman said her Faux-blood magic actually gave her a completely new tin-chai, but it didn't develop until later in life. It's all still a mystery how that crossover works."

"Interesting," I said. But I was only half paying attention. I wanted to learn more about medical studies. "Are only emerald-blooded Faux-bloods able to produce antidotes for mind diseases? And are there other cures they can create for physical ailments that don't already have remedies?"

"My research has been specifically on the emerald-blooded and mind diseases."

I nodded. "I see. I hope you don't mind all my questions."

"Of course, I don't mind. If you want to know more, just ask."

"Rilla's already working at the clinic for experience, and I'm encouraging her to apply to school," Aiden said. "But I never knew that about you, Sito. When you were a kid, you changed your mind every few months on what you wanted to do. You wanted to be an inventor for a while, then a litigator. At one point you went through a classic theater phase and read all the ancient plays. Said you were going to be a famous thespian. I guess that's what happens when you're smart in every subject."

"I didn't know medicine was my real dream until I discovered my tin-chai," Sito said. "You were already gone two years by then."

Aiden's eyes widened. "Tin-chai? My ah-fu and ah-mu never told me you got one, but I guess it never came up in conversation."

"I was a late bloomer," he said. "I—"

Attendant Bin interrupted whatever Sito was going to say. "I'm so sorry, but there's a call from the clinic. Counselor Ponch is desperate for Miss Rilla to go over. A girl is sick. Poisoned herself. They say she's hysterical and refuses help. They're asking if you can use your tin-chai on her."

Aiden stood. "I don't want you going alone. I'm coming with you."

"I'll go, too," Sito said. "I might be able to help calm her."

I didn't know what Sito meant by that, but there was no time to ask. I sprang out of my seat and followed Attendant Bin downstairs to get a coach. Aiden and Sito followed right behind me.

When we got to the clinic, screams echoed in the courtyard. A group of women were gathered outside in a semicircle, whispering to one another, but they stepped aside as we approached.

Ponch was pinning a girl down to the ground. The girl was strong, and Ponch was barely able to hold onto her. I realized Ponch was wearing thick, weighted gloves. I wondered why until I saw the girl's skin phasing in and out, turning to what looked like rock. Was she an Ailo?

Galai stood in front of them, trying to talk to the girl. "You need to see a doctor. You can't do this to yourself."

Blood soaked the girl's dress and dripped from the sides of her mouth. The girl struggled to break free.

"Let me go! I want to die. Why can't you just let me die?"

She coughed. More blood spurted from her mouth.

"Miah, please," Galai said. "Let a doctor help you."

Miah? This was the girl who had come with Galai from Cedar Palace.

I approached them, but Miah glared at me. "One step closer, and I'll bite my own tongue off. I'll kill myself."

CHAPTER 8

✦ ✦ ✦ ✦ ✦ ✦ ✦ ✦ ✦ ✦

She didn't look like she was bluffing. I couldn't risk attempting to help her if she might hurt herself before I could finish singing. Even if I did heal her, in her current emotional state, she would only try again.

Sito moved next to me, his footsteps silent. He whispered in my ear. "Hold on, I know what to do." He looked at the girl and said, "Calm." His voice reminded me of the ocean waves taking over the shore. Despite its gentleness, it commanded domination.

Miah's gaze locked on his. In an instant, she stopped screaming, seeming to be mesmerized by the sound of the single word.

Galai stood and charged at Sito. "Who are you, and what are you doing to her?"

It was obvious Galai was closer to Miah than she'd let on earlier when we'd talked.

Sito backed up. "I promise I'm just trying to help. I won't hurt her. I'm using my tin-chai to calm her down."

"It's all right, Galai," Ponch said. "Prince Sito is studying to be a doctor, specializing in the mind."

Galai eased back, still looking wary but making no further protests.

"Let go of your pain," he said to Miah. "You are stronger than you believe, and you will get through this."

Even I found myself feeling calmer.

Miah's wild eyes calmed, now peaceful, and her body loosened up. Her eyelids drooped.

Sito turned to me. "My tin-chai has to do with the power of suggestion. The words I speak make people feel a certain way. Calm, angry, sad, sleepy. Now you can use your tin-chai to heal her wound without worrying that she'll harm herself."

I nodded and sang.

"Do not attempt to control me,

I'm no longer caged in fear;

And if you ever try to stifle my voice,

My song will haunt your ear."

Color returned to her cheeks. Ponch let go of her slowly, but Miah didn't stir. A snore broke from her throat. The tension in her body eased completely.

One of the counselors stepped forward. "All right, everyone. Back to your rooms. Counselor Ponch and Counselor Rilla have things under control."

The other patients dispersed.

Aiden looked at Galai. "I remember you. You're one of the girls from the last showcase."

Galai panicked. "You won't make me go back, will you?" Her gaze darted around as though she were looking for an escape route.

Aiden put his hands up. "Relax, I would never force you to go anywhere you don't want to go. If my memory is correct, you're from Rilla's hometown. Any friend of my future wife is under extra protection here."

I stepped forward. "That's right. You're safe. So is Miah."

Galai relaxed. "I—I'm sorry. I know we're safe now, but I still feel like we're running. Always running. I'm so tired. This is my fault. She must have had the poison before we came to the clinic and hidden it under the floorboards. I should have double checked her. And I shouldn't have helped her lie when we were asked if we'd had suicidal thoughts before."

"It's not your fault," Ponch said. "I check on her every afternoon and inspect her room. Today, I heard her drinking something, but when I went to check, she just had a cup of water in her hand."

"You heard her?" I asked.

"Yes, my tin-chai. I try not to use it in order to give people privacy, but I have excellent hearing. Anyway, the liquid in her cup looked like water. I even smelled it. The poison was unidentifiable. Even so, I should have been more thorough and taken it away to be tested."

"Don't blame yourself either," I told Ponch. "Miah seemed determined to take her life. If you'd caught the poison, she might have tried something else. No one could fully protect her from herself."

Galai wiped her eyes. Sito handed her a handkerchief. Galai sent him a grateful look.

"Perhaps we should step away and give you some privacy with your counselors," Sito said.

"No," Galai said. "I think you all may take an interest in what I'm about to say. It involves politics and Emperor Carrick." She sank down onto a stone bench and looked at me. "I'm so sorry. I didn't tell you the whole truth earlier about who Miah is. She asked me not to. She was afraid you'd send her back to Carrick. Her real name is Kinsemiah. She's the *zhume* who became Carrick's faela a few months ago, and I served as her trifle."

"*Zhume*," Sito repeated. "She's an Ailo princess."

Aiden frowned. "Yes, I heard about that. The marriage helped Carrick build a stronger alliance with Ailo Kingdom. Ailo promised to come to his aid in times of war and to continue giving him tribute. I know he did it to increase his forces against us. But the last I heard, the *zhume* took her own life a few weeks ago."

"We faked her death," Galai said. "You see, the Ailo didn't want that stupid alliance with him. Carrick had his soldiers take Miah against her will. If she or her family disobeyed, Carrick would have them killed and establish a new Ailo family on the throne to control. Miah said she'd be better off dead, so no one could use her to get to her family and her people, but I managed to stop her from trying anything. Always made sure she didn't have any sharp objects and rarely left her alone."

I felt the burden Galai carried in her words. It must have been difficult for her to care for Miah. And on top of that, she had to deal with her own trauma.

Galai played with the hem of her dress and looked up at me. "Everything I told you at the clinic was the truth. After I found the novelties and Carrick mistook me for you, Radi intended on sending me away. But I couldn't leave Miah. I asked Radi if Miah could come with me. That way Miah would no longer stand between her and Carrick. Radi came up with a plan to smuggle both of us out of the palace. She faked Miah's death. Had it look like suicide by poison. That must have been where Miah got the idea. Once we were out of the palace, we were on our own. The empress didn't want anyone to know she helped us."

"And you managed to get to Emberwood and come to the clinic," Ponch said.

Galai nodded. "I thought she was getting better. But after dinner tonight, she got sick. I saw her bleeding and tried to help, but she started crying and yelling. I've never seen her so hysterical. She confessed to drinking the poison. When Counselor Ponch went to check on her today, she pretended to be drinking water. Even though we saved her this time, I'm terrified she'll try it again."

Ponch placed a hand on Galai's shoulder. "We'll keep monitoring her. The best thing we can do is let her know that we're here and hope that one day she'll find the will to heal."

Galai turned to Aiden. "Your Highness, may I ask a favor of you? Miah has been devastated believing she'll never return home again. Her family believes she's dead. Would it be possible to send someone to let them know Miah is alive? Perhaps they can even write her a letter. Of course, it must be done without alerting Carrick. It might help Miah to hear from her parents."

"Yes, I'll send a secret envoy at once," Aiden said.

She bowed. "Thank you."

Ponch cleared her throat. "Prince Sito, Prince Langdon, and Rilla, you can return to the palace. I'm sure you have important matters to attend to. I'll keep Miah under surveillance."

She and Galai bowed, and we took our leave.

CHAPTER 9

✦ ✦ ✦ ✦ ✦ ✦ ✦ ✦ ✦ ✦

Over the next week, I was so busy with wedding preparations that I couldn't go to the clinic. But Ponch sent me a full report. Miah hadn't tried to hurt herself again. Both she and Galai had been joining more group activities at the clinic. And Miah had cried when she heard we'd sent someone to tell her parents she was safe. It was a good sign, Ponch said.

Since Sito was staying for a while, I suggested that he take up a volunteer position at the main clinic with Doctor Flamyor, and he agreed. I saw him most mornings before he left for work. He was always whistling, and it was clear he enjoyed the job. I wished I could go with him and focus on work, but my dreams had to be put on hold for now. In these uncertain times, I wasn't sure if I'd ever return to the clinic.

King Ashbel and Queen Leonora still wanted to pretend they had the Will of Heaven. They wanted to make this announcement at the banquet reception after the wedding, but we still fought them on the issue. In the end, they compromised, saying they'd wait until after the wedding and see what Carrick's move would be before making any decisions regarding the scepter's reveal. But they were still determined to take responsibility for the Will of Heaven in our stead. Welder had told Aiden and me that he also thought the idea was ridiculous.

"But I'm not the king, so I can't fight him on this," Welder had said.

"Just focus on your wedding for now. We'll worry about your parents' delusions later."

We had just finished the rehearsal the evening before the ceremony. Though there was still much to be done, Queen Leonora had sent both Aiden and me to our rooms to rest. She reassured me that she and the servants would take care of the last-minute details. Having reconnected with Sito, Aiden finally had a friend to celebrate with. Which left me alone.

I was at my desk, using this rare quiet time to catch up on my correspondence. I ruffled through my letters. There was the one letter from Rell and Nia to which I had yet to reply. A note from a patient thanking me for healing their gout. Another thank you letter from a patient's mother, whose daughter had been suffering migraines until I helped her. There was also a list of guests Leonora had left me to review and add to, not that my opinion mattered. I made a face. I'd work on that later.

Then I picked up a letter from Sago and Wyle in Yao Kingdom, sent two weeks ago. I still needed to reply. If someone had told me two years ago that I'd befriend a fox Yao and her son, I would have told them they were insane. I missed Sago and Wyle a lot. We had already exchanged a few letters in the past months, but the post was slow. In this last letter I'd received, Sago wrote that she would try to come to Emberwood for the wedding if she could, but it was unlikely. She was busy with the Southern Yao Clans' current problem. Shyan poachers were increasing in number and robbing her people of their gemstones. Sago said that ever since Carrick had become the emperor, the number of crimes in Yao Kingdom had increased. She also wrote that she was sad to learn Carrick didn't turn out to be the leader we'd thought him to be, and she asked if the rumors were true about war between Seracedar and Emberwood being inevitable.

A knock sounded on the door, immediately followed by the entrance of a maidservant.

"Excuse me, Miss Rilla. The prince is requesting your presence."

I frowned. "I thought he was celebrating with Prince Sito."

"There's been an interruption," she said. "Both princes and General Welder are with visitors who have just arrived at the palace. They wish to speak with you as well."

"Who are they?"

"I'm afraid I don't know their names," the maidservant said. "But two of them said they're your friends. One is a beautiful woman with hair the color of snow, and she has a young son."

"Sago and Wyle?" I breathed a sharp inhale. They'd made it after all.

"They aren't alone," the maid said. "Two Ailo men are with them."

I followed her out, wondering why Sago had brought two Ailo with her. It must have something to do with Miah, their *zhume*.

I went up to the Gold Song Courtyard and entered the meeting room. A flash of downy white fluff crossed my vision. Then sixty pounds came crashing into my arms.

"Rilla!" Wyle cried. "I missed you."

I ruffled the boy's hair. "Missed you, too, kid."

"Hey, you never said you missed me." Aiden flashed Wyle a mock scowl. "And where's my hug?"

Wyle head butted into Aiden. "Of course. I missed you, but I'd rather hug Rilla. She's prettier."

We all laughed at that, including Sago. She was as beautiful as ever, observing us with a semi-amused smile, which was rare considering she was usually so serious.

"Wyle," Sago said, "why don't you go ahead and find a place to practice your martial arts in one of the courtyards? I have matters to discuss with the others."

"Yes, Mama." Wyle flounced out the door.

I went to Sago, and we embraced warmly. "I've been meaning to reply to your letter," I told her. "I'm so glad you're here."

One of the Ailo men cleared his throat, the sound deep and low, and I remembered our other company. The two Ailo were so short that Sago's figure had hidden both of them. Now they emerged, looking a bit awkward to be caught in the middle of this reunion. Sito and Welder also stood quietly to the side.

"I'm sorry, I should make the introductions," Sago said, standing by their side. "Aiden, Rilla, this is Mottle." Mottle was a stout, hairy man with bright, cherry cheeks. He watched Aiden and me warily, unsure we could be trusted. I didn't blame him. Even though this wasn't Seracedar Kingdom, we were still Shyan. And the Shyan people had enslaved his people.

"This is Brix." Sago indicated the second man, this one clean-shaven and a good three inches taller than Mottle, but still two feet shorter than me. His face was lively and good-natured. Unlike his friend, he seemed less suspicious of us.

In fact, his voice sounded animated and filled with emotion. "Prince Langdon, Miss Rilla. It is a pleasure to finally meet you. Sago and Wyle have been constantly talking about you both the entire journey to Emberwood. And we've also just made the acquaintance of Commander Welder and Prince Sito."

Aiden cleared his throat, taking on his proper royal manner. "It's a pleasure to meet you, too. And please, call me Aiden. I'm only Prince Langdon to my parents. Do I dare to guess that your visit has something to do with your *zhume*? Rest assured, she is doing well."

"Actually," Sago started. "I brought them—"

Brix cut her off. "We must discuss the *zhume* at one point. But we have a more pressing matter to bring to your attention, if I may speak."

Mottle interrupted. "Enough of your proper speech, Brix. Why are you asking for permission? Let me just spit it out." He scowled. "We want you to take Carrick down."

Aiden paused, taking this in. "Are you telling me you want to be our allies?"

"Secret allies," Mottle said.

I looked at Sago since she had brought the men here. "What exactly is this meeting about?"

Sago opened her mouth, but Brix went off again.

"It's like this. A few weeks ago, ten miners were buried in a shaft. The Shyan supervisors were having a banquet. Refused to help. The miners were dead before we could use our meager equipment to dig them out. The Shyan could have used their tin-chai to move the rocks within minutes. They could have saved them. Carrick did nothing to punish them. We know conditions are not going to improve with Carrick on the throne, and we want someone to take him down."

"We know the current antagonism between you and Carrick, and we're rooting for you to win," Mottle said. "They outnumber the Emberwood army, but you've still got a good chance seeing as Seracedar is in a state of complete disarray. The people are discontent."

"I know for a fact that Carrick does nothing but sit around drinking all day," Brix said. "Even his advisors are tired of him. They have to make all the decisions. Morale is low, and most of the kingdom is in complete poverty. So in this way, you've got the advantage."

"I'm afraid I still don't understand," Aiden said. "Not that I don't appreciate the information, but are you here just to give me a report?"

Welder moved away from the wall and spoke. "The Ailo want us to defeat Carrick, but they want to watch as spectators."

Mottle glared at him. "Look, we aren't cowards. If that's what you're accusing us of, we might as well leave now, you bas—"

Sago whipped her tail against the wall. Everyone jumped at the sound of the lash and turned to her. "Allow me to speak, please."

She looked annoyed. "Finally. Thank you for your attention. I brought the Ailo here because both Yao and Ailo Kingdoms have the same goal in mind. To gain our independence from Seracedar. I spoke with the Yao Clan leaders about joining Emberwood in this war, but unfortunately, they are concerned that Seracedar's army far outnumbers you. I reached out to Ailo Kingdom, and the Ailo king shares the same concern. If we join the fight and don't win, Seracedar will make conditions in our kingdom more miserable."

"That's what I was explaining," Brix said. "I—"

Sago's voice rose, cutting him off. "Excuse me, I wasn't done talking."

I had to repress a snort. Sago caught me and smiled. "Now as I was saying, given my fondness for both Rilla and Aiden, I want to be of service to you. And the Ailo king appreciates that you have given his daughter, the *zhume,* a sanctuary. He sent Brix and Mottle with me. We want to support you against Seracedar. You can think of us as private mercenaries. We've got networks, friends who travel between kingdoms unnoticed. We'll be your eyes and ears, deliver messages, complete any secret mission you require."

"Thank you, we'll take that into consideration," Welder said. "But I've already got spies in place."

"Excuse me, sir, but I didn't say we were working for you," Sago said. "Any mission we take will be at Rilla or Aiden's request. And we report to them alone."

Welder sulked but remained quiet.

"Thank you, Sago," I said. "And thank you, Brix and Mottle. I can't think of any assignments at the moment. The war hasn't started."

Sago's gaze sharpened. "Hasn't started? But you made the first move. A bold statement if you ask me."

Aiden frowned. "What are you talking about? My ah-fu has ordered us to wait for Carrick to initiate."

"That isn't what I heard," Sago said. "Brix, tell them what you told me."

"Twice a month, I go to Cedar Palace and deliver tribute to Carrick," Brix said. "That's why the king chose me to help you. There was an assassination attempt on Carrick a couple of weeks ago. Poison in the seal of a letter that Prince Langdon and Rilla sent him. The palace advisors think Rilla made the poison."

"I never sent him a letter," Aiden said.

I scowled. "That's outrageous. I wouldn't use poison to kill him. Too kind."

Welder sighed, looking impatient. "Did you witness this attempt personally? If not, then it's just a rumor."

"I didn't see the letter, but I saw Carrick in person," Brix said. "He was in bed, still sick from touching the poison in the seal."

"Too bad it didn't kill him," Mottle said. "Would save us so much trouble. Next time add double the poison, Rilla."

"I told you, it wasn't from me," I said. "Someone else did it and must be trying to set us up. This means Carrick's plotting revenge for sure."

"Which leads me to the other part of what I heard," Brix said. "The guards were gossiping that the Fauxhemian queen sent an emissary to speak with Carrick. It made me think. Carrick probably wants to persuade them into an alliance with him. I wonder what he offered them."

Sito, who had been quiet all this time, perked up and gave Brix a sharp look. "I find it unlikely that the Fauxhemians would agree to join Carrick."

Welder frowned. "As I said, rumors are just rumors." He turned to me and Aiden. "Are you sure you want these Ailo men acting as your spies?"

"Don't insult us," Mottle said. "We don't have to help you."

Aiden gave Welder a look. "Don't be rude. I trust them." He turned back to our guests. "Thank you for all the information. Sago, I can't tell you how much I owe you."

"Yes, I know," she said. "Now I need to find Wyle. I'll see you later."

She took her exit, leaving Brix and Mottle with us.

"There is still the matter of the *zhume*," I said.

"Yes," Brix said. "The king and queen say she can't come back to Ailo in case Carrick gets wind that she's still alive. She must stay here. We'll check in on her whenever we come to visit. Can we see her now?"

"Of course," Aiden said. "Attendant Bin, please take Brix and Mottle to the clinic."

The moment they were out of earshot, Welder said, "Are you sure they are to be trusted? You just met them."

"I trust Sago," Aiden said.

I nodded. "So do I. And if she trusts the Ailo, then I believe them, too. I'm concerned about who sent Carrick that letter. Someone might be trying to provoke him into an attack by framing us."

"And what about the Fauxhemians?" Aiden said. "If Carrick is offering them something for an alliance, we have to stop it. Maybe we can offer more. Ask them to join us instead."

Welder reared up. "Absolutely not. I despise the Fauxhemians. They're hypocrites, advocating for peace, yet they stand for nothing."

I was taken aback by his vehemence. I'd never seen him get so emotional, nor had I realized he hated the Fauxhemians so much.

"I find the people, especially the king, a bunch of hedonists," Welder said. "Not to mention inauthentic. The current queen consort acts as regent now. She cares more about her reputation than the people. You needn't worry about her joining Carrick if he indeed made an offer. They're not going to join us either. No use asking. She won't go to war, not if it means lowering the public opinion of her."

Sito made a face at Welder. "They are not as bad as you say. I met the queen, and I'm friends with Prince Lymere. He is kindhearted. His stepmother is a bit cold, but I don't think she has evil intent." He looked at Aiden. "Cousin, I think you should clarify what's going on. Visit Fauxhemia and ask the queen if she even sent that emissary. I can go with you."

"I think it's worth a try," Aiden said.

Welder opened his mouth. "I don't—"

Aiden held up a hand. "Enough. Tomorrow is my wedding day, and I've already got more on my plate than I can handle. Let's deal with this later and focus on getting through the wedding. Make sure to tighten security, Welder."

"Yes, already on it," Welder said.

"I want more guards to watch over Rilla," Aiden said. "Since we're almost positive Carrick is going to do something tomorrow, I want to be sure she's safe. I don't know what to expect from him. He might even try to abduct her to get to me."

I gasped. "Wait, you think he'd really try to kidnap me?"

"I wouldn't put anything past him."

Welder nodded. "I agree. Rest assured, my men will be on high alert."

"Now I need some peace and quiet alone with Rilla."

Welder and Sito dismissed themselves.

"Alone at last," Aiden said. "I'll walk with you back to your room. I was thinking of staying the night. We haven't seen each other all week."

I was looking forward to talking with him, too. "We can talk for a bit, but we should still sleep early."

A maidservant slipped through the door.

"Your Highness, the king and queen wish to speak with you regarding last-minute details for tomorrow."

"Of course, Rilla and I will be right there."

The maidservant gave us an awkward look. "The king and queen said they wish to speak to you. Alone. They said it's a family matter."

A pang of hurt twisted and turned like a knife in my heart. A family matter? Even though I was getting married to their son tomorrow. This exclusion made it seem like Aiden was married to them, and I was to be just a faela on the side.

Ugh. What a terrible thought. What was wrong with me? They probably didn't mean to hurt my feelings, and with everything that was going on, I shouldn't be feeling this way over something so petty. But it still felt a lot like rejection.

Aiden sighed, looking exhausted. "I'll be right there."

"Tell them you're tired," I said. "You don't have to go."

He gave me an apologetic look. "Sorry. They're my parents. Get some rest. We'll see each other at the wedding."

He marched away, looking like an animal on the way to being slaughtered. This was all too much for him and for me. Why couldn't Leonora and Ashbel see that we were capable of making decisions on our own? We had been through battles before, yet they still didn't believe in us.

It made me wonder what would happen once Aiden and I were married. Would they continue to have private meetings without me? What about when we had children of our own? Would his parents interfere in how we raised them? And as for the Will of Heaven, once we won the war, would they try to control the way we chose to rule Seracedar?

If they continued treating Aiden as a child and not as a leader, who was supposed to be my partner, I wasn't even sure we could win the war. And now I was having doubts about surviving a marriage.

I hoped we could all figure out our roles soon and be amenable to change, or we were doomed.

CHAPTER 10

✦ ✦ ✦ ✦ ✦ ✦ ✦ ✦ ✦ ✦

On the morning of the wedding, I woke up to a line of servants coming into my room with makeup, hair extensions, and my traditional wedding attire. I didn't even have time to pull the bedcovers off before a maid hauled me up and had me sit in a chair. Then someone was applying creams to my face while someone else tugged at the tangles in my hair. A third person gave me a container of dried fruit and nuts to eat while I got my hair done.

Queen Leonora entered the room. She looked uptight. Nothing like her usual perky self. "We're behind schedule. Why hasn't anyone done her makeup yet?" She threw me a short smile. "Good morning, dear. Don't worry, today's going to be perfect."

Leonora pointed at the makeup artist. "Apply more color on her cheeks." Then she circled me, examining my hair, and frowned. "What are you thinking? That updo is sloppy. Do you want it to come undone mid-ceremony? Oh, get out of the way. I'll do it."

She pushed the hairdresser to the side and proceeded to pin up my hair. I looked at her reflection in the mirror. "Leonora, there's no need to be here stressing yourself out about how I look. You should be resting and preparing yourself for the big day."

"I don't need much time to get ready. It's not every day that my only son gets married. For years when I thought he was dead, I never dreamed

I'd get to have this day. So you'd better believe I'm going to make sure it's perfect."

She stood back and assessed her work. "Yes, that should do it."

I could hardly recognize myself in the mirror. The updo was tight on my head, every curl in place. This reminded me of getting ready for the showcase at Cedar Palace. It felt uncomfortable and inauthentic. But at least this time, I was getting married to the love of my life at the end of the day.

Queen Leonora blinked as though she were about to cry. I turned in the chair, trying to look at her, but she stopped me. "Don't move or you'll ruin your hair. I'm fine. But I think you're right. The stress must be getting to me."

She took a vial from her pocket and dabbed an ointment on the pressure points of her forehead. "This should help. It's really been helping with my stress. Cures my headaches and all the tension in my body." She placed the vial on the table next to the makeup.

Then she beamed at me through teary eyes. "You look beautiful. I'm so happy you're going to be my daughter. Now let's get you dressed." She addressed two maids. "Get the wedding attire. Do not mess up the hair."

The maids helped me slip into a silk wedding gown, a royal lavender with a gorgeous floral design that buttoned to the side. It tightened to a close fit against my body.

"You're ready except for the veil," Leonora said. "I'm going to get ready now. Sit here, and the maids will lead you to the courtyard when it's time."

With one last warning to the maids to not mess up my hair, she left my dressing room. I saw her vial of ointment on the dressing table.

"Leonora, you forgot—"

She was already out of hearing distance. I'd return it to her after the ceremony.

I waited for an hour, then another. I couldn't eat or use the chamber pot for fear of messing up my makeup or hair. It was a good thing I hadn't drank much water, and I was glad I'd eaten the dried fruit and nuts earlier.

Finally, two maids entered the dressing room. One of them carried a purple silk veil. They placed it on top of my head and covered my face. I couldn't see anything.

"This way, Miss Rilla," one of them said.

I took slow steps, letting them lead me and hoping I wouldn't crash into anything.

Then I heard the murmurs of an audience. Someone was talking, his voice amplified through his tin-chai. Probably the Crocus who was presiding over the ceremony. "The bride has entered the courtyard. All guests please rise."

I heard the squeaks and clatters of people pushing their chairs back and standing. I let the maids guide me forward.

"The bride is approaching the holy table where she will stand with the groom, His Honorable Highness Prince Langdon Ai. His and Her Majesty, parents of Prince Langdon, are seated at the table, to be honored in the joining of their son and Miss Rilla Marseas."

The Crocus's voice boomed through the courtyard, projecting out to wherever the sound was received. I wasn't entirely sure how it worked, but I'd heard there were Shyan with the tin-chai to receive sound. They would report the entire ceremony in different parts of the entire kingdom through special sound boxes that amplified their voices.

I continued my walk, imagining the guests who were watching. Sago and Wyle. Welder and Sito. Some of the king and queen's friends. News reporters.

My maids stopped, preventing me from going forward. They adjusted my position, nudging me a bit to the left. Then they fell away from me, and I heard them step back. I felt Aiden's presence to my right, smelled a familiar hint of camphor oil that was part of his signature fragrance. Though he said nothing, I could picture him smiling.

I cast my gaze down, past the end of the silk veil and to the ground. Aiden's feet were pointed forward, the only indication that we were both facing the pagoda and the Crocus presiding over the ceremony.

The Crocus cleared his throat. "First bow. Pay honor to Old Grandfather Heaven."

We both bowed to the front.

"Second bow. Turn to your right. Pay honor to your parents and to your ancestors."

We bowed a second time.

A cry broke out, followed by wailing. The king shouted something I couldn't understand. The crowd gasped.

Something was wrong.

CHAPTER 11

✦ ✦ ✦ ✦ ✦ ✦ ✦ ✦ ✦ ✦

I threw the veil off my head.

The king and queen were still both seated, but their eyes were glazed over. King Ashbel shouted and flailed his fists at the heavens. "This is my fault. I should have protected him." He hit himself on the head again and again.

Aiden jumped in, holding his father's arms back so he wouldn't hurt himself. Several guests helped him.

Then I saw the queen. She was sobbing, so hard that her whole body shook. She couldn't stop, just like that night at dinner.

Everyone was busy with the king, they hadn't noticed Leonora. I went to her and placed a hand on her shoulder. "Are you feeling all right?"

She cried out in anguish. "Why have you stolen my son from me? Where is he? Where did you take him?"

She clawed out at me. I jumped away, dodging her thrashing arms. Now others took notice. Sito came with some other guards and tried to hold the queen back. She lashed out at them.

"Something's wrong with both of them," Aiden said. "Rilla, please help."

I sang, unleashing my wyis into the king first. Nothing happened.

He continued his tirade, struggling against the people who held him back.

The guests gasped, watching the scene from the side of the room.

Again, I sang, this time directing my wyis into the queen. But she continued to cry. It wasn't working.

"Leonora," I said. "Can you hear me?"

She wailed louder. "You took him away. My son, my only son."

"Whatever's happening to both of them, it's not physical," I said. "I think it's in their minds."

Next to me, Sito stirred. "Could it be Fauxhemian poisoning?"

I looked at him. "What?"

"Fauxhemian blood can be used to poison the mind," he said. "I remember my aunt mentioning to me that the new chef is Fauxhemian. What if he poisoned their food?"

A man from among the guests called out, "Someone find the chef. He could have poisoned us all." Other echoes cried out, echoing their concerns and fears.

Leonora wrenched her arm free and struck out, catching Sito in the face. He handed her to a guard. He took a deep breath, and in a strong, commanding voice, said, "Calm. Both of you go to sleep."

In a few seconds, both the king and queen slumped over, fast asleep.

"We'll have to keep them that way until we get the antidote," Sito said. "Take them both to the clinic. The medical team should be able to care for them. Some of the nurses have sleep-inducing tin-chai to keep them in a coma."

The servants jumped in, carrying the king and queen away.

Welder shouted at his men. "Secure the palace doors and make sure no one leaves."

The guests had all gathered at the side of the room, continuing to watch us. They were murmuring to one another and looked uncertain about what they should do next. I caught Sago's worried glance and saw Wyle whisper something into his mama's ear.

Welder motioned to the guests. "The wedding is postponed until further notice. Attendant Bin will direct you to a waiting area. For the safety of everyone here, we ask for your patience while we apprehend the suspect."

He gestured to Hu, one of his men. "Hu, take five others and search the palace for the Fauxhemian chef. When you find him, bring him to me."

Attendant Bin tried to maintain order and directed the guests away from the courtyard. Sago looked over at me again, but as the guests moved, she and Wyle followed them.

Aiden spoke, turning my attention back to him. "Are you sure it was poison from Fauxhemian blood?"

Aiden, Sito, and Welder were studying the chairs and table where the king and queen had been seated.

Sito held up a handkerchief. He used it to sweep across the wooden tea table standing between the king's and queen's chairs. "Not entirely, but there's a good chance of it. We need to find the source of the poison to confirm."

Welder's man, Vay, ran up to us. "General, you have to look at this. It was just delivered to one of our staff anonymously."

Welder took the letter from Vay. "It's addressed to Aiden and Rilla." He broke the seal and read it. "My dear friends, congratulations on your happy day. I sent your wedding present to your parents. A Fauxhemian chef. Enjoy. Consider this my official declaration of war. Signed, Emperor Carrick of Seracedar."

Welder looked up, his expression grave. "At least now we can confirm it is Fauxhemian blood poisoning. Must have been in their food or in something the chef gave them personally."

Aiden clenched his fists. "How could he attack my parents? He got personal. This is my fault."

I put a hand on his shoulder. "No, it's not. We knew he was going to do something. The important thing now is to find a way to cure your parents."

Aiden nodded. His gaze went to the wine glasses on the table. He lifted them and sniffed. "They've had similar symptoms before, but Rilla cured them. Why couldn't she do it this time?"

"Maybe he used a smaller dose the first time," Sito replied. "Something still curable with Rilla's singing. But if it's been slowly accumulating over time, or if he used a larger dose, the long-term effects on the mind are something Rilla probably can't cure. That would be my guess anyway." He gazed at the metal cups of wine that Aiden held. "We better have the lab inspect the wine. It might be the only thing they drank that no one else did. If we can trace the poison, maybe we can see if an antidote already exists."

A thought crossed my mind. "No, check the ointment Leonora used. She had it this morning. It's in a vial on my dresser. I remember she gave some to the king to try."

"That's right," Aiden said. "She said the chef made it to help relieve her stress. Both of my parents have been using it for a few weeks now."

"A daily dose of poison makes sense," Sito said. "That must be it."

"I'll go find the ointment and take it to the lab." Welder took his leave.

"Sito, what if there is no cure?" Aiden asked. "Can we make one?"

"Every emerald-blood has a different type of effect on the mind, and each has a different antidote," Sito said. "I can do some research to see if there have been similar cases. Maybe we'll be lucky if an antidote was already developed. If not, then we need blood from the person who poisoned them."

"Please find whatever information you can," Aiden said. "I'm going to the clinic to check on the situation."

"I'll go with you," I said.

"Actually, I could use your help," Sito said. "I've got books and case studies in the library, and I need someone to bounce ideas off of."

I nodded. "Of course."

Aiden reached over and kissed me on the forehead. "I'm so sorry. A part of me actually believed we would get through the wedding without Carrick pulling something like this. I shouldn't have let my guard down."

"None of this is your fault," I said. "It's Carrick's fault. Go see your parents. I'll let you know if we find some answers."

Aiden rushed off, while Sito and I headed in the opposite direction. Two maids trailed after me, holding the hem of my dress up. I didn't have time to change, so they would have to come with us.

Ten minutes later, I was seated at a desk in the library with a pile of newspapers and research articles in front of me. I had called in Ponch to help us. She had been a wedding guest, and she was familiar with reading case studies of mind illnesses, having been through school herself before becoming a counselor. Ponch sat across from me, and Sito stood, sorting through the papers, at the front end of the desk.

The school was on hiatus for the week due to what should be a celebratory time, so all was quiet. No one was in the library except for the three of us. The medical textbook section was at the back, and the books filled the whole wall of shelves.

"Remember, look for a similar case," Sito said. "Even if the suspect isn't alive anymore, the blood of the suspect's relative might work. Families usually share the same color of blood and may have a similar kind of poison if they are close kin."

Ponch pinched her reading glasses closer to her face. "Here's a case." She summarized an old research article. "After eating a chocolate truffle, a man was overcome with love for a woman. Believed she was his dead wife. His sister suspected poison and found an antidote, and sure enough that woman had used her blood to convince the man that she was his dead wife because she had been in love with him."

"That's too different," Sito said. "He may have been overcome with emotion, but in my opinion, our king and queen were overcome by grief and guilt, not love. It's important to distinguish the feelings involved in these cases. Poisons vary and target specific emotional experiences."

"What about this one?" Ponch cleared her throat. "An emerald-blooded man poisoned a rival who loved the same girl. The victim was overcome with rage and was convinced to kill the girl. The emerald-blood did it out of revenge when the girl picked the victim over him. When the victim was cured, he didn't remember a thing."

Sito drummed his fingers on the desk, looking thoughtful. "No. That was rage and the power of persuasion to commit murder. We're looking at grief and guilt over something that happened in the past. My aunt couldn't stop crying. My uncle was blaming himself for something."

"I think it was about Aiden's disappearance," I said. "Leonora kept asking why her son got taken away. Ashbel kept blaming himself for not protecting his son better."

Sito clapped his hands and pointed at me. "Rilla, I think you're right. After Aiden disappeared, my aunt and uncle blamed themselves. They said they must have spoken too harshly to him about his school marks. If they had let him continue martial arts training, maybe he wouldn't have run away and put himself in a position to be kidnapped. They regretted not placing better guards in front of his room that night to protect him. They said it was their fault for allowing their son to get kidnapped and killed, as we had all thought my cousin was dead. Maybe this poison targets parents who blame themselves for losing a child."

My gaze passed over an article about the Fauxhemian king. *King Lieka Said to be Mind Poisoned with Grief. Suspect Remains at Large.* I scanned the article.

"This is interesting," I said. "Did you know the Fauxhemian king was poisoned into grief? For the last ten years, he's been closeted away in his room, either crying or blaming himself over the death of his daughter, Princess Bree, because he sent her to become Emperor Terran's faela. I had heard King Lieka had descended into madness, but I didn't know it was from mind poisoning."

Sito dropped the paper he was holding and stared at me. "How could I not have seen it? That case is similar enough. Ten years ago, King Lieka was mind poisoned, and the suspect was never found. He experienced similar symptoms as my aunt and uncle. Grief over the tragedy of losing his child. A parent who blames himself for his daughter's death."

I scanned the article further. "Says here the suspect was the king's chef, Dribin Clox, who disappeared and was never caught."

"Chef?" Sito repeated.

Ponch froze. She looked at us and put a finger to her lips. "We're not alone," she whispered. "I heard someone twitch." Her gaze traveled to the back of the library. "There. Underneath the unoccupied desks."

CHAPTER 12

✦ ✦ ✦ ✦ ✦ ✦ ✦ ✦ ✦ ✦

The three of us looked around at one another, and I knew we had the same thought. Whoever was hiding might be our suspect.

We all stayed quiet, listening to the silence.

Ponch squinted, a concentrated look on her face. She nodded to a lampshade on one of the desks. I saw what she meant. The tassels dangling from the lamp were shaking.

The three of us stood. Ponch, the best fighter of the three of us, readied herself into a fighting position. "We know you're here. Show yourself."

A figure sprang up and hurled the lamp at us. Sito pushed me aside. The lamp clipped the side of his head, and he yelped in pain. His hand went to his ear and came away with blood.

"Sito!" I cried.

"I'm fine." Sito sprang up and turned, facing the attacker. Ponch and I did as well. It was a tall, muscular man. He had fine features and pale, smooth skin. Fauxhemian features. This had to be the chef.

I was surprised to see that he hadn't bothered to hide his face now that he was exposed. His gaze darted to the door.

Sito got there first and blocked the exit. "Don't even try."

The Fauxhemian grinned. He was two feet taller and at least twenty pounds heavier than Sito. I realized he had no intention of letting Sito stop him.

"Sito, get out of his way!" I shouted. Too late.

The man ran at Sito, planted a fist in the prince's face, and knocked him over. Sito fell like a blade of grass.

The Fauxhemian chef jumped over Sito and bolted out the door. Ponch ran after him. "Stop! Someone stop that man."

Crumpled on the floor, Sito groaned. I knelt, getting closer to inspect him. His nose was bleeding, and he had a black eye. He winced as he attempted to get up.

"You are a scholar, my friend, not a fighter," I said. "You shouldn't have attempted to block someone built like a brick wall. You should have waited for Ponch."

"I'm a man," he said. "It's my job to defend women. You're the weaker gender."

"First of all, don't let Ponch hear you say that. And second, why didn't you just use your tin-chai on him?"

"I didn't think of that," Sito said. "I'm such an idiot."

"Nothing's broken," I said. "But I'll fix you right up."

I sang, healing Sito of his bruises and bloody nose.

"Thank you." Sito pulled himself off the ground. "Do you think Ponch got him?"

Our answer came before I could make a reply as Ponch returned disgruntled. "He got away. Jumped out a window. I expected to see his dead, broken body on the ground, but he wasn't there. I don't know how he survived unless he had an accomplice. I already told Welder, and his men are searching outside."

The door to the library opened again, and Welder walked in. He looked furious. "I can't believe this. The one place we failed to search."

"It's my fault," Sito said, casting his gaze down at his shoes.

"Mine, too," Ponch said. "I'm sorry I let him get away."

Welder's expression softened. "No, I should have had my men be more thorough. I didn't think he'd hide in the library." He sighed. "I do have one bit of hopeful news. The chef registered his name as Dribin Clox. The name rings a bell, but I can't recall where I've heard it."

"That's the suspect in the article," I said. "The one who may have poisoned King Lieka."

"That's right," Welder said. "I remember reading about the chef who mind poisoned Lieka."

"How incredibly foolish of him to use his real name," Ponch commented. "Especially since he's already wanted for poisoning another king."

"Unless he wanted us to know him," I said.

"We've got to find him," Sito said. "That man is our only hope at a cure for my uncle and aunt."

"I already have someone drawing his likeness to post all over the kingdom," Welder said. He paused, tapping his chin. "As I recall, some Fauxhemians didn't believe the chef was guilty. They suspected King Lieka's former mistress. She killed herself because of the backlash, and then there was a scandal when, shortly after, he married her daughter, the current queen, Esmeralda."

Ponch shook her head, tsking. "What a complicated situation."

Sito frowned. "Why do you bring that up, Welder? Do you think there's a connection between Queen Esmeralda and Dribin Clox?"

"The Ailo man from the other day said a Fauxhemian emissary was at Cedar Palace visiting with Carrick," Welder said. "If the Fauxhemians are in alliance with Carrick, he could have asked them to hire Clox to poison our king and queen."

"I find it unlikely," Sito said. "Why would Esmeralda hire the same man who poisoned her husband? Especially since he's been a fugitive for ten years. And also, doing so would only bring back the scandal with her mother."

Welder shrugged. "Just a thought. I don't want to rule out anything."

The library door swung open and Aiden walked in.

"How are the king and queen?" Welder asked.

"Stable for now," Aiden said. "We've got a care team and Doctor Flamyor working together to keep them asleep until we can find a cure."

"We have findings to report on that," Sito said.

"I'm afraid that'll have to wait." Aiden's face was grave. "I have other bad news. Cindertrance City was attacked. Carrick has started the war."

My stomach tightened like I'd been punched. Everything was happening at once. It was clear Carrick had orchestrated all of this to punish us on our wedding day. And it occurred to me now that, since the ceremony had been interrupted, Aiden and I weren't officially married yet.

But that would have to wait. We needed to strategize our defense.

Welder looked at Aiden and me. "I've instructed the wedding guests to remain at the palace until further notice. Meanwhile, both of you need to address the kingdom. Now that the king and queen can no longer make decisions, the two of you need to take responsibility. I'll make arrangements for your appearance together. You have one hour to get ready." He regarded me. "And Rilla, prepare the scepter. You will be giving a public display of its power."

The scepter was still in the form of a flute. I took it out from my cloak pocket. Welder touched it, and the wood became heavier. The carvings on the base appeared, and the scepter returned to its original form.

"We don't need to hide it again," Welder said. "From now on, all will know you hold its power."

Aiden and I sat on the sofa in the stateroom alone, next to the double doors that would lead out to the balcony, where we were expected to address the kingdom in fifteen minutes. We'd rehearsed what we were going to say, and now we waited in silence. I couldn't help noticing how tense Aiden seemed. His shoulders looked like they carried a load of a thousand bricks. And when he'd rehearsed his speech, his tone had seemed so robotic. I could sense the uncertainty in him, so unlike the charismatic man I thought I knew him to be. He must be stressed about taking over his parents' role and worried over their current state. It was a lot of pressure, and I wished I could take some of it off of him.

"We can do this," I said. "You know that, right? This is just another obstacle, another battle, and we can get through it."

He set his lips in a grim line. "I hope so. But I feel so unprepared. My parents are the king and queen of Emberwood. What if I can't lead our people without them? What if I can't be the king everyone needs? I've never had so many lives that depended on my decisions. All of the responsibility rests on my shoulders. One wrong choice could result in Emberwood's collapse and thousands of deaths. Back in Cedar Palace, if I made a wrong move, I could have died, but it would only have affected my life. Carrick could have found another guard to replace me."

"Your decisions affected Carrick, too," I reminded him. "That's why he trusted you. And during our travels, I always trusted you to make decisions with me. You've always been my strength."

Aiden kept his gaze focused on the ground. "You give me way more credit than I deserve. The confidence and strength you saw in me was nothing but bravado. I was just trying to impress you. Truthfully, out of the two of us, I think you're the stronger one. Your voice is far more powerful than my fire tin-chai."

"It's not fair to make a comparison like that," I said. "Our tin-chai are meant to do completely different things. Besides, you throw the strongest, brightest flames I've ever seen. And so quickly, too. No one can outrun them."

"Only because I trained myself to be stronger and faster."

"Which is an amazing feat." I hit his shoulder lightly. "Don't you dare put yourself down. You worked hard to become the warrior you are today."

He looked at me, searching my face. "Can I confess something to you? Something I've never admitted out loud?"

"Of course."

"I always wished I had been born with a more unique tin-chai. To have a fire tin-chai is quite common in Emberwood even if I do throw the biggest, fastest fire bombs."

I stared at him incredulously. "Where is all of this coming from?"

He shrugged and sighed. "I guess I've been feeling a little jealous. Especially when I found out Sito had a latent tin-chai that was so unique. I love my cousin, don't get me wrong, but when we were kids, I had the satisfaction of knowing even though he was great at everything else, he didn't have a tin-chai while I did. And now to know that he has one that's so incredible, to control people's moods with his words, I no longer feel special. Don't ever tell him I said that."

"This has to be your parents talking in your head," I said. "They should never have compared you to Sito. You need to tune that voice out."

"I know. But it's just something I've been thinking about lately. You and Sito have tin-chai that can help the world through your words. Even Welder's tin-chai is unique in a way I envy. The ability to transform objects or environments into whatever he envisions. It's like he's changing reality."

"We can't all be the same, which is why we work best as a team. Especially on the battlefield. Welder is naturally gifted at strategic moves, which his tin-chai helps him to accomplish. Hiding things in plain sight. You don't know what's real and what's not until it's too late. It's a great defensive move against an enemy. You, with your fire tin-chai, were born to be a fighter and lead the offense. Then there's Sito and me. Healers. Our strength comes in the aftermath, taking care of the wounded so they can live to fight another day."

"Except you were born with the ability to heal *and* to kill," he said. "The whole package."

"Yes, but the killing part doesn't come naturally. Only when I feel like I have no other choice. But that's not my point. Tin-chai aside, I'm saying we prefer to help people in different ways. I'd rather use my knowledge of healing to help people. While you would rather fight than study, and your skills allow you to protect people. That's why we complement one another."

"Yes, yes, I know," he said. "Yin versus yang energy. Night versus day. We can't have one without the other. I'm just saying if Old Grandfather Heaven had given me a more unique tin-chai, maybe I'd feel more worthy to be a king."

"I helped amplify your tin-chai, didn't I?" I said. "You have the ability to turn into light, which I think is unique."

He let out a self-deprecating laugh. "Sure, I can turn into light, but it doesn't seem to last for long. I tried it once after the first time you gave me the power. Couldn't sustain it for more than five seconds."

"Maybe with more practice."

"It doesn't matter. I'll never be as gifted as you and Sito."

I gazed into his eyes. "The way I see it, Old Grandfather Heaven gets to decide which gifts we get and what roles we're born into. We can't control that. But Old Grandfather Heaven did give us a choice in deciding how to use what we've been given. Whether we're a non-magical koong or we have a one-of-a-kind amplified tin-chai, whether we're the daughter of a pauper or the only son of a king, it's our responsibility to take what Old Grandfather Heaven gave us and make use of it to be a blessing to others, not a burden. I believe someone wise once said to me, 'Your worth isn't dependent upon your tin-chai, and a person can have all the talent in the world, but if he doesn't have love, he becomes worthless.'"

I imitated Aiden's deep voice when I quoted back his words.

"All right, maybe that wise person had a point," Aiden said with a laugh. "I'm glad you remembered his words when he forgot them." He sobered. "Still, maybe if I had a healing tin-chai or half the brains you and Sito have, I could cure my parents."

"We'll find a cure together," I said. "We've got enough brains between the three of us."

Aiden took my hand and squeezed it. "Thank you. I guess I'm just feeling the pressure of all that's happening. I'm glad you're here with me to talk the craziness out of my head."

"Yes, that's also why we're partners," I said. "We're stronger together because we balance each other out. When one of us feels discouraged, the other gives encouragement."

I looked up and saw Welder watching us. I jolted up, not expecting to see him there.

"How long have you been there?" I asked.

"I guess you didn't hear me come in," he said, not answering the question. "It seemed like you were discussing something important, so I didn't want to disturb."

I'd never met anyone so stealthy. Even Aiden, judging by his look of surprise, hadn't heard Welder. He could have at least cleared his throat or made some noise. Had he been eavesdropping on us?

But Welder gave no indication that he thought he'd done anything out of the ordinary.

"Judging by your presence, I suppose you came to tell us it's about time for our address," Aiden said. "Although I thought Attendant Bin would give us the signal."

"I wanted to be here for support, so I came first," Welder said. "You ready? We've got quite a crowd out there."

Aiden nodded. At least he looked more confident now.

Welder nodded. "Good. I trust you'll be splendid."

Some servants, along with Attendant Bin, now entered the room. They brushed at our outfits and hair one final time. Then we stood in front of the double doors, and Attendant Bin opened them. Aiden and I walked out onto the balcony together. Within my cloak pocket, I felt the scepter's true shape. It was bulkier and longer than it had been as a flute, but I could still conceal it in my cloak until reveal time.

The evening sky was filled with the pastel colors of sunset. Embers stood below us, all wearing somber faces. No cheers, just a sadness that could be heard through a wave of hushed murmurs. Aiden addressed them.

"Thank you for joining us on what was supposed to be a joyous occasion. Unfortunately, the wedding was interrupted when my ah-fu and ah-mu were mind poisoned. King Ashbel and Queen Leonora are in stable condition, and we are working on finding an antidote. Until they are in good health again, Rilla and I have decided to postpone our wedding."

I took note that he seemed calmer now, more confident. For that, I was glad.

"The laws of this kingdom state in the event that the current king and queen are incapable of ruling, their titles and responsibilities shall be given to their progeny and the life partners of their progeny. Therefore, from this day forward, I shall be your king until my ah-fu and ah-mu are restored to health."

The audience roared in approval. Aiden waited for them to quiet down before continuing.

"I have chosen a different name for myself. My parents named me Langdon, but I have lived as Aiden for most of my life. Therefore, I will be known to you as King Aiden."

More applause and shouts sounded.

Aiden raised a hand, indicating he had more to say. "I thank the Emberwood people for your support and wish to address another matter that you must have heard already. Emperor Carrick of Seracedar has attacked Cindertrance City and declared war on our kingdom. Furthermore, he has admitted to hiring the assassin who poisoned my ah-fu and ah-mu. He will not go unpunished. We will fight back and overthrow him. Rilla and I have been given this responsibility by Old

Grandfather Heaven, and we have the proof right here."

I brought the scepter out and raised it. Gasps came from the crowd.

"Behold, the Sacred Cedar Scepter. We have kept this a secret, hoping we could talk Carrick into surrendering peacefully," Aiden said. "We never wanted to go to war. But his actions show that he is a corrupt man."

Murmurs sounded among the crowd, but Aiden spoke louder, and the sound amplifiers rose above the sound of the people.

"Emperor Carrick deceived everyone with a fake scepter, but Old Grandfather Heaven allowed Rilla and I to find the true scepter. Some of you may be wondering how we can prove we're not lying. Allow me to demonstrate."

Aiden raised his hands, and a flame lit up in each palm. "You all know I was born with the tin-chai to form fire in my hands. But the scepter has amplified my tin-chai, a symbol that I have been blessed with the right to rule."

He touched the base of the scepter. A visible energy zinged through the atmosphere. Aiden's whole body morphed into fire. Several seconds later, he returned to his original form. Oohs and ahhs echoed through the people.

Aiden gestured to me. "Rilla's tin-chai was also amplified, giving her the right to rule together with me. She is able to give tin-chai and take it away from any Shyan person. She already amplified my tin-chai further, giving me the power to transform into light."

He disappeared. A ray of light showed in his place, darting across the balcony and rushing through the crowd before returning by my side and changing back to his normal self.

Shouts of awe resounded in the crowd.

I raised the scepter. Another bolt of visible energy emanated from the scepter into the air.

"I'll demonstrate my power in front of you tonight," I said. "Don't worry, I'm not about to take anyone's tin-chai away, and I don't intend to unless absolutely necessary." No need to mention I didn't actually know if I could. Though the scepter's song said it was part of my amplification, I'd never tried it yet, nor did I want to. It felt morally wrong to remove someone's tin-chai. "But I will give two volunteers tin-chai amplification. Any takers?"

Wary looks were exchanged among the crowd, but a few brave people raised their hands. I chose two of them standing at the front. One woman, and one man. Servants escorted them up to join us on the balcony.

I faced the woman first. "Show us your tin-chai."

She touched the balustrade of the balcony. Daisies sprung up where she'd made contact even though the balustrade was made of stone, not dirt.

"Ah, a gardener," I said. "That's beautiful."

I focused my wyis on the scepter, then concentrated its power on her, and I sang a melody. She gasped, standing straight as though electricity had shot through her body.

"I can feel it," she said. "My wyis has grown stronger. My tin-chai has expanded."

She pointed her hands at the ground beneath the balcony, away from the outskirts of the crowd. This time, the ground rumbled, and a sapling shot up from the earth, quickly growing into a tall tree. Blossoms sprouted on the branches, growing into ripe, red apples.

"I've only grown flowers before," the woman exclaimed. "This is my first fruit tree."

Gasps and cheers echoed throughout the crowd.

I turned to the second volunteer. The man's gaze was still on the apple tree. He looked stunned.

"Your turn, sir," I said.

He slowly swung his gaze back to me and nodded, still looking shocked. He raised his arms, extending out his palms, and they morphed into water.

I channeled my wyis through the scepter and into him, and I sang again. In seconds, his entire body liquefied, melting down into a puddle of water. Then the puddle built back up, reforming into his normal body.

"I can't believe this," he cried. "I've never been able to change my whole body into water."

The crowd went wild with their applause and cheers.

Aiden raised his hand again, signaling for them to quiet. As the noise subsided, he continued his speech.

"Old Grandfather Heaven has given both of us the Will of Heaven. I am already your king, but because Rilla has been given the Will of Heaven and is to be my wife, she will be given the title of queen as well. She and I are partners, and we will lead you from this day forward. Emberwood separated from Seracedar long ago, but we have never forgotten our Shyan history. Corruption in Seracedar's recent emperors has brought instability to their people as well as to the surrounding kingdoms of Ailo and Yao. And now the man on the Seracedar throne is a threat to Emberwood. We, the Emberwood people, can no longer abide watching our neighbors and our Shyan brothers and sisters suffer. We may not like war, but Old Grandfather Heaven has given us the responsibility to reunite the two Shyan kingdoms and to establish a new, peaceful era. One kingdom, one rule."

Applause erupted from the crowd. A choir of voices chanted in unison, "One kingdom, one rule. One kingdom, one rule."

CHAPTER 13

✦ ✦ ✦ ✦ ✦ ✦ ✦ ✦ ✦ ✦

Aiden and I made plans to travel to Cindertrance City on the northern coast of Emberwood, the site of Carrick's first attack, where we would assess the damage and try to help those affected. Welder would follow in a day after he helped Captain Kang and Colonel Beyling take care of setting up defense around the capital and Linlang Palace. Sito stayed behind as well, helping to care for Leonora and Ashbel.

We took an overnight coach with Ponch and Jun, who had personally asked to come. They would act as my bodyguards. Ponch had been a lieutenant in the Emberwood army before becoming a counselor, and she was still a well-known legend among the soldiers for her combat skills and light-footed approach. No one could hear her coming until they found themselves on the ground with her foot planted against their back. And although Jun hadn't seemed to like me at our first meeting, she had warmed up to me since then. Since she had been an assassin, she told me this was the perfect job for her.

"I need to do this," Jun had said to me. "If I have to sit one more day at the clinic and listen to more sob stories, I'm going to kill someone. I might as well kill the cronies following that bastard, Carrick. It'll make my life worth living again."

So with Ponch's permission and Jun's promise not to go rogue, we had allowed her to come.

During our coach ride, we reviewed the reports from the attack, launched two nights before. Three Seracedarean ships had fired some kind of seed bomb into the city, causing earthquakes as huge plants uprooted from the soil and splintered the ground. Though I wasn't sure of the extent of the damage, it had to have caused buildings to tumble and road blockages. Worst of all, we were told the hospitals were filling up with wounded civilians, and there were still more missing people buried beneath the rubble.

The Seracedarean ships had left once the damage was done, but we had to be prepared for them to return for another attack.

As our coach drove past the district line into Cindertrance City, we came to an abrupt stop. I looked out the window. Sycamore trees blocked the roads, preventing us from moving forward. But it was far worse than that. The once bustling coastal city had become an unrecognizable jungle.

Tree roots, some as thick as five men lined side by side, dug deep into the earth. They curved menacingly like the jagged edges of a saw, twisting themselves into houses, uprooting buildings, and taking over the city. Monster vines twisted and tangled around lampposts and shops. Leaves sprouted from the rooftops of homes, splitting rooms apart, rending furniture into a million pieces. Everything had been destroyed.

From outside the coach window, I heard a child crying for her mother. At the same time, an elderly man yelled for his son. Then I saw a man pinned down by a tree.

I opened the coach door and jumped out, barely hearing Ponch and Aiden call after me. The man's breaths were fading. A branch had speared him right through the thigh. He must have been stuck here since the attack started. I couldn't believe he was still alive.

I mustered up my strength to fight back the tears. There were too many patients to attend and heal. I couldn't waste time crying.

The branch came out of him as I sang, and the gaping hole in his thigh sealed up. Once his breathing became regular, I moved on to the next victim, a young child whose face had been torn by the thorns as she'd tried to make her escape. I worked as fast as I could, trying to heal as many as I could.

Ponch, Jun, and Aiden had joined me. They pulled people from the wreckage and brought them to me to heal. It was impossible to save all of them. We worked nonstop for hours until I felt like fainting from exhaustion.

From the corner of my eye, I saw Aiden slip a bit, as he tried to hack away at some brush. The ax fell from his grasp, nearly falling on his foot.

I shrieked. Ponch and Jun gasped, too.

"King Aiden," Ponch said. "You need to get some rest. Let the other rescuers take over for a while."

"No," he said. "There's too much work to be done."

"You won't be any good if you collapse from exhaustion," I said. "This was one attack, but we need to prepare ourselves for another one. You know it's only a matter of time before Seracedar strikes again, and we need another plan. We need our king to lead us, and you can't fight with a severed foot."

Aiden hesitated, but he finally nodded.

We lodged overnight at an inn that had opened its doors to those who had lost their homes. People slept in the lobby and filled out the dining area. Aiden and I found an empty space on the floor and plopped down. Jun and Ponch propped themselves up against the wall. Despite the noise of the crowd, we managed to doze off for a few hours.

Sometime at dawn, I woke from the pangs of hunger. Aiden, Ponch, and Jun were still asleep, but I knew they had to be starving, especially Aiden with his insatiable appetite. I decided to look for something to eat for all of us.

The dining area was still full of sleeping people. A line had formed near the kitchen, and three of the inn's staff were handing out meat buns. They were generating more food in a matter of seconds using their tin-chai.

I stood at the end of the line. No one seemed to notice me, thankfully. They must not recognize me as the queen. A man came up next to me. I looked up and saw Welder.

"What are you doing here?" he asked with a scowl.

"What do you mean? I'm lining up for food."

"The future queen of Emberwood and Seracedar shouldn't be lining up for food," he said. "You, handing out the buns, how dare you make the queen wait for breakfast? Serve her at once."

The workers looked at me and their eyes went wide. One of them rushed forward and bowed so quickly, he almost fell. "Queen Rilla, forgive me. I did not recognize you."

He handed me a plate of meat buns, and I took it with a smile.

"And I'll bet you didn't recognize His Majesty either," Welder said. He looked around, glaring at everyone. "You probably made him sleep on the floor the whole night. You should all be ashamed."

"Welder, stop," I said. Why was he making such a big deal about this?

"You're a queen now. Act like it," he said.

I looked at the people around me. "It doesn't matter. Don't think anything of it. Continue as you were."

The workers and people cautiously returned to what they were doing. Welder went to one of the tables and motioned the people sitting there away. They fled immediately. He sat and gestured for me to do the same.

I glared. "You're being incredibly rude."

"I'm showing you how to act like a proper ruler. These people won't respect you if you sleep on the floor or wait at the end of the line for food. Your subjects need to fear you. Sit."

"I don't want people to fear me," I told him. But I sat.

"I have other news," Welder said.

"Let's wait for Aiden. He's still sleeping." I bit into a bun. The savory-sweet filling was delicious.

"I'll tell you first then. There's something I'd like to discuss with you alone."

I frowned. "What's going on?"

"Good news. Carrick is going broke. His father already exhausted the resources coming from the Ailo mines. Now, the only way he can generate gold is using his wife's tin-chai, but she hasn't been able to do so for a while. I heard her depression is worsening, which inhibits her tin-chai."

"That's not good news," I said. "Radi is my friend."

"Was your friend," Welder corrected.

"How do you know what's going on in Cedar Palace?" I asked. "Did Sago and the Ailo men report this to you?"

"I have my own network and spies set in place around Seracedar and elsewhere," he said. "Men I used to command when I was in the Seracedarean army. These men are eager to take down Carrick, so they're acting as my agents now."

I wondered how many men were at Welder's beck and call. And did Aiden know about this?

"Now for the bad news," Welder said. "Daki is probably dead."

He said it so matter-of-factly that it took me a second to register. Then the shock came. I felt an onslaught of heat rising to my eyes but forced myself to hold back from crying. "What happened?"

"His ship sank," Welder said. "He was on the way to Emberwood. We suspect he was on a secret mission to attack us at another point. Thankfully, our men saw his ship and set fire bombs on it. Someone saw him jump ship with the others, but no one appeared to have survived. Look, I know Daki was once on our side, but he decided to work for Carrick. We can't grieve when it's an advantage for us. With him gone, Carrick has lost his best naval commander."

The way Welder was talking sounded like he couldn't care less about

Daki. Had he even considered Daki a friend? War was certainly making him ruthless. Or had he always been this ruthless and only pretended to care for whoever was on his side at the moment?

Welder continued on, unaware of my distrust. "Carrick's power is weakening. But we can't let our guard down. I anticipate another attack here at the port. However, we need to start going on the offense. Take the war out of Emberwood and into Seracedar. We'll start for the weakest villages. The only problem is Aiden needs to give me the permission to attack. He's far too peaceful and won't want to hurt innocent people."

"Neither do I," I said. "Why must we strike at the villages?"

"The best way to capture the kingdom is by convincing the weakest link that we are better than their ruler. We have to make them submit to us through any means. I don't care what you have to do to convince Aiden. Seduce him. Whatever you need to do to make him agree with me."

The smell of fresh meat buns wafted in the air. The inn worker was afraid to interrupt us, but I motioned to him to come over. He laid down another plate of buns in front of us. "I brought more in case the first serving wasn't enough. I can bring fresh buns over to the king as well. Where is he?"

"I'm here, good man. No need to look for me." Aiden strode toward us and sat next to me. The inn worker placed a plate in front of him.

The man trembled. "I'm sorry, Your Majesty. I should have recognized you and offered you a room. I should have asked some of the guests to clear out. I apologize if you were uncomfortable last night."

"What are you talking about?" Aiden grinned at him. "I've slept on the ground for the past ten years. More comfortable than a bed in my opinion. Thank you for your service. Tell your cook this breakfast smells delicious."

He grabbed a meat bun and stuffed his mouth.

Welder tapped his foot impatiently. "Aiden, act more serious. You're a king now."

"I always take my meat buns seriously," Aiden said.

Welder grew three shades of red darker. I could almost see steam coming out of his head. He forced his tone to remain even. "Aiden, please."

Aiden chewed, swallowed, then focused on Welder. "All right, this is me being serious now. And I'm serious when I say I'd appreciate being called for an important meeting as you seem to be having with Rilla."

"That's my fault," I said. "I should have called you, but I wanted to let you sleep longer."

"And thank you for that, darling. But Welder could have waited just fifteen minutes more, I'm sure." The happy-go-lucky Aiden was gone, replaced by his warrior shadow side. His eyes gleamed. "I heard you trying to manipulate Rilla into manipulating me. Thank Old Grandfather Heaven she's too smart for that. But the next time you want me to agree to something, maybe you should try asking me directly."

"Fine," Welder said.

I looked at Aiden, tears in my eyes. "Welder said Daki's dead."

Aiden blinked, and shock came over his face. "How?"

"As I told Rilla, his ship sank," Welder said. "We believe he was ordered to attack us on a secret mission, but our men caught on and fired on his ship first."

Aiden wrung his hands. Like me, I could sense him holding back his tears. "I can't believe it. He was such a good man. A good friend."

"Yes, but this is war, and he was serving the enemy," Welder said. "We can grieve for him later. There are more important things to discuss. So put away your sadness for now."

Aiden cleared his throat. His tone was gruff. "What is it you want to discuss, Welder?"

"I want to send our men to attack the villages and take them by force. You and Rilla will go, too. You'll use the power of the scepter to make them pledge their loyalty to you. Burn their homes if they refuse to surrender. Once we conquer them, we'll use them to fight Carrick in the major cities and the capital."

"There will not be threats or burning," Aiden said. "We'll give them the choice to surrender when it's time to take over the villages. But not yet. We need to focus here."

"You're stubborn just like your father," Welder said. "We can't only focus on defense. We need to go into the villages and establish your right to rule. Instill fear into the people."

"Let's not talk about this now," Aiden said. "At the moment, we're here to help the people in Cindertrance City. And since we anticipate another attack from Carrick, we have to be ready."

Welder pursed his lips, but he didn't object further. "Oh, one last piece of news. My men tracked Dribin Clox but lost him when he crossed the Enyi Ocean and went back into Fauxhemia. I think the three of us should make a trip to Fauxhemia and find him. He's the only way to find an antidote for your parents."

"Wait," I said. "There are more important matters here with the war. We can't just leave and go chase down Clox, even for the antidote. Right, Aiden?"

Aiden hesitated. "Can we have men go search for him?"

"Not without Queen Esmeralda's permission," Welder said. "And given the suspicion that Carrick may be conspiring with her, it would be dangerous. My suggestion is for us three to have a formal meeting with Esmeralda. Given the working relationship between Prince Lymere and Prince Sito and our universities, she wouldn't openly attack you during a friendly visit."

"That's not a bad idea," Aiden said. "This I can agree on. Sito is sure there was just a misunderstanding and the Fauxhemians would never ally themselves with Carrick. I'm sure talking to her will clarify this. Then I'll ask her for help finding Clox."

"We're getting sidetracked," I said. "The Fauxhemians and Dribin Clox are not a priority."

Aiden scowled at me. "Not a priority? My parents are my priority. I thought you of all people would understand that, Rilla."

"That's not what I meant," I said. "Your parents are being kept in stable condition, and we can find Dribin Clox and an antidote after we win this war. But there are people in worse condition right here, and Carrick could attack again at any moment."

"I'm not going on a side quest," Aiden said. "I'm going to assess Queen Esmeralda's intentions. To see if we should consider her an enemy or potential friend. It's called killing two birds with one stone."

"I think that's a wise move, Your Majesty," Welder said. "I do hope we can get the queen's permission to find Dribin Clox while we're in Fauxhemia. It's important that we find an antidote as quickly as possible."

I frowned, wondering why Welder had brought up this topic. He was the last person I would have suspected to prioritize Dribin Clox and finding an antidote when Cindertrance was in shambles and we were bracing for another attack. Besides, the last time we'd spoken of the Fauxhemians, he had made it clear he didn't have a high regard for them or their queen.

I was about to address this, but Emberwood soldiers rushed into the inn. "Your Majesty, General Welder, Seracedar ships are coming closer to the Port of Candlelace. We need you."

"Let's move," Welder said.

Minutes later, Ponch, Jun, Aiden, and I were in the coach with Welder, heading to the Port of Candlelace. The port was on the northeastern tip of Emberwood Kingdom, ten miles east of Cindertrance. We'd have to cross a mountain to reach the city of Candlelace, where the port was based. It would take us half an hour to get there, but Jun was driving. The woman sped like we were being chased by a stampede of wild man-eating godogs.

The Seracedarean fleet now blocked the port, and none of the ships could leave or get in. Since this was Emberwood's biggest hub, all imports and goods were being prevented from getting into the kingdom. Not only would it severely maim our economy if this lasted, there would be a food shortage.

Our hope was to surround the Seracedarean fleet so they couldn't get their ships closer to the port. They couldn't stay forever. Eventually, they would run out of supplies, too. It was a game of who could outlast who.

Our coach sped forward down a mountain road. To the right of our coach, all we could see was the cliffside. And to the left was the edge of the mountain. I hoped Jun was careful. One wrong turn on this twisted road and our coach might drive right off the cliff.

Jun made a sharp turn, and I nearly jerked out of my seat.

"Sorry," she said.

But then the road straightened again, and the ocean appeared out the window. The waters were brightly illuminated under the sun, a blinding silver like the skins of Miyu.

Miyu. The word echoed in my mind. The Miyu had promised to help us and had even given me a conch to call them. I had the conch in my knapsack. If I called them, would they really come? And would they come in time?

Once we got to Candlelace, I'd blow the conch. It wouldn't hurt to try.

Ponch perked up and looked out the window. "I hear something strange. Like a storm's coming."

"But there aren't any clouds," Jun said.

I looked out to the horizon above the sealine. Everything looked peaceful. No ships were sailing our way. But as I continued to observe, I could see the waves starting to roll quicker. With each passing second, they became bigger and more violent.

I shook Aiden's shoulder. "Aiden, is it just me, or do you see that, too? The waves are growing bigger."

The waves crashed on the shore now, foreboding. If this was a tidal wave, we would be in deep trouble.

Aiden poked his head out the coach window. "You're right. I think something's coming out of the water."

Large gray bodies rose from the sea. At first, I thought they were monsters from the deep, but I realized they were machine-like, made of metal.

From beside me, Welder stirred into action. "Ships coming from underwater."

They stopped at a distance from the coast, but they were twice as big as any ship I had seen.

"I didn't think Seracedar had the technology," Welder said. "It must be Daki's invention. He's found a new way to raid our coastline."

Boom! A cannon fired from the first metal ship.

CHAPTER 14

✦ ✦ ✦ ✦ ✦ ✦ ✦ ✦ ✦ ✦

The coach lurched sideways, tossing us out of our seats. Rocks pelted down from the side of the mountain, landing on the front window. The glass cracked.

Ponch shouted. "Jun, look out!"

A boulder from the rockslide was in the middle of the road.

Jun shouted a string of curses and swerved. The brakes screeched. We stopped, but the coach careened, tilting forward and sliding off the road. The front of the coach teetered off the edge of the cliff.

"I've got this," Welder said. He carefully took off his outer cloak. "Aiden, hold on one side of my cloak to balance me. I'll hold onto the other end and try to lean out the window. I can transform the cliffside and make the road extend beneath us. Everyone else, try to lean your weight to the back of the coach. One more shift forward, and we'll all fall into the ocean."

Aiden held onto one side of the cloak, and Welder tied the other side around his arm. Then he slowly shifted to the side window, reaching for the cliff to our right. The coach rocked.

Welder swore and froze. We stopped rocking, and he tried again. He leaned his entire torso out the window and extended his fingertips to the edge of the mountain. He made contact.

We stopped wobbling. The ground was stable. I looked out the front window and realized there was more road where we had previously been hanging off the cliff. I'd almost forgotten that Welder's tin-chai went beyond object transformation, and he could change the environment as well. But now I remembered seeing before that he had changed the back entrance of Linlang Palace to become a row of oak trees, protecting the palace from trespassers.

"Thank Old Grandfather Heaven for your tin-chai, Welder," Aiden said.

We all breathed sighs of relief.

"Sometimes it can be convenient to envision what I want and have anything become exactly that," he replied. "But still, my tin-chai can't beat Rilla's. What would I give for a voice like that?"

Another tremor reverberated below. Outside the window, I could see what was happening on the shoreline. The metal ships fired boulders, which broke apart in the air and fell down onto the bustling port. Debris smashed onto everything in sight. People were running, shouting.

"Let's go, Jun," Welder said. "We've got to get down there."

Jun sped the rest of the way to the scene. But by the time we got there, the attack had stopped—for now, at least. The devastation was massive. Another day of this, and we wouldn't have a city left.

We parked at the docks and got out of the coach. The soldiers had made their camp by the pier.

Hu, Welder's next in command, ran toward us. "Your Majesty, this was delivered to us right after the attack. Someone found it. We think it was dropped in one of the bombs." He held a large red envelope addressed to His Majesty King Aiden and Queen Rilla.

"Don't open it," Welder said. "Whatever's in it might be dangerous."

"We already had that assessed," Hu said. "One of the soldiers looked inside with his tin-chai. It's just paper. Something's written on it. I'll open it for you."

Hu cut open the envelope and took out the parchment. On it, a warning was written in big red letters.

"Surrender Candlelace to Emperor Carrick by sunset," Welder read out loud. "This is your last chance. If you refuse, we will spare no one."

"We're not going to surrender," Aiden said. "Prepare our troops."

"Those with the strongest tin-chai will be in the frontlines," Welder said. "Let's go."

Jun stepped forward. "I'll fight."

"Me, too," Ponch said. "Put us in front."

"No," Welder said. "Your tin-chai can't do anything against those bombs."

"We came here to fight," I said. "Not sit back and watch. My voice is my weapon. And besides that, I can amplify the soldiers' tin-chai."

I called to some of the soldiers. "Line up along the docks, and show me your tin-chai."

The idea played in my mind that I might be able to control how their tin-chai was amplified according to what would be best for the individual. I'd never done it before and simply allowed the scepter to work on its own, but there was no time like the present to see if it could be done.

Several soldiers formed a line on the docks. Behind them, several ships swayed to and fro. The sea, still turbulent from the recent battle, sprayed up on the wharf.

I walked up to the first soldier. He lit up a spark of fire in one palm. It was a blue flame.

"I can't light up anything bigger," he said. "But my flames are extremely hot."

I placed my wyis into the scepter and focused on him, willing his amplification to give him larger flames while I sang.

The fire grew in his hand, still blue. And in his other hand, he formed a second flame.

The next soldier also had a fire tin-chai, and he had no trouble forming large flames. "I could burn down entire buildings," he said.

Again, I concentrated my wyis into the scepter and sang. This time I willed him to have the ability to manipulate fire so it would spread wherever he directed it.

He set a flame in his hand and sent it to the ground, forming a zigzagging line. He closed his palm, and the fire stopped. Then he opened his palm again, and the flames reignited before coming back to him completely.

Welder came to me with another soldier. "This man is a koong. Can you give him a tin-chai?"

"I've never done it, but I can try," I said.

Singing, I put in my wyis into the scepter and focused on the man. I felt power rippling through the scepter. Light glowed from the scepter, but I couldn't sustain it. I didn't have enough power. In another few seconds, the light flickered out.

I shook my head. "I'm sorry. It didn't work. I don't think my wyis is powerful enough."

Welder simply nodded. "It was worth a shot. At least now we know the limits of your amplification power."

I continued down the line of soldiers. A few more had fire tin-chai, some had the tin-chai to move rocks, and others could manipulate the wind.

For those who could control rocks, I amplified their tin-chai so they could hold larger boulders or build rocks from the earth to catapult at the enemy if necessary. And for those with wind tin-chai, I allowed them to have the ability to form bigger windstorms or direct a windstorm in whatever path they willed.

"Amplify those with shield tin-chai, too," Welder said. He gestured to the frontlines. I felt those soldiers' wyis, which were concentrated in front of them. A combined force field, invisible to the eye.

But a wave of dizziness overcame me, and my knees wobbled. Aiden caught me before I fell. "That's enough. You're exhausting yourself. You can't possibly amplify every soldier's tin-chai."

"He's right," Welder said. "You've helped enough."

"But I can do more," I said.

"No." Aiden stopped me from moving toward more soldiers. "When the fighting actually starts, I want you behind everyone. Carrick already hurt my parents, and I'd never forgive myself if something happened to you."

"But—"

"This isn't just to protect you," Aiden said, lowering his voice so only I could hear. "Have you considered that you might be pregnant? If you'll recall, we weren't exactly trying to be careful. I don't want anything to happen if you're carrying our child."

"Even if I am, I can still amplify the soldiers' tin-chai. I'll just stay back from the frontlines."

"No. Too much exhaustion and stress could be harmful, too." He turned to Jun and Ponch. "Make sure you protect her."

Ponch nodded. "Yes, Your Majesty."

He and Welder took off, leaving me with Ponch and Jun.

Jun scowled. "Misogynists, all of them. I can fight better than most of those soldiers. And it's not like we know for sure that you're pregnant."

"There has to be something we can do to help even if they don't let us fight," Ponch said.

"We're not listening to them," I said. "We're joining the fight whether they like it or not. For now, get some rest, since they won't let you join in with the other soldiers. I'm going to call reinforcements. I'll be right back."

"Reinforcements?" Ponch repeated. "Who?"

I reached into my bag and withdrew the conch that Queen Yisa had given me as a reward for saving her daughter, Princess Amika. "The Miyu."

"Shouldn't we inform Welder and the king?" Ponch asked.

"No time," I said. "We'll tell them if this works."

"We're going with you," Jun said.

The three of us walked away from the docks to a more private place down the shoreline. There, I blew the conch. Then we sat and waited.

"Do you really think they'll come?" Ponch asked.

"I'm not sure, but Princess Amika is a friend. The Miyu promised if I ever need help, I just have to play the conch, and they'll come wherever I am."

At least I hoped they kept their promise. I couldn't help but have my doubts. Had they actually heard my call? And if they had, how long would it take for them to arrive?

We waited, staring at the sea. An hour passed. There was no sign of the Miyu.

I must have fallen asleep at some point because the next thing that woke me up was Aiden's angry voice calling my name.

"Rilla, there you are. What are you thinking, sleeping out here?"

I opened my eyes and looked up. Jun stirred beside me. She had fallen asleep as well. But Ponch was awake.

"The three of you gave me the scare of my life," Aiden said. "I was looking everywhere for you. You could have been attacked or abducted."

"I wouldn't have let that happen, Your Majesty," Ponch said. "I was keeping watch."

"I only fell asleep for a minute," Jun said. "The queen called the Miyu. We were waiting for them to come."

Looking at the horizon now, I realized the sky was shaded with a hint of orange and pink. The sun was starting to set. The Miyu hadn't come.

"You two might be experienced fighters, but I doubt you would have been able to overpower several men at once," Aiden said. "Carrick's spies might be here already, scouting out the city. If they saw Rilla, they'd do anything to take her back to Carrick."

I hadn't considered that. "Sorry. I thought I was close enough to our camp that it wouldn't be a danger. And I didn't intend on staying here overnight."

I could see the Seracedarean ships in the distance. They had lit fires, the brightness blending into the pastels of the horizon. They were getting their men ready to attack again.

I stood and faced Aiden. "I'm sorry for worrying you."

"Ponch, Jun, return to camp first," Aiden said. "Rilla and I will walk behind you. I wish to speak to her in private."

The two women bowed. "Yes, Your Majesty." They turned, walking a distance away out of earshot.

Aiden and I followed. He indicated the conch in my hands. "How long ago did you call the Miyu?"

"Maybe an hour ago."

Aiden was silent for a moment. Then he sighed. "It was a good idea, but I don't think we can depend on them if they haven't responded by now."

"The Miyu queen and Princess Amika said they would help me with anything," I said. "They might still be on their way."

"Even so, there's no guarantee they'll agree to help us fight. They'd be placing their people in danger by allying themselves with us. The Miyu and Seracedar have had a shaky treaty for many years, and I don't know if Queen Yisa will want to start a full-scale war again." He sighed. "Doesn't matter. The Seracedarean fleet is going to attack again at any moment. There's no time to talk to the Miyu and convince them to help us. We have to prepare to defend ourselves alone."

The sunlight streamed across the sea now. We only had an hour or so before Seracedar would strike again. Aiden was right. We had no one to help us but ourselves.

Aiden and I returned to the camp. Our soldiers were already up, preparing for battle. Our army marched onto the beach. The soldiers with the strongest defensive tin-chai, amplified shields, stood in front, ready to stave off the tidal waves and earthquakes from hitting the city.

Aiden took me behind a cover of rocks. "Stay behind this."

Jun and Ponch joined me.

"Take care of her, guardswomen." He kissed my cheek, then hurried to join the men in front.

I looked out to the horizon where the Seracedarean ships inched closer. One of the ships led the others. On the leading ship, men stood on the edge of the deck. They dived off the stern and into the water.

Seconds later, the earth rumbled beneath us. The ground shook, and the ocean rose. Our men stood strong, deflecting the first wave, five feet high. It tumbled back into the ocean.

The earth shook again, this time so violently that I lost my balance. Ponch caught my arm before I tumbled down. The quake stopped, but in front of us, the waves rose five feet, then ten, and still grew. Our men shouted, pulling together their tin-chai to shield us. They blocked the tidal wave, but they wouldn't be able to hold out for long.

Ponch grabbed my arm. "We need to get further back."

I resisted. "Not without Aiden. I won't leave him."

"There's no time. He'd never forgive me if I let something happen to you." She pulled me, but I broke away.

"I can't leave Aiden and the rest of them to die," I said.

I pulled out the Cedar Scepter from my cloak and ran toward the frontlines.

Aiden spotted me. "Rilla, I told you to get to safety."

"I'm not going anywhere," I said. "More soldiers could use tin-chai amplification. I can do this."

I sang, letting my wyis flow in the scepter.

"These wings may have been broken and torn,

But my dreams will breach these sealed doors."

I felt the scepter's vibrations, its power, flowing into the soldiers around me. The six soldiers who shielded against the tidal wave shouted, and their bodies transformed, morphing together into a twenty-foot wall of steel that shielded us and the city behind us. The wave crashed against the wall and yielded back into the sea.

A roar of victory echoed among the troops.

"Bravo," Welder said, his expression in awe. I couldn't recall seeing him look impressed before. "Aiden, I know you want to protect her, but we really could use her help in the frontlines."

"Fine," Aiden said. "But be careful."

Boom! The cannons fired from the Seracedarean ships.

"It's not over yet," Welder shouted. "Prepare for whatever new tricks they have up their sleeves."

Black balls of kelp hurled through the air and landed on the shore. The kelp pieces lengthened and morphed, growing larger until they found each other and coalesced, further enlarging. They dug into the sand, forming feet and legs, now taking on the appearance of a single kelp monster. It burrowed into the sand, tunneling through the shore and coming behind us, then racing toward the pier. It plowed through part of the docks and took out several ships. Debris flew everywhere.

The kelp monster continued forward, heading toward the city. It took out the foundation of a seaside cottage, and the entire structure collapsed in under five seconds.

Aiden touched the scepter and let its power fill him. With his amplified tin-chai, he turned his whole body into fire. He ran into the monster. It lit into flames, burning to ash.

Then he transformed back and addressed the other soldiers with fire tin-chai. "Get ready. More of them are coming. Destroy the kelp with fire before it reaches monster form. We can't let any kelp monsters reach the city."

Fresh kelp flew onto the pier. Aiden led the men with fire tin-chai, including the men whose tin-chai I had amplified earlier. They destroyed what they could, but more kelp bombs were thrown, too quickly for our men to burn. The kelp quickly morphed, and three monsters were born, racing down the wharf and toward the city.

"After them," Welder shouted, and he and five soldiers chased the monsters. Now we had fewer men left on the beach to destroy the kelp that was still being thrown. It wouldn't be long until more kelp monsters overcame our defensive line.

I could use the scepter to amplify tin-chai again, but there weren't enough soldiers with fire tin-chai. Was there another tin-chai that could counter the kelp? *Think, Rilla, think.*

I heard shouts, but they didn't come from the Ember soldiers. The voices came from the Seracedarean ships. I looked out to the horizon. Monstrous forms circled the ships. Sea kaigon. I gasped. The Miyu were here. They had heard my call for help.

The sea kaigon intercepted the cannons and tore them away from the ships. The men firing the cannons shrieked as they lost their footing and fell overboard where the Miyu's shimmering bodies waited. The shrill voices of the Miyu pierced the air in a sharp battle cry as they grabbed the falling soldiers and dragged them beneath the water.

As the battle raged, a small group of Miyu swam to shore. In the center of the Miyu sentinels was Princess Amika. I recognized her at once and fought to suppress tears at the familiar sight of my friend.

"I can't believe you came," I said.

"Of course, we did," Amika said. "My mother and I promised to come to your assistance whenever you were in need. We'd heard of the Seracedarean attack on your people and were already preparing our sentinels to come to your assistance. We were already on our way when we heard your conch call. Rest assured, we aren't leaving until we drive the enemy away."

She turned her attention back to the ocean. "I'll join up with you later. There's a battle to be won."

Amika swam out to meet the Miyu sentinels. An army of them rode on the backs of their sea kaigon. They encircled the Seracedarean fleet, preventing them from moving forward to land. The only way they could go was backwards if they retreated, or they would run into the Miyu.

Commanders from the Miyu army cried out, instructing their sisters and kaigon. "Forward, destroy."

The Miyu charged. The sea kaigon smashed into the ships, splintering them into millions of pieces. The Seracedarean soldiers who hadn't already abandoned ship were catapulted into the air by the forceful winds the sea kaigons had created. The few ships that had avoided destruction were steered away as they tried to retreat.

The Miyu surrounded the ships, trapping them from returning to sea. From one of the ships, I saw a white flag being raised. The Seracedareans had surrendered. Victory belonged to us.

CHAPTER 15

✦ ✦ ✦ ✦ ✦ ✦ ✦ ✦ ✦ ✦

With our victory in the battle at the port, the last of the Seracedarean ships not taken by the Miyu retreated. On what was left of the pier, Aiden and I waited to meet with Queen Yisa and Princess Amika to thank them for their help. A few ships were still docked in a single row, the sole survivors from the attack. Wooden boards and debris floated on top of the water. Amidst all of it, the Miyu poked their heads above water to greet us.

Queen Yisa and Princess Amika swam closer. They came onto the boardwalk, their tails morphing into legs and scales becoming long, flowing robes.

We bowed, and they did the same.

"Thank you," Aiden said. "We couldn't have won this battle without the Miyu."

"You're welcome," Princess Amika said. "We'll always be your ally."

Queen Yisa agreed with a nod. "Seracedar is our common enemy, and you're our friends. We wouldn't hesitate in helping you fight them in this war."

"I don't think Carrick will target these waters again," Princess Amika said. "But I'll have some of our sentinels remain in the area to monitor for any new activity."

"We can't thank you enough," I said.

Amika grinned. "You saved my life before. You don't need to keep thanking me. If there's anything else we can help with, call us again."

"Actually, there are two small favors I'd like to ask of you," Aiden said.

"Oh?" Amika raised an eyebrow. "Please ask away."

"Our friend Daki was killed recently," Aiden said. He had to pause, attempting to keep the grief out of his voice. "Welder thinks he was on a secret mission for Carrick, and our men fired on his ship."

"I'm sorry to hear the news," Amika said. "He was a nice man. Surprises me that he took Carrick's side."

A stray tear slid down my cheek. "Seracedar was his home. He wanted to rebuild and defend his kingdom."

Aiden sighed. "Even though he was on Carrick's side, he was still our friend. I wanted to see if you could find his remains in the ocean. I'd like to give him a proper burial if possible."

Amika turned to her mother for an answer. Queen Yisa nodded. "That may be difficult, but we can try. I'll update you if we find anything. And your second favor?"

"I need help finding a Fauxhemian man named Dribin Clox," Aiden said. He gestured to a man behind us who came with a scroll. Aiden unrolled the scroll, and in it was Clox's likeness. "Carrick hired Dribin Clox to poison my parents. We think he's in Fauxhemia now but have lost track of him. Your sentinels are able to transform and mingle with land dwellers. They can talk to the locals and maybe find where he's hiding."

Amika and Yisa studied the portrait.

"I'm not sure our sentinels will be able to find him if he's in Fauxhemia," Yisa said. "Queen Esmeralda doesn't like us. She seems to believe the myths that we are seductresses seeking to lure men into our beds."

Amika rolled her eyes. "As though those men don't willingly agree."

"Yes, well, those are the same men who have perpetuated the myths about us," Queen Yisa said. "In any case, I've told our sentinels to stay away from where we're unwanted. If they're discovered to be Miyu, they could be in danger."

"Please," Aiden said. "Clox's blood is our only means of finding a cure. I beg you to help me. I'll do anything."

I jumped in. "Queen Yisa, you've already done so much for us, coming to our aid. Aiden and I don't want to trouble you further or put your sentinels at risk. Clox might leave Fauxhemia and run to another kingdom. If he does and your sentinels manage to learn anything, please notify us then."

Princess Amika hesitated, looking at her mother. For a moment, I felt a tug of anxiety pulling at my heart. I hoped we hadn't offended our allies by pushing the matter, but also, for his sake and his parents' sake, I hoped they accepted.

Queen Yisa nodded. I let out a sigh of relief.

"You both have my word," the queen said. "If one of my sentinels finds this man, we will notify you at once. If he had harmed one of my family members, I'd do anything to track him down as well."

She smiled at me and Aiden. "Take care of one another. You make a good team."

With that, she and Amika swam away.

Our victory in securing the Miyu's support and winning the battle at the port was overshadowed by the number of casualties in both Candlelace and Cindertrance. I did my best helping other healers to save who we could, but it was too late to save others.

We held a day of remembrance at the Port of Candlelace for the fallen soldiers and civilians who had been killed. And though we couldn't publicly declare it, we also grieved for Daki. Despite his decision to fight for Seracedar, he had been a good friend to us, and I remembered our adventures together through Yao Kingdom and the Miyu Islands.

The sky was overcast, and a somber stillness blanketed the streets of Candlelace City. Aiden and I led a procession through the streets as citizens gathered on the sidelines to watch. Once we reached the docks of the harbor, Aiden lit a candle. From this one flame, together we lit up dozens of candles contained in floating lanterns and let them drift in the water. We asked Old Grandfather Heaven to bring all those taken from us safely into the afterlife.

After the ceremony, we returned to the camp for the evening. I expected that tomorrow we would return to Linlang Palace.

Aiden and I came to our tent. He opened the door for me. "You go ahead and sleep first if you want."

I pivoted, facing him. "Where are you going?"

"I've scheduled a meeting with Welder to discuss our next move against Seracedar."

"Then I'm coming, too."

Aiden looked hesitant. "You don't need to. I mostly want to talk to him about finding Dribin Clox and getting a cure for my parents. That's my responsibility, and you don't need to get involved when there's already so much going on. After all, they're my parents."

"Well, then it certainly involves me. They're going to be my parents, too. You can't leave me out of such an important discussion. We're a team."

He didn't refuse but instead gestured for me to follow him. Welder was already waiting for us by the fire outside his tent. He stood with his gaze to the fire, a pensive look on his face.

"Welder," Aiden called to him.

Welder startled. "Oh, you're here."

I wondered what he was thinking about to make him so unaware of his surroundings when he was usually alert.

"I didn't see you at the vigil," I said.

"I had to take care of some business," Welder said. "Rilla, I have a question for you. I've been giving this much thought. Have you attempted to take away someone's tin-chai yet?"

I shook my head.

"Perhaps you should try," he said. "You have no problem amplifying tin-chai from what we've seen. But taking away tin-chai might be more of a struggle for you."

I cringed. "That's like taking away someone's life purpose. I don't really want to use that side of my tin-chai at all."

"Yes, but it may become necessary at some point," Welder said. "Your regular tin-chai has a dual nature. So does your power through the scepter. Healing comes naturally to you, but you didn't realize you could use your voice to kill until you were pushed to do so. It was a dormant ability. I have a feeling this might be the case with your amplified tin-chai's duality as well."

"Welder's right," Aiden said. "Giving tin-chai is easy for you, but taking it away might require more power. Or it might require some secret technique. You might not be able to do it on the first go. Maybe you should practice. Figure out how to unlock it."

"Practice on who?" I asked. "That would mean I have to actually take away someone's tin-chai."

"Criminals," Welder said. "Prisoners we take captive during this war."

"I still don't want to do it," I said, feeling uncomfortable.

"All right, if that's how you feel," Aiden said. "Don't push her, Welder. She'll use it when she's ready."

Welder looked annoyed, but he sighed. "On to other matters then. We're fortunate that the Miyu are helping us survey the northern waters, but I still wanted to assign some men to stay at the port to keep an eye on things before we return to the capitol."

"I shudder to think what would have happened if the Miyu hadn't been there for us," Aiden said. "Under no circumstances can we let

Seracedar come that close to taking the port again."

"I don't think they'll make another attempt," Welder said. "We're prepared for them. I think Carrick will be concentrating on the southern border now. They'll push into our territory by trying to conquer city by city."

"That's what I'm anticipating as well," Aiden said. "I'm worried about the size of their army. Their troops outnumber ours five to one. I've decided to go to Fauxhemia tomorrow instead of returning home."

"What?" I blinked. "When did you decide this? We never talked about it."

"Sure we did. Back at the inn in Cindertrance," he said.

If we did go to Fauxhemia, then maybe we could visit my family. But there was too much going on.

"Are you sure it's a good idea to make a trip there when we're at war?" I asked.

"Welder said it was a good idea to clear the air with Queen Esmeralda. It must be a misunderstanding that she's working with Carrick. More importantly, I need to ask her to let us search Fauxhemia for Dribin Clox. And while we're there, maybe I can persuade her into an alliance with us."

I frowned at Welder. "You once said you didn't like Queen Esmeralda or the Fauxhemians. Why are you suddenly changing your position?"

Welder looked between us and scowled. "First of all, I never changed my position. I do hate the Fauxhemians and everything they represent. Second, I don't think Esmeralda is innocent of the claim that she's working with Carrick. Of course, she would never tell us so, but we can better assess if she's lying if we visit her in person. Also, an alliance with Fauxhemia is a horrible idea."

"Why would an alliance be a bad idea?" Aiden asked. "The Seracedareans outnumber us. We need more soldiers. If we can say for certain that Esmeralda isn't working with Carrick, wouldn't it be worth trying to ask for her help?"

Welder shook his head and furrowed his brow. "I don't trust Queen Esmeralda. Even if she hasn't taken Carrick's side, I don't think we should bother asking for anything from her except permission to find Dribin Clox, which I know is your main motivation for going to Fauxhemia. No need to hide it using other reasons, Your Majesty."

"I'm not trying to hide it," Aiden said. "Yes, finding Clox is important, but so is finding more soldiers to fight with us. Sito said that Esmeralda wouldn't ally with Carrick or anyone. I don't see how it would hurt to at least try to sway her to our side."

Welder sighed. "This is dangerous thinking, Aiden. You're already assuming Esmeralda is innocent of all the rumors. Perhaps Sito is right, and Esmeralda hasn't allied with Carrick formally. It doesn't mean she wouldn't help him in secret ways."

"You mean Dribin Clox," I said. "You think the rumors might be true that she sent Clox to Carrick."

Welder nodded. "The Ailo man, Brix, said a Fauxhemian emissary was in Cedar Palace, sent by the Fauxhemian queen. That Fauxhemian could have been Dribin Clox. Prince Sito believes King Lieka was poisoned in the same way as your parents by the same man. But some say King Lieka's former mistress was involved. That mistress was Queen Esmeralda's mother. There has to be a connection."

Aiden curled his hands into fists. "If that's true, then why? What would motivate her to help Carrick poison my parents? Fauxhemia has always had a shaky relationship with Seracedar."

"Exactly," Welder said. "Fauxhemia and Seracedar border each other, but they have never had a stable relationship. That makes it hard to trade with each other. Fauxhemia has had to trade with Emberwood and Exentria instead, but getting goods shipped across the sea is expensive. An alliance with Carrick means establishing trade agreements. Carrick might have also promised her a part of Emberwood if he wins the war. Esmeralda knows your father and mother are the strength of Emberwood, but you are new to your position. That makes you weak."

"Still," I said. "The Fauxhemians have never been antagonistic toward anyone. They're known as peace-loving folk. In the days of King Lieka, the king said peace was the Fauxhemian way."

Welder scoffed. "King Lieka was a pretentious coward. He claimed peace was the Fauxhemian way as an excuse for his own fear of taking a stand against anything."

He spat into the fire. Welder couldn't contain his vehemence toward the old king, which surprised me. Usually he was good at hiding his feelings.

Welder lifted his gaze back at Aiden. "Esmeralda and the crown prince are in power now. They might be more ambitious. You need to be wary of them."

Aiden picked up a twig and threw it into the fire. "Sito wouldn't agree. He thinks Crown Prince Lymere is a saint."

"Your cousin is naive," Welder said. "He didn't know his teacher was a murderer and a kidnapper, and he knew that man all his life. Sito is better suited to medicine than politics."

Aiden stilled. "Good point."

Welder sighed. "Look, you're the king, and if you think an alliance can be made, that's your decision. I simply urge you to remain cautious. Also, you're too fixated on finding Dribin Clox."

Aiden opened his mouth.

"Don't deny it," I said. "I'm in agreement with Welder there."

"My parents need that antidote," he said.

"Yes, they do, but you can't let Queen Esmeralda see your desperation," Welder said. "She'll use this to manipulate you. Force you into making deals that shouldn't be made. You need to keep a clear head and not let personal feelings or motivations cloud your judgment."

"I agree," I said. "You can't believe anything anyone says, not even someone you consider a friend. Much less so a queen like Esmeralda who could seek to gain political advantage if Carrick wins this war."

Aiden looked thoughtful. He nodded. "I promise to try not to get manipulated. We can count on you to go with us, right, Welder? If not, I understand."

A strange look came over Welder. I sensed hatred and grief melded together. "Yes, of course. I would never allow you to go there unprotected."

"I'm sure we're safe," Aiden said. "Sito is friends with Lymere. They're working on projects together that would benefit both our kingdoms. Besides, even if the queen is involved with Carrick, she wouldn't ambush us during a cordial meeting. You said so yourself. She cares too much about her reputation in the world."

"Yes, I suppose you're right," Welder said. "I'll have one of my men take a letter to Fauxhemia Castle ahead of us, stating our intention to visit. We'll leave tomorrow."

He bowed and took his leave.

I turned to Aiden and asked, "What does Welder have against Fauxhemia and the royal family?"

Aiden watched Welder's retreating form in the distance. "Welder spent his childhood in Fauxhemia with his mother before he moved to Seracedar to live with his father's family. His mother was a concubine, but she didn't live with his father. I don't know his history in Fauxhemia, but Welder doesn't have fond memories of the kingdom or its people."

"Still, I've never seen such hatred in his eyes as when he spoke of King Lieka," I said.

"Yes, I guess so," Aiden said. He looked distracted.

"What else is on your mind?" I asked.

"I'm worried. If Esmeralda did send Dribin Clox to help Carrick poison my parents, then she won't want us poking around her kingdom trying to find him."

"We don't know for sure that she was involved," I said. "Let's just wait and see what happens."

Aiden gave me a look of determination. "I don't care what she says. If she doesn't agree to let us search, I'll send my people in secret. I'm not going to leave Fauxhemia until we find Clox."

There was something in his expression that worried me. What would he do if Queen Esmeralda denied our request to search for Clox?

He turned. "I need some alone time to think about what to say to Esmeralda. You don't need to wait for me. Get some sleep."

I watched him walk away, and a flickering fear crept into my heart. Until we caught Clox and found an antidote, would Aiden ever be able to focus on winning this war or bearing the Will of Heaven?

What if he left me to deal with the Will of Heaven on my own while he focused on the antidote? What if I had to figure out how to navigate all of these responsibilities on my own?

No, he wouldn't do that to me. He had never abandoned me before, and he knew that I needed him. I prayed that I never had to face a day when I had to be without him.

Because without him, I feared I would fail on my own.

CHAPTER 16

✦ ✦ ✦ ✦ ✦ ✦ ✦ ✦ ✦ ✦

Late the next morning, Aiden and I approached the sea coaches that would take us across the Enyi Ocean to Fauxhemia. These vehicles transformed from land transportation coaches to sea ferries as needed and were faster than regular ships. Welder and a line of a dozen men stood on the docks waiting for us.

"I've assembled a team of the best bodyguards to accompany us," Welder said. "My newest recruits, Oren and Ret, will be among them. They need to gain experience."

The two young men stepped forward and saluted in acknowledgement. I'd never seen them around before. They must be new guards. Oren had silver streaks in his hair, which he'd styled in spikes. Ret had a clean-shaven head. They both looked younger than me. I wondered why Welder had chosen them to come with us if they lacked experience.

I assessed their wyis. Ret was strong, but Oren's wyis shocked me. The only person whose wyis had felt stronger had been Androgy Haming. Oren must have an incredible tin-chai. What was it?

"Are you sure it's a good idea to let them gain experience now?" Aiden asked Welder.

"They look so young," I added. "What are their tin-chai?"

"I trust them," Welder said. "And both of you should trust me. Besides, there are more experienced guards coming, too. Aiden's favored guards, Spince and Klay. Also, two of your guardswomen were selected, Rilla, if that makes you feel safer."

It didn't escape me that he hadn't answered what the two new men's cin-chai were. But Ponch and Jun waved and came over to greet me, so I let it go for now.

"I'm glad you're coming, too," I said. "I didn't expect it. Especially Ponch. I thought you'd be returning to the clinic."

"We're part of the queen's personal team now," Jun said. "Of course, we're coming. We asked Welder if we could join."

"I left Counselor Trine in charge of the clinic," Ponch said. "There are enough counselors now for things to run smoothly in my absence."

A coach pulled up. The door opened. Sito jumped out.

Aiden's brow lifted in surprise. "What are you doing here, cousin?"

"I sent for him," Welder said. "We could use his expertise on the Fauxhemians and his friendly relationship with the royal family."

"It was painful waking up at the crack of dawn," Sito said. "But I took a nap in the coach. I wouldn't miss a trip to visit Fauxhemia for anything."

"How are my parents?" Aiden asked.

"Still stable. Don't worry, I made sure to leave them in the hands of the best care team. Already read the note Welder sent and caught up with the details of this trip in the coach. We'll catch Clox and get an antidote, I just know it. I've got a good feeling. And I'm sure Esmeralda and Lymere have nothing to do with Carrick or hiring Clox. You'll see."

Sito was a true optimist. I worried for him.

Aiden scrunched his face. "I don't like the idea of you coming with us. You're the next in line for the throne after me. What if something bad happens to both of us?"

"Nonsense," Sito said. "Esmeralda and Lymere are lovely people. You'll see how hospitable they are. Nothing bad will happen to us on Fauxhemian soil."

"Prince Sito might have a point there," Welder said, his lips tight.

"The Fauxhemians are more likely to attack you behind your back in your own home than on their territory."

Sito narrowed his lips. "You're such a sourpuss, Welder. Don't hate on the Fauxhemians. Peace is the Fauxhemian way."

Welder rolled his eyes and said nothing further.

The journey to the Fauxhemian capital city, Dawning, would take two hours by sea and the rest of the day and the following morning on land, so we'd have to spend the night camping before continuing to the castle. The trip across the Enyi Ocean was fast and pleasant, but as our sea coaches transformed back into land coaches, I got a glimpse of the Fauxhemian desert terrain. The roads were dusty, the sun burned hot, and my skin soon grew heated and sticky. Looking outside the window, I saw nothing but sand for miles, but our drivers seemed to know the way. At least I hoped they did. I didn't want to get lost in this place.

Again, it crossed my mind that maybe we could visit my family now that we were in Fauxhemia. But it might be out of the way, and Aiden had a lot on his mind. I didn't want to add another request to his plate. A visit would have to wait until another time.

We stopped for the night and set up camp in a forested area that the Fauxhemians had created for travelers. A man-made oasis in the middle of the desert. Since we were far from any of the main cities, we wouldn't find an inn.

We ate a modest supper of berries, toast, and moonrabbit jerky. I sat close to the campfire and watched Sito and Aiden entertain our team of bodyguards with stories from their childhood.

Welder sat a distance away from the others. He had a melancholic expression and took sips from a canteen, which I suspected had some kind of alcohol in it. He took something out from his cloak. A woman's hair ornament, a simple, wooden hair stick. I'd seen elaborate ones that the faela used, but this one looked like it had been crafted by an amateur and might belong to a commoner.

I scooted closer to him.

"You look like you could use a friend," I said. "But if not, then I can go away."

"No, you can stay." He offered me the canteen. "Blueberry rice wine?"

I shook my head. "No, thank you."

"Suit yourself." He took another gulp, then stared into the fire. "I'm going to get drunk, and I don't care."

"This is the first time I've seen you drink more than one cup of wine," I said. "I didn't think you ever got drunk."

"There's a lot you don't know about me," he said. "I used to smoke cigars. One after another. A vice I finally got rid of when I worked for Terran. But occasionally, I still miss a smoke and indulge when no one's looking."

I shrugged. "I won't judge you for it."

He sighed. "Old Grandfather Heaven, I hate this kingdom. Everything about it makes me want to hurl."

"You want to talk about it? You don't have to, but I've learned from the clinic that it helps to open up to someone you trust. I promise I won't spill your secrets."

He was quiet, his expression still and grim. I thought he wouldn't say anything further, but then he said, "You may have heard from Aiden that I have Fauxhemian roots."

I nodded. "On your mother's side."

"My father was a Seracedarean diplomat who came on occasion to Fauxhemia. He'd stay with my mother and me during those visits. But most of my childhood, it was just my mama and me. She was a teacher who worked for the royal family. I was raised in close proximity to the king's children before Mama was discovered to be a rainbow Faux-blood and persecuted for it."

"Persecuted? Why?"

"Rainbow Faux-bloods are a mix of all four colors of Faux-bloods, but their blood is a normal red. They're even rarer than the emerald-blooded. Fauxhemians fear the rainbow-blooded because they can absorb the blood magic of any Faux-blood type. The queen, Prince Lymere's mother, dismissed my mama from her position, and no one else would hire her. They smeared her name. Accused her of crimes she never committed. She ended up killing herself from the humiliation."

"No wonder you don't like Fauxhemia," I said.

"I hate Fauxhemia, but I despise Lieka more. He was a coward and a hypocrite."

"Why? It was the queen who dismissed your mama, not Lieka."

Welder spat into the fire. "In my opinion, he and Terran are cut from the same cloth."

"There's no way you can compare him to Terran. I've never heard of King Lieka being anything but kind to his subjects. He never kept a harem, not even before his mind poisoning. I know he's had three wives, but not at the same time."

Welder took a shot of wine before replying. "You don't know him like I do. Sure, he didn't have hundreds of faela. But he always had dozens of mistresses. All of them look the same as his first wife. I'll bet he's still supplied with a few mistresses despite his current state, just to make him believe his first wife is still alive. Probably at the request of his current wife, Queen Consort Esmeralda, who also perversely has a resemblance to his first wife. Oh, and her mother became one of the king's mistresses when Esmeralda was just a child of eight or nine years."

I didn't know much about the Fauxhemian court or the relationships within the royal family, but everything about them sounded strange to me. "Why would Esmeralda encourage that? Wouldn't she be jealous? Empress Limera hated any woman who took Terran's attention away from her."

Welder sighed. "Old King Lieka is fifty-seven, and his queen is nineteen. Esmeralda never loved the king the way Limera loved Terran. The king married her because she was his nurse, and she happened to look like his first wife. She probably agreed because she wanted the power."

"I'm so curious about how she became his wife when her mother was once his mistress. Aren't there laws against that sort of thing?"

"Hah! Not in Fauxhemia. Esmeralda's mother was accused of being involved in the king's mind poisoning. Either hiring the chef or framing him for her crime. She killed herself as a result. Esmeralda was a servant, and the king, in his madness, was taken with her. No matter that her mother was involved in a scandal. Somehow Esmeralda made everyone forget about that and became his third wife. The king's close advisors believed she could help comfort him as he descended into madness. Now she acts as regent along with the crown prince."

Well, Esmeralda was turning out to be quite an interesting character. I wondered how she had managed to avoid the scandal and climb the ladder to attain her power. She must be a force.

"No wonder you said we have to be careful around her," I said. "Have you met her or the crown prince?"

Welder shook his head. "I left Fauxhemia when the crown prince was still an infant. His mother was still alive then. She died soon after the prince was born. Everything I learned about Esmeralda is what I studied and read in papers. 'Know your opponents better than you know yourself' is my motto."

I wondered who else he considered an opponent he needed to know.

"Didn't you say you were raised with the other royal children? What happened to them?"

"Yes, I knew the king's three daughters. Unfortunately, they are no longer alive."

A flash of rage sparked in his eyes, but it faded as quickly as it had come. If I hadn't been gauging his expression, I might have missed it.

"I'm sorry," I said. "You must have been close as children."

"Yes, and I was also reacquainted with them when I returned to Fauxhemia on assignment."

I raised an eyebrow. "Oh? You mean when you were in Terran's army?"

He made a face. "Unfortunately. I hate that I chose to stay blind to Terran's corruption at that time in my life. I was too focused on making my way in the world. After my mother died, I went to live with my father, his wife, and their daughter. My stepmother and stepsister didn't like me, and I hated living with them. As soon as I was old enough, I enlisted in the Seracedarean army. I worked hard to rise in the ranks. One year, I was sent on special assignment to Fauxhemia to act as a spy, posing as a diplomat. I had to gain King Lieka's trust and learn his secrets, then report to Terran on any of Fauxhemia's weaknesses. According to Terran, I was the perfect candidate, having grown up close to the royal family."

He smiled, a fond look coming into his eyes. "I suppose Terran was right. King Lieka remembered me. So did his daughters. In particular, the eldest, Princess Bree. Actually, she has a connection to you. She was friends with Lady Arlyn. I never mentioned it before because I don't like to speak of that time in my life, but I knew Arlyn. King Lieka entrusted me to escort Bree and Arlyn to Cedar Palace."

I sat up straight. "I remember now. Lady Arlyn spoke of Bree. They were both in the showcase and were chosen to become Terran's faela. She said Bree killed herself."

Welder nodded. His eyes were hooded and sad. "I should have helped them escape, but I chose not to compromise my allegiance to Seracedar. I was in love with Bree." He lifted the hair stick. "I made her an ugly thing like this once. For her birthday. She loved it. Wore it in her hair every day until she was forced to take it off at Cedar Palace."

There were tears in his eyes. It shocked me. I never thought I'd see the day when Welder shed tears. He must have loved Bree dearly.

"If I'd known how evil Terran truly was, I would have abandoned everything. Run away with her. But, fool that I was, I still believed Terran had the Will of Heaven. He believed Seracedar was destined to take control of the world, and therefore, so did I."

"King Lieka must have trusted you deeply since he assigned you to escort Bree and Arlyn."

"I thought I had King Lieka fooled. But no. One day, he cornered me and said he knew I was Terran's spy. And that I was in love with Bree. He didn't arrest me as I expected. He was afraid of Terran and thought he could make a peace offering, prove that Fauxhemia was an ally. Bree and Arlyn were that offering. If they became Terran's faela, King Lieka believed he could create an alliance. I had to deliver Bree and Arlyn to Cedar Palace and tell Terran that Fauxhemia wanted nothing more than peace with Seracedar. If I did not, Lieka threatened to tell Terran that I was a traitor so I could never return, and he said I could never stay in Fauxhemia, or he'd find my mother's last living relatives and kill them."

"That's awful." I shook my head in disbelief. "You're right. Lieka was not a nice man."

"It gets worse," Welder said. "After I took Bree and Arlyn to Cedar Palace, I discovered how Terran and Limera mistreated the trinkets. I found out how they intended to torture Bree and Arlyn. I wrote to Lieka, telling him to rescue his daughter and Arlyn, but he wrote back, saying they were a sacrifice he was willing to make for the sake of peace. I made a plan to rescue them on my own, but it was too late. Bree was dead."

I curled my fists. "How could Lieka leave them there, knowing the cruel fate they would suffer?"

"As I said, he was a coward and a hypocrite." Welder twirled the hair stick, and it changed into a regular twig. Ah, not the real one, but a replica he'd made with his tin-chai.

He tossed the twig into the fire. "King Lieka only cared about his comfort and legacy, the assurance that his subjects revered him. He would have sent all his daughters if it guaranteed Terran wouldn't attack

Fauxhemia. Bree's two younger sisters ran away, fearing they would be sent next, and no one knows where they are now. Probably dead. When Lieka found out Bree went missing and his other daughters had left, he didn't try to fight Terran or figure out the truth. He didn't look for his other daughters. But I'll bet he was wracked with guilt. That's why it was so easy for Dribin Clox to target him and poison his mind."

Welder laughed. I realized he was pleased by Lieka's misfortune. There was a darkness I hadn't expected in him. It scared me.

"He deserves his madness," Welder said. "Deserves to be haunted by his guilt. I was glad when I heard about his mind poisoning. It was his fault Bree died. And his punishment isn't over. He'll pay for his mistakes even further, like Terran did. Until the day I die, I'll pray for Old Grandfather Heaven to see to it."

Something burned in Welder's eyes that looked a lot like the desire for vengeance. Did he really believe Old Grandfather Heaven would render justice upon the old king, or did he intend on doing it himself? The old king was already poisoned with madness. What other punishment did Welder expect Lieka to suffer beyond that? I was scared to find out what was going through his mind.

But then Welder blinked, coming back to himself. "In any case, the king's useless now. It's Queen Esmeralda we need to worry about."

I nodded. "Esmeralda and the crown prince."

Welder laughed, the sound condescending. "The crown prince? Prince Lymere is just an accessory. An ornament Esmeralda uses to decorate her hair."

"What do you mean? I thought Esmeralda is only helping to act as regent with the crown prince. He is to become king one day, not her. If she's involved with Carrick, Lymere would also know and approve, right?"

The look Welder gave me said he thought I was an idiot.

"This is why I forced myself to come along on this stupid mission. You and Aiden have been stuck in the shadows of Cedar Palace, isolated in Seracedar. You know nothing of the outside world. Prince Lymere might be next in line for the throne, but Queen Esmeralda makes the decisions whether Lymere knows the details or not."

I shook my head, still not understanding. "But why? And how does she get away with that?"

"For some reason, the advisors don't question her. The Fauxhemians think she's an emerald-blood and has some kind of control over the advisors' minds. But she can't control all the citizens, and they agree to go along with her as long as the kingdom is prosperous. This is why she cares so much about her reputation."

"What about Prince Lymere? Does she control his mind, too? Surely, he must care if he's not involved in the decision-making."

Welder snorted. "I doubt in his case it's his mind being controlled. Prince Lymere is only two years her junior. Esmeralda's got the prince in the palm of her hand. It's a well-known fact they're having an affair."

I gasped. "Isn't that illegal? In Seracedar, that would be considered a death penalty once they were discovered."

"Fauxhemians don't think the way the Shyan do. In any case, Esmeralda controls the Fauxhemian army, the aristocrats and advisors, and Prince Lymere. This is why I warned Aiden not to let her manipulate him. Though I've never met her, I've heard she's charming. She'll put you at ease. Make you believe you're on the brink of earning her favor. But the moment you leave the room, she'll arrange to have you killed. Even if she makes a promise, there's no guarantee she'll keep it."

He stood and took another shot of blueberry rice wine. "It's going to be an early morning, and we both should get some rest. Good night, my lady."

I watched him walk away. I'd known Welder had a past, but I hadn't realized until now how intricately tied he was to politics in every kingdom he set foot in. Emberwood, Seracedar, Fauxhemia. He had history with all three kingdoms. He had the makings of a very dangerous man, one whose intentions could never truly be figured out. I was glad he was on our side.

And I hoped that would never change.

CHAPTER 17

✦ ✦ ✦ ✦ ✦ ✦ ✦ ✦ ✦ ✦

Early the next morning, Aiden and I stepped onto the coach that would take us to Fauxhemia Castle. Cousin Sito was already seated. But Welder was absent.

"Where's Welder?" Aiden asked. "He's never late. Or is he in the coach behind us?"

"Actually, Welder's not coming," Sito said. "He told me to tell you he woke this morning with a stomach ailment and feels too nauseated to travel. He's going to stay at the campsite. He sends his apologies. He said nine guards will come with us and the rest will stay here with him."

"Oh, he could have sent for Rilla to heal him," Aiden said.

I remembered how much Welder had been drinking last night. What he was suffering wasn't a stomach ailment. It was a hangover.

"Let's leave him," I said. "It must be hard for him to be here in Fauxhemia and have to confront the bad memories of his past."

Aiden sighed. "It's just that he's better than me at assessing if someone's lying." He looked at his timepiece. "But we're running late. We'll have to get by without him."

"You need to go in the other coach," Sito said. "We can't be in the same one. Protocol, you know."

Aiden looked annoyed and tense. I didn't blame him. We'd been counting on Welder to be there with us.

We both switched to the second coach. I watched two guards step into Sito's, while Jun and Ponch came with us. In a third coach, five more guards climbed aboard. I doubted we needed so many guards to protect us, but I supposed it was better to be safe than sorry.

Aiden signaled to the driver, and we sped off. The drive would take another two hours. I dozed off for the first half. When I woke up, I looked outside the window. We were no longer in the desert but the city. This must be Dawning, the Fauxhemian capital. We rode through the streets and passed through a neighborhood. Trees lined up in perfect rows down the street. Golden leaves were scattered all around, a reminder that it was the middle of autumn. The Fauxhemian houses were grand. There was simply no other word that could describe it. Each house was unique, a work of art in itself. One house had an entrance framed with marble pillars. Another had a pair of lion stone sculptures standing on either side of the front gate.

The coach soon slowed to a stop, and this time, we were on a wide paved path, parked in front of a white domed building that sparkled like snow under the sun. It was at least ten times larger than the other houses we'd passed, and the dome stretched so high into the heavens, I couldn't even see the top. On either side of the driveway, gardens extended for miles. This must be Fauxhemia Castle.

The driver opened the doors, and we stepped off. Sito joined Aiden and me, while the guards followed us.

We walked through the gardens that surrounded the castle. Green stretched out in every direction toward the horizon. Clean, manicured grass, decorated with rows of outdoor statues. Carved by the master artists, I assumed. After all, Fauxhemians were known for their art and storytelling. I remembered how talented Arlyn was with her paintings.

We walked down the paved path, and I looked at the plaques of all the statues. They featured famous Fauxhemians throughout history, characters from mythology, and even the pets owned by the royal family. There was a gigantic statue of the Fauxhemian deity called San, surrounded by statues of renowned priestesses who had dedicated their lives to serving their gods. I didn't know much about the Fauxhemian religion other than that they worshipped many deities, each ruler of some part of nature. But the deity of deities was called San, the most powerful being who oversaw the universe. There were holy priestesses who offered prayers to the deities and acted as the conduit for communication between the Fauxhemian subjects and San.

At the end of the statues, we were greeted by a tall woman with sharp glasses. She wore a form-fitted dress in an unflattering green that reminded me of overcooked spinach. Her body was drenched in perfume, an overpowering floral scent. I tried to breathe through my mouth. Aiden sneezed three times in a row, and Sito pinched his nose in an effort to hold back his sneeze.

"Greetings." The woman bowed. "My name is Zelda. I'm the Chief of Diplomatic Affairs. It's an honor to meet you, Your Majesties. We here in Fauxhemia are saddened to hear that King Ashbel and Queen Leonora were mind poisoned. May our deity, San, be with you in this difficult time. I've asked our priestesses to pray for their recovery."

I wondered if she had brought that up on purpose or if she was truly offering her condolences. Any nuances in her tone could indicate Queen Esmeralda's guilt. I had to be on the alert.

Aiden stepped forward and bowed. "Thank you, Zelda." He sneezed again. "Excuse me. We have come bearing—ah-choo!" He sniffled and rubbed his nose. "We've come—ah-ahh—"

He pinched his nose and caught that sneeze.

I decided to help the poor man out. "We have gifts for the king, queen consort, and crown prince." I gestured to the boxes in Sito's hands. Thankfully, Sito had brought them with him from Emberwood before coming to meet us, or we would have been empty-handed. "Dragonkiwi tea for King Lieka's health. Pearls from the Cascasea Sea for Queen Consort Esmeralda, and some of the newest technological inventions from Emberwood for Prince Lymere."

Zelda snapped her fingers, summoning two men to her side. The men took the boxes from Sito.

"Make sure to check for any questionable content before presenting these to the royal family," Zelda said. "The royal taste tester must first sample the tea for poison."

Sito gave a humble bow, but beside him, Aiden tensed. I forced myself not to burst out at the woman. Implying in front of our faces that we might try to poison anyone? This was a direct insult.

And it certainly didn't bode well. Maybe their distrust of us was a sign that Esmeralda was working with Carrick and thought we were onto her.

Still, we couldn't march out now. We had to try to be cordial while on foreign soil.

Zelda's gaze narrowed at us. But her expression was blank, as though she didn't realize she'd insulted us. "The guards behind you will stay here. Only the three of you will come. Follow me."

Aiden looked at me, jaw agape. He whispered, "Did that just happen?"

"Let's hope Queen Esmeralda is a bit more hospitable," I muttered.

Sito put a finger to his lips. "I don't think Zelda meant to insult us. After all, the queen consort is known to be blunt. It isn't a surprise if her hired staff has been trained to be direct as well."

Zelda turned and looked at us. "Well?" she snapped. "Come along. We can't keep Queen Esmeralda waiting all day."

We followed Zelda through the entranceway of the palace. The ceilings were so tall that the oldest tree in Seracedar would have fit inside it. The walls were filled with portraits of proud royalty and aristocrats. The last portrait just before we turned into another hallway caught my eye. The girl posed on the bank of a river, and her smile seemed to be directed at someone behind the artist who painted her.

I stopped. I didn't recognize the girl, but the style of the painting was familiar. This was Lady Arlyn's work, I was sure of it.

"Excuse me, Zelda," I said, not caring when she glared at me in annoyance. "Who is this?"

"That is Princess Bree," Zelda said.

"And who painted her?" I asked.

"I don't know. Likely a master artist. Please, let's not dawdle. I'll give you a tour of the castle later."

Zelda marched forward. Aiden and Sito followed. I paused another moment, glancing at the artist's signature in the bottom corner. Sure enough, Arlyn's name was scrawled there. Her legacy lived on in Fauxhemia Castle.

I took a deep breath, closed my eyes, and said a quick prayer in remembrance to Arlyn and Princess Bree. *May both of you rest in peace.*

With that, I turned and followed after the group.

CHAPTER 18

✦ ✦ ✦ ✦ ✦ ✦ ✦ ✦ ✦ ✦

We walked through golden doors into a spacious room. The first thing I noticed was the vibrant red wallpaper that covered all four walls. It looked like the room had been bathed in blood. Bookshelves piled high to the ceiling, and every book cover was in some shade of red. Even the curtains were red. Six chairs with scarlet, velvet cushions were set around a circular tea table.

"Please have a seat," Zelda said. "Queen Esmeralda and Prince Lymere will arrive shortly."

She hustled out the door. We took our places around the table, but no sooner had we sat than the door opened.

Zelda stood by the door. "All rise for Her Majesty, Queen Consort Esmeralda, and His Royal Highness, Prince Lymere."

We rose.

Queen Esmeralda strode in, her back straight and tall. She wore a shade of crimson that matched the curtains. Her gown was extremely modest, covering most of her skin including her neck, as she'd buttoned the collar, and the sleeves ended at her wrists. It looked positively squelching to wear an outfit like that, yet the queen didn't show any sign of discomfort. Not a single sweat drop appeared on her. She carried a purring maocat in her arms.

Prince Lymere followed in her wake. He was a young man with a tall, thin build and looked sixteen or seventeen years old.

As he entered the room, his attention swung to Sito. A wide grin spread on Lymere's face. "Sito, my friend. Guess you just can't stay away. Didn't we see each other a month ago?"

Sito grinned back. "Yes, well, life gets too boring without you."

He and Lymere exchanged some kind of hand greeting that only they seemed to know.

Queen Esmeralda cleared her throat and gave them a look of disapproval. "Boys, this is a formal meeting for official kingdom matters. Please save your strange handshakes and other shenanigans for later."

Lymere's grin fell. "Yes, Essie."

Queen Esmeralda seated herself, and Prince Lymere sat beside her.

I watched the two of them, and Welder's assertions about the relationship between the queen and crown prince came to mind. Lymere's soft, eager gaze focused on Queen Esmeralda as though she were his entire world. It was clear Welder hadn't made it up.

Esmeralda motioned for us to sit. "Greetings," she said. "It's a pleasure to meet you all. Congratulations on your recent coronation, King Aiden, though it was the result of such difficult circumstances. I was sorry to learn that your mother and father were mind poisoned by a Fauxhemian criminal. I suppose that's the reason for your visit."

Well, she certainly did get right to the point.

"Yes," Aiden said. "As a matter of fact—"

"We'll discuss Dribin Clox and finding an antidote for your parents in a moment," Esmeralda said. "Please make yourselves comfortable first. Drink some tea. I want you to feel at home here."

Esmeralda settled the maocat in her lap. It contented itself and purred at the queen's constant stroking. As comfortable as the maocat seemed, it also appeared the queen took comfort in the maocat as well.

A servant poured each of us a cup of tea. As we waited for him to finish, Esmeralda regarded us. I sensed hesitation in her wide green eyes, but there was no fear. Quiet confidence covered her demeanor. Her skin was flawless except for one cheek, which had a red burn mark. It wasn't a brand like my scar, though. I wondered how it had gotten there.

"I am sorry my husband, the king, cannot be here," she said. "I hope you find the company of the prince and myself adequate for your visit to our humble kingdom."

Her tone was soft-spoken and pleasant. But I reminded myself to stay wary. Welder had said she made people feel at ease only to stab them in the back when they least expected it.

Prince Lymere grinned at us. He had a friendly face. "Yes, I know I also speak on my father's behalf when I say welcome to Fauxhemia. Sito has told me about you, King Aiden."

"Good things, I hope," Aiden said. "And allow me to introduce you to my future queen consort, Rilla."

"A pleasure to meet you, Prince Lymere," I said. "And Queen Esmeralda."

Esmeralda made a brief sound of acknowledgment but said nothing further.

Lymere's gaze shifted to me. "A pleasure, my lady." His attention went back to Aiden. "Your return from the dead was the story of the century. I was in Emberwood working on a project when the headline broke. Sito was in shock when he came to the university, weren't you, old boy?"

Sito blushed. "In shock is an understatement."

"It certainly is," Lymere said. "Especially since you exiled yourself from Linlang Palace." He turned his gaze to Aiden. "The poor man was wracked with guilt. Didn't speak for days."

Aiden shifted his gaze down at the floor. "Yes, that's something we'd all like to forget about."

"Well, I'm glad you cousins were able to get past all that drama with Mr. Rino," Lymere said. He lifted the cup of tea to his lips and drank, seeming oblivious to the awkwardness of this conversation.

"Rino was not the man I thought he was," Sito muttered. "But let's not speak of the dead."

Lymere nodded. "Believe me, I was as astounded as you. I took a class from him once. Thought he was a brilliant man. Never imagined him to be evil."

Was Prince Lymere purposely trying to make things awkward, or did he just lack social skills?

Maybe it was time to shift the subject. "How long have you been friends with Sito, Prince Lymere?" I asked.

Thankfully, Lymere took the bait. "A few years. We met in that Faux-blood Genetics course, remember Sito? You were an exchange student here."

"I'll never forget that class," Sito said. "Remember how much Teacher Kun hated us?"

"Just because we called him out on his mistakes," Lymere said. "If he didn't want us to make him look like a fool, he should have studied more on the subject he claimed to be an expert on."

"And he hated that I was allowed to take his class even though I'm from Emberwood," Sito added.

I kept my gaze on Esmeralda, who made no show of including herself in the conversation. In fact, she seemed bored. Her gaze shifted to her maocat, and she continued stroking its fur.

Without looking up, she spoke. "Lymere, that's quite enough chit-chat of memories only you and Sito share. You're being quite rude, not including our other guests or me in the conversation."

Lymere's face burned red. His voice lowered in embarrassment. "I apologize, I didn't realize I was being rude. I know I talk too much sometimes. Thank goodness I have Essie to remind me when I'm being clueless about social etiquette."

Queen Esmeralda finally looked up at him and smiled. "Yes, I don't know how you'd function without me."

Prince Lymere beamed at Esmeralda's smile as though he'd been gifted a precious gemstone. “I’m so grateful for Essie’s presence during my father’s illness. If not for her, I would never be able to lead this kingdom on my own. I can’t imagine what it’s been like for you, King Aiden, to be thrust into the role so suddenly. To have to make big decisions and deal with the threat of war. But I’m sure your future queen consort is a big help to you as well.”

I was beginning to get a sense that Prince Lymere was too open with his thoughts, not guarded at all like Esmeralda. I didn’t necessarily see that as a weakness. Lymere seemed far more authentic than the queen, and I liked authenticity.

“Yes, Rilla has been very supportive,” Aiden said. “I’m glad I have her on my side.”

“I bet I can guess one of the reasons you’ve come to see us,” Lymere said. “Seracedar is our common enemy. Emperor Terran is the reason my sister, Bree, is dead. And now it seems Carrick is following in his footsteps. If you need us to be your ally against—”

“Dear Lymere,” Esmeralda interrupted. “Let’s not presume why our guests have come to visit us. We should listen to King Aiden speak first and then determine if their goals align with what your father would want for our kingdom.”

Lymere’s grin faded, and his head drooped as though he were a child who’d been caught stealing a piece of candy. “Oh yes, of course. I hadn’t considered that. You’re quite right, as always, Essie. Maybe I should keep quiet now and let you speak.”

“I think that would be wise,” Esmeralda said.

The maocat in Esmeralda’s lap struggled to extract himself from his owner’s arms. He made a sound of displeasure. Esmeralda placed him on the ground, and the maocat sauntered off, disappearing behind some bookshelves.

The queen returned her attention to Aiden and me. “You may proceed with whatever you wish to discuss.”

There was a coldness to her eyes, I thought. But otherwise, her expression was unreadable. The opposite of Prince Lymere. Welder was right. She was the one we needed to watch out for.

Aiden took a sip of tea, then set the cup back on the table before proceeding. "As you guessed, my main reason for coming here is Dribin Clox. There are rumors that I don't want to believe but I can't ignore."

"Ah, I see." Now that the maocat was out of her arms, Esmeralda picked up her teacup and took a sip. "The rumor must be that Dribin Clox poisoned my husband, and because it's the same man who poisoned your parents, you want to know if there's a connection. Perhaps I sent Clox to Carrick. Or I intend to become Carrick's ally against you."

"I told my cousin it's preposterous," Sito said.

"It *is* preposterous," Lymere exclaimed.

Esmeralda spoke with her teacup still lifted, hiding her mouth. "Oh, but why would it be preposterous? In your position, I would find the circumstances suspicious, too."

Aiden looked caught off guard. "You would?"

"I've been accused of many things," she said. "My mother was my husband's mistress. Of course, people would accuse me of being like her. I've heard people accuse me of helping my mother hire Clox to poison the king. Of using my charms to seduce Lieka. And now I do the same to my dear Prince Lymere."

"It's ridiculous," Lymere said, scowling. "People shouldn't be gossiping about things they don't know."

"I don't fault them for it," she said. "By all appearances, it looks like I'm guilty of something."

"Are you guilty?" I asked.

She smiled at me. "You are blunt, Queen Rilla. I like that. I can see we're kindred spirits."

"Answer the question," I said. "Were you involved in poisoning your husband? And did you help Carrick hire Dribin Clox to poison King Ashbel and Queen Leonora?"

"Does it matter if I am guilty? My reputation has already suffered."

For a moment, a pained expression overcame her, the first time I felt she'd revealed anything real about herself. But she caught her slip, and her mask came up again.

"I had nothing to do with King Ashbel and Queen Leonora's poisoning."

Interesting. No denial about being involved in her husband's poisoning.

"Can you prove your innocence?" I asked.

Aiden nudged me and sent me a look. He must think I wasn't being diplomatic enough. But this wasn't about diplomacy. This was about making Esmeralda tell us the truth or pushing her to reveal that she was hiding things.

Lymere sent me a glare. "How dare you? Essie doesn't need to prove anything."

Esmeralda waved Lymere off. "I can fight my own battles, my dear." She regarded me, anger in her dark blue eyes though the rest of her revealed no emotion. "You can believe it or not. But it's the truth. I've spent years trying to make sure I don't do anything to support my naysayers' claims. Sullying my reputation further by associating with Dribin Clox is the last thing I'd do. His blood has nothing to do with me."

She sat forward in her chair and set her cup down on the table so hard, I was surprised it didn't chip. "And I'd never help Carrick. Peace is the Fauxhemian way. We haven't been at war in over two hundred years. Why would I become the first ruler to break that record and risk my people's disapproval?"

"That makes sense to me," Aiden said. "I believe you. I hope you didn't find Rilla's questions to be offensive."

It was my turn to send him a look. We were supposed to be on the same side. How dare he make it seem like I was being rude when I was trying to help him?

Esmeralda looked between the two of us as though sensing my displeasure. "As I said before, I like your fiancée's frankness. You should appreciate her more, King Aiden. She's willing to ask me the tough questions while you sit back and try to make me like you."

Aiden gaped. "I didn't mean to—"

"You want me to like you, and I wonder why," she said. "Is it because you wish for my permission to search for Dribin Clox in my kingdom? Or is it because you wish to ask Fauxhemia to join your fight against Carrick?"

Welder was right about her. She was a force. I wondered if she was a Faux-blood and if that gave her the ability to read minds. Or maybe she was just perceptive.

Aiden seemed speechless. He didn't say a word, only continued to stare at Esmeralda like she was a maze he didn't know how to find his way out of. I had never seen him look so befuddled.

I decided to intervene for him. "Your Majesty, that is exactly why we came here today. We wanted to ascertain if you were involved with Carrick, and now you've declared your innocence. So first, we wish to ask for your help to find Dribin Clox in your kingdom. Sito says Clox's blood is needed to make an antidote for King Ashbel and Queen Leonora. And second, we want to seek your help in defeating Carrick. He is a threat not only to us, but to you. If he wins this war, he could come for Fauxhemia next."

Prince Lymere stood. "Of course, you have our permission to—"

"Dear, please don't interrupt," Esmeralda said. "I was about to speak."

"Sorry, Essie," Lymere muttered.

Esmeralda turned back to me. "You have my permission to search for Dribin Clox in Fauxhemia, but you'll do it without my help. I cannot have my name associated with that man."

Aiden finally found his voice. "Thank you, Your Majesty. I'm determined to find him. I won't let my parents continue to suffer because of him. Once we find an antidote, we can save King Lieka, too."

I sensed Prince Lymere tense his shoulders. His gaze went to Esmeralda as though assessing her emotions. His reaction didn't make sense to me. Neither did Esmeralda's lack of reaction. Wouldn't they be happy to have the antidote to save their king?

Esmeralda only smiled. "How noble of you, King Aiden. The love of a son outweighs all his other responsibilities. While you're chasing Dribin Clox, who will be fighting Carrick? Because I can tell you now, you won't be using Fauxhemian soldiers to do so. I already told you I won't be the one to break two hundred years of peace in our history. Not for Carrick, and certainly not for you."

"Please hear me out first," Aiden said. "I can find Dribin Clox and fight this war at the same time. But Seracedar outnumbers the Emberwood army. I know you advocate for peace, but what happens in this war will affect your future, too."

Esmeralda narrowed her gaze. "Let me be honest with you, King Aiden. My reluctance to join your cause isn't simply to protect my name. I've also been researching you, and I've made observations about you during this visit. Frankly, I don't like what I see. You can't be trusted as a leader. Even if Seracedar poses a threat to Fauxhemia, I don't think it would be wise to ally ourselves with you in a war I'm not sure you can lead us to win."

Aiden recoiled as though he'd been burned. I felt anger stirring in my chest but bit my tongue from lashing back.

Sito stood. "Queen Esmeralda, my cousin does not deserve such—"

Aiden put up his hand, stopping Sito from saying more. "You don't need to defend me. I want to know why the queen feels this way about me."

Esmeralda nodded. "All right, I'll tell you. For most of your life, you served Carrick faithfully. You were a willing bodyguard of the enemy. I don't understand how you let Carrick deceive you for so long. It took you years to return to your family and reclaim your birthright. Had

Terran not died, you would have stayed by Carrick's side to the end and let your own parents continue believing their only son was dead. That only changed after you met Rilla, and your loyalty to her overcame your loyalty to your previous master. You had no choice but to finally take responsibility as Emberwood's crown prince, or you'd risk losing Rilla to Carrick. Someone like you doesn't know who he is without someone else to dictate what path he should take. You are a follower, not a leader. Too easy to be controlled. Why should I risk my kingdom and my reputation allying with one such as yourself? You haven't proven yourself to me."

I clenched my fists and forced myself not to say something I might regret. Esmeralda certainly had researched our story thoroughly. But even though I hated hearing her say these things about Aiden, I had to admit she had a point. Even I worried at times that Aiden didn't quite know who he was yet, and that he wasn't ready to become the king when he'd spent the majority of his life following Carrick in the shadows.

Still, Esmeralda didn't see what I saw. How Aiden cared for the wellbeing of everyone he met. Even though he was going through self-doubt, he had the potential to become a great leader. I believed in him, and I couldn't let her destroy his confidence further when he was already having a hard time.

"Queen Esmeralda," I said. "Aiden stayed as Carrick's bodyguard because he believed in his cause to take the throne from Terran. He didn't know Carrick would choose to go down a dark path. Besides, he may have been in Carrick's service, but the best leaders are those who have experienced humility and know how to serve others."

"Rilla is right," Sito said. "My cousin is far from being a follower. He would give up his life to defend others. He's done it for Carrick for most of his life, and he's done it for me. I'm the reason he was kidnapped and brought to Seracedar in the first place. My mother conspired with my teacher to get rid of him because they wanted me to take the throne. My cousin stayed away from Emberwood and never exposed them because he was protecting me. Even when he came back, he made sure to keep my mother's name out of it so the scandal wouldn't affect me as much."

"Of course, you both defend him," Queen Esmeralda said, rolling her eyes.

Lymere turned toward Esmeralda and placed a hand on her knee. "Essie, don't you think we should give King Aiden some grace? After all, he and Queen Rilla did defeat the slimy bastard that murdered my sister. And if you or I were in his place, Carrick might have fooled us as well. No one expects their best friend to turn evil."

"Speak for yourself, Lymere." Esmeralda pushed the prince's hand away. "You might have been fooled, but not I. But more importantly than being fooled, he chose to stay with the enemy instead of returning to his family and his kingdom. He hid from his responsibility as the Emberwood prince and as a son to his poor, aging parents. This is a character flaw I cannot extend grace to. I hope you do find Clox. You owe it to your parents to give them an antidote."

Aiden hung his head, looking so guilty I wanted to kill Esmeralda for her words.

"You're right," Aiden said. "I should have returned to Emberwood instead of evading my duty. Thank you for allowing me to search Fauxhemia for Dribin Clox. But as for an alliance, is there anything I can do to persuade you to change your mind? What if I find Clox and get the antidote for your king?"

Lymere's gaze passed from Esmeralda to Aiden. He looked like he wanted to say something, but I sensed that he lacked the confidence to speak his mind at risk of opposing Esmeralda.

"I told you finding Clox will be near to impossible," she said. "But if you do find him, I may reconsider joining you against Carrick. On top of that, you would need to help me prove my innocence in my husband's poisoning and find a way to guarantee that my subjects won't criticize me for bringing them into a war."

Aiden's expression fell. I realized Welder had been right in his assessment that Queen Esmeralda cared about her reputation more than anything else.

Esmeralda sniffed. "You see, I don't think you can work miracles, so I'm afraid there's nothing you can do to change my mind."

She stood. "I wish you and Emberwood the best, King Aiden." With that, she swished her skirts about her and made her exit.

Prince Lymere bowed. "I'm sorry to have wasted your time. I wish we could help you fight Carrick, but Essie has made up her mind. I do see her point, and my father would likely have made the same decision."

"Can you help us talk to her again?" Sito asked. "Seracedar's aggressions may affect Fauxhemia in the future as well."

Lymere grimaced. "I know, but until Carrick actually becomes our problem, Essie won't want to deal with it. She's a stubborn woman. She's determined to keep peace in Fauxhemia, which is what our people favor. If we join your fight, I'm afraid we'll have internal strife with the majority of our people who disagree with a war. Essie doesn't want to get blamed for that. We already have enough criticism. You may already have heard about our relationship. Essie has critics who are determined to see her fall. They claim she controls me through her seductive wiles, and they're looking for reasons to keep us apart."

"Your relationship doesn't have anything to do with stopping Seracedar," I said. "Your father sent Bree to appease Terran and stop a potential invasion, but what he should have done was fight Terran to protect his family and kingdom. You could make that decision now. Protect Fauxhemia by facing the problem, not avoiding it."

Lymere looked uncomfortable. "You just don't understand. It's complicated. I don't want to jeopardize my future with Essie. And if Essie doesn't think it's a problem for the present, then I can't argue. Even if I don't agree with her, it's best to let her have her way. I don't want her to get angry with me."

"Lymere," Sito said. "You're my friend, and I've got to be honest. I know you love her, but you can't spend the rest of your life being afraid of standing up to Queen Esmeralda. Or the rest of the kingdom for that matter. You're the crown prince. She's just acting as regent until you become king. You have a bigger say in making decisions for Fauxhemia. Maybe if you start leading the kingdom, your critics will see that Queen Esmeralda isn't controlling you. Maybe they'll back off."

Lymere's eyes narrowed. "You don't have the right to comment on my relationship with Essie or my role in Fauxhemia. I don't want to talk anymore."

"Lymere, please," Sito said.

The crown prince glared at him. "I said, we're done here." He turned to the doorway. "Zelda, please see our guests out."

Zelda said nothing as she guided us back out of the castle to our coach, where our guards and drivers were waiting. We got on our way, watching the castle disappear from view. And with it, our hopes of an alliance against Carrick.

CHAPTER 19

✦ ✦ ✦ ✦ ✦ ✦ ✦ ✦ ✦ ✦

Aiden and I were quiet in the coach, both of us sullen. Jun and Ponch sat across from us. Sito rode in the second coach, but I wished he was here with us to commiserate.

"From the looks on your faces, I'm guessing the meeting didn't go well," Jun said.

"It was horrible." I turned to Aiden and placed a hand on his shoulder. "Don't take it to heart, all the cruel things she said about you. She doesn't know you."

Aiden folded his hands in his lap and stared out the window. "She didn't say anything that isn't true."

"What did she say?" Ponch asked. "I hope she didn't admit being in league with Carrick."

"No," I said. "She claimed to be innocent, and I believe her there. But an alliance with us is out of the question. Welder was right. She cares too much about her reputation among her subjects."

I hoped that now Aiden would forget about the Fauxhemians. We didn't need them to win. But I did need Aiden to stop getting distracted by other goals like an alliance and an antidote for his parents. I couldn't make decisions without him or lead our people alone.

I sighed and looked out the window. We had left the city and were driving through a quieter neighborhood.

"Did she at least give us permission to search for Clox?" Ponch asked.

I nodded.

"Then the meeting wasn't a total disaster," Jun said.

Aiden turned away from the window to look at me and scrunched his brow. "Do you believe that she's innocent of her husband's poisoning? I find it suspicious that she never denied it."

"I caught that, too," I said. "She made it clear that she had nothing to do with Carrick and poisoning your parents, but she never outright said she wasn't involved in King Lieka's case."

Aiden addressed Ponch and Jun. "Esmeralda won't help us search for Clox. She said we need to find him on our own."

Jun pressed her lips in a disapproving line. "She might as well have admitted her guilt. The only reason she wouldn't want Clox's blood is if she doesn't want to find a cure for King Lieka."

"Do you think Prince Lymere knows?" Ponch asked. "Wouldn't he want to save his father?"

"Lymere didn't seem particularly excited about our search for Clox either," Aiden said.

"He's in love with her," I said. "He's probably covering for her."

"At least she gave us permission to search for Clox," Aiden said. "That's all that matters."

I looked out the window again. I was surprised to see that we were turning onto a busy street. The sidewalk was filled with shoppers walking to stores and buying food.

"Are we in a town?" I asked. "I thought we were heading back to camp."

"King Aiden told us to make a stop here," Ponch said. "It's a small town called Morrow."

Aiden snapped to attention. "Oh, yes, all this drama with Esmeralda made me forget to tell you." For the first time during this coach ride, his frown turned into a genuine beam. "We're visiting some special people. I think you'll love seeing them."

It took me a second to make the connection. "My family?"

At his nod, my lips broke into a smile. "I can't believe this. I didn't think we'd have time, so I didn't bother asking."

"I know," he said. "And I also know you wanted to ask but didn't want to burden me given everything that's going on. Your family is close enough to the capital to take a detour without losing too much time, so I decided to go for it." He sobered, gazing into my eyes. "I'm sorry I haven't been attentive to you lately. But please, in the future, don't be afraid of asking or telling me anything that's on your mind. I'll always do my best to accommodate you."

I kissed his cheek. "Thank you. Does my family know we're coming?"

"I sent word as soon as I knew we were making the trip to Fauxhemia," Aiden said.

I knew Aiden had helped relocate them to Fauxhemia when the Seracedarean capital had threatened to kill them if I tried to escape from the palace. Only he knew their exact location.

"And you're sure it's safe?" I asked.

"They've started a new life here," Aiden said. "No one here knows their real names. We'll be discreet. I'll have the guards wait at the local canteen not far away. Jun and Ponch will come with us as security. Sito has insisted on going with us, too. He wants to meet his future cousin-in-law's family."

We stopped at the end of the street.

Sito got off his coach and came to join us. "This will be a nice visit after the one we just had."

The bodyguards walked a distance behind us so as not to attract too much attention. The Fauxhemian citizens paid us no mind and went about their business. We came to a restaurant with outside seating. The smell of smoked meats wafted from the kitchen to the tables where customers sat waiting for their food. The guards sat, filling two empty tables. They would rest here and get some food while they waited for us.

"Your brother's family set their residence down the road," Aiden said.

"He told me in a letter that he's opened up his own practice," I told Ponch and Jun. I couldn't stop a grin from spreading wide on my face. I felt like skipping all the way to Rell's house.

Aiden set the pace and led the way. Sito strode next to him, and the two cousins started their own discussion. It sounded like they were talking about that dreadful visit with Queen Esmeralda.

I didn't want to think about her or any politics at the moment. I didn't want anything to spoil my mood. I'd been waiting for this moment for so long. I couldn't believe I was about to see my family again.

Ponch and Jun walked on either side of me.

"This must be exciting for you," Ponch said.

"How long has it been since you left home?" Jun asked.

"Almost two years," I said.

Down the lane, we passed a bookstore and a florist. Then we came to another storefront made of brick. Through the door, I could smell the mustiness of herbs.

The words "Office of Doctor Ting" were printed on a metal sign above the door. Ting was Nia's maiden name. Of course.

I knocked, the sound echoing the thud of my heartbeat, and waited in anticipation. Footsteps sounded on the other side.

The door opened, and there my brother, Rell, stood. He was thinner, and white hair was beginning to grow on his sideburns.

I took a step forward and embraced him, felt his arms go around me, and we were both crying. His tears fell on top of my head.

"Thank Old Grandfather Heaven," Rell said. "He has brought us together again."

We all went inside. The apothecary was downstairs, and there was a small alcove with a desk that I assumed was Rell's office.

He nodded to my guards, who remained in the doorway. "You're welcome to come in and make yourselves at home."

Ponch and Jun stayed by the front door.

"We'll keep watch from here," Ponch said. "Give the family some privacy."

Rell turned to Aiden. "I'm so glad to see you again. You've saved our family. When you brought us here, I had no idea you'd end up being the Emberwood prince, or that you would marry Rilla."

"We're not exactly married yet," I said. "The ceremony got interrupted."

"Yes, I read the news," Rell said. "I'm sorry to hear about your parents, King Aiden."

"I hope to have the antidote soon," Aiden said. "Once my parents are well, maybe you'll be able to attend our second attempt at a wedding."

"If you think it's safe at that time, then we will," Rell said. "Whenever the wedding happens, it's an honor to have you as part of our family." My brother regarded Sito. "And you must be the king's cousin, Prince Sito. Rilla has talked about you in her letters. I hear you're pursuing a career in medicine. Mind healing? That's admirable."

Sito beamed and bowed. "Yes. It's a privilege to meet you, Doctor."

"We live on the second floor," Rell said. "Come on up."

I nodded and continued to follow Rell. We climbed a flight of wooden stairs, the boards rickety. I stumbled over a loose board, but Aiden steadied me before I fell.

"Sorry, I forgot to warn you about that step," Rell said. "I haven't had time to fix it."

We reached the landing and stepped into what looked like a common area, filled with a child's toys. I barely had time to take in anything beyond that as the door to the kitchen opened. Nia burst into the living quarters. A toddler was strapped to her back. That was my nephew, Tristan. I couldn't believe I was actually meeting him. I'd only dreamt of this day, but now it had come true.

Nia rushed toward me with a cry. She hugged me so tight I couldn't breathe. "How long I've prayed for this day to come."

We sat on cushions around the tea table. I caught Rell and Nia up on all that had happened after escaping from Cedar Palace. I'd told them some of the stories in my letters, but not everything. Nia gasped as I revealed that the princess who had saved Mama turned out to be Androgy Haming.

"What a twist," she said. "I can't believe he knew your mama."

I went on to tell them about how Aiden, Daki, and I finally made it to Emberwood, only to have almost been killed by Mr. Rino.

And then I finally told them that the pan flute I'd found on the Miyu Islands turned out to be the scepter, and it had granted me the ability to amplify tin-chai.

Rell raised his eyebrows at this, but he waited for me to finish my story before he spoke. "I wish I had the chance to talk to Androgy Haming. As delusional and manipulative as he was, he might have been the only one who knew what Mama was like before she changed her name and went to Cascasea Village. Did he mention what Mama's tin-chai was?"

I shook my head. "Only that it was similar to mine."

He nodded, looking deep in thought. "Interesting."

I held my nephew in my lap. He was already sounding out words like "wa" for water and "keke" like a cough when he was thirsty. I couldn't believe he was already this big. I'd missed out on his first year and a half of life. And I still had to miss out on his life until the war with Seracedar was over.

I sighed, thinking about the task at hand. The responsibility I'd been given along with the scepter. "It's scary to have such great power. I'm worried I might not be qualified to be a leader. What if I make the wrong decisions? Like how I spared Haming's life, but that almost got Aiden killed."

Aiden placed a hand on my shoulder. "That wasn't your fault."

"I know, but I feel like Old Grandfather Heaven chose the wrong person for this job, and if Aiden wasn't chosen alongside me, I would try to ask Old Grandfather Heaven to choose someone else."

Rell gave me a sympathetic look. "Old Grandfather Heaven wouldn't have chosen you if you weren't qualified for the task. He chose to give you the scepter, but you also have to make the choice to have faith and obey the calling. And so far you have."

"Yes," Nia said. "You need to trust yourself more. You've survived the showcase, escaped from the palace. You've gotten this far because you're capable."

Tristan cooed, drawing our attention back to him. Feeling him in my arms, I took comfort in knowing at least he'd be safe living in Fauxhemia, where no one could link him to me. Even if it was sad that he had to live by a fake surname, it was for the best to keep my family safe.

"I'm glad you've been able to build a life for yourselves here," I said. "It sounds like you're doing well, which is all that matters."

"Yes," Nia said, but there was hesitation in her voice.

"Is there something wrong?" I asked.

"I don't mean to sound ungrateful," she said. "I know Aiden risked a lot, bringing us here, but Terran is dead now. Do you think it's possible to go home soon?"

I looked at her in surprise. "I thought you were adjusting here."

"I am, but it's not the same. I miss Cascasea Village and the old house. Your parents' house."

"Isn't Rell's practice doing well? Or is there something you're not telling me? Are the Fauxhemians treating you differently for being Shyan?"

Rell coughed, looking uncomfortable. "It's nothing like that. Our

Fauxhemian neighbors have been kind, and I have been able to take on more patients. They trust me. But it does get exhausting not being able to use our real names. I'm Mars Ting here, and Nia goes by Fenia. We want to go back to our true identities. We want our son to know his origin and live under his real family name."

"We don't want to continue living here forever," Nia said. "I know Carrick has started a war with Emberwood, and it isn't safe to go home yet, but perhaps we can return to Emberwood with you. At least then we'd be with family."

"I hate being the bearer of bad news," Aiden said. "But even Emberwood isn't safe for you. Carrick knows the way to get to me is through Rilla, and the way to get to Rilla is through you. He's already sent an assassin to poison my parents. I'd rather not risk jeopardizing your safety. I never told him your location or your new names when I brought you to Fauxhemia. Nobody here knows your connection to Rilla or to me."

"I agree," I said. "Until Emberwood secures victory in this war, I think you should remain here. Don't worry, I'll write you letters, and as soon as the war is over, I'll send for you."

All too soon our short visit was over. I didn't want to leave. Though I wanted to be optimistic, the reality was this war could last for years before I could see my family again.

As we got ready to go, Rell placed a hand on my shoulder. "Can I talk to you for a moment in private?"

"Of course." I followed him to the kitchen.

"I just wanted to talk to you about Mama and give some brotherly advice," Rell said. "You said that the scepter has amplified your tin-chai, so with its power, you can give tin-chai to others. I don't know how to confirm, but I have a strong feeling Mama's tin-chai allowed her to do the same."

"What makes you think so?"

"I remember I went to the market with Mama one day," he said.

"There was a young man begging on the streets. Mama gave him ten Seran and told him to go make use of his life after that day. A few months later, the village was full of news about a young man who was caught gambling with wood chips he'd transformed into money. The money turned back into wood chips after several days. He was sentenced to death for his crime. He'd been koong at birth, had no family or money, but one day, a stranger gave him ten Seran and a blessing. At the words of her blessing, he felt power enter his body and discovered he had a tin-chai. When asked if he was sorry, he said no. All he did was use his new tin-chai for survival, so why should he apologize? After hearing the story, Mama cried. I asked her what was wrong. She said she needed to pray for Old Grandfather Heaven's forgiveness. I was too young to figure out why she was asking for forgiveness, but when you said the scepter gave you the power to bestow tin-chai to others, that memory came back to me."

I gave him an incredulous stare. "Now I feel a hundred times more anxious. What if I amplify the wrong person's tin-chai, and he ends up becoming another Terran? Or worse, what if someone with a tin-chai more powerful than mine forces me to serve him and amplify the tin-chai of all his followers? I might be forced to create an army of evil super soldiers."

"You have quite an imagination, always forecasting the worst-case scenario," Rell said. "It wasn't my intention to give you more anxiety. The opposite, in fact. I suspect giving that boy a tin-chai may have been the last time Mama used her power. We know she was scared of her tin-chai, and that's why she discouraged you from using yours. It's a shame. Think about how much good she could have done for others. But you aren't Mama. You've used your tin-chai and grown so much during your journey. No matter who has tried to control you and your tin-chai, you've found a way to break free. I know you'll use your powers for good and figure out a way to stop those who may try to use you just as you did with Terran and Androgy Haming."

"Still, I'm not sure I would have survived if Aiden hadn't been by my side the whole way," I said, worrying my bottom lip. "I've always been able to depend on him."

Rell frowned. "I sense a *but* coming. What's wrong?"

"He's changed from the man I once knew. Throughout our journey, we were great at working together. He was confident and always felt like sunshine. But recently, he's felt distant. He seems to doubt his decisions more. I sense fear in him when he's always seemed so fearless. I was the one who was afraid."

"Maybe it has something to do with his parents being mind poisoned," Rell said.

I nodded. "I know it has to do with that. But it started before then. Ever since he returned to Emberwood, I've seen his confidence waning. He said he's not sure he can be the leader Emberwood needs if his parents aren't here to support him. I've told him he can lean on me as his support, but he said he doesn't want to bother me. It's like he doesn't want me to see his weaknesses."

"Then he'd better learn," Rell snapped. "You're Aiden's partner now, not his parents. The two of you should be making decisions as a team. If he can't figure it out, then I don't want you marrying him."

I was surprised by Rell's rebuke. It probably showed on my face because my brother's expression softened. "I don't mean to sound harsh. And I don't want to overstep either. I just hope you can figure out how to talk to him about your worries. The two of you were chosen to hold the scepter together. It must mean Old Grandfather Heaven believes you're stronger as a team than on your own. But we all have times when we struggle. No one is perfect, and no one can be someone else's sunshine every day. Maybe Aiden needs to figure out what he's dealing with on his own, and one day, he'll regain that confidence you saw in him before."

"On his own?" I repeated. "We don't have time for him to figure things out on his own. If I can't depend on him, then how are we supposed to win this war? Lead Emberwood? I can't bear the Will of Heaven without him."

"I didn't mean he'll leave you to deal with everything alone," Rell said. "Obviously, he wouldn't do that. But you can't rely on him so much when he's got his own internal struggles. You have to learn to be strong without him. If he doesn't trust himself to make decisions, then you have to. I know I tried to overshield you when you were young, but listening to your adventures made me see how much you've grown. You can protect yourself now. I never want you to hide behind someone again. Not me. Not Aiden. You're capable of standing on your own."

I nodded. "Thank you, Rell. Every now and then I could use the reminder."

He hugged me. "Now I suppose it's time to say goodbye again. Let's hope this war ends soon."

Ponch, Jun, Sito, and Aiden were already waiting outside. With one last wave goodbye to my family, I headed to join them. We walked back to the canteen where the Emberwood soldiers were resting.

One of our men was pacing by the entrance. When he saw us, he looked relieved.

"Your Majesty," he said. "A man is waiting for you. Looks like a guard from the Fauxhemian castle. He won't speak to anyone but you and insists on waiting in his coach until you arrive."

"Bring us to him," Aiden said.

We headed to the coach waiting by the wayside where we had parked our own.

Aiden knocked on the driver's side window. The door opened, and out stepped a man with long hair and a beard.

I looked over at the man and wondered why he seemed so out of place. He might be in his mid-thirties, but it was hard to tell for certain. His beard made him look strange and much older than he probably was. Based on the clean-shaven look of all the Fauxhemians who served Queen Esmeralda at the castle, I hadn't expected to see a guard with such an old-fashioned beard. He looked more like the men in the portraits hanging on the castle walls. He also faintly smelled of smoke like he'd been puffing a cigar before arriving.

He looked at me and the guards behind us. "No, only King Aiden. Everyone else needs to go."

"My fiancée and my cousin stay," Aiden said.

The man nodded. "Fine." He waited for the guards to walk out of hearing distance before continuing.

"I come on behalf of Queen Esmeralda. She wants King Aiden to return to the castle at once. She can give you the antidote you need."

CHAPTER 20

✦ ✦ ✦ ✦ ✦ ✦ ✦ ✦ ✦ ✦

The man handed Aiden a note. Aiden scanned it. "I've been invited back to the castle. Queen Esmeralda says she can get me the antidote without hunting down Dribin Clox."

I raised an eyebrow. "How is that possible?"

"She knows someone else with similar blood," Aiden said, continuing to read the note.

"A relative of Clox with the same blood might share the same poison," Sito said. "Their blood could also be used to create an antidote. But why wouldn't she have told us this when we were visiting her?"

"The queen will explain everything when King Aiden returns to the castle," the man said. "But only two men may accompany him."

I frowned. "Why such secrecy? She just kicked us out of her home two hours ago. And why are only two men allowed to go with the king? That isn't adequate protection. This doesn't sound right."

The man folded his arms across his chest and scowled. "Two men only. Her Majesty's words, not mine."

"Rilla's right," Sito said. "Something about this sounds off." He turned to the guard. "Do you have proof that Queen Esmeralda sent you?"

The man held up a seal. "I'm one of Her Majesty's personal guards."

Sito studied the seal. "It looks legitimate. But still, the king needs more protection than two men."

The queen's man glared at us. "This is the queen's request. If you refuse to comply, I will return to her and say you rejected her invitation and insulted us. You'll never get an antidote for your king and queen."

"No, wait," Aiden said. "My cousin had no ill intent. I apologize for his rudeness." He sent Sito a look.

Sito sighed. "If you insist on going, then I'm coming with you as one of the two men."

"I'm coming, too," I said. "I won't be left out."

Aiden smiled at the messenger. "Give me one moment of privacy with my family please. I promise I'll make this quick."

He took Sito and me aside. "Neither of you can come. Sito, I know you don't want the throne, and you're meant to be a doctor, but nevertheless, you're next in line. Also, I need you to protect Rilla. There's the possibility she might be carrying my child. In case something happens to me—"

My hands shook. Aiden saw my face and gave me a sorry look. "Oops, wrong choice of words."

"Don't go," I said. "This sounds too risky. The queen already gave her consent to find Dribin Clox. Why would she suddenly say there's another way? What if this message isn't coming from the queen? Someone else could be leading you into a trap."

"I know it could be a trap, but I've got to take that chance," Aiden said. "For my parents' sake. It could take much longer to hunt down Clox."

"Then let it take longer," I said. "You have other responsibilities, too. Clox can't be your only priority."

Aiden frowned. "This is for my parents, Rilla. I can't turn away an opportunity to find an antidote. The sooner my parents are cured, the sooner I'll be able to focus on the Will of Heaven and the war against Carrick."

He gave me a reassuring smile. "You return with Sito to camp first. I'll be back in two hours."

"I don't want to go back to camp," Sito said. "You can't go by yourself. Let me go with you."

"Sito, don't be difficult," Aiden said, sending his cousin a warning look.

"Aiden, please don't go," I whispered. "You want the antidote so much that you're not thinking clearly. What if Queen Esmeralda is lying and she really is involved with Carrick and Clox?"

"Then I'll meet with her and find out. One way or another, I'm going to get that antidote. Don't worry, I can take care of myself. I lasted ten years in Cedar Palace, didn't I?"

I wanted to stomp my feet in frustration. "That was different. You were a bodyguard then, hiding in the shadows. You're a king now. With a responsibility to lead your people. Wherever you go, your enemies are going to target you."

"Rilla's right," Sito said. "You can't go gallivanting off on your own. I can't let you leave again. The last time nearly destroyed me."

Aiden gave both of us a stern look. "I have to do this. Please understand. If this is a trap, I'll fight back and survive like I always do. I'll figure out who is targeting me and my parents." His eyes glinted the way they did when he was about to attack the enemy. "And then I'll kill them."

Nothing was going to change his mind. He couldn't focus on anything except finding that antidote. I would just have to accept it and hope that he was successful. Maybe then he would finally be able to refocus on the Will of Heaven.

"Wait. Take this." I unhooked my necklace with the glass ship pendant from my neck. It was the same ship I thought I'd broken and lost forever, but Aiden had put it back together for me.

I fastened it around his neck. "It's a symbol. A reminder that you've always been there to protect me. And now, I hope it brings you protection. You have to bring it back to me personally."

He kissed me, then turned and called to his men. "Klay, Spince. You're with me."

Oren stepped forward. "Your Majesty, let me come with you. General Welder would never forgive me if I stayed behind."

"You and Spince then," Aiden said. He turned to address the queen's man. "My men and I will be riding in our own coach. We'll follow you."

"No, you will ride with me."

Aiden stood his ground. "I've already compromised enough. We will take our own coach."

"Fine," the man barked. He got back into his coach.

Aiden and the two guards got in a coach. I watched them disappear, the dirt kicking up from the wheels of the coach. A queasy feeling squeezed my stomach.

Sito stayed still, his frown deepening. Then he sprang forward, getting into the driver's seat of another coach. "I'm going after them. Sorry, Rilla. It will kill me if I sit here doing nothing and end up losing him again. Ponch and Jun can take care of you, right?"

I nodded. "Don't worry about me. Just make sure Aiden doesn't do anything stupid."

"If we're not back in four hours, send help," Sito said.

"Be careful," I called after him as he took off. "Please make sure you both come back alive."

I watched Sito drive off. And even though Ponch, Jun, and six other guards remained to accompany me back to the Emberwood camp, I felt like I'd been abandoned to fight this war on my own.

We returned to camp.

"Where is Welder?" I asked the soldiers. "I need to speak with him."

Ret saw me and approached. "He's still feeling sick, but he went for a walk to get some fresh air. Is something wrong? Where's the king?"

"The king went back to Fauxhemia Castle, but I'm worried it might be a trap."

"I'll go find Welder at once," Ret said. He rushed off, his feet carrying him faster than a speeding coach. Now I knew his tin-chai.

I waited with my guardswomen. The minutes ticked by. Pacing the camp, I wondered what was taking so long. I sat for a while, but my anxiety was too high, so I stood and paced some more. I felt Ponch and Jun throwing worried glances my way.

"You should sit and take some breaths," Jun said.

I shook my head. "I can't."

Ponch came and handed me a canteen of water. "At least drink some water. You look like you're about to faint."

I took the canteen and sipped. The water quenched my dry throat. I didn't realize how thirsty I'd been until now.

Jun looked at her watch. "It's been half an hour. Welder must be really sick and throwing up in the woods because with Ret's speeding tin-chai, I can't imagine what else would be holding them up."

Then I saw a blur zooming down the road. Ret slowed to a stop, carrying Welder with him.

Welder took hurried strides toward us. He was drenched in sweat.

"Finally," I said. "Where have you been?"

"I'm sorry. I was trying to recuperate from last night and thought a walk might help. But that's not important. What's happened? Where are Aiden and Sito?"

I explained everything that had happened.

Welder glowered. "Of all the idiotic stunts. Aiden is blinded by his desire for an antidote. We need to send someone after him and Sito. Which two men did Aiden take with him?"

"Oren and Spince."

Shouts sounded in the distance. A rider on horseback approached our camp. The rider slumped forward, barely able to hold onto the reins. As he grew closer, I saw that it was Oren, one of the guards who had accompanied Aiden.

He came to a stop and stumbled off the horse. Blood poured from a wound in his side. He staggered forward and fell to the ground.

"Rilla, come help him," Welder said.

I sang, healing Oren of his wounds. He opened his eyes.

"I'm sorry, my queen," he said. "I've failed you. I don't know what happened to the king, but I fear the worst."

My entire body grew chilled like I'd been thrown into an icy lake. My legs wobbled, threatening to collapse under me. I grabbed onto Ponch for support and forced myself to remain poised. I couldn't lose my senses now. Aiden said he could take care of himself. He'd promised to come back.

"What happened?" Welder roared.

"Fauxhemians ambushed us," Oren said. "The queen's messenger led us into a forest, and a dozen Fauxhemian royal guards jumped out of the trees, attacking us with swords. Esmeralda sent them to kill us."

"I knew Esmeralda couldn't be trusted," Welder said. "Oren, explain how you made it out alive. What happened to the king?"

"We fought them off," Oren continued. "Spince and I paired up. King Aiden was doing fine on his own. But then Spince deflected a blow. Saved my life, but he went down. Everything after that is a blur. I killed seven, then looked up, and the rest were dead. Burned bodies. I assume the king used his tin-chai on them. I counted them as the exact number of attackers. I searched for the king. Called for him. But no answer. However, I did find this."

He pulled out a necklace. My necklace.

"It was caught on a bush near a cliff," Oren said. "I think—I think—"

I tuned out the rest of his words. I wanted to curl into a ball on the ground. Still, I forced myself to listen to Oren. There was no way Aiden could have tumbled down that cliff.

I faced Oren, forcing my tears back. My voice shook. "What about Sito? Did you see him? He went after you."

Oren shook his head. "Prince Sito followed us? I saw no sign of him."

"Damn it." Welder pointed to several men. "Go. Search for the king and the prince." He looked back at Oren. "How are you certain it was Esmeralda who sent these assassins?"

"The Fauxhemian messenger with the beard who led us into the ambush wasn't dead," Oren said. "He came up behind me. Stabbed me. I thought I was a goner. He said the queen was following up on her promise to Carrick. Dribin Clox was supposed to have poisoned King Aiden, too."

"So, she was in league with Carrick and Clox," Welder said. "How did you escape?"

"I found a rock and bashed his head in," Oren said. "I was lucky. Old Grandfather Heaven must have been on my side." Oren looked at me with sad eyes. "I'm sorry. So sorry. I didn't want to leave without finding His Majesty, but I needed to return here alive and tell you."

I stared at him. I heard his words, knew Aiden was missing. But I couldn't accept it.

Welder slapped Oren on the back. "You did well, my man. Thanks to you, we know Esmeralda's true intentions. Don't beat yourself up over the king or the prince. We'll continue looking for them."

Through my grief, the thought came through to me that something about Oren's account seemed strange. But I felt too numb to figure out why.

Aiden was missing. Sito, too. What if we never found them? What if they were dead?

I couldn't move. I couldn't breathe.

Welder's voice sounded distant in my head. "You, and you. Put together a search team and scour every inch of Fauxhemia if you have to. Just find the king and the prince. Be careful, the Fauxhemians won't like that we're trespassing without their queen's permission. Ponch and Jun, take Rilla back to Emberwood immediately. It's not safe here. Rilla. Rilla? Do you hear me?"

He touched my shoulder. I jumped. Gave him a blank stare.

"You need to go," he said.

I remained frozen.

"I think she's in shock," Welder said. "Ponch, help get Rilla into the coach."

Ponch took my arm. I felt her tugging me away. Dots swarmed in front of my vision. Aiden was missing. Aiden could be dead. What was I going to do without him?

Darkness overcame me, and I surrendered to it.

CHAPTER 21

✦ ✦ ✦ ✦ ✦ ✦ ✦ ✦ ✦ ✦

Time passed in a blur. Somehow, I found myself in a coach, then sailing across the sea, and finally, back at Linlang Palace. I felt like I was living in another world. An alternate reality.

For three days after returning home, I stayed in my room and refused to talk to anyone. Not Ponch or Jun, and not even Sago, who had come to see how she could help. I wanted to stay in bed and never get up.

But on the third day, I rose from my bed, a sudden realization spinning into my head. Oren's story didn't make sense.

I found a rock and bashed his head in. Oren's words replayed in my mind.

Something about the story wasn't adding up. It was strange. Staged. Why hadn't the queen's man killed Oren with the first stab? Instead, the man had stabbed Oren, only to reveal that Esmeralda was responsible for conspiring with Carrick and Clox. It was almost as though he'd wanted Oren to return to tell us this.

Also, it seemed too convenient that Oren would have found a rock to kill the man before he got killed himself. Had Oren really killed that man?

Why had Welder accepted Oren's story without question?

You did well, my man. Thanks to you, we know Esmeralda's true intentions.

He'd acted like Oren had done a noble deed. No criticisms that one of his men had failed to protect the king. Welder rarely praised his men, especially not after a mission had gone wrong. Then there was the fact that he hated Esmeralda and had been acting strange the whole time we were in Fauxhemia. Getting drunk, claiming he had a stomach ailment so he wouldn't have to visit Esmeralda with us, encouraging Aiden to chase down Dribin Clox in the first place. If Welder hadn't brought up Clox back in Cindertrance City, Aiden might not have been sidetracked into going to Fauxhemia.

Most importantly, Welder hadn't been at the camp when I'd returned. Why had it taken so long for Ret to find him? And when he'd finally arrived, he was drenched in sweat like he'd just been exercising. Or been in a fight.

A horrible thought occurred to me.

What if Welder, not Esmeralda, was responsible for Aiden and Sito's disappearance? Oren, Ret, Hu, Vay. Were they all in on it?

I didn't know much about Welder's men. Hu and Vay carried out his commands and had always seemed to be competent, but I hadn't ever gotten to know them. I'd seen Ret use his tin-chai, the ability to move at fast speeds. I didn't know what Oren's tin-chai was. But his wyis was so strong, he had to have a tin-chai. What I did know was these men were loyal to Welder and would do anything he said, even kill the king of Emberwood.

I didn't want to believe Welder would do such a thing, but I'd never trust him again unless I was sure. I had to do my own investigation.

I washed up and put on a fresh set of clothes. Then I stepped outside my room and found a maid.

"Is Sago still here?" I asked.

The maid looked surprised. "Your Highness, it's so good to see you up. And yes, Ms. Sago hasn't left yet. She's been waiting to speak to you."

"Please find her and tell her to meet me in my room."

The maid bowed. "Yes, Your Highness. At once."

I went back into my room, sat down at my desk, and penned a cordial letter to Queen Esmeralda. I asked if she had heard anything about Aiden or Sito's whereabouts. I didn't accuse her of anything, but I did tell her I wanted to meet with her and clarify the situation before it escalated.

I signed off the letter and sealed it.

A knock sounded on my door. Sago's voice came from the other side. "Rilla, can I come in?"

"Yes."

She opened the door, and the sight of her concerned face brought fresh tears to my eyes.

Sago embraced me and I cried into her shoulder. "Oh, my dear child, I'm so sorry. Don't lose hope yet. You must remain strong. It's what Aiden would want. He named you as his successor, so you have to muster up the strength and courage to continue on and lead Emberwood without him."

I pulled away from her in surprise. "What are you talking about?"

"I know you haven't heard yet because you've kept to your room since your return. The royal advisors, upon hearing that both Aiden and Sito went missing, took out an official decree Aiden signed before both of you left for Cindertrance. In the event that both Aiden and Sito are deceased or incapacitated, the throne will go directly to you, Aiden's future queen consort. If you're with child, even if conceived out of wedlock, he acknowledges the child as his, and they will become the legitimate heir when they are of age."

I blinked away tears. "I didn't know he did that. He must have done it to protect me in case something happened to him. But is it really possible if I'm not legally married to him?"

"Apparently so," Sago replied. "I talked to Ponch. She's been eavesdropping on the advisors. Under Emberwood law, if the king has no heir in his bloodline, he will name his successor. You're to rule in Aiden's stead until he and Sito are found. And I refuse to give up on them.

Neither should you. I sent Wyle with a group of Yao to Fauxhemia. They're helping with the search. I heard Esmeralda doesn't like that we're there, but she's allowing a week-long search to prove she has nothing to hide."

"So she denies that she had anything to do with that ambush?"

"She claims someone is trying to ruin her reputation," Sago said. "She wants to meet with you on neutral ground. She maintains she has never been in league with Carrick and never helped him hire Dribin Clox. But Welder already refused her invitation."

I scowled. "He had no authority to do that. He's not the king."

"I agree. There's something not right with that man."

I looked into her eyes. "What do you mean?"

"I'm not sure yet. Just that I don't quite trust him." Sago frowned. Worry lines creased her brow. "Ponch told me about your visit with Esmeralda. The whole situation seems strange. I think we need to investigate further before casting blame on anyone, but Welder is biased against the Fauxhemians."

I took the letter off my desk and showed it to Sago. "I need you to help me deliver this to Esmeralda. I want to hear what she has to say. It's important that Welder doesn't find out."

She took the letter. "I'll go at once. I promise to return soon. Have courage. I don't believe in your Old Grandfather Heaven, but I believe in you."

Sago hugged me again, then took off. Once she was gone, I went to the Gold Song Courtyard to find someone to tell me what Welder was up to. I knew he was back from Fauxhemia. Maybe it was because I had already formed suspicions against him, but it seemed peculiar that I hadn't heard from him since his return. If he was up to something, I had to keep a better eye on him.

Up in the Gold Song Courtyard, I found servants bustling to and fro, bringing fresh tea into the meeting room. I went into the room and found a group of a dozen men sitting around the table. Most were older gentlemen, the usual group who had advised King Ashbel. But there were two younger men who I'd never seen before. Then I saw Lord Tu, a familiar face.

I went up to him. "Hello, my lord."

He looked surprised to see me. "I'm glad you're well enough to join us today, especially since we're to vote on whether to declare war on Fauxhemia. I was so worried about your wellbeing, having not seen you at any of the meetings the past few days."

"Meetings? I wasn't told about any meetings."

"You weren't? Welder said you've been overcome with grief, so I assumed that was the reason. You poor child, I'm so sorry for all that's happened, but I believe the king is still alive. You can't give up hope either."

"Thank you," I said. "Has Welder been calling these meetings?"

"Yes, we've been discussing how to handle Fauxhemia. Today we're supposed to vote on whether or not to declare war on Esmeralda."

Welder entered the room. His gaze met mine. He paused but showed no sign of surprise to see me.

"Oh, good to see you're here today," he said. "I wasn't sure whether to call you, but I'm glad you were notified."

"You could have told me about these meetings," I said. "I would have come."

"I wasn't sure what your condition was. The servants all said you wouldn't get out of bed and didn't want to see anyone."

I didn't say anything further because he did have a point. I'd refused to see anyone for three days. Why had I allowed my emotions to get the better of me when there were important matters to discuss? Life didn't stop just because I was sad.

The other council members were staring at us. They gave me pitying looks and shook their heads.

"Poor girl," I heard Colonel Beyling whisper to Lord Tu. "What will she do now? They were never officially married, and she's expected to take his place. I'm surprised it's even allowed."

"Emberwood laws have always been too liberal, in my opinion," Captain Kang said. "But King Aiden signed off, and it's done. I can't imagine a woman leading this kingdom without a husband. But perhaps she'll surprise me and prove herself worthy of the position."

We took our seats. I took a sip of tea to quench my dry throat. Welder began the meeting, his voice confident and unwavering.

"I state once again that we need to retaliate against the Fauxhemians," Welder said. "They are just as much our enemy as Seracedar. Esmeralda is waiting for us to fall. She helped Carrick because she wants him to destroy us."

Lord Pan cleared his throat and stood. "Welder, you continue to accuse Esmeralda of treachery, but you have yet to provide proof. Although Fauxhemia has never been our ally in war, we've always had a friendly relationship. Prince Sito and Prince Lymere started the education program that allows Emberwood and Fauxhemia university students to study together. Our kingdoms have established fair trade agreements that have been in place for decades. We share oil and coal to provide energy resources for them, and they give us stone and natural minerals for building projects. Why would Queen Esmeralda risk ruining everything we've built together?"

I took another sip of hot tea before speaking. "I agree. Besides, Esmeralda was clear when we visited her. Her reputation is of utmost importance to her, and she would never start a war and risk her people's disapproval. She wants nothing to do with Clox because of the rumors associating her involvement with her husband's poisoning."

"Esmeralda is a cunning woman," Welder said. "She says one thing but does another. I can't explain her motives, but today, I can provide evidence of her duplicity."

He gestured to the two young men who sat among the council.

The men stood, and one of them addressed me. "It's true, Your Highness. We were sent to Seracedar as spies a month ago, and we saw Queen Esmeralda at Cedar Palace. She met with Carrick."

The other man nodded. "I listened in on their conversation. Esmeralda said she would help Carrick behind the scenes. First by taking down Ashbel and Leonora, then King Aiden. She said Emberwood would never survive with Prince Sito, a scholar, on the throne. Guess she didn't expect Prince Sito to go missing, too."

Lord Tu scowled. "But why? I can't think of a reason she'd want to hurt us."

"Prince Carrick promised that if he wins this war, he will give Fauxhemia the northern quarter of Emberwood," the first man said. "And better access to trade with Seracedar, which Fauxhemia has never had. She'd be the most remembered female ruler in Fauxhemian history to mend the relationship with Seracedar. And no one would remember the gossip about her involvement with King Lieka's poisoning."

"There you have it," Welder said. "It's all about making herself revered in the eyes of her subjects."

"There's one more piece of news we learned," the second man said. "Esmeralda doesn't want anyone to find Dribin Clox. She told Carrick that if Clox shows up in Seracedar, she wants him killed. Also, she called Clox her uncle."

"What?" My gaze snapped to him. "Uncle by blood or a friend of the family?"

"Her mother and Clox shared the same father, though Esmeralda's mother changed her name after she estranged herself from her family."

"No wonder she had Aiden ambushed," Welder said. "If he found Clox, there would be a chance we'd find out his connection to Esmeralda. She could have worked with her uncle to poison King Lieka. She didn't want anyone finding Clox for fear that her secret would be revealed to her subjects."

"Why didn't you bring this to our attention before King Aiden went to Fauxhemia?" another advisor asked. "We could have warned our king. He would still be here with us."

The first man cowered. "We couldn't return without blowing our cover, so we sent a letter. Unfortunately, the general never received it, and we only were able to sneak out recently, but the king was already in Fauxhemia."

This all seemed too suspicious. Were they telling the truth? Or had Welder set this up? Was it really true that Esmeralda and Dribin Clox were related? My mind drew a blank. I didn't know what to say. How to challenge them.

I couldn't think. I didn't want to think about Esmeralda or war or anything. I just wanted Aiden to be here. The grief was overwhelming.

I took a deep breath. I couldn't be overcome by emotions in front of the council.

Standing, I faced Welder. "I think we shouldn't be so hasty in judging—"

The room started to sway around me, preventing me from continuing. Strange, why was I suddenly dizzy?

"You don't look well, Rilla," Welder said. "Perhaps you should go to your room and rest. Forgive me for being insensitive. I should have insisted that a woman like you have time to grieve in privacy instead of trying to conduct business."

The other men grunted in agreement.

"That's not necessary," I said. "I'm fine. King Aiden has left me in charge in his absence, and I won't let him down."

But the room wouldn't stop spinning. The dizziness was getting worse. And a cramp squeezed in my abdomen. I needed to lie down.

I fell back into my chair and braced my head in my hands. Why was this happening? Was it really because of my grief? I glanced at the cup of tea I'd been sipping. I hadn't felt dizzy until drinking it. Who had offered it to me?

Welder stood and called outside the room. "I need assistance."

A maidservant came at once.

"Please escort Her Highness back to her room," Welder said. "She needs to rest."

He turned back to me. "Don't worry. The kingdom is in safe hands with me and the rest of the royal council."

Back in my room, I lay on the bed. The room swayed. The pain in my abdomen was growing worse. I forced myself to take deep breaths. What had set this off? Was it possible Welder had someone put something in my tea, or was I being paranoid?

I hated not knowing his true intentions, but it was clear to me that he was trying to frame Esmeralda. He must have hired those men, those so-called spies, to say all those things at that meeting. But the royal council believed it. They trusted Welder.

I had trusted Welder.

And now I didn't even know who to trust anymore. What if it wasn't just Welder who wasn't happy that Aiden had left me in charge? What if he'd swayed members of the royal council to his side? What if some of them were conspiring with him against me?

I reflected on Welder's history. He had stolen the scepter before. And he had proved that he was capable of doing anything for a cause he believed in, even if his actions put others in jeopardy. What if he had a reason for being in Emberwood, for helping Aiden and me? A reason that wasn't as selfless as he claimed.

What if—

Sharp pain squeezed my abdomen, worse than before. I folded forward and groaned.

And then I felt it. A gush of blood soaking into my undergarments.

Oh no. My monthly bleeding had come. Could this, coupled with stress, explain the dizzy spell? Or had someone really put a draught in my tea? I couldn't know for sure.

But then the horrible realization came crashing in. I was not with child. I was not going to have Aiden's child.

If Aiden really was dead, I had nothing left of him. I'd never see a resemblance of his golden sunshine. I'd never have a part of him to hold onto. Never again.

My entire body was numb, but I forced myself to clean up and change my undergarments. Then I lay back on the bed. The pain in my abdomen felt unbearable, and I curled up, trying to will it away.

The emotions I'd held back in front of the council finally gushed out like a thunderstorm. My shoulders heaved, and I cried into Aiden's pillow, even as I tried to catch any remnants of his lingering scent. I sobbed harder than I ever had before. I cried until there were no tears left.

I drifted off to sleep, but soon woke, pain coursing through me. I realized the bed sheets were soaked in blood. This had to be more than just my monthly bleeding. I made my way to the door and cried for help.

A guard rushed in. He took in the blood. "Your Highness, I'll call the doctor."

Soon, a team of nurses came into the room. Doctor Flamyor was right behind them. When I saw her, tears gushed down my cheeks. I sobbed.

"I'm right here, dear girl," she said. "Let's see what's happening."

She took some time to examine me, and a grave look came on her face. "Rilla, I'm sorry to say this, but you had a miscarriage."

Emotional pain came flooding back. "What?"

"It was early enough not to have lasting ramifications," Doctor Flamyor said. "But I want you on bed rest for a few days, and I'll continue to monitor you."

I couldn't speak. I stared at her, frozen. How could this have happened? Of course, there were several possible answers, but I couldn't stop myself from suspecting there had been something in the tea that Welder had given me. Did he want to make sure I didn't have any children with Aiden? To make sure there were no future threats stopping him from taking control of Emberwood?

Doctor Flamyor and the team of nurses eventually left me to rest, but there were two nurses who remained on duty outside my room in case I needed them.

For the next few days, I couldn't get out of bed. I slept most of the time and had never felt more exhausted. Ponch and Jun took turns caring for me, and I woke long enough to take my medicine. They refused to tell me anything related to politics or Welder.

Never would I trust Welder again. And I certainly would never drink or eat anything he gave me. If he had really done this to me, I wanted to make him suffer. Take away what he valued most.

I'd never felt so depressed in my life. A part of me wondered if Old Grandfather Heaven was angry with me. Maybe this miscarriage was punishment for sleeping with Aiden before we were officially married. Maybe I deserved it.

This deep sadness was even worse than the days I'd been in a novelty cage. At least then I'd had Aiden's visits to look forward to. I remembered how he used to request that I sing *Lady of the Sea.*

I'd written that song based on Auntie An, the woman I worked for in my village. She had been such an inspiration to me. Her tin-chai was finding gifts from the sea anytime she went fishing. From seafood to pearls to seashells, she sold whatever the sea gave her and had run a successful business. I remembered her telling me that when her fiancé had been killed at sea, she had thought many times about throwing herself into the ocean to join him. But one day, she came across two starving children begging for food. The sea had given her fresh fish and kelp that morning, so she cooked the food for the children to eat. It was that day she realized she could do a lot more good in the world if she decided to live instead of die. And she knew it had been her fiancé who brought those children to her that day. Ever since, she lived with the purpose of using her tin-chai to help others.

"I never want to fall in love," I'd once told her. "It was already terrible enough losing my mama and baba. But it would be unbearable if the person with whom I chose to share my life and to bare my intimate secrets suddenly left me."

"Love is worth it," she'd said. "And everyone leaves eventually. Not always by choice, mind you."

"Exactly. I don't think I'd ever get over the sadness."

"Probably not. Grief never really goes away. I still cry when I think of my Jalius. But I know he wants me to live out my purpose, and that inspires me to be strong. I used to write him letters to tell him everything I wanted to say. Still do. When the grief feels unbearable, I find writing my feelings helps. Words can be powerful and healing."

Auntie An was a wise woman. Words were powerful and healing. I, of all people, should know. I got out of bed and went to my desk. I took out a pen and some parchment, and I began to write a letter, pouring out my words to the only person whom I wanted to talk to at the moment.

My dearest Aiden,

I don't know what to do. You've left me, and I'm so mad at you. I'm angry you let yourself disappear and you're letting me feel this much grief. I've never experienced this level of sorrow, not even in the days I was trapped in the novelty cage. At least back then you were there. But now you're completely gone, and I don't know how to move forward. I feel as though the sun will never shine again.

I'm told that Esmeralda and Clox are related. If it's true, Esmeralda could have given us her blood to find a cure for your parents, but she didn't. Is it proof that she's a liar? Or is that just another lie about her to get me to believe she plotted the ambush on you?

And now my suspicions are cast on Welder, the man we regarded as our friend. I don't know his intentions or his true heart. What if he betrays us? I don't know what to believe or who to trust. I don't know how to do anything without you. But I have to figure it out. People are counting on me.

Tears ran down my cheeks and blotted the paper, smearing the ink. I was finally admitting it to myself. Aiden might be dead. It was a reality I didn't want to accept, but I couldn't deny it any longer.

I can't believe you might be dead. I can't believe you might not be coming back. I keep hoping this isn't the end of you, of us. But if you are still alive, wouldn't you have given me a sign by now?

I continued to write. Everything that I wanted to tell Aiden poured out of me onto the page.

Even if you never come back to me, I'll always love you until the last ember of starlight flickers out in the night sky.

I put the pen down and lay back on the pillows. I stared at the ceiling blankly, feeling as though my entire soul had been sucked out of my body. It was a cold night, but I didn't have the energy to get up to light a fire. I didn't even want to get under the blankets or call a servant for help. I didn't want to see anyone. My hands were frozen, and I'd likely catch a cold, but I didn't care.

I closed my eyes, felt the tears fall down my cheeks again, and wished I could sleep forever.

I dozed off. I didn't know how long I was sleeping, but a sound woke me. I looked around at my surroundings. I was in my bedchamber, and I was no longer cold. My fingers and toes had regained all feeling. A mound of blankets was piled over me, and a blazing fire roared in the hearth. I heard the same sound that woke me. A scratching noise. The window was open, and a tree branch scratched the pane. I didn't remember leaving it open. I sat up straight and gasped.

Not only was the window open, but the letter I'd been writing and my pen were gone, too. I swore I'd left them on the bed when I'd fallen asleep.

I thought back to my days at Cedar Palace. Whenever I'd fallen asleep outside, I'd always wake up covered in a blanket. Later I found out that Aiden had been watching over me. Was it possible that he had returned?

I called his name, threw off the blankets, and searched the room. But no one was there.

I opened the top drawer of my desk. There, tucked in front, were my letter and the pen.

That smidge of hope died again. I cursed myself for believing he'd come back. Though I had locked the door, a maid could have asked for a key to come check on me, and not wanting to wake me, lit a fire, covered me in blankets, and put my letters in the drawer for safekeeping.

That wouldn't explain the open window, though. Wouldn't the maid have closed it? Maybe it hadn't been locked tight.

In any case, it couldn't be Aiden. He wouldn't have come in here and not revealed himself to me. That would be too cruel.

I got back into bed, but this time I didn't sleep. I thought about the last moment Aiden and I had been together. He'd promised me he would come back. But more importantly, I had promised him I would be strong and protect the kingdom if he couldn't return.

And I also remembered Rell's words to me.

You can protect yourself now. I never want you to hide behind someone again. Not me. Not Aiden. You're capable of standing on your own.

Thinking of my brother's encouragement brought comfort to me. He believed in me. I had to believe in me, too.

Life couldn't stop just because Aiden was no longer here. Emberwood and Seracedar were still embroiled in war. Emberwood needed reassurance and motivation more than ever. I didn't have time to mope, while the citizens were desperate for leadership. I couldn't allow chaos to take over the kingdom.

Even if Aiden never came back, I still had to keep my promise to him. I would protect Emberwood. And with the Will of Heaven, I would restore peace to both Shyan kingdoms.

CHAPTER 22

✦ ✦ ✦ ✦ ✦ ✦ ✦ ✦ ✦ ✦

It took about five days before I regained enough energy to feel more like myself again. I took it slow, and Ponch and Jun finally gave me some updates on Welder. He was still trying to convince the royal advisors to declare war on Fauxhemia, but he didn't have the majority vote yet. Most of the advisors were concerned that we were spreading ourselves too thin and needed to finish the war with Seracedar first.

One morning, I felt well enough and knew I couldn't stay away from my duties any longer. I got up and dressed in a new gown. I'd been saving it for a special occasion, but wearing it now gave me the confidence and strength I needed. It was in a cerulean shade like the Cascasean Sea in summer. It reminded me of my roots, that I was just as responsible for my hometown in Seracedar as I was for Emberwood. I did my makeup and covered the blotches and bags under my cried-out eyes. Then I finished the outfit with my necklace—the glass ship pendant with the Yao diamond in the center of it. I didn't know what I was about to face, but I did know that I was a queen. A leader. And I had to lead my people.

I looked into the mirror and practiced putting on a brave face. An unreadable face.

I had to meet with Welder. His recent behavior was not sitting well with me, and I needed to find out what was going on in his head without him knowing I suspected him of ulterior motives.

This would be tricky. I was facing a general, a man who was known for his strategizing. But, I reminded myself, I had stood up to Empress Limera, Emperor Terran, and the minions of Cedar Palace. I'd defeated Androgy Haming. And I had the Will of Heaven. I might not be a general, and I might be ten years Welder's junior, but I had faced battles all the same. I could not discount myself.

A knock sounded on my door. "Rilla, it's me, Ponch."

I opened the door. Ponch looked distressed.

"What's wrong?" I asked.

"I didn't want to worry you, but I'm afraid there's a problem that can't be ignored any longer. If you're not feeling up to it, Jun and I can try to deal with things on our own, but it's something you should know."

"Tell me," I said. "I'm feeling fine now."

She came in and shut the door behind her. "Yesterday morning, two Fauxhemian ambassadors arrived to speak to you. Queen Esmeralda sent them. Prince Lymere is one of them, and the other is that woman we met at Fauxhemia Castle."

"Zelda?"

"Yes, that's her name."

Sago must have delivered my letter to Esmeralda by now. Esmeralda must have sent Lymere and Zelda to reply to me.

"For her to send two important Fauxhemians says they are looking for peace," I said. "Why didn't Welder send for me? Even if I have been ill, he should have alerted me."

"Because Welder has gone and lost his damn mind. Prince Lymere said there must be a misunderstanding, and they were not behind His Majesty's attack. But instead of informing you, Welder accused the prince of lying and sent them away."

I gaped. "He has no authority to do so. Why is he undermining me?"

"That's not the worst of it," Ponch said. "An hour ago, in front of the royal council, he made it sound like he was sending Prince Lymere and the woman home, but I listened in on a secret conversation he had with his men. He ordered them to go after Lymere and Zelda and keep them where no one would find them. Said he would deal with them later. Jun has gone to see if she can figure out where he's taken them."

My suspicions were growing despite wishing it wasn't true. I didn't know what Welder was intending, but it was clear Welder hated both the Fauxhemians and the Seracedareans. He may have lied about other things, but not about his love for Princess Bree, which was apparent when he'd spoken of her that night while drinking. It was the only time I'd seen his vulnerability. He'd forgotten to put on his mask that night, which had allowed me a moment to see the pain motivating him.

And now, with all the male heirs to Emberwood's throne out of the picture, he was making his move to seize power over Emberwood.

A man could do a lot with power. The question was, what was Welder planning on doing if he succeeded in gaining it?

But more importantly, I knew this meant Welder had no intention of looking to me as a leader. Even with the scepter in my possession, if I got in his way, he would try to get rid of me. Just as I suspected he had gotten rid of Ashbel, Leonora, Aiden, and Sito.

A knock sounded on the door. "It's Jun. Can I come in?"

Ponch opened the door. Jun looked frustrated. She closed the door behind her with a bang and let out a string of curses. "I'm sorry. I lost them. Welder's men took Lymere and Zelda in a coach, and I couldn't follow."

"It's all right," I said. "We'll find them another way."

"I don't understand," Ponch said. "Why is Welder doing this? And why are the guards listening to him instead of their queen? Aiden left you to take over the throne."

"Ponch, Jun, I need you to swear to be discreet about what I'm about to tell you," I said. "From the moment I met him, I knew Welder was a complicated man. A calculating man. I suspect he came to Emberwood with the intention of getting King Ashbel to trust him. Then he could control the army and use Emberwood to defeat Seracedar and Fauxhemia. He has a vendetta against both kingdoms."

Ponch nodded. "It's apparent he wants to frame Fauxhemia. And he must have been behind King Ashbel and Queen Leonora's poisoning. He and his men probably made it look like Fauxhemia was behind King Aiden and Prince Sito's disappearance. I'm pretty sure something went wrong with Welder's plan, though. I don't think he managed to kill the king or the prince."

I looked at her, my heart leaping. "Do you think so?"

"If he was sure they were dead, he wouldn't have his men still searching for them," Ponch said. "And he would have brought the bodies back to Emberwood as proof. It would make it easier for him to seize power if he could snuff out the kingdom's hope of them still being alive."

"Do you think he's conspiring with Carrick as well?" Jun asked.

I shook my head. "No, he's making it look like Carrick and Esmeralda are working together so that Emberwood has reason to fight both kingdoms. I'm still hoping I'm wrong. I truly regarded him as a friend, and Aiden trusted him. His betrayal is devastating. I still don't want to jump to conclusions, but it's clear we need to be wary around him. He managed to rise in the ranks of the Seracedarean army, and now he's infiltrated the Emberwood army with his own loyal men."

Ponch frowned. "I understand why he hates Seracedar. No one likes the current emperor or the last two. But why Fauxhemia?"

"He grew up there. He has a history with the royal family. Welder was in love with Princess Bree and blames her father for sending her to Cedar Palace to become Terran's faela. And he happens to be the soldier who escorted Bree there."

"Can you use your authority as queen to find Lymere and Zelda?" Ponch asked. "Tell the royal council Welder instigated the attack on King Aiden."

"Honestly, I'm not sure if that's a wise move," I said. "I think Welder has been planning things for a while. He may have already gained loyalty from some of the council members and army officers. I don't know who might be conspiring with Welder. They might already have a plan against me if I claim Welder is a traitor."

Jun scratched her chin, looking deep in thought. "Unfortunately, I think you have a point. I was a witness to another mastermind, Androgy Haming. The androgy bid his time for years, gathering support among the Lotuses without suspicion until he was ready to strike. What if Welder has been hatching his scheme since years ago when Bree was killed? He stayed in Seracedar and gained Terran's trust even though he must have hated the emperor for what happened to Bree. Then he stole the scepter. Despite losing it, he still came to Emberwood and first gained Ashbel's trust, then became a confidante to you and King Aiden. In that time, I'm sure he's gained rapport and respect among the Emberwood army and the noblemen. We have no idea who could be in on his plan."

I nodded. "Until we figure out more of Welder's plot and who is loyal to him, we can't expose him. We'll have to find Prince Lymere and Zelda on our own. Our relationship with Fauxhemia cannot be damaged further. We can't afford to fight them while we are already at war with Seracedar. If Welder intends to wage war on both kingdoms, he will drive Emberwood into ruin."

Ponch bit her bottom lip and stared into the distance, looking lost in her thoughts. Then she lifted her gaze to me. "I know who might be able to find them."

The three of us went to the clinic. Some of the ladies were practicing martial arts in the courtyard. Ponch went straight for them. Among them were Galai and Miah.

Galai stopped when she saw me. "What's going on?"

The other ladies stopped their practice and gave us curious looks. Galai and Miah came to stand next to me.

"Sorry to interrupt," I said. "We have an emergency."

Ponch gestured to two young women in their twenties. The two Fauxhemians at the clinic, Nena and Wray. They were both diamond Faux-bloods, from what I remembered, though I had never seen them use their blood magic yet.

"Wray, Nena, we need your help," Ponch said.

Nena stepped forward. "Of course."

"What's going on?" Wray asked.

"Prince Lymere and a Fauxhemian woman visited the palace today," Ponch explained. "Could you work together to use your magic and see if they are still in the kingdom? And also find out what Welder has planned for them."

Nena nodded. "On it, Counselor."

"I'll see what my invisible friends can discover," Wray said.

Nena took out a needle and stabbed her index finger. Wray did the same. I winced for their sakes, but neither of them even batted an eye. Maybe they were used to it.

Their blood trickled from their fingers, sparkling and shimmering a vibrant silver hue. I'd never seen diamond blood before. The sight fascinated me. I wondered how their blood magic worked.

Nena smeared her blood on the branch of a tree, then closed her eyes and lifted her palms to face the sky. She breathed in deeply. Wray flicked her blood into the air and whispered a chant.

Galai and Miah stared at them.

"What's happening?" Galai whispered. "How does their blood magic work?"

"I'm not sure," I said. "But I think diamond Faux-bloods have seer abilities."

"I thought Fauxhemians had to make someone drink their blood for their magic to work," Miah said.

"As I understand it, that's only for emerald Faux-bloods," I said. "If someone drinks their blood, they get poisoned with mind or emotional manipulation, which is why the researchers focus on emerald blood to find cures for mind illnesses."

Ponch looked back at us. "Nena's diamond blood gives her the ability to communicate with nature. More specifically, the trees. This tree will talk to the next tree, and so forth, until one of them locates Prince Lymere and Zelda. Wray can summon the dead and talk to the spirits in the area. She calls them her invisible friends. She can ask them to listen in on Welder and his men to find out what they're up to."

"Would they be able to ask the trees and the spirits to find Aiden and Sito?" My heart thumped faster at the possibility, but Ponch shook her head, instantly snuffing out that spark of hope.

"Unfortunately, Nena can only reach the trees within a certain range, and Wray can only talk to local spirits. Ghosts are contained within a few miles of the place they haunt and can't travel beyond that area. Hopefully, Prince Lymere and Zelda aren't too far, or this won't work to find them either."

We waited another minute. Then Nena gasped and opened her eyes.

"The trees say two Fauxhemians are still in the kingdom. They're on palace grounds." Nena closed her eyes again, concentrating. "They've been bound in iron shackles and chained to the ground. Like animals. They're locked in the ticket booth at the old coach station, about two miles from here."

I looked at Ponch. "There's an old coach station?"

"The new coach station was built a few years ago right outside the clinic," Ponch said. "The old one was left standing, but it's now abandoned, and the city uses it to keep all the out-of-service coaches until they can be turned into scrap metal."

"My friends have followed Nena's tree trail," Wray said. "They say there are five men guarding the Fauxhemians, and they can hear them talking. Welder plans to execute the Fauxhemians in the morning."

Ponch turned to me. "An execution? Surely Welder wouldn't go that far."

"I wouldn't put it past him," I said. "No one except us knows he's holding Lymere and Zelda against their will. He could easily kill them and clean up the mess without anyone knowing."

"Once Queen Esmeralda realizes they are missing, she'll question if we killed them," Ponch said. "Welder will deny it, but there will be no proof. This is exactly the kind of incident that would rally the otherwise peaceful Fauxhemians to want to go to war. In that case, Esmeralda's reputation would take a dive if she *didn't* retaliate."

"Why would he do that?" Galai asked. "What's going on, Rilla? First, King Aiden and Prince Sito go missing. And now Welder is trying to kill two diplomats."

The other ladies echoed her sentiments. "You can trust us," Miah said. "We want to know and help if we're able."

I addressed the women. "I've discovered that Welder is up to something. I don't know his full plan, but I do believe he had something to do with Aiden and Sito's disappearance, and he's using that as a reason to instigate war with Fauxhemia."

"Well, we can't let that happen," Felicity said. "We need to rescue them."

"Yes, how can we help?" Venn asked.

I looked around at the ladies. Many of the Shyan women had tin-chai. Among them were Venn, Yin, and Felicity, older women who were experienced fighters with strong tin-chai. Galai, Jun, and Lina were younger Shyan, who also possessed tin-chai. I couldn't recall all of their tin-chai, but I did know Galai could turn into water, Jun had the power of invisibility, and Venn could disguise a person into anyone else. Then there was Counselor Trine, who was a maocat Yao, Nena and Wray, both Fauxhemians, and Miah, an Ailo.

The question was who among them could use their tin-chai to help rescue Prince Lymere and Zelda?

A plan began to formulate in my mind. "I have an idea. I'll need to enlist help from several of you if you're willing."

"You can count me in, of course," Ponch said.

"Me too," Nena said. "Just let me know what to do."

The other ladies echoed in agreement.

"I appreciate your willingness, but I'm in need of specific powers," I said. "Powers that Galai and Miah possess."

Galai and Miah looked baffled.

"Our abilities aren't that useful," Miah said. "Galai turns into water, and I'm a rock Ailo. There's not much use in transforming my skin into rock."

"But that's exactly what we need you to do," I said. "You can break and smash things. Like chains and shackles. Galai will turn both of you into water. You'll blend into the groundwater and flow underground into the ticket booth. Miah will use her skin to cut through the chains. Once Lymere and Zelda are free, Galai will turn all of you back into water and get out the same way. The guards standing outside won't even know what happened."

"One problem," Galai said. "I can only turn myself into water. Not other people. I also can't sustain my power for over twenty minutes."

"But I have a way," I said. "I can use the scepter to amplify your tinchai so you can transform others with you. As for the amount of time . . ." I looked around at the other ladies, trying to improvise. This wasn't easy.

Then I spotted Jun. "What if Jun makes you all invisible while you go out to the old station? Then you'll only need a short amount of time in your water form to get in and out of the ticket booth."

"I'm in," Jun said. "I can make as many people as we need invisible as long as they're holding onto me. Let's do this."

Galai's eyes grew wider. "I don't know. I'm scared. What if we get caught?"

"Then I'll say I put you up to it," I said.

She still looked skeptical.

I placed a hand on her forearm. "Look, I know you can do this, but I don't want to force you into it."

Miah turned to Galai. "Please Galai, we can't let them die. Emberwood has become our sanctuary and our home, and if those Fauxhemians die, it could instigate more war. We're already fighting Seracedar. I don't want Emberwood to suffer from having to fight against both kingdoms. Do you?"

Galai took a shaky breath. "All right. I'll try my best."

I took the scepter from my pocket. Its power coursed into my veins. I sensed that it wanted to help us. It wanted to use me to amplify Galai's tin-chai.

I sang a refrain.

"These wings may have been broken and torn,

But my dreams will breach those sealed doors.

Singing words to break these chains,

I'll rise again in a glorious blaze."

The power from the scepter jumped into me, through my ha, dai, ji, and kai channels, and united into Galai's body. She jolted at the spark. It took mere seconds, and the electricity subsided.

Galai tested her power, first turning herself into a rivulet. She surrounded Miah's feet, and Miah liquefied into water. This bigger pool of water surrounded Jun, and she, too, turned into water.

"Okay, I guess we did it," Galai said. Her voice sounded morphed like she was talking underwater, but I could hear excitement mixed with terror in her voice. She transformed back into her normal self as did Miah and Jun.

Jun wrapped one arm around Miah, and the other around Galai. The three of them disappeared from view. I heard Jun's voice. "Give us the better part of an hour. It will take longer to tow four people with me on the way back."

"Bring them back here," I said. "I need to talk to them personally. Then we'll work on smuggling them out of the kingdom."

"You can do this," Ponch called after them.

I hoped for everyone's sake that this worked. If Welder found us out, we'd all be doomed.

CHAPTER 23

✦ ✦ ✦ ✦ ✦ ✦ ✦ ✦ ✦ ✦

We waited with bated breath. Some of the ladies began to pace. Time had never passed so slowly. Twenty minutes ticked by. Then forty.

"Do you think they're all right?" Felicity asked.

"My friends say they left the old station twenty minutes ago," Wray said. "But they're going slow. Jun is tired from keeping everyone invisible. Welder's men are getting suspicious, too. They haven't heard a peep from the prisoners and think they should check on them."

Ponch looked at her watch. "It takes twenty minutes to walk back here from the old station. But if Jun's struggling, it will take longer. Let's wait five more minutes before we send someone to help them."

I paced the courtyard. The minutes felt like hours.

"Oh," Wray said, jolting up. "My friends say they're back."

I felt a presence on the grass. Jun reappeared first, then around her, holding onto her arms, were Galai, Miah, Prince Lymere, and Zelda.

Lymere and Zelda looked terrified, but they appeared unhurt. Their gazes traveled around at the other women, then pinned on me.

"You're both safe now," I said. "I'm going to make sure you get home."

"Queen Rilla," Prince Lymere said. "Thank goodness."

"This is intolerable," Zelda screeched. "May San damn your souls. Our queen sent us to make peace with you and clear up misunderstandings, but you tried to have us killed. When she finds out, you can believe we're going to have problems you can't even—"

"Enough, Zelda," Lymere said. "I don't believe this was the queen's fault. She sent her people to save us, after all."

I bowed, trying to convey my sincerity. "I'm so sorry for everything that's happened to you. General Welder acted on his own, but I won't let him hurt you. We're going to get you back to Fauxhemia."

Lymere and Zelda took a seat on a stone bench.

Zelda coughed, still looking annoyed. "I need some water first. We haven't had anything to eat or drink in hours."

Ponch rushed off to the residence hall across from the courtyard. In two minutes, she returned with a tray. On it were two tall porcelain cups filled with water. She handed them to the Fauxhemians. Lymere gulped down the water. Zelda took a sip, tasted it in her mouth as though testing it for poison, then drank the rest.

"We'll leave you to talk in private," Ponch said. She gestured to the other women, and they went across the courtyard, though I could see them looking back with curiosity.

Zelda finally looked appeased and less flustered. "Queen Esmeralda sent us to clear up the circumstances of the attack on King Aiden. We're sorry to hear the news of his and Prince Sito's disappearance, but if any Fauxhemian was behind this, it was not under our queen's orders."

Lymere took another sip of water and cleared his throat. "Your general seems convinced that we're guilty. He said if we didn't admit to what we've done and return the king and prince at once, he would execute us at dawn. No matter what we said, he accused us of lying. He accused me and Essie of colluding with Seracedar. It's ludicrous. Sito is one of my best friends. I'd never betray him or his family."

Zelda scoffed. "That imbecile Welder makes no sense. Queen Esmeralda sent us here to tell you that you have our cooperation to investigate the matter and find King Aiden and Prince Sito. We're determined to clear our queen's good name. If she really were behind all this scheming and colluding, I hardly think she'd make this much of an effort, much less send the crown prince and her best assistant into unfriendly territory. We told this to Welder, but he said it must be a trick."

"I believe you," I said. "Unfortunately, I think the general is trying to create discord between our kingdoms. In fact, I think he may have set all this up. I think he had Dribin Clox poison Ashbel and Leonora, but he made it look like Esmeralda and Carrick were colluding. I also think he plotted the ambush that led to Aiden and Sito's disappearance. All to have an excuse to declare war on Fauxhemia."

Lymere set his glass down and frowned. "Why would Welder do this?"

"Revenge," I said. "Welder was in love with your sister, Bree, and blames your father for her death. You must have been too young to remember. Welder wants to destroy your kingdom and Seracedar. King Ashbel was against a war with Seracedar, but he was poisoned and incapacitated. And Aiden didn't believe Esmeralda was colluding with Carrick even though Welder tried to make it seem so. Aiden wanted Fauxhemia as an ally. So Welder got him out of the way, too. At least that's my theory. I can't prove it yet."

Zelda shook her head in disbelief. "Welder is not Emberwood's ruler. Can you not do anything to stop him? You are queen. King Aiden placed you in charge, didn't he? And you have the scepter. Don't the Shyan believe the person who bears the scepter has the right to rule?"

"Aiden and I were given the Will of Heaven together," I said. "Our right to rule applies to Seracedar, but not Emberwood. As for my authority over Emberwood, I'm afraid if I go against Welder, he will try to discredit me. He is the commander of the Emberwood army, and without Aiden, many of the men will turn to Welder to lead them, not me. I heard the men in the royal advisory council say they don't trust a woman to lead this kingdom without her husband. They might not believe me. Some of them might already have betrayed the Emberwood throne and could be involved in Welder's plot. Until I have proof that he is behind everything, I can't make a move against him."

Lymere stood. His fists were curled in anger. "I won't let him destroy my kingdom. What can I do to help you stop him?"

"First, I ask for your help in finding out what's happened to Aiden and Sito."

"Of course," he said. "That was already a given. That is, if Zelda and I make it home alive."

"I have a plan," I said. "I'll make sure you get back to Fauxhemia in one piece. As long as you promise to help me. Also, I'm hoping you can confirm or deny a rumor. Is Dribin Clox related to Queen Esmeralda? I was told he's her uncle."

Lymere's face turned white. "Who told you that?"

"It's true then," I said.

Zelda narrowed her gaze. "What? The queen never told me this."

"It's a carefully guarded secret," Lymere said. "No one outside of Clox, Essie, and I are still alive to tell it. So who told you, Rilla?"

"One of Welder's spies said he heard Esmeralda confess it to Carrick when they were conspiring together," I said.

"Impossible," Lymere said. "Essie never conspired with Carrick, and she would never tell anyone her darkest secret."

I wasn't sure what to say. He seemed sincere. But how could he know what Esmeralda was doing behind his back?

Lymere's eyes widened. "You said Welder was close to my sister. Essie and Bree were friends when Essie's mother lived with my father. Bree might have known that Essie was an emerald Faux-blood. Maybe she mentioned it to Welder. He could have learned other details about Essie. Connected her to Dribin Clox. Then Welder found Clox and confirmed the rumors. He could have also hired those men to lie to the council about Essie meeting with Carrick."

"That makes sense," Zelda said.

"You have to believe me, Rilla," Lymere said. "Essie hasn't been in contact with Clox since my father was poisoned. She had nothing to do with what happened to King Ashbel and Queen Leonora."

I regarded Lymere, narrowing my gaze. "Queen Esmeralda's blood could save Aiden's parents and your father. Why would she withhold that information and not want to save them?"

Lymere's cheeks heated. "I'm sorry, but it's complicated. I can't get into the details. Except that Essie can't have anyone know of her association to Dribin Clox. He was my father's chef, and he was blamed for poisoning my father. But there are still rumors that Clox was framed by my father's mistress."

"Esmeralda's mother," I said.

"Since Clox was never caught, no one could prove it was his blood that poisoned my father," Lymere said. "And Essie's mother refused to give anyone her blood. People suspected she was an emerald Faux-blood, but she drowned herself in the sea before the authorities could collect her blood. The priestesses refused to pray to San for her soul to be at peace because of the accusations against her. It was the darkest time in Essie's life."

Zelda sighed. "The poor child. I was there as her companion and witnessed everything. She didn't even have time to grieve over her mother. Both Esmeralda and her mother looked like King Lieka's first wife. When Esmeralda's mother died, Esmeralda replaced her as the lookalike to comfort Lieka. He wouldn't let anyone else near him. She had to care for the king during the beginning of his madness. She became the target of criticism, especially when she ended up marrying the king, even though it was the king's advisors who encouraged the match."

Lymere nodded. "It was incredibly unfair, but Essie pushed through it. She worked hard to prove herself worthy to lead Fauxhemia as regent, and the gossip eventually faded to mere whispers. But once word comes out that she and her mother are related to Clox, all of that history will resurface. That's the only reason she didn't donate her blood to research. But I hope you believe she's innocent of conspiring with

Carrick and had nothing to do with that ambush. It has to be Welder."

"I do believe you," I said. "But that doesn't help with proving Welder is behind this. I need your kingdom's help to stop him."

"You can count on me," Lymere said. "Just tell me what to do."

"I need you to tell Queen Esmeralda our suspicions about Welder and ask her to reconsider an alliance with Emberwood. The first step of that alliance is using her blood to find a cure for King Ashbel and Queen Leonora. And then we need to find Aiden and Sito. I can't stop Welder on my own, and I can't win a war against Carrick on my own either."

Ponch gestured at us and ran back to where we sat. "Nena says the trees are telling her Welder's at the old station. He knows Prince Lymere and Zelda have escaped. We don't have much time. How do we get them out of here?"

I gave Jun a questioning glance, but she winced. "I can try, but I'm not sure I'll last long enough to cross into Fauxhemia, especially having to turn two others invisible with me."

"Maybe I can help," Venn said. "What if I disguise them?"

"Good idea," I said. "How long will the disguises last?"

"As long as needed if I'm there with them," Venn said. "I can take them back to Fauxhemia. But I could use another person to help me in case we need to fight."

I looked at the group of women. "Any volunteers?"

Yin stepped forward. "I'll do it."

Venn placed a hand on Prince Lymere's shoulder and closed her eyes. She seemed to be focusing her wyis into the prince. His body shortened and thinned, and his face transformed into a younger version of himself. A boy of about six or seven years old.

Venn turned to Zelda next. She put her hand on Zelda, who slightly cringed at the touch. Venn closed her eyes. Zelda morphed, her body growing plumper. Crease lines formed in her forehead and around her jawline. A mole grew on her chin. She looked like a middle-aged auntie.

"Nobody give me a mirror," Zelda said. "I feel older, and I don't want to know what I look like."

"Yin and Venn will escort you back to Fauxhemia," I told Lymere and Zelda. "You'll take the regular coach to the harbor so as not to attract attention. Yin and Venn are the best fighters here. I trust them to get you home safely. Now go."

We watched them leave. Just in time. Fifteen minutes later, I heard the receptionist call out, "You can't barge in here. Group therapy is in session. Stop."

Seconds later, footsteps marched toward us. I looked up and saw Welder and three of his men. They strode through the corridor and onto the grass where we sat in a circle, pretending to do group counseling.

"Welder," I said, rising to my feet. "This is a clinic, and there are rules against people barging past the front desk. You're violating these patients' privacy. If you wished to talk, you should have sent word and waited for me back at the palace."

"Apologies will have to wait," Welder said. "Two dangerous prisoners have escaped, and I need to find them immediately. Have you seen them?"

I regarded him, but his face revealed nothing. "No. What prisoners? I wasn't notified of anyone being held captive."

"Two spies from Fauxhemia were caught, and I detained them for further questioning. Not thirty minutes ago, they managed to free themselves without being seen. The lock wasn't broken, but the shackles were left behind."

He looked around at all the women, his gaze shrewd. Missing nothing. I was sure he suspected us.

"I know a coach took off for the harbor ten minutes ago," he said. "I sent Ret to the harbor to stop the ferry leaving for Fauxhemia and search all the passengers to see if the prisoners are among them."

Ret, the speedster. He'd catch up to them for sure. But he wouldn't be able to recognize them. He also had never come to the clinic, so he didn't know Yin or Venn. There was a chance they could still escape.

"Let me know if you catch them," I said. "Thank you for coming here to check on us."

"Are all of the clinic's patients accounted for?" Welder pressed. "Because I'm certain the prisoners had help escaping. As I recall, one of the patients here has the power of invisibility. Perhaps she had sympathy towards the prisoners. What was her name again? She came with us to Fauxhemia as your personal guard, didn't she, Rilla?"

Jun pinned her gaze on Welder. Her eyes were black, and her hands curled into fists. I could see her temper threatening to spiral out of control. I gave a silent prayer that she would remain collected.

I stepped in front of Welder. "General, I've been at the clinic all day, and I didn't see anything suspicious. I trust these women. They are noble and would never help anyone who is a danger to this kingdom. They would fight to the death to defend Emberwood just as your soldiers would."

Welder smiled. "Of course. I apologize if I offended you, Your Majesty. If you do hear anything about these prisoners' whereabouts, please let me know. But now that I know you're safe, I'll take my leave."

He bowed, and his men followed suit, making their exit.

I watched them leave. Making an enemy of Welder was a scary game. I couldn't accuse him without having a strategy and knowing exactly what he was up to. He was a mastermind, one who had made a career of strategizing against his opponents and being two steps ahead at all times.

He was also a man. No matter how I wished the world was different, most people still trusted men over women to lead them. Without Aiden by my side, it would be difficult to gain authority on my own even with Aiden's decree that I would rule in his stead.

"What do we do now?" Ponch asked. "I think he suspects us."

"I *know* he suspects us," I said. "But I'm a queen, and Aiden left the throne to me. Also, I have the scepter. Welder knows he can't win against Seracedar without me. And he can't take complete power over Emberwood unless he kills me."

"We're not going to let that happen," Jun said. "I'll cut his throat in his sleep."

"No," I said. "He won't be that easy to take down. He's a fighter. Even if you succeed, he has many men working for him. I need to know exactly what he's planning and who may have turned against Emberwood to side with him."

"Then until we find out, we'll protect our queen," Ponch said.

Galai nodded. "The women here are your army. Let us be your eyes, too. We can spy on Welder and spy on the men. Find out who's a traitor."

"Thank you for your support," I said. "Maybe together we can find evidence of his motives. It's the only way to convince the royal council to remove him as general and make him leave the kingdom. Otherwise, it's my word against his, and the council will say I'm just imagining things."

"That all-male council of old geezers." Jun scoffed. "Why am I not surprised?"

"Until we can prove Welder's guilt, we should focus on the one goal we share with him," I said. "To defeat Carrick and Seracedar. He won't be able to fight a war with Fauxhemia at the same time. I think it would make sense if he wanted to take over the Seracedarean army first. Then with the combined forces of Seracedar and Emberwood, he'll look to conquer Fauxhemia. Let's go along with him for now and be careful not to do anything to antagonize him. I want to make him believe I'm on his side, so he lets his guard down."

"You can count on us to support you whatever you decide," Ponch said. "When you want to make a move, we'll be there to help."

The other women echoed agreement. For the first time since Aiden's disappearance, I no longer felt so alone.

CHAPTER 24

✦ ✦ ✦ ✦ ✦ ✦ ✦ ✦ ✦ ✦

Ret was unsuccessful in finding Lymere and Zelda. I heard that he'd searched every passenger on the ferry, but the prisoners hadn't been among them. Having no reason to detain the ferry further, the passengers had grown furious, and he finally allowed them to leave the harbor for Fauxhemia. The news made Welder rage, and he took it out on the soldiers during training.

I managed to avoid Welder for the next two days as my schedule was full. I made my address to the kingdom, and Emberwood made public vows to accept me as their queen.

The day following my public address, Yin and Venn returned, reporting that Lymere and Zelda had made it across the Fauxhemian border safely. I hoped the prince would follow through with his promises and convince Esmeralda to donate her blood. If we could cure Ashbel and Leonora, at least they would believe me when I told them about Welder's ulterior motives. They would have no trouble convincing the royal council. I wouldn't have to deal with Welder or with Seracedar on my own.

Thankfully, Welder didn't pursue his interrogation of me or the women at the clinic. I knew he still believed we had helped the Fauxhemians escape, but his attention shifted from Fauxhemia back to Seracedar.

The Miyu had confirmed that all was peaceful in the Enyi Ocean. Since the attack at the Port of Candlelace, things had been relatively quiet on Carrick's side, which made me wonder what was going on in Seracedar. Either there was some kind of internal strife preventing Carrick from attacking us further, or he was planning a bigger surprise for us.

Welder claimed his spies had gone to investigate, and he had an answer. We gathered for a meeting with the royal advisors to discuss his findings.

"I have good news and bad news," Welder announced. "The bad news is my spies say Carrick is determined to burn Emberwood to the ground. After their failure to take Candlelace and the death of their admiral, the advisors have asked him to reconsider negotiations of peace with us, but he swears he'd rather fall on his own sword."

Captain Kang cleared his throat. "If he's against peace, then what is he planning? It's been too quiet."

"That's where the good news comes," Welder said. "There's a reason the advisors asked Carrick to negotiate with us. They aren't sure they can win. Seracedar's finances are quickly draining. Carrick doesn't have the money to pay his soldiers, and many of them are refusing to fight until they receive compensation. He doesn't have enough men to both defend the capital and launch further attacks on us."

"Then we need to act quickly," Colonel Beyling said. "Now that we know he's weak, we can attack the capital."

Welder shook his head. "Not the capital. Not yet. That's where he'll be the strongest. The soldiers who remain loyal to him are protecting the palace, guarding him from us."

He had a glint in his eye. Something was up his sleeve. "Then what do you propose should be our strategy?" I asked.

"Our strategy is to anticipate his next move and stop him from making it," Welder said. "So let me ask you this. What do you think will be his next move when he's losing soldiers?"

Lord Pan furled his brow. "Finding new recruits. Since he refuses to negotiate peace, he'll need more men if he wants to continue waging war."

Welder nodded. "Correct. And where will he find men who are willing to fight for him without pay?"

"He's not," Lord Tu said. "He's probably going to enlist men from rural villages. Poor citizens who will have no choice in the matter."

"Exactly so," Welder said. "And my spies have informed me that Carrick's already enlisting men from Province Sen, in towns close to the capital, forcing one male from each family to join his army, or pay an outrageous penance if they refuse. If he does this to every village in Seracedar, he'll be able to grow his army tenfold. We need to get to some of those villages first. Recruit Seracedareans on our side before he has the chance to take them."

"I like this strategy," Colonel Beyling said. "It takes care of several issues at once. We can grow our army to become as great as Carrick's while also making his subjects no longer accessible to him. And in doing so, these villages will surrender to our rule."

"We'll march from the industrial towns in the west all the way to the fishing villages on the southeastern coast," Welder said. "They are the furthest away from the capital. We'll force the villages to surrender to us before Carrick can reach them. Then we'll give them a similar option that their emperor would have offered. Either fight for our side or be put to death if they refuse."

I froze. "Put to death? No. I don't want to hurt anyone. The small fishing communities have suffered enough. They don't deserve to be pillaged and killed when they don't have the means to defend themselves."

Welder rolled his eyes. "Relax. You have the scepter. Once you prove you've got the Will of Heaven, I'm sure these small-town folks will pledge their loyalty. They're superstitious enough."

"And while Commander Welder and Queen Rilla lead this campaign,

Colonel Beyling and I will ensure our home base is kept protected," Captain Kang said.

Lord Tu grunted in agreement. "I approve. The queen is also a native from a sea village, isn't she?"

Everyone's gazes turned to me.

"Yes," I said. "But—"

"Good," Lord Pan said. "Then the fishing villages should be easy to take over. The people who share a common background with you will find you more trustworthy."

"Maybe, but what if some of the villages refuse to surrender?" I asked. "What if demonstrating the power of the scepter isn't enough to convince them? Not everyone will be happy about letting Emberwood take power over Seracedar."

"If they resist after we give them a chance to surrender peacefully, then we'll kill them," Welder said. "We can't waste time showing mercy on anyone who hinders our cause."

The advisors murmured together in agreement.

"What you're proposing sounds like murder, not warfare," I said, not able to contain the anger within me. "I understand that in war, we can't spare everyone or show signs of weakness, but many villagers will want to defend their homes. And the poorest people in Seracedar don't stand a chance against us. How is what you're proposing different than what Carrick is doing? It's just as wrong."

"I never said Carrick's forced enlistment was wrong," Welder said. "It's what I would do if I were in his place. And that's why we're using the same tactic."

"But—"

Welder cut me off. "My queen, you don't need to worry. As long as you demonstrate the power of the scepter, I'm sure the villagers will surrender. They'll see that we're the better choice over Carrick."

"Welder is right," one of the advisors said. "This man was a born leader and strategist. You can't be so soft, Queen Rilla, if you are to lead

Emberwood to victory over Seracedar. Women always give into mercy. But mercy has no place in a war."

Welder smiled. "Then it's decided. We leave tomorrow."

Early the next morning, we left for the western border of Seracedar. Welder led a thousand soldiers, with his most trusted men by his side. He also ordered my guardswomen to come.

"Ponch and Jun, of course," he said. "They are two of the best fighters I've seen. Also, Yin and Felicity. They have powerful tin-chai. You can bring others, too. Just make sure they have useful tin-chai and can fight."

Once these women were recruited, others among the women at the clinic wanted to come, too. Venn, Lina, and Galai. Also, Miah, Wray, and Nena, who were not Shyan but said they could contribute with their abilities, too. Now that they knew Welder was plotting to take over Emberwood, all of them wanted to be part of the guardswomen who protected me as we tried to figure out Welder's next move.

We traveled to the border of Seracedar by coach. The journey took a full day, and by nightfall, we were in the Emberwood city of Kitein. Tomorrow, we would march across the border into the first village Welder wished to capture, Bellflower. The town was a farming community also known for making the finest silverware, pottery, and china in all of Seracedar.

We set up camp for the night and ate a quick meal. As I settled down by the fire, Welder approached me.

He gestured to the spot next to me. "May I sit?"

"Go ahead."

Welder sat. I felt his gaze and turned toward him. He looked pensive and a little awkward. "Listen," he said. "I want to apologize to you."

His words surprised me. Was he being sincere, or was he trying to make me take down my guard? "Oh? What for?"

"I know it's been a difficult time for you with all that's happened," he said. "I can't imagine the grief you must be going through. And I haven't exactly been the greatest friend or shown much empathy. I've been so occupied with figuring out Fauxhemia's motives and strategizing against Seracedar. But I want you to know we're on the same side. You're my queen, and I serve you,"

"Oh." I struggled to find a response. "Thank you."

He tugged at his shirt sleeves, and I noticed he was wearing a wristwatch with shiny leather bands.

"I've never seen you wear a watch. Is that new?"

"Oh, I received this as a gift from some of the advisors as a good luck charm on our crusade."

The advisors hadn't given me anything. Not that I wanted a gift, but it showed that they now looked to Welder as their leader over me. They didn't care that I had the Will of Heaven or that Aiden had given me authority of Emberwood in his absence.

"Look," Welder continued. "Everything I do is for the good of this kingdom, even if we don't see eye to eye all the time. The truth is, without you and your guardswomen, we may not be able to win this war against Seracedar. Most Seracedareans are deeply religious and believe in the Will of Heaven. You can win many of them over without a fight. But there will be some who put up more of a resistance. Corrupt magistrates and noblemen who've lived with wealth and power far too long. Bellflower, for example, won't be an easy village to capture."

"How do you know this?" I asked.

"The people are loyal to their village magistrate, Jangle Rife. He's a corrupt man and happens to be one of Terran's brothers-in-law. Though he didn't support Carrick as emperor, it would be worse to surrender to Emberwood. Cedar Palace supports his pockets and his status. He's not about to let anything destroy those privileges."

"You seem to know a lot about this Jangle Rife," I said.

He tossed a twig into the fire. "We were acquainted when I worked for Terran. Actually, he was a friend. The first aristocrat I knew when I came to the palace with Bree. He pretended to encourage me to run away with Bree. Then after she died, Rife helped plan the coup against Terran, but he betrayed Daki and me."

"I'm sorry to hear that," I said. "How horrible of him."

Welder straightened his posture. "Yes, well, our history isn't important. I need our goals to align when we go into battle, or we'll fail in capturing this town. Rife is an evil man and needs to be killed. So do his followers. Can I trust you to do what's necessary to win? To kill those who oppose us?"

I folded my arms across my chest and kept my expression stoic. "I share your goal of defeating Carrick. I never said I refused to kill the enemy, but I won't kill civilians. Some people had no choice but to live under Cedar Palace's tyranny, and they should be shown mercy."

"Yes, and I promise we'll give them that option. But remember, not all will. We have to do what's necessary to take power over these people. Doesn't matter that you have the scepter. Many Seracedareans won't like the idea that you've joined with Emberwood and are using the enemy's army to take over their kingdom. They'll view you as a traitor. Also, the truth is, the Seracedareans have stronger tin-chai than Embers in general. The Emberwood soldiers, including the men who work for me, are good fighters, but most of their tin-chai aren't that impressive. My tin-chai, as well, is useless on the battlefield."

He cracked a grin at his self-deprecation, and I feigned a smile.

"I mean, what good can camouflaging objects do in battle except turn a rock into a spear to kill a few opponents? Even if you were to amplify my tin-chai, I think I'd still be limited in what I can do."

"I've seen you transform the side of a cliff to extend the road beneath us," I said. "You're powerful enough."

"Thank you, but I'm still not as powerful as you. Fortunately for us, it was just a small portion of road that I had to transform. And transforming the landscape beneath my enemies' feet might incapacitate them for a moment, but it won't necessarily kill them. Whereas you can sing and take down the entire frontline at once. What I mean to say is, you and many of your guardswomen are Seracedarean with some of the greatest tin-chai I've ever seen. Not only that, but I've also seen your guardswomen fight, and they're more skilled than many of the male soldiers. Your tin-chai and abilities are needed to defeat Seracedar. Your guardswomen will listen to you, not to me. And you have the power of the scepter to amplify all of our tin-chai. So I hope you agree that we have to be aligned and work as partners if we're to succeed in winning this war. I want you to tell your guardswomen this, too. I want to be able to trust them. If they use their tin-chai and fight for our cause well, they'll be rewarded."

Even though I'd ever be able to trust him again, I had to make him think I was amicable with him.

"You're right," I said. "We'll do our best."

He smiled, the first time in a long time that I felt it to be genuine. I wished I could believe it. "Good. Friends again?" He stuck out his hand, waiting for me to reciprocate the gesture.

"Y-yes. Of course." I took his hand and shook it.

He stood. "Get some rest. We have an early start tomorrow."

I watched him walk away. Now I realized the real reason he had wanted me to come with him to battle. Why he had told me to bring my guardswomen. It wasn't just because he wanted me to show that I had the scepter. It was because he needed my tin-chai. My amplification ability through the scepter. And he needed my guardswomen's tin-chai. He intended on using us to win this war. Which meant he didn't think he could do it on his own. His only reason for trying to patch things up with me after our disagreement over Fauxhemia was because he believed I'd go along with whatever he wanted if I thought we were friends.

Sure, I'd go along with him for now. After all, I wanted to win the war, too. But he was wrong if he thought I would ever be friends with him again. Especially if I found proof that he had killed Aiden.

The next morning, we marched across the border and continued towards Bellflower.

"Rife's tin-chai is dangerous," Welder told us. "Leave your swords and any weapons made of metal at the campsite. Rife controls metal, and if you have any on you, he'll turn it against you. Use wood, rocks, or tin-chai instead. Watch out for the other townspeople and their tin-chai as well. They know we won't have metal weapons on us, so they'll use that to their advantage."

We passed the arched entrance into the village. The place looked deserted, with not a soul on the streets. The shops were closed, and there wasn't a single light in any of the windows.

The wind gushed through the empty village in an eerie high-pitched squeal, like a choir of ghosts competing to sing the highest note.

Welder's eyes narrowed as he scanned our surroundings. "Don't be fooled. They're here. I feel their wyis."

So did I. The wyis of many Shyan were hiding in the buildings. I could imagine them spying on us, waiting for the right time to attack.

There was a tinkling sound, like wind chimes, the music so beautiful that the hypnotic bells almost succeeded in putting us off guard from their true source. Suddenly, we found ourselves surrounded by glinting objects, almost blinding in the sun. My eyes strained to see more clearly. Thousands of metal blades were in midair, the sharp ends pointed in our direction.

"It's Rife!" Welder shouted.

Without a second warning, the knives flew at us. Our soldiers stepped forward, summoning their wyis. Some men lifted rocks into the air with their tin-chai, deflecting the first few knives. Others took control of the wind, creating air tunnels to knock down more knives.

I channeled my wyis into the scepter, amplifying these soldiers' tin-chai to make them stronger. Create more wind tunnels. Summon more rocks.

It was working. Most of the knives had fallen to the ground.

But then they stirred, reanimating themselves into the air.

"We need to find Rife," Welder said. "He's got us on defense. We need to stop him from using his tin-chai. Rilla, use the scepter. Take away his tin-chai. Now's as good a time as any to try. But we've got to find Rife first."

The knives came at us again.

"I got this," Yin cried. She summoned electric sparks in her hands and aimed it at the knives that barreled toward us. All of them clattered to the ground at once.

But in mere seconds, they lifted into the air yet again. More shouts echoed around us. Battle cries. Villagers ran out of the shops and buildings, charging at us with swords.

Now we not only had to defend against the flying blades, but we had to do so while fighting off the villagers' attacks.

Pained cries resounded all around. Knives stabbed some of our men, instantly bringing them down. These knives flew back into the air, now dripping with blood.

"Yin, cover me," I said and crouched beside the fallen soldiers. Yin stood in front of me, deflecting the knives.

"I'll help," Miah said. She turned her skin to rock and caught blade after blade, throwing them to the ground.

My other guardswomen joined the Ember soldiers. Those with deflective tin-chai focused on the knives, while the others battled the villagers.

I sang to some of the fallen soldiers, quickly healing them of their wounds. They recovered, slowly sitting up. I moved toward more wounded men.

And then from the corner of my eye, I saw a shadow behind a boulder. Hands lifting this way and that like a puppeteer pulling strings.

"There!" I shouted. "He's hiding behind that rock."

Yin pointed to the rock, and electric sparks emitted from her fingertips. She sent the electricity into the rock, and it splintered into a thousand pieces that crumbled onto the ground.

A slender man emerged. That must be Rife.

"Rilla, take away his tin-chai," Welder shouted.

I aimed my wyis into the scepter and targeted Rife. The scepter glowed. I strained. I needed more power. The light faded. I felt depleted of energy. Why wasn't it working? It had been easy to amplify someone's tin-chai.

Rife turned knives away from the battle and targeted them at Welder.

"Oren," Welder yelled. "The queen has failed. Use your tin-chai. Just don't kill Rife. He's mine."

Oren stood tall. "Finally." He held his hands in the air like he was summoning something toward him. I felt a great charge of wyis entering his body from Rife, who screamed as though he'd been burned. The knives shifted direction, turning away from Welder and toward Rife.

The villagers shouted, coming to his defense. But as they came at us with their swords, Oren waved his hands in the air, and the swords lifted away from those who held them into the air. Oren twirled his hands, and the swords reversed. The villagers realized they were no longer in control of their weapons and ran. Too late. The swords pierced their bodies one by one. Men fell to the ground, dead.

I froze and stared at Oren, who looked proud of himself. What exactly was his tin-chai? Did he share Rife's ability to control metal? No, it had to be more than that. It was like he'd stolen Rife's tin-chai. Oren had disarmed Rife first, inhibited him from using his tin-chai, and then Oren had taken control.

A dozen knives flew toward Rife. He ran but came to a wall. Our men cornered him from the opposite end. The knives pinned his clothes to the wall, missing his flesh by a mere fraction.

He struggled and cursed to no avail.

A huge smirk grew on Welder's face. He strode toward the man.

"Well, well, Rife. So glad to meet you again after all these years."

Rife reminded me of a raccoon, the way his glasses framed his eyes in perfect, tight circles. He had an extremely long, slender neck that seemed to stretch even further as he glared up at Welder. "I should have killed you myself as soon as I found out you had betrayed Terran."

"You should have, but you didn't. What a shame."

Rife laughed and looked around at the Emberwood soldiers and at me. "Do they all know about your motivation? It must be why you came to my village first. To get your revenge on me."

Welder blanched. "Stop talking. You know nothing."

"Don't I? I saw you bring that Fauxhemian princess to the palace. Saw how you looked at her. And I know it must have eaten you up that she became Terran's whore. Before you kill me, I should tell you I had a taste of her, too. She was a tasty morsel. Pity she killed herself before I could have a second lick."

He laughed as Welder's expression changed to one of utter fury.

Welder slapped the man so hard that blood spurted from his broken lips and smashed teeth. Rife fell to the ground, though he still laughed, pleased to have unsettled Welder's usually stoic nature.

"By the time I'm finished with you, you'll wish you were dead," Welder snarled. Then he motioned to his men. "Tie him to a tree. I'll deal with him. In the meantime, Oren, gather up the rest of the villagers."

Welder marched away with two of his men, who carried a bound Rife with them.

Meanwhile, more villagers were dragged out of their homes and onto the street.

Welder's men started beating a few of the older townsmen.

"Stop!" I shouted. They ignored me.

One of the townsmen's spectacles fell off his face. He searched for them, but Oren grabbed the spectacles from the ground and tossed them to Ret, who then ran circles around the man. The two laughed.

I stepped in front of Oren and Ret, glaring at them. "Stop that. He's not fighting you anymore. There's no need to torment him."

Oren folded his arms across his chest and gave me a dirty look. "I don't take orders from you. Welder said I'm his second in command. I'm allowed to do whatever I want."

He grabbed the spectacles, threw them on the ground, and smashed them beneath his heel.

"How dare you speak to your queen that way?" Jun said. "I don't like bullies."

She turned invisible, but in two seconds, we could see her again. A horrified expression grew on her face. "I can't use my tin-chai."

"Ah, but I can," Oren said. He grinned and turned invisible. The sound of a punch landed into Jun's stomach. She grunted and keeled over. We could hear Oren laughing. He became visible again. "Don't try to stop me again, bitch."

"Why, you little jerk," Felicity said. "Someone needs to teach you a lesson."

She sang three notes but stopped. "It's gone. I don't have my tin-chai anymore."

Oren opened his mouth and sang a taunting tune. At the sound, Felicity choked and fell to the ground. She was in pain.

Oren had stolen her tin-chai, too. I was sure of it now. "Stop!" I cried. "You're hurting her."

He ignored me and continued singing. Felicity writhed, turning blue.

"Please stop," I begged. "You're going to kill her."

"Hey, what's going on here?" Welder's voice broke through, and Oren stopped singing. Felicity took a gasp of air. The guardswomen crouched down to make sure she was okay. But I confronted Welder.

"Oren hurt two of my guardswomen, and he almost killed Felicity. He disrespected me when I tried to stop him from tormenting a villager who did nothing to him. We need to discipline him."

"They used their tin-chai to try to hurt me first," Oren said. "I was only defending myself."

Welder gave Oren a calm stare. "Apologize to your queen for being disrespectful."

"But—"

Welder gave him a silencing look.

"I'm sorry, Your Majesty," Oren said to me. He looked at Welder. "But I was only carrying out your orders."

"I know, and you're not in trouble," Welder said.

"Not in trouble?" I said. "We need to discipline him for what he did to the villagers and to my guardswomen."

"Discipline him then," Welder said. "Take away his tin-chai."

"General, no," Oren yelled.

"Calm down," Welder said. "The queen hasn't been able to do it yet. I don't think she has enough power. Maybe she never will." He gave me a challenging look. "So try it. If you succeed, I'll submit to your authority."

I aimed my tin-chai into the scepter again. Oren couldn't be allowed to keep his tin-chai. I had to take it away from him before he became too powerful. The scepter glowed. But again, I couldn't sustain its power. In another second, the light died.

"That's what I thought," Welder said.

The dispute between us was getting more attention. Other Emberwood soldiers and the villagers watched with curious stares.

"There's nothing to see here," Welder said. "Soldiers, return to your tasks and finish gathering up the villagers. They will sign over their surrender and promise to join our army against Carrick. You have my permission to kill those who refuse. After they sign over their loyalty, burn down the village."

"No," I said. "Soldiers, stop. As your queen, I assert my authority to show these people mercy."

Welder glared at me. "You have no authority here. This is my army. These are my men."

"And I'm your queen. You agreed to show mercy to those who surrender. Why must you burn their homes?"

"I am showing mercy. I should kill them all for following Rife."

I tilted my chin up, standing my ground. "They must have done so out of fear."

Welder looked back at me and my guardswomen. Jun still clutched her stomach, but she glared at Welder defiantly. Felicity looked like she was breathing normally again, but she looked pale and scared. I hated that Oren had done this to him and that Welder was allowing him to get away with it. Welder was defying me, making it clear that he controlled the army, not me.

"Let's get one thing clear," Welder said. "Your guardswomen are not to use their tin-chai on my men again. If they do, I won't be stopping Oren next time. We're all here to fight against the enemy, not each other."

Oren shot me a triumphant look.

Now I understood why Welder had kept Oren's tin-chai a secret. It must have been his plan all along to use Oren to control me and my guardswomen.

"You can use Oren to ensure everyone obeys your commands," I said. "But that boy is immature. How do you know he won't turn on you one day?"

Welder smirked as though he held another secret. "Oren knows better than that. Don't you, Oren?"

Oren nodded and saluted. "I serve you to my dying day. If this woman has a problem with you, she has a problem with me."

"No need to go that far," Welder said. "Rilla is still your queen and my friend. She has the Will of Heaven. You need to respect her and Old Grandfather Heaven. Prove that you're becoming a mature man."

"Yes, sir."

"I may be your queen, but I'm most certainly not your friend after all this." I had never felt more furious. "I might not be able to take away tin-chai right now, but I still have my other powers. I can use them to take away your authority."

The dark look he threw at me would have scared me if I was still a mere village girl.

"You can try, but you won't succeed," he said. "I meant it last night when I said I need you, the power of the scepter, and your guardswomen to win this war. But let's make one thing clear. You may be the queen, but I command this army. I command Oren. And I will tell him to use his tin-chai to keep anyone who thinks about revolting in line. Including you, my queen." He pinned his gaze on my guardswomen. "Do I make myself clear?"

My guardswomen stared at him in fear. No, I couldn't let Welder make us feel powerless, like we were living in cages, used for our tin-chai again. I had to stop him. He might have Oren, but he didn't have Oren's tin-chai. I glanced quickly at Oren. He was distracted, giving gloating looks to my guardswomen.

I could hurt Welder with my voice, reminding him that I could easily kill him before I ever allowed him to control me or my guardswomen. All in front of these soldiers.

I sang three notes, exerting my wyis into my tin-chai and directing it at Welder. A feeling of sudden coldness doused my entire body. Emptiness. Something was wrong. I couldn't sing. My voice had gone silent.

Welder stood tall, towering over me. "How dare you? Using your tin-chai on me? After I thought to play nice and mend our friendship.

Well, as you can see, it didn't work, and now I'm going to show you what I will do if you try it ever again."

He sang. Not at me, but at my guardswomen.

They shrieked. Galai and Miah developed boils and rashes on their skin. Felicity, Wray, and Nena grew wrinkles on their faces, instantly aging twenty years. Jun and Ponch keeled over, throwing up on the street. Venn, Yin, and Lina's bodies contorted, shrinking. Their skin grew translucent, threatening to disintegrate altogether.

I screamed, but no sound emerged. I shouted at Welder to stop. I was sorry. But the words slipped off my tongue into silence. He'd stolen my voice. I rushed at Welder. Threw my fists at him. He shoved me to the ground. I landed face down. I felt a cut on my lip and tasted blood in my mouth.

Welder stopped singing. "This is what happens when you disobey me. I have the power to harness Oren's tin-chai and through it, I can steal anyone else's. So you can either use your tin-chai to fight for me as my soldier, or I'll turn your tin-chai against you."

But how? How could he have gotten Oren's tin-chai? It was a completely different kind of tin-chai from his own transformation tin-chai, one that couldn't even come about from amplification.

Many of the Emberwood soldiers were staring, fear on their faces. Welder's loyal men snickered.

"The same rules apply to all Emberwood soldiers," Welder said. "Let it be known to all your comrades. King Ashbel and Queen Leonora are asleep and will not wake up. King Aiden and Prince Sito are dead. And your king may have left this woman to be the queen of Emberwood, but she has no real power. I am in command of you. Anyone who disobeys me will be at my mercy."

I felt my wyis re-enter my body. I cleared my throat. My tin-chai had returned.

"Heal your guardswomen of their wounds," Welder said. "See? I'm reasonable."

I rushed forward, singing to heal my friends. One by one, they returned to health and their normal age.

My whole body shook as I faced Welder again. I couldn't speak, still shocked. I hadn't felt this powerless since I'd been Terran's novelty.

"I see I've finally gotten through to you," he said. "From now on, remember your only job here is to use the scepter as I see fit. You will amplify the tin-chai of anyone I tell you to, and you will show the villagers you have the Will of Heaven to give them the option of surrendering to me. Are we clear?"

He took me by the arm and dragged me across the town, where the villagers had been forced to gather around a podium. We went up onstage.

"I won't hurt any of you if you pledge loyalty to Emberwood and fight on our side," Welder said, addressing the villagers. "The Queen of Emberwood has the scepter. And in the wake of King Aiden of Emberwood's death, Old Grandfather Heaven has chosen me to replace him as the queen's partner."

Lies. He spewed lies with such ease. Oh, how I wanted to spit in his face.

He continued, "We have the right to rule over you and dethrone Emperor Carrick. Take in the truth with your own eyes and believe it."

He placed one hand on the scepter above where my hands held it. Then he gave a show of appearing to place his wyis into the scepter.

"Use your tin-chai on me, Vay," he said. Vay raised a rock in his hand and sent it at Welder. But Welder took control of the rock, reversing its direction and letting it fly away.

"My tin-chai was amplified in an unconventional way," Welder said. "My original tin-chai is the ability to camouflage and transform objects. But now I can camouflage my tin-chai to take on someone else's tin-chai."

That had to be a lie, too. How would his tin-chai have been amplified? I'd never used the scepter on him. There must be something else giving him the ability to take on Oren's tin-chai and now Vay's.

"And now I'll allow the queen to demonstrate her amplification ability." Bending down to whisper in my ear, he ordered, "Amplify Vay's tin-chai."

Even though he was powerful enough on his own, he still wanted me to use the scepter as a way to demonstrate his control over me.

I forced myself to raise the scepter. Singing, I channeled my wyis through the scepter and into Vay. He beamed with triumph as I finished.

Vay lifted a hand and waved it. A sword from one of the other soldiers came to him. "I could only control rocks before. Now I can control metal just like your previous chief magistrate."

Welder's voice boomed through the air again. "The Queen of Emberwood is able to amplify anyone's tin-chai through the power of the scepter. Carrick has been lying to you all along. We have the true scepter. Old Grandfather Heaven has granted his Will to both of us. We will reunite Seracedar and Emberwood to become one Shyan nation."

The villagers fell to their knees and kowtowed, bowing until their foreheads touched the ground. Five men remained standing.

"I will not bow," one of them shouted. He looked brazen. Ready to die. "Emberwood stopped submitting to our emperors and the Will of Heaven when they separated from Seracedar long ago. Why should I obey them now? Even if Carrick lied, I would rather die than fight for the enemy and see the reunification of the Shyan kingdoms."

The other four men echoed shouts of agreement. "We will not bow."

"So be it," Welder said. "Take them away and tie them up with Rife."

The soldiers gathered up the five men, who struggled and shouted. Tears burned in my eyes. But I couldn't do anything for them. Welder's men and all the Emberwood soldiers marched through the streets at Welder's command. They entered houses and buildings, pillaging everything in sight.

Now that Welder had used me and the scepter to exert control of the village, he left me alone with my guardswomen. We watched helplessly as the village burned to the ground. The smell of smoke and burned flesh filled the air.

"What do we do now?" Jun asked, looking at me and Felicity. "My tin-chai has returned. What about you two?"

"Mine is back, too," Felicity said.

I nodded. "So's mine. At least we know what Oren and Welder did isn't permanent."

Tortured screams resounded in the air from the direction where Rife and the dissenters had been tied to a tree.

"I don't think we can fight back," Galai said. A look of despair came across her face. "Welder's made it clear that he and Oren will steal our tin-chai and use it back on us or the people we're trying to protect."

"They might be able to steal tin-chai, but they can't steal my rock-solid skin," Miah said. "Or Fauxhemian blood magic from Nena and Wray."

"We can't fight against Welder, though," Nena said. "We're outnumbered by his loyalists."

"And now the Emberwood soldiers are scared, too, after seeing what he did to Rilla," Jun said. "Even if they want to be loyal to King Aiden and Rilla, the thought of being stripped of their tin-chai and having it turned on them must be terrifying. Who knows how many Shyans' tin-chai Welder and Oren can steal at one time? I thought I was brave, but I never want to experience that feeling of powerlessness again."

All my guardswomen turned to me, looking for direction.

"Do as he says for now," I said. "I don't want any of you to get hurt. We need to learn more about Oren's tin-chai and how Welder acquired it into himself. Then maybe we can find a way to fight back. Welder won't get away with this."

I didn't know what Welder did to those men who refused to pledge their loyalty or to Rife, nor did I wish to know, but by morning, their bodies had been burned. Nothing was left in the village except ash.

The Seracedarean army never came to stop us. Welder's spies reported that Carrick was having problems with his troops. They weren't getting paid and refused to fight. Even the commanding officers were getting frustrated with Carrick, who rarely left his chambers or gave any orders at all.

"The number of soldiers willing to fight will only cover the defense of the capital city," one of the spies said. "Lieutenant Kenbo and Colonel Laht are the only commanding officers left on Carrick's side. They've ordered their men to barricade Senlin City, preparing for the day we arrive."

"Good," Welder said, his face lighting up. "Our army is increasing. If this keeps up, we should have no issue taking the capital. Return to Senlin and keep watching them."

I was certain word of the battle in Bellflower had traveled back home to Emberwood. But I heard nothing from Colonel Beyling and Captain Kang.

I sent Venn, disguised as a hawk, with a letter. Not two miles from camp, she was shot down, lost the letter, and came back half dead. I used my voice to heal her, and thankfully, she survived. I was certain one of Welder's men had shot her, but he never mentioned it.

So I used the scepter on Lina, amplifying her tin-chai so she could carry sound directly to a specific area. I sent a message to the royal advisors, including Captain Kang and Colonel Beyling, addressing my concerns about Welder. I told them he was a danger and I needed support to stop him.

A week later, I received a reply. I read it aloud to my guardswomen.

Dear Rilla,

The royal council has evaluated your accusations against Welder, and we admit to being confused by your conflicting messages. In the letter you wrote to us last week, you stated your relief in having Welder lead the Emberwood army. You said he was doing an outstanding job, and the battle in Bellflower was a success. You told us Welder had received tin-chai amplification from the scepter, and you accepted him as your partner in King Aiden's stead. You even signed over complete control over the army to Welder, giving up your authority of the troops. You said it was too stressful, and the soldiers weren't listening to you. And we agreed. Told you so in our reply. As a man and general, Welder is more qualified to handle the soldiers.

I paused, looking at my guardswomen. "I never wrote such a thing. If it was my signature on that letter giving Welder control, he must have used his tin-chai on the one I tried to send with Venn. He must have changed what I wrote and made it appear to be in my handwriting with my signature."

"This is outrageous," Jun exclaimed.

"That's not all," I said, and I continued reading.

We heard your message through your sound amplifier, and we're concerned. Your story this time is completely different from what you shared in your letter. You say both Oren and Welder have the ability to steal tin-chai. But as we understand it, Welder told us of Oren's power before he left on the crusade. He said it was necessary to keep it secret to train Oren to be humble. And you said yourself before changing your story that Welder received amplification to camouflage his tin-chai into someone else's, which isn't the same ability as Oren's.

Furthermore, you said Welder tried to kill your guardswomen and strike fear into the Emberwood soldiers. We have already asked Welder for his account of the incident. He said he was disciplining your guardswomen for their lack of respect, and he would never have tried to kill them. We understand Welder might have tough methods, but he has the experience to lead us to victory. Going forward, Colonel Beyling and Captain Kang are supporting General Welder's decisions, and we are encouraging Welder to discipline the Emberwood troops if they fall out of line to his command. Welder said you must have changed your story because of a little row between the two of you. He disciplined one of your guardswomen, who tried to leave the soldier camp without his permission, and it must have ruffled some feathers, as he explained it.

Venn let out an angry curse. "That bastard. He's taking credit for shooting me down and taunting us for not being able to do anything to him."

I finished reading the last paragraph.

And so, the royal council has decided that Welder is not at fault. Queen Rilla, we understand you must still be grieving for King Aiden. We all loved him, and maybe your grief in having to let Welder take his place as your partner under the Will of Heaven has caused you to lash out in this disturbing way. We advise you to take control of your emotions and not to be so overly sensitive. We're at war, and though you no longer hold authority over the soldiers, you're still expected to set a proper example.

"There's a little more, but I don't want to read it," I said. "They're just scolding me and telling me to follow Welder's orders in battle."

"How could they just believe him like that?" Nena asked. She looked disgusted. "He actually convinced the royal advisors that he received the Will of Heaven in King Aiden's place."

"It's because he's a man, and I'm a woman," I said. "Plain and simple. They already didn't like the idea of Aiden naming me as his successor. I still have a say in other matters pertaining to the kingdom, but they don't want me to have authority of the army. This is just the excuse they need to take it away from me and give it to Welder. Blame me for being too emotional just like a woman."

"What do we do now?" Galai asked. "Is there no way to convince them that Welder's lying?"

"They're not going to listen to me until it's too late," I said. "So I have to find other people who will listen. Lina, send another message, this one to Counselor Trine."

Counselor Trine had remained at the clinic in Ponch's absence.

"Tell her to pass on our message to anyone who might be looking for me," I said. "Welder is a danger, and we need help. From the Fauxhemians, from Sago and the Ailo men, from anyone."

"On it," Lina said. She screeched out her words into the air, aiming them in the direction of Emberwood. We couldn't hear what she was saying, but the sound would carry directly to the clinic.

"Are you sure you haven't had any word from the Fauxhemians?" Ponch asked. "Or from any of your other friends?"

"If so, the message isn't getting to me," I said. "Maybe Welder is intercepting it. I have no way of knowing."

Since sending the Fauxhemians back home, I'd received no word from Lymere or Esmeralda. Even if they hadn't tried to contact me, I knew that Sago and the Ailo men would. Yet I hadn't heard from any of them.

When I'd left Emberwood, Sago and the Ailo men told me they were still in Fauxhemia, helping me search for clues to Aiden and Sito's disappearance. Maybe it was because I was on this crusade with Welder, making it difficult to reach me without Welder knowing. I had no way of contacting them either. I didn't know where they were, and I couldn't send out one of my guardswomen without Welder's knowledge. My only hope was that they would come to Emberwood looking for me, and Counselor Trine could get my message to them.

"We can't do anything else for now," I said. "The best we can do is continue going along with Welder until we can discover his weakness. Find proof of his crimes. Then maybe we can convince the royal council that we're telling the truth."

And so, we marched on. At every town we came upon, I went along with Welder, parading the power of the scepter in front of the villagers and convincing them we both had the Will of Heaven. I said nothing to disagree with him. Did nothing to rebel again.

What could I do? He held all the cards, and he knew it. He had control of the Emberwood army and all of our tin-chai. The royal advisors believed him over me. I couldn't convince the Emberwood soldiers to fight him since Colonel Beyling and Captain Kang were on his side.

My guardswomen and I were too afraid to go against him. I just needed to survive. As long as I went along with him, I could buy enough time to figure out a plan. To discover how he'd gotten Oren's tin-chai and find a weakness in it. Maybe he had a Yao gemstone. If so, I had to take it away.

And even with Oren's tin-chai, Welder couldn't control non-Shyan magic. But I didn't have enough non-Shyan guardswomen to win against all his men.

For now, the wisest move I could make was to let Welder take control and stay silent.

CHAPTER 25

✦ ✦ ✦ ✦ ✦ ✦ ✦ ✦ ✦ ✦

A month passed as we made our crusade to the southern coast. The day came when we drew close to Cascasea Village. It filled me with dread. How many of my neighbors would surrender without a fight? And how many would Welder kill?

We came over a sandy hill, and I smelled the ocean. Salty spray wafted into my nose. Then I saw the sea. Free and tumultuous as it had always been, like a soul who refused to have a permanent home. The waves caressed the shore, and gulls soared above us. I wished I could stay here forever. But Welder didn't stop. We continued marching, making our way to the busiest part of town, the port.

As we drew near the harbor, a man stood on the pier. No one else was in sight. As we approached, he kneeled on the docks.

Galai touched my shoulder. "I think that's Chief Magistrate Khan."

"You're right," I said. We'd known him since we were children. It felt out of place to see him kneeling before us.

Chief Magistrate Khan touched his forehead to the ground. "I represent Cascasea Village, and we surrender to the Will of Heaven. Queen Rilla, please remember your townspeople and spare our lives."

I urged the chief magistrate to stand and glared at Welder. "I won't let anyone get hurt. They'll have to kill me first."

Welder crossed his arms and flashed me a look. "Before you decide to give up your life, remember the people you're leaving behind. I still have power to control their tin-chai. Threatening to kill yourself isn't beneficial to anyone and would probably demoralize your guardswomen further, don't you agree?"

Damn him. How was I going to take him down?

He gave me a smug smile. "There's no need to give me that look, and certainly no need to be so dramatic. Your townsfolk have already surrendered. I have no reason to resort to force. You have my word, not a hair or a brick will be touched." He turned to Chief Magistrate Khan. "Good man, you don't have to be afraid. You're on our side now. But where are all the other villagers?"

"They remain in their homes waiting for the word that our surrender has been accepted and our lives will be spared," Chief Magistrate Khan said.

"We'll sign an agreement of peace," Welder said. "Tell your townsfolk to gather all their able-bodied men sixteen years and older and send them to the beach, where we will be setting up our camp. They will join the Emberwood army on our crusade to defeat Carrick."

Chief Magistrate Khan bowed. "Thank you."

"Meet me with all your men in an hour," Welder said.

We headed to the shore to wait for the villagers. Welder told the soldiers to set out their tents for the night.

In another hour, Chief Magistrate Khan came with over thirty men to join the Emberwood army. I stood by Welder as he and Khan signed a peace agreement, but I didn't say a word. Welder had me on this crusade for no other reason than to control me, the true wielder of the scepter. If Old Grandfather Heaven were really on my side, how could he have let this happen? Why wasn't he giving me answers on how to defeat Welder? And why didn't I have enough power to take away tin-chai? I should be able to do it.

Maybe I'd done something wrong. Angered Old Grandfather Heaven. Maybe I hadn't been good enough, strong enough, brave enough.

My faith in myself and in Old Grandfather Heaven was crumbling. Everything I'd come to believe to be my destiny felt like a lie.

I marched back to my tent and paced. Thousands of thoughts raced through my head.

From here, I knew Welder's plan was to head back north and lead the crusade into the eastern villages of Seracedar. We would make our way to the big cities and the capital, where we would take over the palace.

The big cities would be hard to invade, but Welder seemed sure of himself. And now that I saw his army growing bigger from all the Seracedarean villages that had surrendered their men to aid our cause, I was starting to believe we would win.

My worry now was for what would happen after we won. Welder's power was only growing, and I had no control over him. I didn't know what his next move would be against me. I still had the scepter, but he had the army. If he decided to use me as a mere figurehead while he held the real power, I wouldn't be able to stop him.

I still needed evidence of his crimes against Emberwood. Evidence of his involvement in poisoning Ashbel and Leonora and making Aiden and Sito disappear.

And I needed to find out how he was using Oren's tin-chai. My guardswomen joined me in my tent.

"Welder seems to be keeping his promise here," Ponch said. "Oren wanted to steal valuables and pillage homes, but Welder said no one's to mistreat the people here because this is your hometown. He said he gave you his word."

"Not that it mattered before," I said. "Why is he bothering now? I just hope Oren doesn't go against him. That boy is unpredictable."

"Welder must have promised him something or have something against him," Jun said. "It's the only way Oren would be that loyal. Oren doesn't fear Welder. He's the only one whose tin-chai Welder can't steal, seeing as he's the source of Welder's power."

"Keep your ears open, Ponch," I said. "Any conversation between the two of them might reveal something."

"Yes, of course," Ponch said. "I have been listening, but Welder's too smart to say anything so close to camp. He doesn't know my tin-chai yet, but he must suspect you've told us to spy on him."

"I've been wracking my brain trying to figure out how he can use Oren's tin-chai," I said. "And I have a theory."

I took off my necklace and showed them the Yao diamond pendant.

"Yao blood magic," Jun said. "I've heard of it. Androgy Haming and some of the Lotuses who followed him used Yao gemstones. A Shyan can put another Shyan's blood on it to use their tin-chai for a short time."

"I had given this necklace to Aiden before he disappeared," I said. "Oren supposedly found it, and he gave it to me. But I've been wondering if this necklace is a fake. Maybe Welder stole the necklace with the real Yao diamond and camouflaged it to wear on himself."

Galai's eyes widened. "But using Yao blood magic has horrible side effects if someone has evil intent in using it. Empress Radi confided in me once when she was drunk and complaining. Emperor Carrick used a Yao gemstone during the early days of his reign to borrow an advisor's tin-chai. It helped him fake the amplification of his tin-chai. But the side effects stopped him from performing in the bedroom and weakened his stamina. Empress Radi wasn't happy about it. She got him to give it up eventually."

"I've heard about the side effects, too," I said. "From Sago. But maybe it's worth it to Welder if he's just using it to scare us for a short time." I turned to Venn and lifted the scepter. "I don't know if I can give you Welder's tin-chai, but I'm going to try."

I sang, sending my wyis through the scepter and into her.

Venn's body glowed, then turned back to normal. She frowned. "I feel amplification, but I'm afraid it's not what you want me to do." She touched my necklace, but it didn't change. "No, I can't use my tin-chai on inanimate objects. But I can do this."

She turned, touched Jun's shoulder, and Jun shifted into a bunny. Venn touched her again, and Jun returned to normal. "Disguising people as animals and vice versa is probably not what you need right now."

"All right, on to plan B then," I said. "Jun, do you mind?"

I indicated the pendant.

Jun pricked her finger with a knife and let her blood drip on the Yao diamond. I felt the blood magic working as I inserted my wyis into it. Then my body disappeared.

"It's real," I said. "Which means Oren and Welder didn't steal it from me."

"But that doesn't mean Welder couldn't have found a Yao gemstone to use for himself," Ponch said. "What about that new watch he's been wearing? He could have camouflaged a gemstone into the watch."

I clapped my hands. "Yes, that's a brilliant thought, Ponch. We'll look at his watch next. We just need to figure out how to get—"

Shouts broke out in the distance, interrupting the remainder of my sentence.

"What now?" I groaned.

Lina and Wray rushed into the tent, their wide-eyed gazes flying to me.

"Two fishermen are challenging your right to rule," Lina said. "They're looking like they want to pick a fight with Welder."

I headed out with my guardswomen. The fishermen stood outside of Welder's tent facing Welder. Ret and Oren were with him. The fishermen were so loud, I could hear their shouts clearly.

"The rest of the village may have surrendered, but we didn't agree to it," the first one said. "We don't want to fight for you."

Oh no. If they started something with Welder, he'd have them killed. I ran to them.

"Where's the girl who they say wields the scepter? She's supposed to be one of us." The second man spat on the ground. White spittle foamed near Welder's foot. He looked annoyed.

"I'm here," I said.

Welder faced me and lowered his voice to a whisper. "You don't have to prove anything to them. Remember, we agreed everyone has a choice. They are easily disposable."

"Cascasea Village surrendered before I had to show them the scepter and tin-chai amplification," I said. "But the other villages saw the proof. It's only fair that these men should get to see it, too."

I took the scepter out of my cloak pocket and showed it to the men. "This is the scepter, and I bear the Will of Heaven."

"As do I," Welder said. "Both of us have received tin-chai amplification."

"Why would Old Grandfather Heaven choose you?" the first man asked. "The daughter of a fisherman? And a traitor who ran away from Seracedar? General Welder, your name is infamous in this kingdom. You betrayed us when you left Seracedar to join forces with Emberwood, our sworn enemy."

The second man nodded. "Anyway, we won't believe it until we see your tin-chai amplification. You, woman, I hear you can amplify tin-chai. We brothers both deep dive. We can breathe underwater, but if you amplify our tin-chai so we can transform into fish, just like fish Yao, then we'll bow to you."

Welder tapped his foot and folded his arms. "We haven't got all day to waste with these fools. Let me deal with them."

I shook my head. "No, I—"

"Who are you calling a fool?" the first man growled. "I should gut you like my morning catch. Traitor."

Didn't they know they were a hair's breadth away from getting killed, and they were insulting the only person standing in the way of their executioner?

I stepped between him and Welder. I stood my ground, giving the fisherman a stern look. "Step back, sir."

Singing, I cast my wyis into the scepter, then into the second fisherman. His body transformed, two slits forming on either side of his chest. Gills. His arms elongated, and his skin grew translucent. They looked like a version of fish fins though the rest of him remained the same.

He looked at himself. "Not bad. I wanted to become a full fish, but this gets the job done. I'll be able to swim better and dive for pearls now."

"My turn," the first fisherman said. "I need to dive for pearls, too."

Welder laughed. "Like I said, you're fools. You think after challenging our right to rule and refusing to surrender, you're still going to live another day to dive for pearls?" He snapped his fingers. "Ret, show these men the consequences of their refusal to surrender with the rest of their village."

"My pleasure," Ret said. He ran circles around the two men, digging out dirt around them until the ground loosened beneath the men. The earth crumbled, and the men cried out as they fell through the ground. Ret threw earth, rocks, and dirt on top of the men, so fast I barely had time to realize his intent. He was burying them alive.

"No," I screamed. I could still hear the men under the rubble screaming for help. "You can't leave them to die. They were going to surrender. It isn't necessary to kill them. Stop this at once, Welder."

"Queen Rilla, I've warned you before about questioning my orders, especially in front of my men," Welder said.

I glared back at him. "Someone needs to question you. You've let power go to your head."

"Do you need me to demonstrate again what happens when you and your guardswomen disobey me?" Welder motioned to Oren. "If one of these guardswomen initiates their tin-chai for a second, you know what to do."

Oren grinned. "Gladly, sir."

My guardswomen drew out their swords, coming by my side to face Oren and Welder. They were in battle mode.

"We don't need to use our tin-chai to defeat this little shit," Jun said. She aimed her stare at Welder before lowering her gaze to Oren. "Or his dungpiece follower."

"That's right," Wray said. "And there are some of us with other magic you can't steal." She held a clear barrel-shaped canister in her hands. It contained liquid. Thick like blood, but it wasn't red. It sparkled like diamonds. The canister had a trigger button on the base.

"Wray," I said with a gasp. "Is that your blood? What do you intend to do with that?"

"My invisible friends can be quite scary when provoked," Wray said. "When I pull the trigger, my blood will shoot into the air and at my enemies. My friends will deal with them."

I hadn't known she'd collected her blood, hadn't asked her to do so. The thought of her blood being shot out was repulsive, but if it worked to defeat Welder, I wasn't about to question her.

Nena stepped forward, too, also holding a canister, which I assumed also contained her blood. "We're prepared to fight. I might not have a tin-chai, but the trees listen to me."

Miah transformed her skin into rock. She glared at Welder. "We aren't going to let you continue bullying our queen or killing people just for the sake of it."

"Ah, yes, two Fauxhemians and an Ailo," Welder said. "True, Oren can't steal your types of magic, but including Rilla and the other Shyan guardswomen, there are only nine of you. I admit you're all excellent fighters, but without the use of tin-chai, do you really think you can go against my entire army?"

I looked around. Though Oren and Ret stood by Welder here, other men were gathered around the campsite, staring at us. And all of them obeyed Welder's orders, not mine.

"Stand down," I told my guardswomen.

"Wise move, my queen," Welder said. "As I've said before, all I want is for you and your team to work with me, not against me. We're on the same side. You can show mercy to some of our enemies, but not all. And in this case, these fishermen challenged us. They'd easily turn on us again even if they surrender now. Now let's return to our tents. It's been a long day."

Ret ogled Wray and Nena. "I've sampled a lot of Shyan women, but never a Fauxhemian. Would one of you like to be my first?"

Oren joined in, laughing. "I'd like to steal some of your magic if you know what I mean." He waggled his eyebrows, and before anyone could stop him, he reached for Wray.

Quicker than a pouncing maocat, Wray flipped Oren to the ground and shot her blood into the air above him. She chanted some words under her breath.

Oren groaned and yelped in horror as he gazed around him. While we didn't see anything, he screamed. "Get away from me, you ugly spirits. No, don't touch me. Ouch."

Then Nena shot her blood before I could stop her. "Trees, help me," she called. A tree root sprung out of the ground and twisted around Oren's ankle. It grew taller, holding Oren so the boy dangled in the air.

Oren shivered. His skin was pale, and he couldn't stop trembling. "General, help me, please. Cut me down, and get that woman to stop these things. They're threatening to drag my spirit out of my body."

Some of Nena's blood had landed on Welder's hand. He looked at it with disgust but did nothing to wipe it off.

"Idiot," he said.

Curling my fists, I stood in front of my guardswomen, bracing myself for his retribution.

CHAPTER 26

✦ ✦ ✦ ✦ ✦ ✦ ✦ ✦ ✦ ✦

Ret glared at us. "You women need to be taught submission or you'll never get a man."

He moved fast, circling us. But to my surprise, he stopped. His face was panic-stricken, and his posture was strange. Frozen in place. Ret's heels were lifted, but his toes were on the ground as though he'd been glued there.

Then I felt Welder's wyis. The general was exerting his wyis upon Ret. Taking away his tin-chai. Ret flopped to the ground like a ragdoll. Some of the other men watching us started snickering. Ret looked humiliated.

"General, what are you doing?" Oren shouted. "Why are you punishing Ret for defending me?"

"You deserved it," Welder said. "Both of you are idiots. I won't have my men disrespecting a woman."

"But they disrespected you first," Oren said. "They tried to rebel against you."

"If any soldier disobeys me, I'll be the one to decide their punishment. And I'd do the same to anyone, no matter what gender. But I won't allow any of my men to get away with acting like Terran or Lieka, treating women as bedtime playthings."

Welder lifted his hand. Nena's blood had left a faded streak. But it absorbed into Welder's skin. "Trees, help me discipline these boys." A branch fell off a tree, seeming to have heard Welder.

Nena gasped. "What the—" She turned to me in horror. "He's using my blood magic. But he didn't steal it from me."

"How is that possible?" I asked. "Did Oren take on your magic, too?"

"I don't think so," she whispered. "If he did, he would have freed himself from the trees by now. Wray's blood landed on Oren, too, but he couldn't stop the ghosts from tormenting him."

Welder grabbed the branch and struck Oren across the back five times. Oren howled with each lash.

When Welder was done, he said, "Let the boy go." The tree root uncurled from Oren's ankle and dropped him onto the ground with a thud.

Ret still remained on the ground, unmoving. But he gave Welder a sullen stare.

Welder stepped toward him with the branch. "You have something to say, boy?"

"We've shown you nothing but loyalty," Ret said. "But instead of making good on your promise, you humiliate us."

"And it'll be far worse if you continue this insolent behavior. My promise can quickly change to a threat. I know who your weakness is."

Ret paled, but he didn't say another word. Welder struck him on the back five times, just as he did with Oren, but Ret remained stoic, refusing to show any sign of pain.

Once Welder was through, Ret stood. He stayed silent, staring at his feet. I wondered what, or who, Welder had on him.

"I've seen both of you fight," Welder said, addressing Ret and Oren. "If not for your tin-chai, any one of these women could kick your pitiful asses. They train much harder than the two of you combined. Don't think for a second that because your tin-chai is useful to me, you get special treatment. Now go take fifty laps around the village as punishment for your impudence. No tin-chai allowed. If I get reports that you cheated, the punishment will get worse. After your laps, I'll consider letting you get your wounds treated."

Ret and Oren went off running, both groaning from the pain of their lashes.

Welder faced me again. "I know you had concerns about Oren and Ret's immaturity and if Oren would turn against me. As you can see, I have no trouble keeping them in line. I'm still more powerful than Oren. I can take on your Faux-bloods' magic, too."

But how? It occurred to me that Welder's mother had been a Faux-blood who could absorb blood magic from the other Faux-blood types. Had he inherited her magic? It still wouldn't explain how he'd gotten Oren's tin-chai, though. There had to be a connection, but I just wasn't understanding it yet.

"You look baffled, my queen," he said. "I suppose you wonder how I've become so powerful. I know you'll figure it out eventually, but it's not important. You've no need to defeat me. I'm not your enemy. I've told you countless times that as long as you and your guardswomen do as I say, I have no reason to hurt you. In fact, I'll protect you. Haven't I demonstrated this already? No man will get away with trying to dominate you or your guardswomen."

"Only you," I said.

He shrugged. "I have to dominate everyone. To ensure submission. The one with the most power gets the most respect and deserves authority. Even his enemies bow down to him, and that is and will always be my purpose of living. Now return to your tent for now. I'll find you again later. I have something more private to discuss, but let me finish off these fishermen."

I gestured to my guardswomen, and we turned away, heads hanging in defeat.

Back in my tent, Galai took a pillow and screamed into it. "I hate this. Those fishermen used to work with my father. They were lazy workers and always argued with my baba, but they still didn't deserve to die this way."

"Are you sure we can't do anything to rescue them?" Miah asked.

"No, I don't want to risk any of you," I said.

"Then we just sit here and wait for them to die?" Yin punched the ground.

I sighed. "I hate this, too, but Welder is just too powerful. Now we've learned he not only steals tin-chai but can steal Faux-blood magic as well."

"I still don't understand how he did it," Nena said. "How could he steal both Shyan and Fauxhemian magic?"

"He's half-Fauxhemian," I said. "He must share his mother's blood magic. She was a rainbow Faux-blood."

Nena gasped. "A rainbow? Those are so rare. Normal Fauxhemians hate them, and even Faux-bloods fear them."

"Still doesn't explain how he's using Oren's tin-chai," Wray said. "Faux-blood magic doesn't cross with Shyan tin-chai. He must have a Yao gemstone in that watch."

Ponch's ears twitched. She swore. "I heard someone declare the fishermen are dead."

"And look, the general's coming here again," Jun said, nodding outside the tent door. "What else could he possibly want to discuss with you, Rilla?"

Welder approached the tent. The sight of him made me want to throw up.

My guardswomen didn't move. But I motioned to them. "It's okay. Return to your tents and get some rest."

Reluctantly, they got up and sauntered away, leaving me with Welder.

"They're quite protective of you," Welder said. "But there are only so many times I'll forgive their defiance. Make sure they learn before it's too late."

"What do you want?" I asked. "Can you make this quick? I'm tired."

"Look," he said. "You don't have to like me. But I have always told you that I want you to be my partner. If I didn't, I wouldn't have let you keep your title as queen."

"I have the scepter," I said. "Without me, you have no control of it."

"That may be true," he said. "But I could have done what Carrick and Terran did. Faked my own tin-chai amplification through the scepter and disposed of you. I believe the Will of Heaven is changeable. Whoever exerts the most power will eventually have the right to rule. If Old Grandfather Heaven were really on your side, would he have let me take authority from you? Wouldn't he have given you enough power to take away Oren's or my tin-chai? And would he have let Aiden die?"

My anger rose. I bit it down, knowing Welder was trying to bait me.

"Get to your point," I said.

"I might not believe in Old Grandfather Heaven anymore, but I do believe in the powers that the scepter gives to certain people. Like you. You were lucky enough to be born with a strong tin-chai. To heal and to kill. And now the scepter allows you to amplify tin-chai. No matter that you can't take away tin-chai yet. You have enough power. With you by my side, we can conquer the world together. As partners."

As if I wanted to be his partner. He knew I'd never willingly let him use my powers to further his agenda without being forced to.

I had to try it again. Taking away his tin-chai. Old Grandfather Heaven had to help me if I believed enough.

"I'm afraid I've been hearing criticisms that Emberwood needs a man to lead them, not a woman," Welder continued. "While the people love you, there is a minority in opposition to your rule, and I don't want that minority to grow. They say they can't trust a woman to rule. The royal advisors are also doubtful of you."

He kept talking. Telling me how I didn't have experience leading an army, and no one would follow a woman with no experience. But my thoughts raced, focused on how I could use the scepter on him without his suspicion.

"Did you hear me?" he asked, drawing my attention back to him. "What are your thoughts?"

"Uhm, thoughts about what?"

He gave me an impatient look. "I said I want you to be my partner for life."

I stared at him blankly. "What do you mean partner for life? You already told everyone we share the Will of Heaven."

"I'm proposing to you," he said.

Proposing. He couldn't possibly be suggesting what I thought he was. I stared at him, mouth agape.

"I know how much you love Aiden, but eventually, you have to move on," he said. "I know it's hard, but you must let him go. We need to do what's best for the kingdom. I want to marry you."

CHAPTER 27

✦ ✦ ✦ ✦ ✦ ✦ ✦ ✦ ✦ ✦

Welder wanted to marry me?

Of all the things I'd expected him to say, that was far from it.

"We would make a good team," he said. "The marriage would be a business arrangement only. I have only ever loved Bree, and I know you'll never have anyone in your heart except Aiden. I'd never try to force you to have a true marriage with me. And I'll benefit from your tin-chai and connection to the Emberwood royal family. I could take over by force, but it would be easier to convince the people to accept me as their ruler if I'm legally bound to you since Aiden already established you as the authority figure in his stead."

I couldn't marry anyone as long as I had hope that Aiden was still alive, but the thought of becoming Welder's wife made my skin crawl.

I already felt like Welder was using me as a puppet. If he became my husband, I'd be in his clutches for the rest of my life. Welder had just said he preferred to become the ruler through legal means instead of force. Emberwood law stated that any children from my future marriage would become heirs to the throne. Welder was dreaming if he believed he could convince me to have children with him.

Yet, as much as I wanted to scream *no* in his face, I had to keep my emotions hidden. Bide my time to make my next move. And maybe this was my chance. I could say yes now and get him drunk as I pretended to celebrate with him. Then I could try to remove his tin-chai.

"You're right," I said. "I agree. I'll marry you."

"You will?" He looked surprised. "I thought it would take more convincing than that."

"It's not like I have a choice. Aiden is dead. At least if I marry you, I'll stay queen. Besides, if I don't agree, you'll force me to anyway. Don't pretend otherwise."

"Yes," he said. "But your consent would make things much easier and more pleasant."

I feigned a smile. "Then what do you say we drink to that? An arranged marriage where we both reap benefits."

I poured two cups of rice wine and planned my next move. I could use the scepter to take away his tin-chai. If he couldn't take off the camouflage effect he'd placed on his watch, where I suspected he hid the Yao gemstone, then he wouldn't be able to use Yao blood magic and would stop being able to harness Oren's tin-chai. Then again, I wasn't sure he was using a Yao gemstone. But if he'd acquired Oren's tin-chai into himself, then maybe the scepter would take away that ability, too. I'd have to figure things out through trial and error, which I didn't like. I wanted more time to know for sure how he was using Oren's tin-chai, but I couldn't let this chance pass.

I needed to take away some of his power. Without all that power, many of the Emberwood soldiers might not fear him as much. Maybe I could win them back to my side.

I handed Welder one of the cups. "To our future victory over Seracedar."

He drank, tilting his head back. In the seconds that his gaze was averted, I pretended to drink, only I tossed the liquid from the cup behind my shoulder.

I poured another shot for both of us. "This one is to toast our future victory over Fauxhemia."

He stopped, looking at me in surprise. "Really? I thought you believed in Fauxhemia's innocence."

"If they were truly innocent, Esmeralda wouldn't have hidden the fact that she and Clox were related," I said. "It's apparent that she ambushed Aiden to stop him from looking for Clox. So no one would ever find out she shares his blood. I want her to pay for what she did. Once we have victory over Seracedar, we can combine their troops with the Emberwood army to conquer Fauxhemia. Our forces will be unstoppable."

"Hear, hear," Welder said. "Rilla, I'm so glad you finally see reason."

He tossed the contents of the cup down his throat. Again, I threw the liquid on the ground and pretended to drink it when he looked back at me.

I lifted the jug to refill his cup, but he shook his head. "Any more and I might pass out on the floor and regret it in the morning."

"Oh, come now," I said, refilling the cup anyway. "I have another toast you can't refuse. This one is for Princess Bree and for Aiden. May their memories live on."

"You're right, I can't refuse that one." He drank the shot. "So you really think Aiden's dead? Have you . . . accshepted it?"

The slur in his speech betrayed him. I could see his eyes start to glaze over. Just one more shot might do it.

I refilled his cup. "Yes, I've accepted it. And I want to see the Fauxhemians pay. I know I kept asking you to show mercy to Seracedar, but I won't ask the same once we march into Fauxhemia. They deserve to have their homes burned to the ground for what happened to Bree and Aiden. I understand your thirst for revenge now, and I'm all in it with you."

"Yes, le-ss drink to that. My Bree will be avenged." He lifted the cup and downed it. His head wobbled, and he keeled over on the ground.

Now was my chance. I grabbed the scepter from my cloak. Concentrating my wyis into the scepter, I focused on taking away Welder's tin-chai.

Old Grandfather Heaven, you said the scepter would help me to give and take away tin-chai. If you have truly given me the right to rule, then give me the help I need to defeat Welder before he gains more power.

The scepter glowed. Maybe this would actually work. I gave everything I had, poured my wyis into the scepter. Sweat dripped from my brow. Giving someone tin-chai had never required this much effort.

More power. I was almost there. I could feel it. Just a little more.

The light from the scepter flickered, threatening to go out. *No. Please, no.* My wyis was fading. I had no power left to give.

The scepter's glow faded. I collapsed to the ground, exhausted. I'd failed. How could this be? Maybe Old Grandfather Heaven was angry about something I did. Maybe he wanted to take away my right to rule and give it to someone else. Maybe I wasn't enough.

Welder stirred. His eyelids flickered and opened. "Rilla, I told you."

I jolted. Had he been conscious all this time? I wiped a tear away from my cheek, forcing myself to pull it together.

Welder sat up, his gaze now sober. "I told you I shouldn't be drinking so much. I always fall asleep." He stretched and yawned. He saw the scepter in front of me and froze.

"Why do you have that out?" he asked. "You should be more careful and keep it hidden in your cloak when you're not displaying its power. Someone could snatch it up."

"Nonsense," I said. "I'm in the privacy of my own tent, and I have my eyes on it."

His shrewd gaze dug into me. My hands shook. What if he had been pretending to be sleeping and knew I'd tried to take away his tin-chai?

"I should retire for the night," I said.

He didn't move. "It's still early. And now that I've had a nap, I'm wide awake, I see a problem."

"Wh-what do you mean?"

"The scepter's true form is much bulkier than it was as a flute. It must add a lot of weight and be hard to carry." He gestured at the scepter. "Let me see it. I'll disguise it again. It'll be more convenient for you."

I paused, trying not to sound suspicious. "It's all right. I'll put it away now."

He grabbed the scepter first. "It will be safer, too. Now that we've established in most of the villages our right to rule, you won't need to prove the scepter's power as much until we've reached Cedar Palace. Transforming it into a different object will add a precaution in case someone wants to steal it." Welder twirled the scepter in his hands. "What form should it take? A flute again?"

"I don't need it to be disguised," I said. "Give it back."

He smiled. It was more of a smirk, like he knew he had me cornered. He flipped the scepter behind him, then back in front of him. Now it was in the form of a pan flute.

He handed it to me. "Here. Why bother with something new when what's tried and true worked?"

I took it from him, and he made his exit. Once he was out of sight, I buried my face in my hands and sobbed. The grief hit all at once as it had every night since the day Aiden had disappeared.

I said a prayer to Old Grandfather Heaven. "I don't know why you didn't help me take away Welder's tin-chai, but I have to believe you have your reasons. I beg you not to abandon me now. Help me find a way to establish my power without marrying Welder. If you have truly chosen me to lead the Shyan people, guide me through what I should do next. And please, if at all possible, let Aiden and Sito be safe."

This was all I had in my power to do at the moment. I drew my cloak closer to my body, lay on my futon and closed my eyes, intending to rest for just a minute. I still had to tell my guardswomen about Welder's proposal, though I had a feeling Ponch had been listening to the whole conversation.

A song played in my head.

"Although you've already left me

Although we've said goodbye

Don't ever forget when you were mine

I will always love you

'til the last ember of starlight

flickers out in the night sky."

I woke up with a start. My cloak had fallen off the futon and onto the ground. The chatter of the soldiers had died down, and I could hear snores. I looked around my tent. My guardswomen were fast asleep in their makeshift cots around my futon. They must have come back and decided not to disturb me. I got up, walked outside, and looked at the sky. The moon was higher than it had been when Welder left. It had to be well past midnight.

I heard the song again.

"Although we went our separate ways

Every part of you that aches

is the part of me that breaks

I will always love you

'til the last ember of starlight

flickers out in the night sky."

This time, the notes felt like they were telling me to follow them. It was just like the first time I'd heard the scepter sing to me, telling me to find it in the lake on the Miyu Islands.

I took out the scepter from my cloak. It looked exactly like the flute that I'd first discovered. But something was wrong. The song I heard wasn't coming from here. It was calling me from elsewhere. And the feel of the scepter was off somehow. I didn't know how I could tell, but this really was nothing but a flute.

Welder must have switched the real scepter for this one, probably when he'd twirled the scepter behind his back. I should have known. Should have been more careful. Why was I failing at everything?

The song called to me again. My ears perked up. The notes were urging me to come after them. To come find the scepter. Maybe Old Grandfather Heaven hadn't forgotten me after all.

Welder must be out there with the scepter. I didn't know what he was doing away from the camp, but I had to trust the song. I had to follow the sound.

I walked toward the source of the music, away from camp. The melody played, taking me to a familiar pathway. A place I'd once known so well. This was the way I used to go to the cliffs by my house, where I'd once spent so much time writing music. It was also where the palace scouts had overheard me singing to heal a bird.

The song continued, beckoning me to the shore.

"Although we stand on opposite shores

I hope you still see the fireworks

through the haze and through the storms."

I passed my old house and couldn't help but stop to look around. A wave of nostalgia hit, bringing me down like a sprout in a storm. It was jarring to see the cobwebs that had built up on the dusty front porch that had once been so well-kept. The garden where flowers had bloomed was now dry and dead. I knew when the war was over, Rell and Fenia would return to make the place sparkle once again. That day couldn't come soon enough.

The song grew louder, reminding me of its urgency.

"I will always love you

'til the last ember of starlight

flickers out in the night sky."

With one last look at the house, I turned around and headed for the shore. One day, I'd come back to the home my parents had built. One day, the kingdom would be at peace again. And I had to make one day possible. I had to find the scepter again.

Only the Lavender Moon was high in the sky tonight, casting a sad, lonely shadow on the water. The song of the scepter slowed, and I knew it had drawn me here. I waited and watched.

A lone figure appeared, walking slowly across the shore. I recognized Welder at once. His hulking frame, the way he stood straight and took calculating steps.

He took the scepter out from his cloak and twirled it. The song crescendoed in my head. Without a doubt, that was the real scepter. He stopped twirling and looked at it. I could imagine the smile, the smugness on his face. He touched it, and it transformed into a wooden hair accessory, a thin, five-inch hair stick. It was far from the elaborate hair sticks the faela had used to hold their coiled buns into place, but more like what a simple village girl would use. He tucked it back into his pocket and gave it an affectionate pat. How was I going to get it back from him?

Another figure walked from the direction of the camp to the shore, joining Welder. I stilled and squinted, trying to identify the person. It was Oren.

I held my breath, listening in on their conversation.

"I thought we had a deal," Oren said. He looked sulky. "You still haven't given me what you promised. And also, I don't like what you did to me today. I didn't sign up to be humiliated or whipped."

"I'm your superior," Welder said. "And you stepped out of line today."

"But you're the one who needs me," Oren said. "Maybe I'll just stop giving you what you need from me. Then what will you do? It's not like you can kill me."

"I can take your blood by force," Welder said. "And I don't need a tin-chai to beat you as I proved earlier today. Your fighting skills are sorely lacking."

Welder reached into his cloak and drew out a small vial, holding it out to Oren. "Now don't make me hurt you again."

Oren slumped, looking defeated. He drew out a knife and pricked his finger, then let his blood drip into the vial.

Now I remembered something Sito had said, though I hadn't been listening closely at the time. Case studies about half-Shyan, half-Fauxhemian persons whose magic crossed over. Welder's ability to take on Oren's tin-chai didn't involve a Yao gemstone after all.

Welder had inherited his mother's rainbow Faux-blood and the ability to absorb another Faux-blood's magic. Being a half-Shyan, half-Fauxhemian, Welder's Faux-blood magic must allow him to absorb Shyan tin-chai through the blood as well.

Welder lifted the vial to his lips and drank it. I suppressed the urge to gag. The lengths he would go to attain more power.

This was an even worse situation than I'd thought. Even without using Oren's tin-chai to steal someone else's tin-chai, Welder could still take their ability as his own if he absorbed their blood. Oren was just a faster way of doing so. Why take in a variety of blood when just Oren's blood would suffice?

Oren watched Welder in disgust. "You could just let it absorb into your skin. You don't have to drink it."

"Drinking it lasts longer," Welder said. "Unless you want to give me your blood every other day instead of just once a week."

"Whatever suits you," Oren said. "I've kept my promise to you. Kept you supplied. When will you fulfill your end of the bargain? You said you'd absorb the queen's blood yourself and use her healing tin-chai on my brother. I wish I could steal her tin-chai myself."

What? Oren had a brother in need of healing? This must be what Welder had over him. But why not simply ask for my help? Oren was an immature boy, but if his brother was sick, I wouldn't hesitate to use my tin-chai to save him.

Also, if he couldn't steal my tin-chai, then it meant he couldn't steal all types of tin-chai.

"As I told you, not until we get victory over Seracedar. We can't make a special trip in the middle of our crusade."

"I can't wait any longer," Oren said. "The doctor said my brother is getting worse."

"He's hung on for a year in his condition," Welder said. "I'm sure he can survive another few months."

Oren stared at Welder in shock. "I can't believe this. I should have just taken the queen's Yao gemstone and stolen her blood when I had the chance. But you told me to give it back to her. You said the side effects were too dangerous."

Again, why didn't it occur to him that he could just ask me? Why bother trying to steal my Yao gemstone or letting Welder control him in exchange for his help?

"I was protecting you. I've heard of some Shyan who couldn't use their tin-chai anymore after messing with Yao blood magic. You've got a powerful tin-chai. You can take on any tin-chai meant to be used for fighting. So what if you can't steal subtler forms of tin-chai like my camouflaging or Rilla's healing? You were born to hold the offense, not the defense."

"All you care about is being able to use my tin-chai," Oren said. "I'm done with you. I'm going to find the queen right now and steal her Yao gemstone and her blood."

Oren stood, facing the campsite.

Welder moved so fast, Oren only had time to yelp before he landed on his back in the sand. Welder held a knife to Oren's neck.

"As I said, without your tin-chai, you're nothing," Welder said. "I could easily gut you now, and then your brother is as good as dead. But I don't want to kill you. I care for you deeply, and I promise, I will help your brother in time."

He took the knife away and extended his hand. Oren looked wary but allowed Welder to help him up.

Welder placed a hand on Oren's shoulder. "Do you remember when I found you and Ret? What I promised?"

"You said if we did everything you said, we'd never feel powerless again. You promised we'd be your right-hand men and be able to rule over our enemies."

"And didn't I give you the chance to get revenge on one of your enemies?" Welder asked. "Didn't it feel great to see the look on King Aiden's face when you stole his tin-chai and threw it back at him?"

I bit back a sound of horror.

"Too bad I missed," Oren said. "He killed my oldest brother. I wish I had been able to make the killing blow to exact revenge. You don't think he and his cousin survived, do you?"

"They haven't come back yet," Welder said. "It's unlikely the king would have left Rilla all alone once he found out I was behind the ambush. I think it's safe to assume he and Sito are dead."

Tears rushed down my cheeks.

"You won't let me kill the queen, though," Oren said. "And you humiliated me today in front of her."

"No, I can't let you bully women," Welder said. "That's my rule, out of respect for Bree."

"What if she figures out how to use the scepter to take away tin-chai?" Oren asked.

"She won't," he said. "Her wyis isn't strong enough on its own. Unlike you, she was born to be on the defensive side, not the offensive. She's got too much healing energy and not enough fighting energy. I suppose that's why Old Grandfather Heaven paired her with Aiden. He really was the yang to her yin. I have a theory that he might have been able to help her unlock the power to take away tin-chai. Good thing she never figured it out."

What was he talking about? How would Aiden have been able to help me?

"Are you sure about that?" Oren asked. "She might still be able to figure it out without Aiden."

Welder made a face. "Nothing's a complete certainty. With enough practice, who knows? She's managed the impossible before, defeating Terran. She's used her voice to manipulate the elements, too. I'd be a fool to underestimate her. Which is why I took matters into my own hands. I stole the scepter from her."

Oren gasped. "You did?"

"She tried to get me drunk, and I caught her attempting to use the scepter on me. Can't believe I almost fell for the oldest trick in the book." Welder patted Oren's back. "Don't worry. I promise once Rilla and I are married, you'll see her suffer at my hands. I'll control everything she does, every note she sings. That's even worse than death, don't you think? Especially since it's her worst nightmare to have her freedom of choice taken away."

"She deserves it," Oren said. "After what she did to my younger brother. Making him an invalid. She took away his freedom to walk and eat on his own. Ret's sister, too. Rilla disfigured her so badly, she was kicked out of the palace. She'll never find work or a man to marry and support her. All they did was serve Emperor Terran because they had to. Aiden and Rilla didn't care about the innocent people they hurt when they brought Terran down. They don't deserve the Will of Heaven."

I bit my lower lip to keep from crying out. Oren's brothers must have served as guards at Cedar Palace. And Ret's sister had probably been a serving trifle. Aiden and I had hurt and killed many of the guards when we'd made our escape. I hadn't wanted to, but I'd justified it in my mind as being the result of war. A means to my own survival. And after winning against Terran and his forces, I hadn't given much more thought about the lives I'd affected or asked for forgiveness.

Here I was, telling Welder he needed to show more mercy. Believing he was callous for stating that we needed to kill to win the war. I was a hypocrite.

Yet, I reminded myself, there was one difference between Welder and me. Welder was using the situation to further his evil agenda even though he didn't care at all who he killed. Whereas I made a solemn vow to Old Grandfather Heaven now that to my dying day, I'd find a way to use my voice to help heal those affected by this war. I wished I could tell Oren how sorry I was. I could save his brother if he was willing to listen to me, but I doubted it. He hated me. Had every reason to. Especially when Welder had Oren gripped in his manipulative clutches.

There was no way I could make up for the lives I'd taken, but all I could do was try to become a better person. A better ruler if Old Grandfather Heaven still willed it.

I heard the song of the scepter again, reminding me of its presence, stowed in Welder's cloak pocket. But Welder and Oren didn't seem to hear it.

"Return to camp," Welder said to Oren. "Make sure nobody sees you. I'll be back in a bit."

Oren walked back to the campsite. I stayed in place, wondering why Welder remained. The song of the scepter rang out a little louder now.

Welder took out a cigar. He lit it and exhaled a ring of smoke. Since when did Welder smoke?

Then I remembered that night he'd told me about Bree. He'd mentioned in his youth, he used to smoke and still occasionally indulged.

Welder paused, looking left and then right. He took his watch off his wrist and flicked it, channeling his wyis to use his tin-chai. The watch transformed into a stack of papers. Letters in envelopes with seals stamped on them. What did they contain?

He rifled through the stack and separated out a few. These he threw onto the sand, then transformed the original stack back into a watch and strapped it back onto his wrist. With a satisfied sigh, he took a few more puffs of his cigar and held it above the discarded letters.

If only I could get a look before he burned them. Maybe a glimpse of the words on one of the envelopes would be a hint at what the letters contained. I inched closer, stooping behind the rocks. One of my steps squeaked in the wet sand.

His gaze snapped towards my hiding spot. "Who's there?"

I dared not breathe. Welder stepped closer to me. Another few feet, and he'd be able to see me. I should have taken Jun with me to make us invisible. Why hadn't I thought of it earlier? I prayed for a miracle.

A loud boom echoed over the ocean, and the sky illuminated in a burst of bright light.

Welder jumped, his gaze swinging from my direction to the sky.

Pop! Pop! Pop! More flashes of light lit up in the sky. Pretty colors of red, orange, and green. Fireworks. Who could be setting off fireworks at this time of the night? A surprise attack from Carrick's forces? Surely not. They would launch bombs, not fireworks.

It had to be one of our men, drunk and careless, using his fire tin-chai as entertainment.

I heard Welder curse. "When I find the drunk idiot, I swear I'll—"

He'd come to the same conclusion as me. He dropped the cigar onto the stack of papers and hurried away, back to camp.

The sky had gone dark again. The only evidence of the fireworks was the faint smell of smoke in the air. Whoever had set them off had saved me from discovery. For that I was glad, but the immature recruit, probably drunk on rice wine, needed to be disciplined. Good thing the village had already surrendered. But if we had been elsewhere in a bigger city with Carrick's loyalists in the majority, the sound of explosives could have launched them into attack mode, starting a fight.

I needed to return to camp before I was missed. Welder would surely force every recruit to wake up and report to him.

But first, I went to the fire Welder had set. I stomped on the flames, smothering the fire. Then carefully, I picked up what remained of the papers. Some had already turned to ash, but I'd managed to save several letters.

One envelope was addressed to Aiden. I recognized the seal on the envelope. It belonged to Carrick. The letter was still inside. I opened it and read what hadn't been burned. It was dated two weeks before the first Seracedarean attack. Before this war had officially begun.

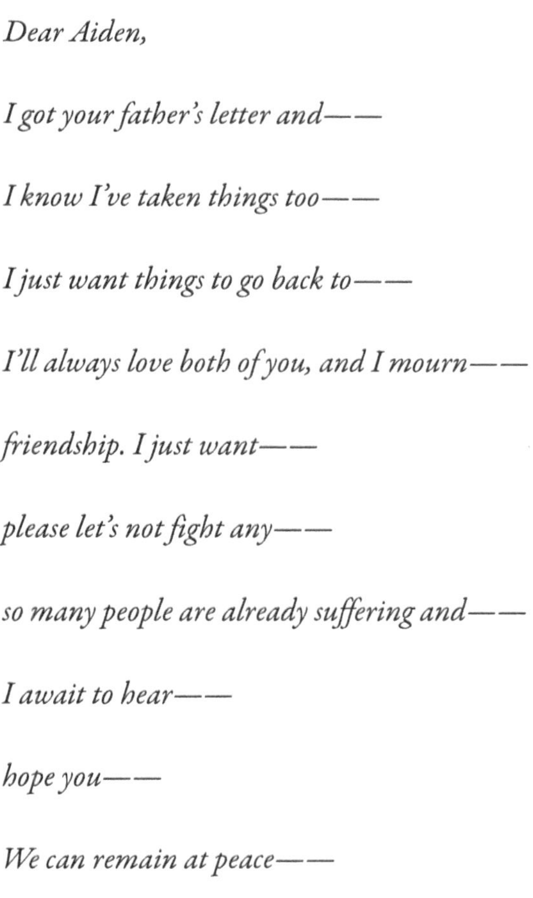

Dear Aiden,

I got your father's letter and——

I know I've taken things too——

I just want things to go back to——

I'll always love both of you, and I mourn——

friendship. I just want——

please let's not fight any——

so many people are already suffering and——

I await to hear——

hope you——

We can remain at peace——

Fainting faela. Had Carrick really written this? Was this a response to King Ashbel's letter to Carrick asking for peace two months ago? King Ashbel might have been right after all. We could have convinced Carrick to avoid war.

Welder had purposely stolen Carrick's letter and made sure we never knew about it. He knew Aiden had a soft spot for Carrick and would have called for a truce if there was a possibility for it.

I read some of the other correspondences. They were from Welder's spies. He'd placed his people in Cedar Palace, Linlang Palace, and Fauxhemia Castle, I realized. Lord Run, one of the advisors on the royal council, worked for Welder. There was even a letter from a spy in Fauxhemia who had gotten the address of my brother's family.

This chilled me. Welder already had enough power to force my obedience, but using my family? There was no way I could go against that.

And here was another letter. This one had barely been burned. A spy in Cedar Palace had written it, and the date was one week before the war had started.

General, your plan worked. Carrick believes Aiden and Rilla tried to poison him, and now he swears there will never be peace between Seracedar and Emberwood. He's angry and hurt, and not even Radi could make him listen when she told him there might be a misunderstanding. He plans to attack Cindertrance seven days from now, the day of the wedding of his former friends. You don't have to worry. If Emberwood attempts to send another letter to Carrick asking to resolve their issues, we'll make sure he never knows.

Welder had known a week before Seracedar's attack that Cindertrance was the target, and he'd done nothing to stop it. He'd sacrificed all those people just to get what he wanted. His first step toward revenge on Seracedar and Fauxhemia.

I didn't think Carrick would believe me if I sent him a letter telling him Welder was behind this, and there was a misunderstanding. I could try, but Welder's spies would probably stop my correspondence from getting through. And then they would tell Welder that I knew what he'd done. Could I ask Lina to use her tin-chai to specifically target Carrick's location? No, that wouldn't work. We didn't know where Carrick was within Cedar Palace, and one of the spies might hear the message instead.

For now, I had no choice but to continue the march to the palace. I had to stay focused on taking back the scepter. I knew Welder had taken it as an extra precaution. To make sure he had another way to control me once he revealed that he'd stolen the scepter. Maybe he thought he could reduce my morale by telling me I'd lost the Will of Heaven since it had been so easy for him to take it from me. Or maybe he thought he could eventually convince Seracedar that he had solely acquired the Will of Heaven and I had lost it, thereby asserting his authority further.

But I wasn't going to let him manipulate me into believing that. Welder hadn't learned at all from when he'd stolen the scepter from Cedar Palace and lost it on the Miyu Islands. No one could manipulate the Will of Heaven. It didn't matter how much I doubted myself or all of Welder's attempts to thwart Old Grandfather Heaven. Now I truly believed Old Grandfather Heaven wanted me to have the scepter, with or without Aiden, or he wouldn't have drawn me out here tonight, alerting me of Welder's schemes. Old Grandfather Heaven had given me another chance to accept my destiny.

You can protect yourself now. You're capable of standing on your own.

My brother's words echoed in my head. Yes, I had the power to protect myself and the ones I loved. I had the power to defeat Welder.

I touched the pendant around my neck with the Yao diamond. If I had a drop of Welder's blood, I could use his tin-chai. Transform the flute I had into a hair stick and substitute it for the real one in his possession. I needed a plan.

I raced back to camp, just in time to see that Welder had raised an alert, and everyone was coming out of their tents to report to him.

Welder was asking all the soldiers one by one where they had been, and he asked the guards who had been scouting the area if they had seen anything suspicious.

"Someone lit up those fireworks," Welder said. "No way our enemy would have lit up something so pretty and celebratory, so I'm guessing it was one of you. Since no one is talking, I'm setting a new rule. From now on, there is to be no alcohol in the camp. Anyone caught with a single shot will get ten lashings. Oren, Vin, you will be in charge of enforcing this rule."

The men saluted. "Yes, sir."

Welder turned around and saw me. He frowned. "Where have you been? I went to your tent. Ponch said you weren't to be bothered."

"I wasn't feeling well. My monthly bleeding started." I knew this lie would prevent him from asking further. Welder had questionable character, but he was a bit squeamish when it came to the bodily functions of women.

"Er, right." He cleared his throat. "I assume you heard the fireworks?"

"Yes, they were quite loud."

"Did you see anything suspicious?"

I shook my head. "I think you may be right that it was one of ours. I agree with your alcohol ban, and I'll enforce it as well."

"Very good then. Get some sleep with what's left of the night." He returned his attention to the troops.

I returned to my tent. One thought occupied my mind. How was I going to get the scepter back? The first step was getting Welder's blood. A hard task, but not impossible. If I could accidentally cut him, I could tend to his injury and steal his blood. It would require stealth.

It was too late to think. I reached under my pillow for the stash of letters that I'd been writing to Aiden. It had become a sort of therapy for me, to write everything I wished I could say to him.

However, this time I realized I was missing one. Worse, I realized the missing letter contained some of my suspicions of Welder. Fainting faela. I curled my fists. What if Welder had been snooping? What if he'd stolen them and knew I was onto him? I shouldn't have been so careless.

Ponch came into the tent. "Rilla, where have you been? We were so worried."

The other guardswomen walked in behind her. All of them had such concerned expressions, I felt bad for not telling them I'd gone after Welder.

"I have quite a story to tell you," I said. "But first, did Welder come into my tent?"

"Not that I'm aware of," she said. "The fireworks woke us up. We went outside to see what was going on, and when we realized you weren't here, everyone except me went to look for you. I stayed here, and Welder came by asking to see you. I covered for you and said you weren't feeling well. He went away after that to wake up the soldiers."

"So you're sure he didn't come inside and look around? I'm missing some important letters."

"If he did come snooping around, it wasn't tonight," she said.

The other women murmured echoes of agreement. They hadn't seen Welder come in either.

That gave me a little bit of relief. I knew I'd had all the letters yesterday. I read them back to myself every night. But if Welder hadn't stolen the letters, then who had? I could curse myself for not being more cautious, but now I had to stay on alert. Those letters in the wrong hands would cost me dearly.

CHAPTER 28

✦ ✦ ✦ ✦ ✦ ✦ ✦ ✦ ✦ ✦

The next morning, Galai woke me with a shout. "Rilla, come quickly. You'll never guess who's here."

I groaned and rubbed the sleep from my eyes. "Who is it?"

Miah pulled at my arm. "Sago, Wyle, Brix, and Mottle. You need to get up. Welder's arguing with Sago. She says she'll only speak to you, but Welder wants her to report to him. Ponch is trying to stop them from getting into a fight."

I lurched up and hurried after Miah and Galai. A crowd had gathered outside, forming a circle around Sago and Welder. They argued so loud that I could hear every word fifty feet away.

"I told you everything you have to say to Rilla should be said to me first," Welder roared. "I'm the commander of the Emberwood army."

"I don't take orders from you," Sago said.

Brix, Mottle, and Wyle stood behind Sago, looking ready to come to her defense. Not that Sago needed it. She was scolding Welder like he was a child.

"Trying to control everyone around you to make up for your own insecurities is simply pathetic," Sago said.

"Why, you Yao bitch," Welder growled. "I can order you to be killed right now."

"And risk the wrath of the Yao and Ailo nations?" Sago countered.

"You're still at war with Seracedar. Even though you're at an advantage, that could change if you make an enemy of two more nations." She sized him up. "Besides, I've heard about how you can steal tin-chai and Faux-blood magic, but you're no match for a Yao like me."

I finally reached them. "All right, that's enough. Why are you two causing a scene?"

"If your spies have information, I have a right to know," Welder said.

Brix stepped forward. "We only report to Queen Rilla. If she feels that what we have to report should be made known to you, I'm sure she'll tell you. Isn't that right, Rilla?" He sent me a look, begging me to help make peace.

"Yes, that's right," I said. "I'll talk to them first, Welder. Then I'll let you know what's going on."

"Fine." He walked away, and the soldiers in the crowd dispersed, still murmuring to each other.

"That man is horrid," Sago said. "He refused to send for you and ordered me around. I don't know how you put up with him."

"I don't have a choice," I said. "Like he said, he commands the army. He's too powerful with his magic, and he has spies everywhere. He has control of Oren's tin-chai and has used it to steal our tin-chai, then used our own powers against us. Let's go to my tent for privacy."

Back at my tent, I had my guardswomen keep watch at the door to make sure Welder and his men weren't snooping.

My guests took a seat in a circle around the table.

"We tried to find you in Emberwood, but the royal advisors refused to talk to us," Sago said. "Welder convinced them we were double agents working for Carrick in exchange for our kingdoms' independence. Thankfully, Counselor Trine found us and told us the situation."

"It took forever for us to track down your actual location," Mottle said. "That's why you haven't heard from us."

"Not to mention the trouble we had in Fauxhemia," Brix said. "But we finally have some answers you'll want to hear."

"You have no idea how long it took us to get an audience with Lymere and Esmeralda," Wyle said. "It's also why it took us so long to get back to you. They were definitely avoiding us."

Sago handed me a note. "This is from Prince Lymere. I can already tell you what it says. Prince Lymere still has no lead on what happened to Aiden and Sito. And no evidence that Welder hired Dribin Clox. Queen Esmeralda refuses to donate her blood, which means no antidote for Aiden's parents. She said Welder has spread malicious gossip about her, accusing her of being related to Clox. Of course, she's denied all rumors. But the damage is done. Many of her subjects don't trust her. Some believe if she hired Clox to poison Aiden's parents, she must also have had him poison King Lieka. Others are asking her to prove she's not related to Clox by testing her blood. They accuse her and her mother of poisoning Lieka themselves. Her detractors are trying to find evidence against her."

I sank back in the chair, my heart heavy. Still, I forced myself to read the letter. It confirmed everything Sago said. "Prince Lymere says he's sorry he can't do anything more for me. I thought he was worried about Welder's plan to one day go against Fauxhemia, but Lymere writes that Esmeralda refuses to do anything about it now. She's focused on restoring her reputation. If we continue to harass her about becoming Emberwood's ally or donating her blood, she'll no longer allow us to search for Aiden and Sito in Emberwood. He can't help us further without her consent."

"After everything you did to save Lymere and Zelda from Welder," Sago said. "They show no appreciation. Prince Lymere is a coward. It's his destiny to lead Fauxhemia, not Esmeralda's. I suppose Welder was right about one thing, though. Esmeralda cares about nothing else except herself and her reputation."

"At least there's good news in Yao Kingdom," Wyle said. "Seracedar has withdrawn their troops, and we've become independent again."

"Same in Ailo Kingdom," Mottle said. "We have our independence.

Seracedar is weakening. A sign that your efforts to take the villages are working."

"It's too bad Welder is in control of the army," Brix said. "Once the war is won, what's to stop him from taking you down, Rilla?"

"Well, he's asked me to marry him," I said. "His intent is to control my tin-chai. He's not really giving me a choice either."

"You can't possibly marry him," Sago said.

"Of course I'm not going to marry him," I said. "But I have to figure out a plan to take him down."

"At least you have the scepter," Mottle said. "He can't use it without you. Why don't you just use it on him? Aren't you supposed to have the ability to take away someone's tin-chai?"

These Ailo men certainly did not know how to comfort someone.

"Actually, I have bad news," I said. "Last night, I tried to take away his tin-chai, and it didn't work. I don't know what I did wrong. Also, right after that failed attempt, Welder stole the scepter from me. He gave me a fake. I'm going to get it back. I already have a plan. I need to get a drop of Welder's blood."

Sago's gaze traveled to the Yao diamond on my pendant. "You need to use his tin-chai?"

"Yes, he's disguised the scepter as a hair stick. I need to exchange it for an exact replica and then transform the real scepter into a pan flute, so Welder won't suspect."

"Wish we could help you," Brix said. "We have other news that might cheer you up. It's about Aiden and Sito."

I gasped. "You've found them?"

"I wish," Mottle said. "Maybe then they could take control back from Welder."

Hope was snuffed out instantly. A stabbing pain formed in my heart. "What news do you have then?"

"We tracked down one of the men who ambushed Aiden," Brix said.

"He played dead during the fight. Escaped when the coast was clear. What a coward."

Mottle looked proud. He flexed his hands, transforming them into rock. "I only had to threaten to break all his fingers before he squealed. He was hired to wear the uniform of a Fauxhemian royal guard and attack. So were a few others like him."

The Ailo men looked at me as though waiting to see my reaction.

"Well, what happened next?" I asked, feeling impatience flaring up.

"You'll never guess who hired him," Brix said. He paused for dramatic effect. "It was an Emberwood soldier who works for Welder. We got a description. Silver spiky hair. Now that kind of hair is unusual. It had to be the silver-haired man who was standing next to Welder today. He was with King Aiden during the ambush."

"Oren," I said. "That's no surprise."

"That's not all," Mottle said. "He said there were Fauxhemian guards who were part of the ambush. But they work for Welder, not Queen Esmeralda. He heard them when he was playing dead. They were talking to a bearded man who told them to keep spying on Esmeralda and to make sure Aiden and Sito were dead. The bearded man said he would make it worth their while. He heard them call the bearded man General."

I nodded. "I already figured out last night that Welder must have disguised himself as that messenger who came to us, telling Aiden to meet Queen Esmeralda for the antidote. I remember thinking his beard looked strange. All the Fauxhemian men, even the middle-aged ones, in Queen Esmeralda's court had been clean-shaven. And the messenger smelled of smoke. Welder smokes when he thinks no one is looking. I should have made the connections sooner. I also heard Welder talking to Oren. They staged the ambush on Aiden, and Sito must have gotten there in time to help Aiden. Oren wasn't successful in killing them. He asked Welder if he thought they were really dead. That means they might still be alive."

Sago gave me a pitying look. "I don't want you to have false hope. After all, if they were still alive, wouldn't they have made themselves known to you?"

Wyle frowned at her. "Mama, don't be such a pessimist." He patted my shoulder. "Don't give up hope. We're still looking for them. Just because they haven't shown up yet doesn't mean they're not alive. Maybe they have a reason."

"Better be a good reason then." Sago sniffed. "Leaving Rilla alone to fight this war and to deal with that unstable man child who blames the world for his own failures. If Aiden and Sito are alive, I'm going to give them a piece of my mind for not protecting you better."

"Thank you, Sago." I looked at the others. "And all of you."

"Well, I don't feel that helpful since you already figured out most of what we came to tell you," Brix said.

"But now I know what's going on with the Fauxhemians," I said. "And just having you here helps so much. I was beginning to feel so isolated dealing with Welder on my own."

"We'll continue the search and see what else we can learn about the Fauxhemians," Sago said. "But promise you'll take care of yourself while we're away."

Ponch came into the tent. She looked agitated. "Welder's asking if you're finished here. He wants to know what they're telling you."

Sago smirked. "Inform the general that if he wants to know, he'll have to fight me. No magic allowed from either of us. First person to draw blood wins."

Ponch blanched and looked between Sago and me. "A-are you serious?"

"Of course, I am," Sago said. "I never joke when I challenge someone to a duel. I hope he's not too scared."

"What are you doing?" I asked her. "You know he'd never refuse."

"Good," she said. "I'm determined to draw blood from him. After all, aren't you in need of some?"

Ah, that was her plan.

Ponch smiled now. "Then it'll be my pleasure to tell him of your challenge." She flounced back out of the tent. I could hear her and Welder exchanging words. Welder's voice roared up.

"Challenge me? Of course, I accept. When I'm through with her, she'll be in so much pain, she won't be able to transform for a month."

I flinched. "Sago, are you sure? I don't want you to get hurt."

Sago smiled. "Have you so little faith in me?"

We cleared away a space in the middle of the camp to act as the dueling arena. Ret ran on the perimeter of the fighting platform, drawing boundary lines in the sand. The Emberwood soldiers gathered on the outside of the lines, some of them whispering to one another. I heard them talking about Welder, so I stood behind them, trying to listen in on their conversation to see where their true loyalties lay.

"Do you think the Yao woman can really beat him?" one asked.

"I hope so. The general would be humiliated. Would prove he's nothing without his magic," another said.

"I'd definitely lose respect for him," a third said. "I don't understand how Beyling and Kang can trust him. If they could see what we see every day, they'd know Welder's up to no good. Too bad the queen can't take away his tin-chai. I wish Ashbel and Aiden were here. They'd never have let Welder gain so much power."

Their words crushed me. I was failing them.

"Quiet," the second man said, noticing me.

The men bowed. The soldier who had criticized me looked embarrassed. "We didn't see you there, Your Majesty."

"Don't let Welder hear you talking," I said. "I don't want him to hurt you."

Then I walked past them to where Sago and Welder faced each other in the center of the fighting platform. My guardswomen, the Ailo men, and Wyle gathered in Sago's corner, while Oren, Ret, Hu, Vay, and a few other men stood behind Welder.

"You can do this, General," Hu said.

Vay clapped. "Beat her to a pulp."

Oren and Ret said nothing, but they prepared water and a towel for Welder. Ever since Welder had punished them in front of us, they had been rather quiet. They were still devoted to Welder, but I wondered how much longer they would follow him. Especially if they weren't getting the revenge they wanted on me as Welder had promised them. I had to keep an eye on those two. If only I could convince them to let me help their family members.

Sago and Welder faced each other. Ponch acted as the referee, standing between them.

"Rules are simple," Ponch said. "There will be no Yao transformation, no Shyan tin-chai, and no weapons permitted as agreed by both fighters. If any of these rules are broken, the fighter will be disqualified and forfeit the match. Fighting is strictly limited to hands and feet. First person to draw blood wins. Fight begins in three . . . two . . . one."

Ponch moved out of the way.

Sago and Welder circled each other. Welder punched out. Sago blocked. She smirked. I knew that look. She had something up her sleeve.

In a sudden movement, she transformed into fox form and lashed out all of her nine tails at once. Two of them caught Welder on the back and shoulder before he reacted, dodging the rest. He hit the ground and rolled out of the way of another tail.

"You're disqualified," he shouted. He cursed, sitting up and touching a lash mark on his shoulder. His hand came away with blood.

"Yes, but I drew blood," Sago said, transforming back into her woman form. "You of all people would agree that rules can be broken in order to win a war."

Welder glared at her. "Doesn't matter. This wasn't war. You broke the rules, so you forfeit. I win."

Sago shrugged. "If it matters to you so much, I forfeit, and you win."

She walked away from the fighting arena and came to me. She whispered into my ear. "You're welcome."

Ponch remained in the arena. I'd given the Yao diamond to her. She was stealthy, and I trusted her to get a drop of blood without Welder's knowledge. She knelt by Welder. "Those look bad. It'll take days to heal. Maybe Rilla can do a fast fix-up." She called me. "Rilla, can you use your tin-chai on Welder?"

"Coming." I ran to the arena and came closer to Welder, pretending to inspect his wounds. "Yes, these look bad."

Ponch stood back, walking behind Welder. She gave me a subtle nod. She'd gotten his blood.

Welder made a sound of discomfort. "Well, don't just stand there looking at them. Sing."

I sang a short verse. The lash marks sealed up, and the blood disappeared. In seconds, Welder appeared healthier than he ever had before. If only I could sing him to death.

"I don't know what's wrong with your Yao friend," he said. "But I don't want her anywhere near me from this day on. If she ever attacks me again, I will kill her, no matter how close the two of you are."

"I'll be sure to warn her," I said. "You should return to your tent and change. Your clothes are torn through."

Welder saw his ruined shirt from where Sago's tails had torn them. He cursed, then stood and stormed away.

Ponch looked around to make sure no one was looking. Then she handed me back the Yao diamond and my pendant, which I quickly fastened around my neck. The blood glinted off the clear gem.

Sago approached us, with Wyle and the Ailo men behind her. "You didn't have to challenge him just to get his blood," I said. "Now he's mad at you. What if he tries to retaliate one day?"

Sago rolled her eyes. "As if I'd be afraid of that man. I can deal with him. I know you could have gotten the blood yourself, but this seemed a faster solution. I wish we could stay and help you get the scepter back, but we should return home. We need to warn the Yao and the Ailo of Welder's activities. We're going to do our best to get our people to agree to help you fight him."

"That we are," Mottle said.

"Thank you," I said. "All of you."

They turned to go, but Welder approached, some of his men in tow. "Not so fast. What makes you think you can leave? I should have you and the Ailo men imprisoned."

I stepped in front of my friends, but Sago pulled me back. She showed no fear and stood her ground. "Do you think that's really wise? I told you before, you can't afford more enemies, especially not those whose magic you can't control. Starting a fight with Yao and Ailo wouldn't benefit you. We're not your end goal."

"That's right," Wyle said. "You can't keep us here, or all the Yao clans will come looking for us."

"The Ailo, too," Mottle said. "Our nation will become the sore stuck so far up your ass, it'll be impossible to scratch."

Brix sent Welder a glare. "I echo my friend's words, though I'd choose to be less crude. That image is unpleasant."

Welder assessed them. My heart pounded, wondering if my friends' bravado would really work. But then he took a step back.

"Your nations are tiny bugs, not worth my time," he said. "Leave. But if I ever see you step foot within my army's camp again, I'll show no mercy."

He and his men turned back toward his tent.

"Go before he changes his mind," I said.

The Ailo men bowed. Wyle and Sago took turns hugging me, and I saw them off.

Wyle waved at me one last goodbye. "Best of luck. You've got this."

CHAPTER 29

✦ ✦ ✦ ✦ ✦ ✦ ✦ ✦ ✦ ✦

That night, my guardswomen and I planned our move. Jun and I would go to Welder's tent and search for the scepter while he slept. It was risky, but I couldn't think of another way. I knew he would keep it close to him. He'd never leave it alone somewhere.

"What do the rest of us do?" Galai asked.

"Wait here," I said. "In case one of the soldiers on duty comes by to check on us a second time."

Ever since the night of the fireworks, Welder had told Oren to have nightly inspections ensuring everyone followed the newly established curfew. Welder had someone come to look in on me and check that I was asleep. For safety reasons, he'd said, but I knew it was just an excuse to spy on my guardswomen and me. A way to make sure we knew he had power over us.

Ponch's ears perked up. "Curfew inspection incoming."

All of us took our positions in our beds. Oren opened the tent door and peeked inside. "All settled in?" He scanned the tent, mouthing a count. "Looks like everyone is accounted for. Good night."

We waited a few minutes before getting back out of bed. I ruffled up my bed covers, making a lump in the shape of a person. Then I took out the fake scepter from my cloak pocket. An ordinary flute.

Ponch cupped her hands around her ears and squinted in concentration. "I think Welder fell asleep. Yes, I definitely hear him snoring. Now's your chance."

Jun took my hand. Though I could still see her and me, I knew we were invisible when the other guardswomen's gazes looked around the room as though they'd lost sight of us.

"I just had a thought before you go," Ponch said. "If Rilla saw Welder put the scepter in his pocket, then chances are he's still keeping it on him. You might want to look there first. No need to search his things and mess up anything that might cause him to suspect."

"I think you might be right," I said.

"Great," Jun muttered. "Now we've got to touch him without waking him up. What a dream job. Are you sure we can't just slit his throat in his sleep?"

"He has too many loyalists who will know it's us," I said. "We'll be tried for treason, and Oren might try to gain power. That will only lead to a whole new set of problems, only we'll be rotting in prison. We need to prove Welder's guilt to the royal advisors and get justice for Aiden and Sito. So no, we can't kill Welder yet as tempting as it may be."

We left my tent and headed for Welder's. Most of the soldiers were asleep, but Oren and several others were sitting around the fire, snickering over some lewd conversation. They took turns drinking from a canister. I suspected it contained wine. If Welder knew about it, he probably didn't care.

Jun lifted the flap of Welder's tent, and we snuck in. Oren and his friends were too busy drinking to notice the door flap open and close. It took a moment for our eyes to adjust in the dark, but there was still enough light from the campfire filtering through the canvas to see around us.

Welder lay on his back in his cot, light snores emerging from his lips.

The song of the scepter played loud and clear. It was calling me again. Sure enough, the sound came from Welder's head. I saw a glint of metal under his pillow.

"There," I whispered to Jun and pointed. "Pillow."

We tiptoed closer to the cot. I slid two fingers under the pillow, grabbed the hair stick and tugged. Welder let out a moan. Jun and I froze. Welder rolled over to his side, giving us his back. The hair stick, no longer held by the weight of his head, slid out easily. I looked at it long and hard, trying to remember every detail. It was surprisingly simple. Made of plain wood with a flowery design. Nowhere near as elaborate as what the faela wore at Cedar Palace. The design wasn't perfect. The flowers weren't uniform in size or detail. Probably made by someone who didn't create hair sticks as a profession.

One thing that couldn't be missed were the letters carved on the back. Bree's name. I wondered if the princess had worn a hair stick like this. Had Welder made it for her? Maybe that's why he had chosen this form for the scepter. I almost felt sorry for him. It was obvious how much he'd loved her.

No, focus, I told myself. He may have loved her, but he was on the path of destroying everything and everyone around him because of his need for revenge.

I put the hair stick into my cloak pocket and took out the fake scepter. Then, feeling the Yao diamond in the pendant around my neck, I channeled my wyis into it. I pictured the image of the hair stick that Welder had. Recalling the details. Plain and simple wood, with Bree's name carved on the back. Uneven flowers. The flute in my hands changed, shortening and bending until it took the form of the hair stick.

With slow, even movements, I tucked it under Welder's pillow. He jerked up, waking with a start. I jumped back, bumping into Jun and stepping on her foot. She let out a yelp.

Welder was wide awake. "Who's there?"

He got out of bed and lit a candle. His gaze looked right at us. Jun and I stood still, not even daring to breathe.

Welder went back to his cot and felt under his pillow. He grabbed the hair stick and cradled it in his hands like it was a precious pet. "Still here. Guess it was a dream."

He tucked the hair stick into his nightshirt, then blew out the candle and got back into bed. Jun and I still didn't move. Finally, we heard a snore.

We backed away and left his tent. Then making sure the coast was clear, I brought out the hair stick. I pictured the image of the flute in my mind. Focused on it. The hair stick wobbled in my hands. It grew longer, shifting into a tube shape and forming several holes in its body until it became a flute. I tucked it back in my pocket. Then Jun and I went back to my tent, where the guardswomen were pacing.

Ponch was the first to look in our direction. "They're back. I hear them breathing."

Jun made us reappear. I waved the flute. "We got it."

Ponch's gaze darted to the door. "Get in bed. Oren's coming."

We all flew back into our cots. Just in time. Oren peered inside. We kept quiet, pretending to sleep. Moments later, he left.

"One day," Galai said. "I'm going to punch that boy's face in. Just wait."

"I'm with you, girl," Jun said.

One day soon, I hoped. But now that the scepter was back in my hands, I could finally sleep well. At least for tonight.

CHAPTER 30

✦ ✦ ✦ ✦ ✦ ✦ ✦ ✦ ✦ ✦

One week passed, and we came close to Senlin City, capital of Seracedar. Welder sent his spies into the city to scope out the situation. They returned within a day with their report.

"Carrick's in deep trouble," one of the spies said to Welder. "Most of the royal army has deserted him. They've all heard of how large our forces have grown during our campaign through the villages, and they also fear you and the queen. They believe you hold the Will of Heaven, not Carrick."

"Word is Lieutenant Kenbo and Colonel Laht are prepared to surrender to us the moment we step into the city," a second spy said. "They are fed up with Carrick and would rather surrender to a former friend than continue to work for a liar and coward."

"Ah, yes, Kenbo and Laht," Welder said. "Glad to know they wish to be friends again. Once they surrender, we should be able to claim victory, and this war will be over."

Welder looked around at his commanding officers and at me. "Even so, don't let your guard down. We march into the city at dawn. Be alert in case Carrick or his men are up to any tricks."

The next morning, our army entered the city. The royal army was waiting for us, with Lieutenant Kenbo and Colonel Laht standing in front, waving white flags of surrender. The moment they saw Welder, they all fell to the ground on their knees.

Welder laughed in triumph, a manic laugh that chilled me from the inside out. "Now we take down the palace. Seracedar is mine."

He stepped forward, meeting with Kenbo and Laht. In silence, I watched him negotiate terms of surrender, but I took no part in it. With the Seracedarean army on his side now, nothing was stopping him from dominating the Shyan people and taking his next step to conquering Fauxhemia.

What was I going to do? I had never felt so helpless.

The moment negotiations were through, Welder took Kenbo and Laht with him to stand in front of our army, now united with the Seracedarean army.

"Today is a day of victory," Welder said. "Not just for Emberwood, but for Seracedar, who for too long has suffered at the hands of a corrupt royal family. Our kingdoms are now one, and we will enter a new future of prosperity. But first, we must officially end the reign of an old era. Together, we march into Cedar Palace and take back our kingdom from Carrick."

Fifty Seracedarean soldiers and thirty Emberwood soldiers were chosen to storm the palace under Welder's command. Laht and Kenbo, along with Ret and Oren, would remain with the rest of the army outside, keeping order in the city and preventing anyone from going in or out of the palace.

"You and your guardswomen will come with me," Welder said.

With a single roar made up of a choir of voices, we marched into Cedar Palace. The Seracedarean soldiers showed no mercy. They were worse than the Emberwood soldiers. They tore the palace to pieces, burning rooms and overturning furniture. They threw expensive porcelain against the walls and destroyed everything in sight. In the Autumn Courtyard, they burned the trees until all the colors of red and gold turned black and ashen gray.

We entered the Dark Palace, where the forgotten faela lived. I shivered, remembering my time here with Lady Arlyn. Some of Terran's faela had remained here after his death, having nowhere else to go. They now fled their treehouses in fear, screaming as they tripped over their heels.

Welder barked at the soldiers. "You can destroy the palace, but don't hurt the women. Just gather them up. We'll figure out where they should go later. If any soldier disobeys me and lays a finger on one of them, I'll chop off that finger and any other unruly body part. Understood?"

The men answered in unison. "Yes, sir!"

One of the men came to report to Welder. "Carrick is not in the palace. We've checked everywhere."

"Not to worry." Welder sneered. "He can't hide now that his commanding officers have surrendered." Welder turned on his heels and gave the order to several men. "Laht and Kenbo already told me if he's not here, he'll likely be at Sagewood Cottage, but only they know the location. Report to them, and they'll lead you to Carrick."

I felt dread settle deep in my stomach. Welder was not going to let Carrick go easily. I had no doubt Welder would torture Carrick before eventually killing him. Terran was dead, so the only way Welder could extract his revenge was to take it all out on the next convenient man. Though Carrick had been less than a laudable man, he still didn't deserve to be punished for the crimes of his father. I had to think of some way to save his life, and I had to find a solution quickly.

Within the hour, the men returned with Laht, Kenbo, and more soldiers. They dragged Carrick from a horse. He was chained, bloodied, and bruised beyond recognition, yet Welder didn't think that was enough. He ordered the men to continue beating him. I heard a scream and looked up, realizing Radi was behind him. She too was bound, and at her scream, one of the men slapped her.

"Shut up, bitch!"

"Stop!" I cried, stepping in to block the man. His fist reared back, readying to hit me.

I refused to budge. I couldn't stand by silently anymore. "If you strike me, you defy Old Grandfather Heaven."

The man got a better glimpse of my face and backed away in recognition. "General Welder told me to put the woman in a novelty cage as punishment. She stabbed two of our soldiers."

"You'll do no such thing," I said.

"Rilla," Welder barked. "I told you not to be soft. That woman is a prisoner. She's loyal to Carrick. She'd kill us all if she could."

"Radi is my friend. She was a victim of Terran's rule. She was already a bauble once. She doesn't deserve this abuse. Don't put her in a cage again. Bree would agree with me, and you know it."

I held my breath but saw the flicker of sorrow in Welder's eyes when I mentioned Bree. "What do you propose for us to do with her then?"

"She can become my companion. Once we return to Linlang Palace, I'll need someone to help me dress and bring my meals."

"Fine," Welder growled. "Seeing as she was Terran's victim as Bree was, I'll show her mercy. However, if she tries to get in the way of anything I do, she's dead. I hold you completely responsible for her."

I nodded. "Of course."

Welder gestured to his men. "You can stop beating him for now. I don't want him dead yet. Take a rest. He's not going anywhere."

The men stopped, and Carrick keeled over, unconscious.

Welder turned to me. "I have other matters to attend to. Come find me as soon as you're done taking care of the woman. Hurry."

He walked off, away from us and Carrick.

I untied Radi and tried to pull her up, but she refused to move. Her eyes remained tearfully rooted to Carrick, who lay bloodied and unmoving on the ground.

I whispered to her. "We'll think of a plan to save him, but for now you have to come with me."

"You and I have nothing to talk about," she said, flashing me a stubborn glare. "We're enemies now. I don't wish to go with you."

"You have no choice." She was frustrating me. Didn't she know I was trying to save both their lives?

Her eyes welled with tears.

I sighed. "Look, I know it's hard, but you must come with me and leave Carrick for the moment."

"They'll kill him."

"No, not yet they won't," I said. He'd likely be tortured before being executed publicly, not that it would help to mention that to Radi. "If you try to stop Welder now, *you* will die, and that won't do Carrick any good."

She still refused to move and remained on the ground.

"Rilla," Ponch called. "General Welder sent me to hurry you along. He said I'm to take over tending to your friend. He wishes for your presence in Treehouse 8. Why that treehouse, I've no idea, but he said it holds significance to you."

Carrick's treehouse. Where I had spent many days by his side back when I was a trinket.

"What?" Radi's eyes flashed angrily. "You have no right to go there. That space is sacred to Carrick and me. I don't want your dirty breath in there."

Ponch growled at her. "How dare you speak to the queen that way?"

I silenced Ponch with a wave. "It's all right. Could you please take care of Radi? She is my friend and is to be treated as such."

"Yes, Your Highness," Ponch said, even while glaring at Radi.

"I mean it, Ponch," I said, and then I turned to go.

Walking along the path to Treehouse 8, I couldn't help but recall the memories of my time at Cedar Palace with Carrick. Back when I thought I was in love with him. I remembered when I'd visit his mother's novelty cage and hope to bump into him. I'd thought he was a good man. One who was capable of bringing about change in Seracedar.

So much had changed since then. Part of me hoped there was still good in him. That he might still change if given another chance. But there was no way Welder would let him go.

Outside Treehouse 8, I saw a crowd gathered, seated in front of the treehouse as though waiting for some announcement or show to begin. There had to be at least fifty people. Several soldiers were there as well as Crocuses and Lotuses who I assumed were from local monasteries. Androgies and serving trifles stood around the seated guests. And to my surprise, a soldier led my guardswomen to stand with the androgies and trifles. All of them were present except Ponch.

I walked over to them. "What's happening?"

Jun shrugged. "We were instructed to come. Welder is about to make an announcement."

A serving trifle came up to me and said, "General Welder wants you to come into the treehouse immediately."

What was Welder planning? I didn't have a good feeling about this.

I followed the trifle into the treehouse. Welder was with several serving trifles, all of whom were helping him dress in clean attire. His boots were shiny, and his black velvet robes might as well have belonged to an emperor. He was already asserting himself as the new ruler, taking over Carrick's chambers and using Carrick's things like they were his own.

He looked up at me, and in his expression, I was reminded of the way a master might gaze fondly at a pet godog.

"Rilla, good timing. We are about to make history, you and I."

"What are you talking about? What's going on out there?"

"You shall see." He looked in the mirror and a pleased grin broke out on his face. "Spectacular. Now I'm ready."

"What do you need me here for?"

Welder grabbed my arm. "We're going to make an appearance together."

"Wait, what appearance? Aren't you going to tell me what's going on?"

"No. Just play along, and all will be well."

He pulled me outside toward the crowd. Now there had to be a hundred spectators.

Two men cleared their throats and tested their voices, amplifying the sound.

"Testing, one, two, three."

"Are you sure the entire kingdom will hear?" Welder asked. "And Emberwood as well?"

"We've got a network of sound amplifiers in place from here all the way to Linlang Palace," one of the men said. "Everyone will hear your announcement, rest assured."

I nudged Welder. "What announcement are you making?"

"Stand next to me and smile. That's your only job."

The sound-amplifying men nodded to Welder. "Whenever you're ready, General."

Welder cleared his throat. An immediate hush overcame our audience.

"Emperor Carrick has fallen," Welder said. "Queen Rilla already rules over Emberwood, and everyone has seen proof that she holds the Sacred Cedar Scepter along with me. We have the Will of Heaven and right to rule over Seracedar. May our two kingdoms unite from this day forward."

The audience clapped.

"I have a second announcement," Welder continued. "Rilla has given her consent to be my bride. With our marriage, we will rule over our unified kingdom together."

My heart stopped. What? I hadn't expected him to make a public announcement yet.

"No, that's not—"

Welder gripped my arm. "You already said yes, and I won't let you back out now," he whispered through his stoic grin. "Look up to your left. My men are ready to kill your guardswomen if you cause a scene."

My gaze went to where three men lay hidden in the trees, their bows and arrows pointed at my unsuspecting guardswomen.

The crowd burst into applause.

"Smile, Rilla," he continued to whisper. "If you do anything to get out of this marriage, I'll make sure you lose everything. Now that I have Seracedar, I can burn Emberwood to the ground if I choose."

I simply stood there, frozen in place, my voice lost to applause and congratulations. And long after the crowd had dispersed and Welder had gone to be hailed by the troops, I remained in the same spot.

My guardswomen surrounded me.

A tear rolled down my cheek. "I couldn't say anything to contradict him. He had men who were about to shoot you."

"Damn that shithead," Jun said. "We should have been more aware."

They took turns hugging me. At least their comfort made me feel less alone.

"You don't have to go through with marrying him," Ponch said. "We'll find a way out before it comes to that. Let's be strong together."

She was right. We would find a way. I had to believe it.

Later that night, I went to visit Carrick. They'd placed him in a cage in the Summer Fields. The cage was not unlike those that had housed the baubles. To say he was in bad condition would have been an understatement. His entire back was covered in blistering lashes, and his face almost unrecognizable. It was battered and swollen, and even as a doctor, I cringed to see him. He'd been left half naked as humiliation, and the way his elbow jutted out awkwardly was evidence something was broken and hadn't been set.

But the proud Carrick did not utter one sound. He sat in as dignified a position as he could muster. When he saw me, he turned away. I dismissed the guards, asking them to give us privacy for five minutes.

Then I sighed and began to sing, trying to undo as much damage as possible without it being noticeable to Welder. I couldn't heal him completely, or I'd be in trouble, but I could at least be subtle about it and reverse the pain, like an anesthetic.

However, as soon as I began to sing, Carrick silenced me. "I don't need you or your pity. Go away."

I watched him, and though he tried to hide it, he was twitching from the pain. I sang anyway. Hummed low, just enough power escaping from my lips to numb the pain.

"I told you to go away!" he screamed at me.

"You still haven't changed at all," I said. "If you were any less selfish, you would ask me where your wife is."

"My wife," he scoffed. "I have no doubt she's safe since you're involved. You'd do anything to protect *her*, but you never cared about me. Neither did Aiden."

He was acting like a toddler.

I flashed him an annoyed glare. "You know that's not true."

"Isn't it? If either of you cared for me, you wouldn't have tried to poison me with that letter."

"That wasn't from us," I said. "You have to believe me."

"Why should I? I wanted to negotiate peace with you. I wrote Aiden a letter, and he ignored me."

"He never got that letter. Welder intercepted it. He made it seem like you hired a Fauxhemian assassin to poison Aiden's parents."

"I wish I had thought of that," Carrick said with a growl. His bitterness was written all over his face. "Aiden chose his family over me, and I hope they all die. In fact, I'm glad he went and got himself killed by the Fauxhemians."

"You don't really mean that," I said. "Welder manipulated everything. He used our circumstances and our emotions to make us misunderstand one another."

"I don't care anymore," he said. "Nothing matters. Welder's going to kill me, and no one can stop him."

"So you're just going to sit back and let him do what he wants," I said incredulously. "You aren't even going to try and fight back?"

"What's the point? I have nothing to live for."

I wanted to slap him. "Nothing to live for? What about Radi? What about your daughter? She has to be a year old by now, right? Cirisa needs her father."

He suddenly sat up, and I knew I'd struck a nerve. "Ciri. Does that bastard have my daughter?"

I honestly didn't know. I'd only brought up his daughter in the spur of the moment, but now I wondered where she was. "I haven't seen her. Was she with you and Radi when Welder's men came for you?"

"No," he said. "We sent her away with her nurse, but I don't know if they made it safely." He swore. "I will strike him down with lightning before he touches my child."

I'd never seen this side of him before. It gave me some hope that there was still something left in Carrick, a part of him that was capable of loving someone. "Carrick, I can help you find—"

"I don't need your help," he spat, proud as ever. "I'll kill Welder myself and escape."

"In your condition? Carrick, you have to stop being so stubborn."

"I told you, I don't need your help." He turned around again and ignored me.

"Well, you have my help whether you want it or not. Especially when that child is out there somewhere. I promise I will find her and keep her safe. And I'll figure out a way to stop Welder from killing you, see if I don't."

I walked away angrily and went to my tent to settle down for the night. Of course, I couldn't fall asleep. My mind raced, thinking of how I could help Carrick escape.

I fell in and out of sleep until sunlight streamed through the cracks of my tent.

A blaring alarm jolted me up.

Shouts came from the guards. "Carrick's escaped!"

I jumped out of bed and ran to the Summer Fields. Sure enough, the lock was broken, and Carrick's cage was empty.

"Where is his whore?" Welder shouted, and he seized Radi, who had been following behind me. "It was you, wasn't it?" He slapped her.

"Stop!" I shielded her. "It couldn't have been her. She was with Ponch and me all night."

Ponch nodded furiously. "I watched her the whole night. She never left our tent."

"Get her out then," Welder yelled. We retreated, watching him pound a fist against the empty cage.

Who had been able to free Carrick? He had been guarded so securely.

Outside the cage, I saw a piece of singed metal. I stopped in my tracks. The metal had been melted down into a lock pick. Someone with a fire tin-chai could have done that.

Aiden. He was the only one who would have cared to jeopardize his own life to save Carrick's, though Carrick was still an asshole.

Was Aiden alive? I didn't dare hope, but I couldn't help it. If he was alive, I needed to find him. And if I did find him alive, he had a lot of explaining to do.

CHAPTER 31

✦ ✦ ✦ ✦ ✦ ✦ ✦ ✦ ✦ ✦

The following week, Welder had several coaches brought to the palace from Emberwood. Now that we had won the war, he was determined to bring Emberwood technology to Seracedar, starting with faster transportation. He declared that we were to have a victory tour, so we drove a coach from Senlin City to the northern coast of Seracedar. Welder took a hundred men, both Seracedarean and Emberwood soldiers, and I took my guardswomen. Since we hadn't ventured to the northern cities yet, Welder had decided we should visit the people and show them the faces of their new rulers.

We spent the majority of the day parading through the main northern city of Hailong. In the afternoon, the city hosted a celebration for us on the shore. I could smell the ocean. This was my chance to speak to the Miyu again.

The Miyu traveled from coast to coast, and the sentinels mingled with the people on land. Maybe they had heard news of Aiden's whereabouts. Or at least had found something out about Daki or Dribin Clox as Aiden had asked them before. Anything they had would be helpful.

I waited for Welder to be busy with his men. Even after our victory, Welder never missed a session of training with his soldiers, both morning and night. When I was certain he was occupied with his training session, I had my guards keep an eye on him.

"If he misses me, tell him I've gone to bathe," I said.

I slipped away to the shore and blew the conch that Princess Amika and her mother had given me. Within the hour, Princess Amika and three of her royal sentinels appeared.

"Rilla, I've been so worried," Amika said. "It's been a long time since you contacted me, and I heard about everything that's been going on. Is it true that you agreed to marry Welder? You can't go through with it."

"I didn't want to agree. He's trying to force me into it. I have no choice at the moment but to go along with him. He's threatened to burn Emberwood to the ground, and he has so much powerful magic, not even my voice can win against him."

"What a horrible, manipulative man," Amika said. "But I'm so glad you didn't actually agree to marry him. You already have a fiancé whom you love."

"And who is presumed dead."

Amika averted her gaze for a moment. "Well, yes, but you can't marry someone you don't love."

There was a strange look on her face. Like she was debating something within herself. What was that all about?

"I hope I don't have to," I said. "But I'm not here to talk about that. I think Aiden is alive. He may have helped Carrick escape from Welder. If it's true, then I don't know why he hasn't revealed himself to me. That's why I called you. I was hoping you might have heard something from Aiden."

Amika turned back to me. "I'm sorry I can't give you the answers you're looking for about Aiden, but we did send our sentinels to search for Daki and for Dribin Clox, as Aiden asked us to do. I can tell you about them." Her eyes gleamed in the moonlight. "Daki is alive. He survived the attack that sank his ship and got stranded on the Miyu Islands, where my sentinels found him."

"Thank Old Grandfather Heaven," I said. "Where is he now?"

"On the search for Dribin Clox," she said.

"Clox?" I frowned. "Does he know about Aiden's parents? Did you tell him?"

Amika hesitated. "Y-yes. He knows and wants to help."

"Then why didn't he come find me?"

"All good questions, which will be answered in due time," she said. "But let's get back to who sank his ship. And why. Daki said he was sent by Carrick on a special mission to deliver a letter to Emberwood asking for a truce. Carrick was rethinking his decision to declare war. He had received a letter from King Ashbel, asking for peace. Carrick realized his kingdom was crumbling, and with his finances drained, he wanted help rebuilding Seracedar."

I gasped. "I found a letter that Welder was trying to burn. It was from Carrick, and from what I could make out from it, he was trying to ask for a truce. Was Welder behind the attack on Daki's ship?"

Amika nodded. "Daki's ship was bombed and hijacked. The attackers came aboard and stole the letter. Before killing all of Daki's men, the attackers made the mistake of revealing they worked for Welder. They left Daki for dead, but they didn't know he's half shatooth Yao. He was wounded, but he managed to transform and swim to shore."

"It all makes sense now," I said. "We could actually have avoided war. King Ashbel was right about that. It must be why Welder got him out of the way."

"That's not all," Amika said. "Some of my sentinels have been spying within Seracedar. After Daki's mission was intercepted, my sentinels heard that there was an assassination attempt on Carrick."

I nodded. "Poison in a letter thought to be from Aiden and me. That was Welder, too. Because of it, Carrick officially declared war on us. Welder set up all these misunderstandings. He used all of us as pawns in his game of revenge."

"One more thing, Rilla," Amika said. She looked hesitant. "Look,

I'm not at liberty to say much, but as your friend, I just can't keep you in the dark. Daki is in your hometown."

"Cascasea? Why?"

"He's looking for Dribin Clox. My sentinels have been working with him. We've been tracking Clox. He left Fauxhemia, and we followed him into Seracedar. But we lost him at the Port of Cascasea. We think he changed his appearance but may still be there. Daki went to investigate in person. I think you should go find Daki and talk to him. He is possibly staying at your house, and he might be able to tell you . . . uhm . . . something I can't."

"At my house? How would he know where my house is? And why are you being so cryptic?" I narrowed my gaze, giving her a suspicious look.

The princess looked apologetic. "Sorry I can't tell you more. Go find Daki. He can give you more answers. And if you need anything else from me, just call again."

She and her sentinels waved goodbye and swam away. What was Amika not at liberty to say? Why all the hemming and hawing?

I had to get back to my house and find Daki. I just needed to convince Welder to let me get away alone.

When I got back to the camp, I went to see Welder at his tent. He looked to be in a better mood as he sipped on a cup of tea and ate a bowl of congee.

"Ah, Rilla," he said. "Sit down and share a meal with me."

I did so, thinking it was better not to refuse and risk souring his mood. He poured me a cup of tea. "Thank you. Seems like you're in a good mood today."

"Well, we've captured Seracedar and secured our victory," he said. "Winning is a glorious feeling and deserves to be celebrated. Now we can finally take a short rest before we focus on our strategy to conquer Fauxhemia."

"You're right," I said. "We should enjoy some time to recuperate.

Which is why I wanted to ask you if I could take a week away from camp. There's a place I need to visit. I'd like to borrow a coach as well."

"Ah, I see." His expression was unreadable. He paused a moment before replying. "May I ask where you are going?"

"My parents' gravesites. It's the anniversary of their death."

It was the truth. I hoped playing the sympathy card would make him more amenable. I couldn't avoid telling him my destination since I needed a coach to get there. I just hoped he wouldn't force me to take one of his men. I had to play this right.

He set his mouth in a thin, grim line. "All the way back to Cascasea? What's to stop you from running away? I know you still have reservations about marrying me, but I thought you were smart enough to know refusal isn't an option."

I knew it wouldn't be easy to convince him. He trusted me as much as I trusted him.

I pulled the scepter out of my cloak and handed it to him. "If you need a guarantee, you can have the scepter back until I return."

My heart pounded. I depended on him not taking it. After all, he didn't know that I had stolen back the real one from him. But what if he took it anyway? This was a bad idea. I shouldn't have been so impulsive.

He looked at it for a moment, then shook his head. "No need. I'll let you go, but not by yourself. I'll have some men accompany you."

"I get to choose who comes with me," I said. There was no way I could have them following me to find Daki.

He folded his hands across his chest and set his mouth in a thin, unsmiling line. "Planning a rebellion?"

"I just want some privacy as I visit my parents' gravesite. If you don't trust me, I'll have most of my guardswomen remain with you. You know I'd never abandon my friends. I would never desert Emberwood or Seracedar either. I take my responsibilities seriously, and I gave my promise to Aiden that I would protect his people. You have my word on Aiden's grave that I'll come back and marry you."

He sighed. "Fine. If you're not back by sunset on the seventh day, I'll send someone for you. If you try to run, I will find you, and you'll never know freedom again."

At dawn the following day, I prepared to leave. I had chosen Galai and Miah to accompany me on the journey. Galai was familiar with Cascasea Village and the culture there, which could be useful if we needed to find Dribin Clox among the villagers. And I knew Galai wasn't going anywhere without Miah. The two were inseparable.

I hated using my other guardswomen as a bartering chip, but it was the only way Welder would let me leave.

"Don't worry about us," Jun said. "He knows better than to mess with us."

"That's right," Ponch said. "We can take care of ourselves."

"I need you to listen in on whatever Welder's saying," I told Ponch. "And the rest of you, keep each other safe and make sure Welder doesn't send anyone to spy on me. I'll be back in one week."

The women waved goodbye. "You can depend on us, Rilla."

I drove the coach, maintaining a slow speed for safety. The roads in Seracedar were meant for horses, not coaches, so they weren't as wide as the roads in Emberwood. But taking a coach was certainly better than riding horses to Cascasea Village. We'd be there by tomorrow evening.

Galai turned to me. "What is it you're really up to? I highly doubt you just want to spend two weeks sweeping your parents' graves."

"We're going to find Daki, my friend who helped me during my journey to Emberwood."

Galai's eyes widened. "I've heard of the name, Daki. Wasn't he Carrick's naval commander? I thought he died."

"I talked to the Miyu princess, Amika. She confirmed that he's alive, and he might be staying at my childhood house. He's searching for

Dribin Clox, who was seen at the Port of Cascasea. Princess Amika was being cryptic, but she told me to find Daki for more answers. It could have something to do with Aiden. I think he's still alive and suspect he was the one who rescued Carrick. I sensed Princess Amika knew more than she was telling me."

Galai and Miah were quiet for a moment, seeming to take that in.

"I don't want to get my hopes up," I said. "I just need to find Daki and see if he can clear up my questions. I need something to use against Welder, something that might spark an idea of how to defeat him. I need more evidence to convince the royal council of his crimes."

"I wish we could just kill him," Miah said. "Rip out his organs and be done with it."

I turned to her in surprise. She was usually so quiet and rarely spoke aloud any violent thoughts.

"I do, too," Galai said. "I don't understand why the advisors choose to believe him over you. How can they believe his lies and call you overly sensitive?"

I sighed. "Unfortunately, it's the sad reality of our culture. The Emberwood royal advisors are of King Ashbel's generation, and they never had a female ruler. Same with Seracedar. Of course, they'd naturally prefer to follow Welder over me. They probably choose not to see how dangerous he is simply because he's a man."

"It's not fair," Miah said. "It's not like that in Ailo or Fauxhemia. In Ailo, many of the leaders are women. And Queen Esmeralda rules Fauxhemia."

"Maybe one day the new Shyan generation will change their mindset from their elders," I said. "But it won't happen overnight. And it certainly won't happen without proof that Welder is a dishonorable man. That's why we need to find Daki. He can testify that Welder manipulated this war from the start by attacking Daki's ship when he tried to deliver a request for a truce from Carrick. It'll prove Welder plans on taking over the Shyan kingdoms for his own gain. If we can make the people and the royal advisors see that his intentions are dishonorable, they may stop looking to him as a leader."

We carried easy conversation for the rest of the day and spent the night at an inn near Tinsai Village. Early the next morning, we drove off again. The drive was scenic and easy, but many villagers stared at our coach, probably because they'd never seen one in their lives.

By early evening, we reached the edge of Cascasea. I parked the coach near the harbor, and we walked the rest of the way to my house, taking the path across the cliffs. The sun was beginning to set, and the sky was an array of pastel purples and pinks.

Then I finally saw my house from a distance. The lights were on inside. Someone was living there.

Galai paused. "Are you sure this is safe? How do we know this isn't some kind of trap?"

"What if it's not Daki?" Miah asked. "What if it's a vagrant or pirates?"

"I can only trust what Princess Amika told me," I said. "Just be cautious. Put up your defenses."

With silent footsteps, we made our way to the front gate. A few weeks ago, dead leaves had covered the front porch and cobwebs had draped the pickets in the gate. Now most of it was gone. Someone had swept up.

Miah shifted, her skin taking on its rocky shell. Galai held her knife in front of her. And I unsheathed my sword.

Footsteps approached. Someone had already heard us. The front gate swung open.

I lifted my sword, but a man spoke, stopping me from swinging.

"It would be rather ironic if you killed me before I got the chance to tell you I'm not dead."

From the flickering shadows of dusk, Aiden emerged, looking healthy and well.

CHAPTER 32

✦ ✦ ✦ ✦ ✦ ✦ ✦ ✦ ✦ ✦

I dropped my sword and leapt into Aiden's arms. He brought me close to him, and I cried into his chest. "You idiot. How could you have disappeared?" I touched his face. "You're not a ghost, are you?"

"I'm sorry." He hugged me tighter. "And no, not a ghost yet."

I wouldn't have let him go if I hadn't heard another familiar man's voice. "Tell them to hurry up and get inside. We don't want anyone to accidentally see us."

I started in Aiden's arms. "Daki. Princess Amika said you'd be here."

"I'm here, too," Sito's voice piped in.

I peeked past the gate and saw both Daki and Sito standing in the open quadrangle.

"Daki's right," Aiden said. "We should all go inside first." He made sure no one else was outside before he shut the gate behind us. "You're sure you weren't followed, right? If we have to move to another hideout, we should do it now."

"I haven't seen anyone following us," I said. "I've been checking, and I also told my team of guardswomen to make sure Welder didn't send someone after me. I trust them to do their job."

Miah gaped at Sito as though she couldn't believe he was real. Galai's jaw fell open as well.

Sito gestured to us. "Come to the kitchen. I'll put on a pot of tea."

We headed to the kitchen. It was strange to see these men here, not only because they had been declared missing and possibly dead but because they were at my childhood home. They had never been here when I lived here.

I looked at Aiden. "Why are you at my house? How did you know this *was* my house?"

"I came here before, remember?" he said. "To take Rell, Nia, and the baby to Fauxhemia."

Oh, yes. How could I have forgotten? He had saved my family when the palace had threatened to kill them if I were disobedient.

"Anyway, we needed a place to stay during our search for Clox," Aiden said. "This was the best shelter I could think of. I didn't think you'd mind. I wasn't expecting you to come."

"I can't believe you're all still alive," I said. "I had hoped you were, but I had no signs. No evidence. Why didn't any of you try to contact me?"

"I did," Aiden said. "Think about it, and you'll know the number of times I tried to tell you I was alive."

I thought back and remembered. "The night I was back at Linlang Castle and woke up with the fire on and blankets over me. That was you?"

He nodded.

"And the fireworks that went off, saving me from Welder's discovery when I saw him at the beach."

Again, he nodded. "That night, I also went into your tent to see if you had left me any clues of what Welder was up to. I came away with these." He held up my missing letters. "They were addressed to me, so I took them."

"That was you? Thank Old Grandfather Heaven. I thought Welder had them."

I heard a clatter of chains at the back of the house followed by a colorful string of curse words. "That's Carrick, isn't it? You rescued him."

"Yes," he said.

"I knew it. That's when I finally suspected you were still alive." I suddenly felt anger rising inside of me. Tears began to build. I felt heat rising into my eyes. "I don't understand why you didn't reveal yourselves to me sooner. Why didn't you give me solid proof you were alive? For months, we've been fighting this war. I've been forced to do Welder's bidding, so he won't turn on me or kill my friends. He even has spies who told him my family's address in Fauxhemia. How could you just abandon us to deal with all this on our own?"

"I agree," Galai said, her annoyance apparent as well. "You have a lot of explaining to do. We've been putting up with Welder's bullshit, believing it was our only option, and meanwhile you three are sitting in here drinking tea. Why didn't you come to our assistance?"

Miah placed a hand on Galai's shoulder. "I'm sure they had a good reason. Let's hear them out."

"Believe me," Aiden said softly. "I wanted to show up and kill that treacherous bastard, but I had to collect all the evidence, figure out all the traitors, and really understand how Welder's powers work."

I took a sip of tea and let the hot liquid coat my dry throat. It was comforting despite all the conflicting feelings raging inside of me. I set the cup on the table. "I know Welder was pretending to be the messenger who tricked you into thinking Queen Esmeralda wanted to talk. He intercepted a note from Carrick asking for a truce. Welder was also the one who hired Dribin Clox to poison your parents, and he sent a letter to Carrick with poison, pretending it was from us. That was why Carrick attacked Cindertrance."

"I found all of that out after the ambush." Aiden grabbed my hand and kept it cradled in both of his. I was still a little flabbergasted by his sudden reappearance. After so many months of not knowing where he was, I felt like this had to be some sort of dream. But the strength with which he grasped my hand, and the calluses that had built on his fingers, told me this was real.

"What happened that day?" I asked.

"We were attacked by a group of mercenaries," Aiden said. "Spince tried to defend me, but Oren was in on it. Oren fought with Spince, and I had to fight off the mercenaries. Then Oren killed Spince and came for me. He stole my tin-chai. I was so surprised when he threw my fire back at me that he almost got me. But Sito pushed me out of the way. We ran."

"Oren came after us," Sito continued. "He kept throwing fire at us. I used my tin-chai, trying to persuade him into calming down. It worked, and he stopped."

"It worked?" I repeated. "Oren didn't steal your tin-chai?"

"No," Sito said. "Aiden and I think Oren can only steal tin-chai used for attacking. He couldn't steal a defensive tin-chai like mine."

"That's what Welder meant," I said. "He said Oren was born to hold the offense, not the defense. That's why he can't steal my healing tin-chai. Anyway, go on with the story."

"Oren stopped attacking us, and I got my fire tin-chai back," Aiden said. "But the messenger jumped down from the trees. He stole it this time. Before Sito could react, the messenger cut him and swiped at his blood. Before I knew it, the messenger had convinced me to stop fighting. It was like I was frozen."

"My tin-chai wasn't effective on the messenger like it was on Oren," Sito said. "I grabbed Aiden. But there was no place to run. We had our backs to a cliff. The messenger threw another fire bomb at us, and this time, I slipped back, pulling Aiden with me. Only by the grace of Old Grandfather Heaven, it wasn't as far as it looked. We skidded down the cliffside and landed on a small ledge. The messenger and Oren started talking, wondering if we were dead, but they couldn't see us. That's when I recognized Welder's voice and realized he was the messenger. It was only later when I remembered he was half-Shyan, half-Fauxhemian, and he must have Faux-blood magic helping him to absorb tin-chai."

"We spent two days hiding from his men," Aiden continued. "I knew Welder would be looking for us. As long as he didn't find our bodies, he would suspect we were still alive. But if we stayed away for longer, he might give up and actually believe we were dead. We already knew Oren was working for Welder, but there had to be more. I also recognized some of my attackers as Fauxhemian guards. They had been in Queen Esmeralda's court the day we visited, and I realized Welder had Fauxhemians working for him, too."

"We returned to Queen Esmeralda," Sito said. "Prince Lymere told us that Welder had tried to kill him and Zelda, but you and your guards saved them. They agreed to work with us, flush out all the traitors in their midst as well. Esmeralda promised to become Emberwood's ally against Welder and prioritize making an antidote for Aunt Leonora and Uncle Ashbel if we could find Dribin Clox."

"Why?" I asked. "She could become our ally and donate her own blood. We don't need Clox."

"She and Lymere are in love and wish to have a true marriage one day, blessed by San, after King Lieka is gone," Sito said. "The Fauxhemians might be open-minded about their relationship, but not if Esmeralda is proven to have lied about her association with Clox and involvement in King Lieka's poisoning. The rumors that she's related to Clox have caused her people to distrust her. They demand that she give her blood to be tested and want proof that she isn't related to Clox. She keeps denying it and refuses to give her blood, but the scandal has added fuel to the fire. If she's ever found guilty of being involved in Lieka's poisoning, neither the public nor the Fauxhemian priestesses would ever give their approval for Lymere to marry her. And once Lymere becomes king, he'll be pressured to take another bride while sentencing Esmeralda to live the rest of her days in a convent under a vow of celibacy as penance to San."

"But she *is* related to Clox," I said. "How will finding him help her?"

"Once we find Clox, we also have to get a confession from him," Aiden said. "Force him to admit that Welder hired him, and Esmeralda had nothing to do with it. Have him admit in a public address to Fauxhemia that he poisoned King Lieka and also say he's not related to the queen."

I scowled. "You mean she wants him to lie?"

"She'll make it worth his while," Sito said. "She'll pay him a fortune if he confesses and then disappears. She'll help him escape from the authorities."

"She said it was best if you had no knowledge of our plan, so you wouldn't have to lie to Welder," Aiden said. "She promised if our plan worked, she would give me a vial of either Clox's blood, if we catch him, or her blood to work on an antidote for my parents as long as we remain discreet. She also promised to help us fight Welder."

"No wonder I heard nothing from Prince Lymere and Zelda after their rescue," I said. "They promised to keep me updated, but when I sent Sago and Wyle to follow up, Prince Lymere said he couldn't do anything further to help me. I thought they had reneged on their promise. But how did you meet up with Daki again?"

"I had heard rumors circulating earlier that Fauxhemia and Seracedar were teaming up to destroy Emberwood," Daki said, "but I knew it wasn't true. Carrick was too busy sulking in his room to plot anything. After I was attacked and realized Welder was behind it, I suspected he had started those rumors, and once he used Emberwood to conquer Seracedar, then he would target Fauxhemia next. I wanted to warn Queen Esmeralda, so I went to Fauxhemia and asked to see her. But Aiden and Sito had already beaten me to it, and they filled me in on the plan."

"So all of you were in on this plan except me." A quiet rage filled me. I'd believed they were all dead. That I was alone. I'd carried the burden of pretending to submit to Welder. And meanwhile, they'd been together, talking out a plan without me.

"You have to understand, Queen Esmeralda made me promise to not reveal myself to you," Aiden said.

"In exchange for the chance to save your parents. Yes, I understand."

"And in exchange for a Fauxhemian alliance. But that wasn't the only reason. Welder is a complex character. He has been plotting his revenge from the moment Princess Bree died. He planted men who are loyal to him in Seracedar, Fauxhemia, and Emberwood. I needed to figure out what he was planning and the extent of his power."

"You're the king of Emberwood. The soldiers and the advisors only listen to him because they're scared. But if you had come back to lead them, if you had told everyone that Welder was a traitor, then I believe they would have had the courage to fight back. He would have been arrested, and he wouldn't have been able to grow his army with all the Seracedarean soldiers."

Aiden sighed. "Do you really think if I had accused him of being a traitor, he wouldn't have found a way to escape, regroup, and try some other tactic? He's got loyal men like Oren on his side, powerful tin-chai at his disposal. I didn't even know if he already had full control of the Emberwood army. If there were turncoats. I had to keep my distance, make him think I had died, so he would set his plan in full motion. It's the only way to catch him. Now I know the men who betrayed Emberwood."

"Maybe the rest of us should leave the room," Galai said. "The king has a lot of apologizing to do to his future wife. Rilla, don't let him off easy." She huffed and gathered everyone out of the kitchen into the other room.

"I kept an eye on you from a distance," Aiden said. "I couldn't stand not seeing you and knowing how devastated you must have been. It was torture."

"Then why didn't you just reveal yourself?" I asked. "I could have kept it a secret from Welder."

"You don't know how many times I wanted to. How many times I almost did. Besides, I thought it would be easier for you. The less you knew, the less you would have to hide from Welder."

Even though Aiden believed in his reasons, I still was hurt that he hadn't considered including me in his plan. "We're supposed to be partners. We have the Will of Heaven together."

"I know. And you did the hardest part. You made Welder reveal his true intentions. That he wants to take over the kingdom. And you made him reveal his weakness. Even though he can steal tin-chai and Faux-blood magic, he still fears the scepter. He fears you. Because you have the ability to take away tin-chai. Isn't that why he tried to steal the scepter from you?"

I looked at Aiden in surprise. "You know about that?"

"I also know you stole it back from him. I told you I've been watching you from afar."

"I haven't figured out how to do it, though," I said. "I overheard Welder talking to Oren. He seems to think you have a role in helping me unlock that power."

Aiden frowned. "Maybe, though I'm not sure how. It's through your amplified tin-chai that Old Grandfather Heaven would allow you to take away someone's tin-chai. Let me think about it more. There must be something Welder sees that we can't."

"I also overheard Oren say that he and Ret have siblings who are hurt because of us," I said. "Welder promised them that he would steal my blood and use my tin-chai to heal them. That's why they're loyal to him, and they hate us. But Welder hasn't followed through yet. I wonder if I can talk to Oren and Ret. Tell them that I can help them if they stop obeying Welder."

"No," Aiden said quickly. "We can't take the chance of letting them know you eavesdropped. As you said, they hate us. Welder's managed to manipulate them, and simply talking to them won't make them switch loyalties. Once we defeat Welder, then maybe we can help them."

I nodded. Aiden was right.

"I heard he has plans to marry you," Aiden said. "That's another reason I know he's scared of you. He wants to keep you by his side to control your tin-chai."

I crossed my arms and glared at Aiden. "I can't continue being his puppet. How long do you expect me to continue this farce? Are you simply going to let him force me into marriage before you finally reveal yourself?"

Aiden shook his head and took my hands into his. "Of course not. I just need a little more time. As soon as we find Dribin Clox and get a confession, we can exonerate Queen Esmeralda. We'll have a chance to save my parents and gain Fauxhemia as an ally. Then we'll have enough power to take down Welder."

"How much longer?"

"Soon. I promise. We have a lead to finding Dribin Clox. Word is he's been spotted among the vendors at the port. I just don't know which vendor. The people here are tight-lipped with those from out of town, and I don't want to tip Clox off if someone tells him we've been asking questions."

"What if Clox escapes again? We don't have any more time to waste. If you come back now, the Emberwood army will return under your control. And we still have the scepter. We don't need Fauxhemia to fight Welder. This is our responsibility, not theirs."

Aiden gave me an uncomfortable look. "Maybe, but I'm not sure we're enough on our own. It would be a safer bet with Fauxhemia on our side. I—"

The sound of glass shattering had us out of our seats and heading towards the back of the house. The others joined us from the living room.

Glass lay scattered around the floor of the back room. The window had been broken.

"Shit." Aiden looked out the window. "Carrick's getting away."

CHAPTER 33

✦ ✦ ✦ ✦ ✦ ✦ ✦ ✦ ✦ ✦

Daki leapt out the window. Aiden and Sito ran outside, and I went after them. From the exit on the other side of the house, Galai and Miah cut him off. Miah, in rock form, tackled Carrick to the ground.

Carrick struggled to get up, but he was already weak from his previous injuries. Miah easily pinned him down.

"Let me go!" he shouted. "I need to go."

"Go where?" Daki growled at him. "You can't go anywhere like this."

Carrick breathed hard, quickly fading in his struggle. "You don't understand."

"I understand enough to know that you need to shut up and rest," Aiden said. "You've been beaten to the point of death. If you go anywhere now, you'll die."

"I can still heal you if you'll let me," I said.

Carrick gave me a stubborn glare. "Don't you dare. I don't need your help."

I stepped back, washing my hands of him. If he didn't want my help, I wouldn't force it on him.

"Since you refuse Rilla's way of healing and want to stay in this sad state, you'll have to heal the natural way," Aiden said. "So stop fighting us."

"But my daughter—"

"We'll help you find her," I said. "But for now, you need to calm down."

Carrick said nothing more. He didn't look at Aiden or me, but he allowed Daki to take him back to the house. There was a mixture of emotions on his face. Anger, humiliation, fear, panic. But mostly I saw pride. Though Aiden had saved him from Welder, he refused to show any gratitude.

We walked back into the house, where Sito and Daki tended to Carrick. Galai and Miah busied themselves by keeping watch outside. Aiden and I slipped into my childhood bedroom. We sat on the side of the bed in silence.

Aiden knew what I was thinking and looked at me sadly. "There's still hope for him. I believe it."

"He can't be saved," I said. "He doesn't want to be saved."

"He can, and he will. I have to believe the friend I once knew and loved is still in there somewhere."

How I wished that were true. Aiden's refusal to give up on people was both his fault and his strength.

"Do you believe Welder can be saved, too?" I asked.

"I don't know, but I hope so," he said. "Love and revenge make people do crazy things. But maybe there's a way to make Welder see that he's wasting his life, and Bree wouldn't want this for him."

I embraced him. "I love you. But your optimism makes me fear for your life."

"I know." His gaze burned into mine. I turned my face towards his, and our lips met. It felt so good to finally touch him again. I sensed his longing, which fueled my own desire. Our kiss lengthened into unadulterated passion.

And then he broke it off, making me groan. I tried to reach for him again, but he stopped me.

"However, if there's one thing that could put someone beyond redemption, it's hurting you. If Welder ever tries to put his hands on you, I *will* kill him." He looked at me closely. "Has he?"

I understood what he meant and shook my head quickly. "I would kill him if he tried. I can protect myself. But he does seem determined to marry me. You are going to come back from the dead before he tries to force me to go through with it, right?"

"I promise," Aiden said. "I'd never let you become a bigamist. It may be the popular thing to do in Seracedar, but in Emberwood, you should know polygamy is against the law."

"Technically it wouldn't be bigamy since we're still not officially married," I said.

Aiden scowled. "I'll kill him before I let him take you as his wife."

"I'm glad to hear that," I said. "But in all seriousness, you know you're the only one for me. I'll kill him if you don't get to it first."

I brushed my lips against Aiden's. He kissed me back and held me. "It was torture not being able to be by your side. There were so many times when I wanted to go to you. I don't want to be apart ever again."

"I don't either, but we'll have to. I have less than two weeks before I need to return."

"I don't want you to go back." His fists clenched. "I wish this were all over. I want to keep you all to myself. Just the two of us."

"We're alone now."

He rose to shut and lock the door. "We'd better make the most of our time then."

I dodged him as he reached for me. "We can't do *that*. Not here. People are out there."

"And they'll stay out there when they realize the door's locked."

But as he started kissing me again, I couldn't resist.

"I missed you," I whispered, treasuring the warmth of his body.

"I love you," he said back, and we tumbled together onto the bed, where we stayed until morning.

The following afternoon was the anniversary of my parents' passing. Aiden and I paid our respects to them. As my parents' ashes had been scattered in the sea, their monuments were on the beach. The waves crashed against the white cliffs as we hiked up the hill behind the house. Sandpipers glided just above the surface of the sea, their bodies barely touching the horizon. It was a warm day, but there was still a chill from the breeze, and I shivered, covering myself more fully with my navy-blue cloak.

Aiden followed me closely. "Are you all right?"

I nodded. I was just in a somber mood, as I always used to be when visiting my parents. Their graves were marked by white sandstone, two rectangular blocks half buried in the sand. I swept away the debris and washed the stone until it sparkled.

It was a sad thought to realize that once Rell and I were no longer in this world, no one would remember their existence.

"I hate that only people who make their way into the history books are remembered," I said. "Especially the villains. Normal hard-working and peace-loving folks are simply forgotten like it never mattered that they existed at all."

"That's not true," Aiden said. "What someone did with the short time they had on this earth matters if they chose to be kind. It matters so much more than spending a long life trying to seize power, fortune, and fame. Your parents' legacy is you and your brother. They raised their children to become kindhearted, selfless people."

My eyes watered helplessly. "You always know exactly what to say."

"Of course, I do." He grinned. "One of the many reasons you love me."

We knelt on the sand in silence, and I looked upon the white stone markers. "Mama, Baba. I'm sorry I haven't been able to visit for so long. I'm sure Rell is sorry, too, so I'll apologize on his behalf. Life has been full of unexpected events. It's been an experience of both tragedy and joy these past few years. I'm still trying to figure some things out, but you taught me to have faith if I just keep doing the next right thing."

I turned to look at Aiden. "I want to introduce you to the most important person in my world. My future husband, Aiden. You would love him."

"I can vouch for that, sir and ma'am," Aiden interrupted, then motioned for me to carry on.

I rolled my eyes. "He's very arrogant, but I love him because he has a kind heart, and that's the most important quality I value in a person."

Here, Aiden took over. "Mr. and Mrs. Marseas, I want you to know that I love your daughter, and I will take care of her for our entire lives. That is a promise I made in my heart since our days as friends at Cedar Palace. But now, I'm making this promise to you."

I looked at him, feeling so much love I could burst. He was everything that was warm and bright in my life. A beacon in a dark, unkind world.

How glad I was that I'd finally found him again, that he hadn't really died. Tears gathered in my eyes.

He turned and brought me into his chest. "Don't cry, or your parents will think I'm bullying you."

"You are a big bully," I replied with a sniffle. "You left me on my own for so long."

His smile faded, all joking aside. "I know. I'm sorry. But you were strong on your own. You did well."

"That's not the point," I said. "I know I could live without you and survive well enough, but I just prefer not to. So don't you ever go and die again."

"Eventually, we'll all have to die, but I can promise you I'll try very hard not to die until we're at least old enough to lose all our teeth."

We slowly headed back to the house, treasuring the precious little time we had together before I had to return to Welder.

Halfway back, Daki came running out to meet us. He looked distraught.

"Carrick has escaped. Went about to do his business and pulled a fast one on us."

Aiden flashed a worried look at me. "In his condition? He'll never last. Where will he go?"

"Your guess is as good as mine," Daki said. "I swear we've searched everywhere. He may be hurt, but he moves fast."

"He's got the motivation of a desperate man," I said. "He went to find his daughter. He thinks Welder has her."

Aiden swore. "That fool. If he's gone back to Welder, we'll all be found out."

"No, I don't think he'll go find Welder yet," I said. "He knows he doesn't have the capability to defeat Welder on his own and in his current condition. He'll go into hiding until he can find time to heal, locate Cirisa, and formulate a plan."

Aiden shook his head. He looked like he wanted to throw something. "We could have helped him. Why would he leave?"

"Because he's prouder and more stubborn than anyone," I said. "He doesn't want to admit that he needs help, especially not from us. We'll have to let him go on his own for now."

"Does Welder really have Princess Cirisa?" Daki asked me. "I thought the nurse took the princess and fled."

"Welder would never stop pursuing until he finds them," I said. "Princess Cirisa is a valuable hostage."

"If he does have the princess, he won't harm her," Aiden said. "Welder will use her as leverage to get to Carrick. And to Radi." He looked at me with a grave expression. "You can't entirely trust Radi right now. She has only two priorities, Carrick and Cirisa, and she'll take down anyone else to protect them. Welder knows this. Be careful."

I hated hearing that. At one point, Radi and I had been best friends, and I would have trusted her with my life. I didn't want to believe she'd betray me.

"Rilla, do you hear me?" Aiden gave me an expectant look.

I sighed. "Yes. Don't worry, I'll be careful."

CHAPTER 34

✦ ✦ ✦ ✦ ✦ ✦ ✦ ✦ ✦ ✦

Before sunset, Daki, Sito, Aiden, and I took off for the port. Aiden carried a written confession for Clox to sign admitting Welder hired him to poison Ashbel and Leonora. He planned to show this to the Emberwood royal council as evidence of Welder's crimes. We left Miah and Galai at the house in case Carrick came back.

We kept the hoods of our cloaks over our heads and our gazes lowered. I didn't know who might recognize them, but the chances seemed slim. One, it was a small village. And two, news had always traveled slowly here. Cascasea was a secluded village, and even if the people knew of the recent politics, they wouldn't have seen pictures of Aiden or Sito. I was more likely to be recognized. But I didn't want to get left behind. I didn't have much time left before I had to go back to Welder, and I refused to spend any second of that time separated from Aiden. Besides, even if I were recognized, it could be to our advantage. Though a few years had passed since I'd left home, some of the Cascasean vendors who I knew could still be here. They might be tight-lipped with outsiders, but maybe I, as a local girl, could put them more at ease.

The sun edged toward the horizon, casting purple and pink shimmers on the water. The beach was silent and desolate, but I could see fishing vessels in the distance, the only sign that there was still life in this tiny village.

"We'll check the port first," Aiden said. "If Clox changed his appearance, we'll have to be subtle when we ask questions, or he'll know we're looking for him. I hope he hasn't poisoned anyone else."

"He wouldn't dare try anything," Daki said. "He's a fugitive in hiding. However, if there have been rumors, the locals would know the gossip."

"I don't think he'd outright poison anyone to the point of madness," Sito said. "But a low dose of his blood might cause someone to be in a heightened state of grief. They might have been driven to do something out of the ordinary and then wake up not remembering the episode."

"Similar to getting drunk?" I asked.

Sito nodded. "Exactly."

We walked down the familiar path I used to travel from my house to the sea market. I hadn't been back there since that fateful day the palace scouts had discovered my voice. Life was so much simpler then. I missed Auntie An and the treasures she found in the sea. The seashells we had sold the last day before my entire life changed. If it wasn't for her inspiration and her story about losing love and then finding her purpose again, I may never have gotten out of bed after Aiden had disappeared.

Evening settled by the time we reached the marketplace. We'd come just in time for the night market. Lanterns hung above the street. The flickering lights brightened the place though it still looked dingy. The last time I'd been here was during the day. It had been in a sad state, with only a few peddlers selling food and wares. I was glad to see there were more vendors out now. Still, there were far fewer stalls than when I'd come as a child.

It was early in the evening, so most of the vendors were still preparing the food. The night rush for suppertime would probably come in about an hour.

A young woman behind one of the stalls was busy marinating fish.

The sign in front of her table said: *Fresh seafood. Caught this morning. All you can eat for 10 Seran until sold out.*

I marveled at this. How could this vendor be able to offer all that seafood for such a cheap price?

The woman looked up at me, and our gazes met. Recognition registered, followed by surprise. She called me first. "Rilla?"

"Auntie An. I can't believe it."

Her face lit up, and she rushed forward, nearly knocking over a bottle of marinade. She embraced me. "Child, I can't believe it either. I had hoped we'd see each other again. I heard about your escape, and stories about your adventures have circulated around the village. I even heard that you were here when Chief Magistrate Khan surrendered us to Emberwood's rule, though I stayed home and waited for the news like most folks. But I never expected to see you standing here in front of my booth on a random midweek evening."

"I can't believe you stayed here," I said. "I thought you would have traveled, gone somewhere to start over. Fallen in love again."

"This is my home. Why would I leave? Just because you made me look young again?" She laughed at my bewildered expression. "I wouldn't expect anyone to understand, but I met my beloved in this village. Even if I were given a million chances to start a new life, I'd never be able to forget him. I'm content with never experiencing love again. It's a choice I've made, and I stand by it."

I respected her decision. I'd experienced love with Aiden and thought I'd lost him. I'd been blessed that he had come back, but in Auntie An's shoes, I might have made the same choice. Some people believed they only needed to experience love once in their lifetime.

"As long as you're happy," I said.

"I am indeed happy. I have everything I need here. Old Grandfather Heaven blesses me with plenty, and I love sharing it with my community. I couldn't ask for more."

She looked at Aiden, Daki, and Sito, who were standing awkwardly behind me. "Care to introduce me to these handsome fellows?"

"My husband-to-be, Aiden, his cousin, Sito, and our friend, Daki," I said. "Everyone, meet Auntie An."

Auntie An's eyes widened. "Oh, I didn't realize I was in the presence of royalty." She started to curtsy, but Aiden placed a hand on her shoulder.

"Auntie An, there's no need for that," he said. "I've heard of you from Rilla, and I consider you to be my auntie as well."

"My, my," Auntie An said with a beaming smile. "This one has manners. I like him. I had heard of your engagement before the emperor banned any news mentioning either of your names after that."

She turned to Daki. "A pleasure to meet a new friend." Her eyes lit up in recognition. "Wait a minute." She kept her tone down. "Aren't you the naval commander I read about in the papers? You're supposed to be dead. Come to think of it, I thought I read that King Aiden and Prince Sito of Emberwood are thought to be dead as well. Didn't you both go missing in Fauxhemia?"

"Old Grandfather Heaven had other plans for us," Daki said. "We're all alive and well, though most people don't know it yet."

"You're one of the few who now know," Aiden said. "Will you do us a favor and keep our secret?"

Auntie An smiled. "Of course. But I must say, this is intriguing."

I could see a question forming in her eyes, though she didn't ask it. Instead, she finally moved her gaze to Sito. "And it is an honor to meet you, Your Highness."

Again, she moved to curtsy, but Sito stopped her this time.

"It's my pleasure as well, Auntie, but please don't curtsy anymore or mention our titles," Sito said. "As Aiden mentioned, no one's supposed to know we're alive. We're here incognito."

"Oh?" Auntie An stood straight, no longer hiding her curiosity. "May I ask what brings all of you to such a secluded village as Cascasea? But if you cannot answer, I won't be offended."

"Actually, maybe you can help us," Aiden said. "We're searching for an assassin." He unrolled a parchment with Clox's profile drawn on it. "Have you seen this man? I'm not sure if he's wearing a disguise, but a source told us they saw someone who looks like him here."

Auntie An studied the portrait. She wrinkled her brow. "I can't say for certain since the hair is different, and this man looks older. But those eyes look similar to the young man who opened a hot pot and flavored tea stand on the other side of the marketplace. He's come here a few times to pick up the seafood I sell during the day. Quiet man, never even acknowledges me. I'd never eat there, and if he is this assassin you're looking for, I'm glad I didn't go anywhere near his place." She lowered her voice to a whisper. "I've heard some crazy stories from customers who say they'll never go back."

"What do you mean?" Daki asked.

"After eating the food, they said they did some crazy things. They can't prove it's because of the food, but in all cases, they were customers who ate there and complained that the service was slow."

"Interesting," Aiden said, scratching his chin. "What kind of crazy things did they do?"

"An older man said he had a dream of his dead son, who fell to his death after cliff diving into the ocean. The man said the grief was so unbearable, he couldn't stop himself from diving off a cliff himself. Thankfully, he didn't get hurt. Another man said he woke up on the beach without a stitch of clothing on and had no recollection of how he got there except that he'd been crying the previous night, thinking of the woman who jilted him at the altar. And a village auntie took up a knife and would have killed her brother had her son not been there to stop her. Said she came out of a trance-like state with no idea of what she'd done. Her son said she thought her brother was their baba, who used to beat them as children."

"That's our guy," Sito said. "Let's go get him."

I turned to Auntie An. "Sorry our reunion was so short. I promise

I'll be back to see you when all of this is over. If I survive."

"You are a survivor, my girl," she said. "And I'll be here waiting. Until then, I'll continue praying for Old Grandfather Heaven to keep all of you safe."

With one last wave goodbye, I headed off with Daki, Sito, and Aiden for the other side of the marketplace. We got a whiff of herbs and spices from the hot pot soup before we even saw the food booth. It smelled delicious.

Aiden's stomach growled. "Even knowing it could contain poison, I still want to eat that."

"Keep focused, cousin," Sito said. "We can make our own hot pot soup after we catch Clox."

We sat at one of the tables and waited.

A man came out of the booth with a pot, which he set in front of a customer. He had shaved his head and wore a goatee, and he'd done something to his face to appear younger. Looked like makeup. But I recognized those dagger-like eyes. It was Clox.

"Quick, look down before he recognizes us," Daki whispered.

Too late. Clox lifted his gaze and saw us. His expression turned to panic. He lifted the bowl of hot soup and hurled it at our table. Aiden dodged, and scalding soup barely missed him. The bowl splintered against the table.

Clox took off running. We went after him.

"We'll split up," Aiden yelled. "Cut him off."

He went right, Daki and Sito went left, and I continued straight. Clox went down an alleyway filled with litter and foul-smelling garbage. He picked up a box and threw it at me. I dodged sideways.

He climbed a stairway leading up to the roof of a vacant building. Aiden was already there. Clox saw him and jumped off the stairs, going left. But Sito and Daki blocked his path.

Clox turned, facing me. He grabbed a wooden board from a heap of garbage and swung it at me. I dove down, out of the way. He slid past me and ran back out of the alleyway.

Fainting faela. I wasn't going to let him get away. Splinters of wood from a broken crate lay on the ground.

I sang.

"Resilient as bamboo unbreakable in the storm,

Let this song define me as my spirit is reborn."

The wood splinters twined around one another, forming a beam. I bent it, shifting the form so that it curled around Clox's foot. He tripped and fell.

Aiden, Daki, and Sito cornered him.

"We've got you now," Sito said.

"You'll do exactly as we say, you weasel," Aiden said. "Or I swear you'll wish for death. First, you'll sign this written confession clearing Queen Esmeralda of hiring you to poison my parents. In addition to this written confession, you'll return to Fauxhemia and give a public statement to your people that you poisoned King Lieka, and you are not related to Queen Esmeralda."

Clox laughed. "Oh, I should have known she would have something to do with it. That bitch never wanted to acknowledge her bloodline. Her family."

"Or maybe she just doesn't want to be associated with a criminal like you," Daki said.

"Criminal?" Clox repeated. "Esmeralda turned me into a fugitive. She smeared my reputation to protect her own."

"Yeah, yeah," Sito said. "Whatever you say. There's no excuse for what you did to my aunt and uncle. Welder hired you, and Esmeralda had nothing to do with it. Now sign."

Daki forced a pen into Clox's hand, and Aiden held out the paper. They made Clox scrawl his messy signature under the confession statement.

"Now we're going to need some of your blood," Aiden said. "I've been waiting to do this for a long time."

Aiden took a knife and sliced a long cut along the palm of Clox's left hand. I winced, but Clox only laughed. Clox's palm was coated in his emerald blood. Aiden took a vial from his pocket. He dripped Clox's blood into it. Then he forced Clox to stamp his palm print on the signed confession.

Aiden let go of Clox. "We'll bring you back to Fauxhemia where you will be tried for your crimes. You'll make a public confession to exonerate the queen of poisoning King Lieka and say you're not related to her. She'll compensate you for the confession and allow you to leave. Make it look like you escaped."

Clox sat back, staring at his bloodied hand. "Paid to become a fugitive for the rest of my life?"

"Better to be a rich fugitive than the life you've been living," Daki said. "It's more than you deserve."

"Deserve?" Clox spat. "And do you believe Esmeralda *deserves* to be sitting on the Emberwood throne, clear of all charges even though she is guilty? I'll confess she had nothing to do with poisoning the Emberwood royals, but I'll never confess to what she did to King Lieka. Not for all the money in the world." Clox sneered. "I was the chef of a king, and she turned me into a villain. She used me, and now she's using you."

I turned to Aiden. "As we suspected, she's been lying and covering up her crime all along."

"There must have been a reason she poisoned Lieka," Sito said. "He was known to have violent episodes."

"Oh, yes, the king was a horrible man," Clox said. "He hit my sister and Esmeralda every time he got drunk. I don't blame her for poisoning him. But she used me to take the fall. Promised she'd help me clear my name. And then she abandoned me when she married Lieka to acquire her own power. She'll never agree to whatever she promised you in exchange for hunting me down. All she cares about is protecting herself."

His gaze flickered to the left, then to the right. A look of desperation came over him. "You'll see I'm right soon enough. Don't let her use you the way she used me. She'll never let you have an antidote if it means healing King Lieka. With my blood or hers, she'll renege on her promises. How is it fair for her to live happily ever after while I'm forced to continue running for the rest of my life? That's not the way I want to live."

Clox's eyes filled with tears. "I have a girlfriend, Marnie. I couldn't be with her for all these years I was on the run. Yet, she continues to believe in my innocence and has been waiting for me to return. Society has snubbed her because of me. How much worse will it get for her if I let Esmeralda win? No, I won't let her use me anymore."

He bared his teeth in a crazy smile as though he had come to an important decision. "The magic in my blood starts to disappear the moment I'm dead. Good luck getting that antidote. Maybe this way Marnie can finally move on."

He grabbed the knife from the ground.

"No," I shouted. Aiden lurched toward Clox.

Too late.

Clox plunged the knife into his chest. He fell back to the ground and stopped breathing. Even I couldn't save him now.

Aiden swore. "I can't believe this. I didn't think he'd be that desperate."

"He didn't want his girlfriend to suffer more disgrace," I said. "I feel sorry for them."

"He poisoned my parents," Aiden said. "He was still a criminal even if he didn't poison Lieka."

"No time to think about that now," Daki said. "There might not be enough magic left to create an antidote if we don't act quickly."

"We need to leave now then," Sito said. "Daki can create a fast transport."

Aiden turned back to me. "I'm sorry, Rilla. I have to get this blood to the lab and this written confession to Esmeralda. She might still accept it and help us fight Welder. I'm not ready to reveal myself to be alive yet. Not without Esmeralda's consent. I can't blow the chance of securing an alliance with Fauxhemia. You'll have to return to Welder for now, so he doesn't suspect anything."

I nodded, too stunned by the suddenness of his departure to say anything. I wasn't ready to say goodbye to Aiden yet. As quickly as he had re-entered my life, he was now leaving again.

Besides that, I had so many things I wanted to tell Aiden, but I knew he'd never listen. What if Esmeralda *was* using them?

Aiden was so focused on getting an antidote and securing an alliance, he was willing to help Esmeralda do anything. Even condemn a man who was framed, driving him to kill himself.

"I'm sorry," Aiden said again. "I hate asking for a favor in these circumstances, but I need your help. Return to the house and ask Galai and Miah to help you bury Clox's body. We don't need him now that we've got his blood, and we don't need the local magistrates asking any questions. Can you do that for me?"

Again, I nodded, not able to find my voice. I couldn't find the words to argue with his decision. It felt like he was abandoning me, but I couldn't say it out loud. Finding an antidote for his parents and securing an alliance were important to him. More important to him, it seemed, than me.

"I promise once I get Esmeralda's agreement, you'll see me again," Aiden said. He gave me a hasty kiss on the forehead, and then he and Sito took off, leaving me behind with Clox's corpse.

CHAPTER 35

✦ ✦ ✦ ✦ ✦ ✦ ✦ ✦ ✦ ✦

I returned to Welder and Cedar Palace earlier than the full week I'd been allowed for my leave. After Galai and Miah helped me bury Clox, there had been nothing left to do in Cascasea.

Welder welcomed me back with a smile, and I did my best not to cringe at his touch as he embraced me.

In the days that followed, Welder spent a fair share of his time changing things around Cedar Palace to fit his taste. He burned the faela chambers and got rid of all emblems of the royal family, and he issued a proclamation to the kingdom that anyone who refused to acknowledge him and me as their new rulers would be put to death. He left me alone to plan for our wedding, which I made sure by all appearances that everyone knew would take place in one month back in Emberwood at Linlang Palace.

Radi was helping me with the planning. I hadn't told her it was a farce. In the back of my mind, though I hated to admit it, I couldn't trust her completely. I had told her, however, that Carrick was still alive, and that I'd seen him during my time away. I said he was trying to locate Cirisa.

While Radi wasn't completely satisfied with my answer and wanted to know where I'd seen him, at least she wasn't being combative. While we weren't exactly friends again—we could never go back to those days—we probably understood each other more than anyone else, and we were grateful for each other's company.

About two weeks after my return, I woke up with a queasy stomach and a headache. Maybe I'd eaten something bad, but more likely, I thought it had to do with my anxiety lately. Between dealing with Welder and constantly being worried about Aiden, while having to keep my feelings from showing, it felt like I was about to explode.

I decided to skip breakfast and took a walk instead. The fresh air helped.

I headed for the old Apple Barrel, deciding to spend some time there. I reminisced about my time as a trinket, preparing for the showcase, and that morning I'd met Radi.

Welder had turned the entire area into a training ground for the soldiers. The men practiced their drills this morning, and on the other side of the courtyard, Ponch led the female soldiers with their exercises.

I stopped to watch them a bit before heading in the opposite direction, towards the lake where Radi and I had skinny-dipped the night I'd first met Aiden and Carrick.

Coming here brought back so many memories. I sat by the lake for a while and stared into the distance, letting the wind blow on my face. The cool air felt nice, and the queasiness slowly disappeared.

A whistle sounded in the trees, startling me. A man jumped down and somersaulted mid-air before landing in front of me. Even though most of his face was covered in a mask, I knew it was Aiden. He wore a cloak over his head and was dressed in the uniform of the Cedar Palace guards, his appearance the same as when he was just Friend to me.

"Pardon me, miss. I came to see if you were interested in skinny-dipping with me again."

Annoyance overcame me. "What are you doing here?" I hissed. "It's dangerous. If they catch you—"

"You worry too much," he said. "I got through this palace unnoticed for years, dressed exactly like this. I know what I'm doing."

"Let's at least take cover where there's a little more privacy," I said.

"Good, I'd like to get private with you too."

"Be serious," I scolded, dragging him off into the cover of some trees.

"I am serious. I want to talk to you about what's going on, and that needs privacy." He waggled a finger at me. "Oh, I see. You were thinking of something a little more naughty. We can do that too, but later."

"Aiden, please," I whispered.

"All right," he sighed, sobering up. He hugged me. "I just needed to see you, to make sure you're okay. I also wanted to tell you, I successfully delivered Clox's blood to Prince Lymere. There should still be enough magic to extract from the blood to create an antidote. We'll know for certain in a few days. We were able to take out Welder's spies within the Fauxhemian court. He won't be hearing from them anymore. I also gave Esmeralda the written confession and confronted her about Clox's accusations."

He wore a grim expression as he said this.

"Why don't you look happy about this?"

"Sito and Lymere said there's still a chance the resulting antidote won't be potent enough because the magic has deteriorated after Clox's death," he said. "We might still need Esmeralda's blood. Now that she's got Clox's written confession that she wasn't involved in poisoning my parents, most of her critics have taken a step back. However, some members of the Fauxhemian court still decided to push for a trial for King Lieka's poisoning. They say Clox never admitted to poisoning King Lieka, and they're out to get Esmeralda. She'll be called to testify next week. Don't worry, there's not enough evidence to convict her."

"What if they make her give a sample of blood?" I asked. "They'll know she's related to Clox and question why she lied."

"Even if they do, it's not proof she poisoned Lieka. Besides, no one can make her give up her blood. She's still the queen, and they need her consent. We're all sure she'll be found innocent."

"But she's not innocent," I said.

"She confessed to Sito and me that she had no choice," Aiden said. "King Lieka kept hurting her mother. She intervened once and Lieka splashed her face with hot tea. It's how she got the scar on her cheek."

"Is that supposed to make us sympathize with her? She had her uncle take the fall, promised to clear his name but never did."

"She said the truth will ruin her," Aiden said. "All of Fauxhemia will hate her. Prince Lymere agrees. They won't be able to get married if public opinion of her remains poor. Clox is dead now anyway. Clearing his name won't benefit him."

"These are all just excuses for her and for you," I said. "How do you know she'll keep her word? Take our side against Welder and donate her blood if Clox's isn't enough?"

"So far, she still agrees that Fauxhemia will help us fight Welder on the condition that the trial goes her way. As for her blood . . ." Aiden trailed off, looking grim. "I don't know if she'd risk it without further incentive. I might have to strike another bargain with her. If I give her something worth her while and ensure secrecy by taking her blood to a private lab in Emberwood, maybe she'll consider it."

"That's a lot of maybes," I said. "The trial might not go the way she wants. She could still back out of her agreement to an alliance."

"I know, but Lymere told me not to bring up the alliance or her blood until after the trial. Esmeralda's mood is mercurial. She might get upset and change her mind about everything. Unfortunately, this means waiting two more weeks before I can come back from the dead and make a move against Welder with Fauxhemia backing me up."

"I'm supposed to marry Welder in two weeks," I said. "If you don't reveal yourself, what am I going to do? Go through with it? And in two weeks, what happens if Esmeralda backs out of all her promises?"

"As I said, I'll negotiate with her," Aiden said. "Lift all tariffs in our trade agreements. There has to be something I can offer to make her agree to my terms."

I shook my head and sighed. "Don't you see? Esmeralda is holding a lot of power over you. As much power as Welder is holding over me. I just want us to work together as a team again and take back our lives."

"I know. But I can't give up yet. We're so close to an antidote and an alliance. No matter what happens in two weeks, I'll come for you."

The sound of laughter came from a distance, alerting me that our time together was up. I pushed him away. "You need to go."

He looked as sorry as I felt. "Two weeks. I promise." Then he jumped into the trees and disappeared.

"We're done here," Welder told me that night. "It's time to return to Emberwood."

"Wh-what?" I stammered, and then hated myself for showing that he'd taken me off guard. "Why? We're not scheduled to leave for another week."

"The Emberwood troops have been away from home too long," he said. "They deserve to rest now that the war is over. Besides, we can plan for the wedding better once we're back in Emberwood."

Was this sudden change really for the reasons he stated? Or did he have something up his sleeve? I wondered if he'd find it suspicious that his spies in Fauxhemia were no longer sending him messages. I should have asked Aiden about that.

I stared at him. "Aren't you needed here?"

"Not really. Everything is stable now, and my men will have everything under control. Kenbo and Laht will be in charge here. They're old friends, and I trust them. I'm taking a hundred Seracedarean soldiers back with us. It will be good to have them at the parade as we formally join the two kingdoms together."

"What parade?" I asked.

"I'm planning a parade the day before the wedding. We'll announce our victory over Seracedar and that from now on, we become one kingdom. Then you'll formally introduce me as your consort and the new Emberwood king. You'll tell the people it's what King Aiden would have wanted and that you want to obey his wishes even though a part of you will always love him."

You have no idea what we want to do to you, bastard, I thought angrily, but I maintained a forced smile. "Of course. If that's what you want to do."

"Glad to hear you have no objections. A bit of good publicity never hurts, you know. I've already told the royal advisors, and they agree." He spun on his heel and left.

There was nothing I could do but hope that Aiden's spies would alert him that we were on our way to Emberwood earlier than planned. Any attempt on my part to send him word might get intercepted by Welder's men, and I could not risk it.

We arrived back at Emberwood two days later. Linlang Palace was preparing for the wedding already. Welder had sent word to the servants to start getting things ready for our arrival. One day passed after another, and I was getting closer to the dreaded moment.

Would Aiden really come through in time? Or would I have to continue playing this game and try to delay the wedding? If only I could figure out how to unlock the power to take away Welder's tin-chai.

I hated that Aiden was forcing me to deal with this alone while he waited for his precious antidote and an alliance that might never come.

The morning before the wedding, I got up and couldn't fall back asleep. The sun hadn't risen yet. I got up and went through the halls. The palace was deserted. Welder had made the announcement for everyone in the kingdom to take a day of rest to prepare for the celebration of our wedding tomorrow, beginning with a parade this evening. The servants had all gone back to their families last night.

I took a walk in the Gold Song Courtyard, where the fire flowers still burned bright in the darkness. They flickered, and once the sun streamed through the windows, they would dim.

"Rilla." I heard my name from the shadows and recognized Aiden's voice. He emerged from behind a stone pillar.

I followed him to a more secluded place, in a corner of a corridor between pillars. Some shrubs provided more privacy, hiding us from view should anyone come across the courtyard.

A smidgeon of light hit his face, and I could see the desolation written there.

"Oh no," I said. "They weren't able to get an antidote."

He shook his head. "It wasn't enough blood. If Clox wasn't dead, we could have extracted enough magic. Esmeralda refuses to donate hers. She's also reneged on her promise to send the Fauxhemian army to our aid."

"I told you. That woman is toying with you," I said, anger pulsing in my veins.

"Clox's written confession wasn't enough to prove her innocence in court. It's only proved that she wasn't involved in poisoning my parents, but the court says there's no evidence to exonerate or convict her of Lieka's poisoning. The ruling has many Fauxhemians rioting in the streets. They're demanding that she give a sample of her blood, but Esmeralda still refuses. She's been in hiding, hoping all this will die down if she lays low. She said if she gets Fauxhemia involved in a war now, it will only make things worse for her."

I gaped. "Did you remind her that Welder intends on destroying Fauxhemia?"

"Yes, but she said she'll worry about it after the criticisms die down."

I leaned against a pillar. Behind us, the fire flowers glowed, illuminating bursts of colored light. "And what about Lymere? He's the real heir to the throne. Can't he address the people? Make decisions without Esmeralda? He can tell the Fauxhemians how dangerous Welder is and why it's necessary to fight him."

Aiden shook his head, giving me a hopeless look. "He says he loves Esmeralda too much. He doesn't want to risk ruining her or their chance at a true marriage after his father passes away."

I shot him a look of disbelief. "They're both full of excuses. Jeopardizing the future of their kingdom simply because they want approval for marriage. They can figure that out later. Opinions always change. She can win over the public and the priestesses if she takes down Welder, the world's most dangerous man at the moment, who is bent on destroying her people."

"I tried telling her that, too," Aiden said. "She told me the only way she'll agree to fight now is if Sito and I help her find another Fauxhemian who is distantly related to her and might have a similar magic in their blood. Bribe them into saying they were Clox's accomplice in Lieka's poisoning. It'll take the focus off her. She's agreed to give me her blood if I succeed."

"You can't be serious," I said, sending him a look of disbelief. "Are you actually thinking of doing as she asks?"

"It might be the only way to save my parents. If I were the one to get poisoned, they'd want to save me, too. They'd say any sacrifice is worth it. And Esmeralda said—"

I burst out at him. "Your parents said. Esmeralda said. And before, it was Carrick said. Can't you listen to yourself and make your own decisions for once? You've always been a follower, but now it's time for you to be a leader."

He stared at me, the shock apparent in his face from my outburst. "I understand your frustration, but there's a lot at stake here. If I mess things up with Esmeralda, I could fail in defeating Welder and in getting an antidote."

I shook my head. "If this new plan fails, then what? I don't believe she ever intends on giving her blood to you or helping us fight. I think she's giving you the runaround. She doesn't care about us. She doesn't even care about her people. She only cares about protecting herself. But you don't need her to fight Welder. All you need to do is lead your people. I think the reason you stayed away from Emberwood for so long and the reason you're staying away now is because you're afraid. Afraid of being a leader. Because if you fail, there's no one else to blame. You'll have to take responsibility for the decisions you made. But don't you see? Not taking responsibility is a decision. Not leading is already failing Emberwood. It's failing me."

He hung his head and turned his gaze toward the courtyard and the fire flowers. "You're right. I am afraid. I don't have the experience to be a leader. My parents have always been the king and queen. They didn't teach me to make decisions for myself, much less for an entire nation. Carrick was the prince. He told me what to do, and I did what was asked. Even in my time with you, you're the one with the plans. I'm just the sidekick assisting you with those plans. It's how I've always been. Catering to someone else's whims is the only plan I know how to follow."

"Is that your decision then?" I felt a burst of pain in my heart. "You're going back to Fauxhemia? What am I supposed to do? How am I supposed to stop Welder?"

"Come with me," he said. "I came here today to take you back to Fauxhemia. We can figure things out there."

"That's your solution?" Tears streamed down my face. "To run away with you and abandon our people? Leave Welder to do with them as he pleases?"

He looked conflicted. A tear slid down his cheek. He wiped it away hastily, "I-I don't know what to do. It's not just about the alliance. Esmeralda's blood is my only chance to save my parents. I can't lose them. I owe them everything."

"Well, I know what I'm going to do," I said. "I'm going to stay here and fight Welder. If you're not going to reveal that you're still alive, I'll do it for you. I'm going to find the advisors and appeal to them once again even if they don't believe me. I'll reveal that Welder used Clox to poison your parents and then he tried to kill you and Sito. You can either stay and lead Emberwood with me, or you can go back to

Esmeralda and be her servant, begging for help that will never come."

"Don't ask me to choose. I don't want to lose my parents, but I don't want to leave you either."

"I'm not asking you to give up on them," I said. "But right now, Old Grandfather Heaven has given us the Will of Heaven. We're serving as vessels to bring peace to the Shyan people. We're fighting for the future. Once we win, then we can figure out how to save your parents, even without Esmeralda's stupid blood."

He watched the flickering lights from the fire flowers playing on the side of the stone pillars. Searched them as though they might have an answer.

"What if she's the only way?"

"No. We can still find another Faux-blood. Maybe there's a distant relative of Clox. Or someone else who has the properties in their blood to make a proper antidote. But we'll find them on our terms and our timing, not Esmeralda's. We can face it together in the future and ask Old Grandfather Heaven for help. But there won't be a future if you can't commit to fighting Welder with me."

His hands curled into fists at his side. "I don't know."

I sighed, finally realizing there was no amount of talk that could make him see reason. "Life would be easier with you by my side, but if you feel like your quest serving Esmeralda is more important than leading your people, there's nothing I can do to convince you otherwise. You do what you want."

I turned from him and walked away. I took one step after another, willing him to come after me. But he didn't. When I turned around again, he was gone.

I slowly made my way back to my room. Radi or one of my other guardswomen was probably looking for me. I composed myself before opening the door.

I froze. Welder stood in front of my bed, waiting for me. Next to Welder's feet lay Ponch and Radi, both bound up with their mouths gagged. Ret, along with two soldiers, had their swords pointed at them. Radi's eyes brimmed with tears, and in her expression, I saw an apology.

My gaze drifted back from Ponch and Radi to Welder, who had a big smile on his face as he looked back at me.

"Checkmate," he said.

CHAPTER 36

✦ ✦ ✦ ✦ ✦ ✦ ✦ ✦ ✦ ✦

Welder's accusing gaze dug into me. His smirk grew ever grander, like a maocat teasing its new toy. "I know Aiden is alive. Do you want to know how I know?"

I remained frozen, refusing to give him the satisfaction of reacting. He must have had me followed, though I thought I'd been careful. I was a fool to believe we hadn't fallen into Welder's trap. He was always three steps ahead.

Welder laughed. "I already suspected it when Carrick escaped. Then my spies didn't report back from Fauxhemia. So I sent someone to investigate. Found out Esmeralda had imprisoned all my spies, and she had a written confession from Clox saying that I had hired him to poison Ashbel and Leonora. Thankfully, I convinced the royal council it's a fake confession. Why else would it be written instead of directly out of Clox's mouth? No one has even found the man yet. But then I thought, who would have gone through so much trouble to help her? It had to be Aiden and Sito. And I just received confirmation."

His eyes flashed to my belly. "I don't even think *you* know the good news, but I'll be the first to congratulate you. Pity it will grow up without knowing its parents, but I'll treat the child well as long as you do as I ask."

I touched my stomach and gasped at the realization of what he was hinting at. "Impossible."

But it was possible. I'd had a queasy stomach and headache some mornings. And come to think of it, my monthly bleeding was two weeks late. I hadn't thought anything of it because sometimes I was irregular.

"I would have thought it impossible as well," Welder said. "After all, the only man you would ever consent to be with is supposed to be dead."

I said nothing, only glared.

He smiled, obviously proud to have outsmarted me. "Your friend, Radi, is an easy target. Why do you think I agreed when you asked me to spare her life? One threat to kill her stepdaughter, and she promised to be my spy. Told me your monthly bleeding is late, and you've been nauseous. No wonder you asked to leave the soldier camp. You must have met with Aiden then."

"You have Princess Cirisa?" I wanted to rip his throat. "Where is she?"

He clicked his tongue at me. "Safe for now. As long as you go through this wedding without any upsets. I know Aiden won't be able to resist coming for you."

So Welder knew about that, too. "So announcing your intentions to marry me was just a way to draw him out."

"No, I still intend to marry you," he said. "But I just want to make sure I kill him for real this time."

"I'll never marry you."

"I thought you might say that. I also suspect you and Aiden have a plan in place."

He thought we had a plan. If I weren't so angry, I would have laughed.

"If I were him, I'd first appear to the men who could help him take back the army," Welder said. "Which is why as we speak, I have Oren leading a hundred Seracedarean soldiers to the Emberwood training grounds. Colonel Beyling and Captain Kang, and fifty chosen Emberwood soldiers were told to meet me there, but my men are going to ambush them. They will be killed unless you tell me what Aiden is planning."

"No, you can't," I shouted. "We don't have a plan. It's true that Aiden's alive, but he's abandoned me. He's abandoned Emberwood. Esmeralda hasn't agreed to donating her blood or to an alliance. She's using those two things as bartering chips to make Aiden help prove her innocence in Lieka's poisoning. Aiden doesn't see that she's using him, and he's staying in Fauxhemia."

Welder froze. "Really?"

"Yes, please stop the ambush. There's no benefit to you killing the advisors and the soldiers."

Welder turned to Ret. "Go tell Oren not to go through with it for now. Once the wedding is over, I might change my mind. Depends how Rilla behaves."

"Yes, sir." Ret bowed and sped off.

"I'm not lying," I told Welder. "I wanted Aiden to come back to Emberwood. But he won't give up on a cure for his parents."

Welder sighed, looking back at me. "I suppose I'll have to send someone to Fauxhemia to check on your story. But you do look devastated. Must be true to some extent. I knew he didn't have what it takes to be a leader. In that case, you're better off with me as a husband. I'd never abandon you. You're too precious. Now I think it's time we get ready for the parade. Attempt to sing one note, and I'll steal your voice and kill your friends. Don't test me."

More men came into the room. Two of them grabbed my arms. I struggled to break free.

"Help!" I cried. Where was everyone?

"No one's going to hear you," Welder said. "Remember? Everyone is taking the day off and getting ready for the parade."

Welder addressed his men. "You, stay here and watch them. The rest of you, search every nook and cranny of this palace and make sure Aiden isn't here."

"Why don't I save you the trouble?" Aiden's voice broke out as he stepped into the room. He punched the two guards who tried to grab him. They cried out and held their broken noses.

The other guards pointed their swords at Aiden and surrounded him.

He came back for me. My first thought was one of joy. Fury quickly replaced it. The idiot was going to get himself killed.

Aiden glared at Welder. "Let Rilla and the others go."

Welder placed a knife to my belly. "I'll tell you what. You come quietly with me, and I'll spare Rilla and your child."

Aiden held his hands up in surrender. "Fine. I'll go with you. Don't hurt her." His gaze went to my belly. His expression was one of shock and fear. He swallowed. "O-or my child. I'll do whatever you want."

"Good," Welder said. His men took Aiden and tied him up. Aiden didn't struggle. The men placed gloves on his hands.

"Special gloves so you can't play any fire tricks on us," Welder said. "Even if you did, I'll remind you I can steal it away. You too, Rilla."

As though I needed the reminder. I'd love nothing better than to kill him with my voice. But he'd just steal it and kill Ponch, Radi, and Aiden.

Welder bound my hands with rope and gestured for me to sit next to Ponch and Radi.

A soldier came into the room. He whispered something into Welder's ear.

"Good job," Welder said. He smiled at Aiden. "Guess you thought Daki and Prince Sito could help you make an escape, but we've already caught them."

Aiden glared at him. "You'll regret it if you hurt them."

Welder shrugged and gestured to his men. "Keep a close eye on the women. I'll deal with them later. The rest of you, follow me."

"Where are you going? What are you going to do with Aiden?" I shouted.

Welder smiled. "What do you think?"

"You can't do this," I said. "Old Grandfather Heaven will never give you the Will of Heaven. The scepter will never amplify your tin-chai. I still have the power of the scepter."

"Is that so?" He pulled out the hair stick, the fake scepter. "Not that I need the scepter with my power to steal tin-chai, but I suppose I should inform you I stole it. The one you have is a fake. Doesn't that prove you've lost the Will of Heaven? Old Grandfather Heaven must have given up on you."

He still didn't know I'd taken it back from him. The only thing I could believe right now was that Old Grandfather Heaven was still on my side. Somehow, I'd find a way out of this mess.

Aiden flashed me a horrified look, and his gaze seemed to be asking, *You have a plan, right?* Why did I always have to be the planner? He should have planned better before storming into this room.

I looked back at Welder and faked my shock. "How did you steal the scepter? What use do you have with it? You might as well give it back. Without me, you can't access its power."

"Foolish girl. I don't need its power, and I don't need Old Grandfather Heaven's approval to rule over all Shyan people. He has no power over me. I'm not using the scepter for amplification. He can't take over my tin-chai. But with my power, I can take any tin-chai I want, and the people will believe it's through amplification."

He placed the hair stick back into his pocket and patted it. "I stopped believing in the Will of Heaven. I believe the man with the most power rules everyone else through fear. Old Grandfather Heaven supposedly chose both of you, yet I was able to acquire authority over you. And now your voice will be at my command. I'll destroy Fauxhemia with you and both Shyan kingdoms under my control."

My worst nightmare was coming true. "I won't let you control my voice."

"How will you stop me? I can have your friends and family killed. I can steal your voice if you use it on me. And when your baby is born, I'll use its life to force you into obedience, too. As long as you do as I say, I'll treat it like my own."

"I'll kill you before I let you anywhere near my baby," I said, struggling against my captors. "I won't let you take this one from me, too."

"Too? Ah, so you know I put something in your tea last time. I didn't intend for you to miscarry, just so you know. I only wanted to make you drowsy and incoherent during the meeting with the advisors."

Aiden struggled against his bonds. His face had turned furious. "You made us lose a baby? I'll kill you."

Welder scoffed. "Kill me? You abandoned Rilla. You don't deserve to be self-righteous. If Bree had been pregnant with my child, I would never have left her side. She'd be my priority. Not some antidote. You don't deserve to be king, and you don't deserve Rilla."

Aiden sneered. "Says the man who delivered the woman he loved right into Terran's hands."

Welder turned a dark shade of red and punched Aiden in the stomach. Aiden keeled over, groaning.

Welder pointed to his men. "Take him away." He turned to me. "I'll return shortly." He gagged me and followed his men, shutting the door behind him.

CHAPTER 37

✦ ✦ ✦ ✦ ✦ ✦ ✦ ✦ ✦ ✦

I tested my bindings. Next to me, Radi and Ponch did the same. But the ropes were tied too tight, and unless we could get something sharp to cut them, we couldn't get them loose.

Five guards stood in the room keeping watch. Three stood next to us while the two others stood by the door. They all looked bored.

I made eye contact with Radi and Ponch. Radi hung her head down as though she'd given up hope, but there was a spark in Ponch's eyes. Her hands moved, and I saw a glint of metal. A letter opener. I didn't know how she'd managed to get ahold of it, but she was amazing.

She sliced through her bindings but stilled. She was free. What was she waiting for? Her ears twitched, and a smile formed in her eyes. She must have heard something.

Two seconds passed, and a commotion sounded outside the door. *Bang, bang*. The room shook. Someone was trying to break down the door. Wood splintered. A hole formed in the door, distracting the guards.

Ponch moved. She planted a fist into the side of a guard's face, kicked him in the chest, and he fell.

I stood and tried to make sense of what was happening. The door crashed down, splintering into tiny pieces. Miah came through first, then Galai. And Carrick.

Carrick was here. I could barely process it. Was he on our side?

Ponch fought off two guards. She dodged their swords.

"I've got you, Ponch. Ha-ya!" Miah bulldozed both guards to the ground.

Galai swooped in, her arms turning into water. Using the amplified tin-chai I'd once given her with the scepter, she plunged her arms into another guard, liquefying his chest and lungs. He gasped for air, turned blue, and passed out.

Three more men entered the room.

"Untie Rilla and your wife," Galai told Carrick. "We'll take care of them."

Carrick came towards me. He cut my bindings. I took the gag out of my mouth.

I gaped at him. "What are you doing here?"

"Would you rather I leave?"

I shook my head. "But I thought you ran away to find your daughter. I thought you hated us."

"Let's just say I think I owe you at least one good deed." Carrick worked on Radi's bindings and got them loose.

Radi rubbed her wrists. Her eyes shimmered as she looked at him. "You came for us."

He nodded. "Of course. We don't have much time. We've got to join the others and save Aiden."

I blinked. "The others?"

He flashed me an exasperated look as though to say, *Keep up, Rilla.* A guard charged us, but Carrick summoned electricity and sent it pulsing through the man's body. A foul burnt stench filled the air. Then the man fell to the ground, dead.

I sang, aiming my wyis at the remaining guards.

"You can try to douse my fire

And spit on all my dreams.

My light will grow brighter

For the world to see."

Boils formed on their faces, and their skin melted away. Bones clattered onto the ground.

Oh, how I'd missed doing that to horrible people.

I faced Carrick. "Now tell me what's going on. Do you have a plan? Is Aiden in on it?"

"No, it's all me, and I'm not lying this time," Carrick said. "I got to the clinic to warn your guardswomen before Welder's men came. We fought them off. I took Miah and Galai to save you three while the others went to find Aiden, Sito, and Daki."

I looked at Galai and Miah. "And you both willingly went with him? Are you okay?"

Galai scowled. "I don't like the idea either, but right now, he seems like the better option compared to Welder. And he did try to apologize. Not that it helps."

"I really am sorry," Carrick said. "For all the lies and horrible things I've done. I know nothing will make up for what I did. To you, Miah, the novelties I kept. And to Rilla and Aiden as well. I'll spend the rest of my life trying to be a better person. And in my next life as well. As many lives as it takes."

"Let's just start with today and go from there," Miah said. Her lips were set in a grim line, and she crossed her arms across her chest. "Actions speak louder than words. But enough talk. We need to move. Any idea where they've gone?"

Ponch nodded. "I heard Welder say they took Aiden, Sito, and Daki to the old coach station." Her ears perked up. "I don't think they made it there. I hear fighting outside. The palace coach garage. The other guardswomen are there. We've got to go help them."

We rushed through the hall and took the elevator down to the entrance. The palace was empty. Welder had done a thorough job in getting everyone out for the day. He must have planned it on purpose. Servants, students, and staff had gone home to their families. Even most of the soldiers, except for Welder's loyal men, were supposed to have taken the day off. But I wondered if they were around at Welder's request for the parade and if Ret had really called off the ambush. If only there were some way of notifying all the Emberwood soldiers that Aiden was alive, and it was time to fight against Welder.

But we didn't have time to chase the soldiers down. Aiden needed us now.

"How did you know where to find my guardswomen?" I asked Carrick. "And how did you know we were here?"

He pointed to his uniform, and I realized he was dressed as an Emberwood soldier. "Been here in disguise for weeks, following you and Welder around. I was hoping to find out where he's holding my daughter. I saw you and Aiden talking earlier, followed Aiden here and when he got himself captured, I went to find your guardswomen for help. Any more questions?"

I shook my head. "Wait, one more. Did you find Cirisa?"

"No," he said. "But we'll worry about that later. Let's save Aiden first."

CHAPTER 38

✦ ✦ ✦ ✦ ✦ ✦ ✦ ✦ ✦ ✦

The elevator reached the ground level, and we rushed out, past the front entrance and to the grounds where the palace coach garage was located.

The sounds of a fight echoed in the distance. Swords clashing against each other, cries of death, fists hammering into flesh and bone.

My guardswomen were in battle with Welder's men, including at least two dozen Seracedarean soldiers. My guards were outnumbered two to one. I scanned the scene. Found Sito and Daki. They had gotten free. The two fought against Welder's best guards, Ret and Oren.

Where was Aiden? My heart raced as I looked from face to face. Then I saw him. Relief rushed into me. He had managed to free himself. He fought against Welder. No tin-chai. Just hand-to-hand combat.

More soldiers flooded into the area. About a dozen of them. Miah and Galai blocked their path before they could get to the others. Carrick, Ponch, Radi, and I flanked the new group of Seracedarean soldiers on both sides.

Another fifty Seracedarean soldiers poured in, moving toward us. We wouldn't be able to last for long with this many soldiers to fight.

And then I heard more cries. In the distance, a blur of gold and red uniforms charged forth. "Save King Aiden," someone shouted.

A hundred or so Emberwood soldiers were here, and at the front, Colonel Beyling and Captain Kang led. Lina was with them. She must have used her sound amplifying tin-chai to alert them. Thank Old Grandfather Heaven for Lina's good sense.

They charged forward, attacking the Seracedareans.

With a cry, I ran into the midst of the fight, joining the Emberwood soldiers. I sang, taking down three who came at me. I turned around. Galai and Miah had teamed up, fighting against two others. Ponch held her own against three, and Radi had taken a branch and beat another over the head. The man was probably already dead, but she kept hitting him.

Another man came in my direction, wind and rocks swirling around him. He aimed the rocks at me. Lightning flashed, striking the rocks and the man all at once. The man's cries subsided as he turned to ash, the gray particles floating away in the wind.

Carrick came to my side.

"Thanks," I said.

"No problem."

Out of the corner of my eye, I saw two men corner Counselor Trine against a tree. She shifted into her maocat form and hissed, springing on one of the men and clawing at his eyes. He shook her off, screaming.

I ran to her, singing. My voice roared through the air, taking them down. They fell to the ground and thrashed around, their skin melting until two piles of bones lay silent and still. Trine shifted back into her human form and nodded to me a quick thanks.

On the other side of the tree, Jun fought against two soldiers. She disappeared, and the two men looked in every direction, surprise on their faces. Then slash marks appeared on their chest, and they shouted in pain as blood gushed from their wounds. They collapsed, dead. Jun reappeared, her sword covered in blood, and a grin of triumph on her face.

"Who's next?" she shouted.

Thunder crashed, and lightning lit up the sky. Rain poured down. Carrick must have summoned a storm. I smelled burning flesh and heard the cries of pain, the *zing* of electricity being sent through bodies.

I looked around. The Seracedarean soldiers were surrounded by the Emberwood army and my guardswomen. Oren and Ret were on the ground, hands behind their heads. Daki and Sito stood behind them, swords pointed to their chests.

"Don't kill me," Ret said. "I still have a sister to take care of."

"You should have thought about that before following Welder," Sito said.

"But he promised me—"

"Silence," Daki said.

I couldn't believe it. We were winning.

Welder shouted, lifting his hands in surrender. His right hand formed a fist in the air. Maybe in frustration. "You win. Arrest me, Your Majesty." He bowed in Aiden's direction.

There was something odd about his tone. But there was no way he could get away now. Even with all the magic he had, he wouldn't be able to get past all the Emberwood soldiers and my guardswomen.

Welder stepped forward. "I want to tell the king something before I'm arrested. I know another way you can get the antidote. There's another relation of Clox and Esmeralda. If you want me to say more, you'll have to be the one to arrest me."

"Don't fall for it, Aiden," I shouted.

Welder shrugged. "Up to you whether or not to believe me. But you should know by now how well I do my research. I make sure I know everything about my opponents."

"And that includes us," I said. "He's using your parents to manipulate you again. You can't listen."

But Aiden raised a hand, urging everyone to step away from Welder. "It's all right. He can't do anything if I don't use my tin-chai. And there are too many soldiers. These three aren't going anywhere."

He cautiously approached Welder.

Welder bent back his arm in the air, his hand still forming a fist.

Like he was holding something. Like he was about to throw something.

I looked down at the dead soldier at his feet. Part of a broken spear jutted halfway out of his chest. One of my guardswomen must have used a spear to kill him.

A spear. My gaze flashed back to Welder in horror. It wasn't anyone else's tin-chai he was using. It was his own.

"Watch out!" I shouted.

Welder threw a Seran coin into the air. As it left his hand, the coin transformed back into the missing part of the spear. It was directed straight for Aiden.

Everything seemed to play in slow motion. I ran. My guardswomen shouted and ran after me.

Then somehow Carrick was there, standing in front of Aiden. The spear went through Carrick's stomach. He stumbled, faltered, then fell to the ground. Blood dripped from the wound.

Radi screamed.

In the distance, I heard Welder's voice. "You may have taken back Emberwood, but I have Seracedar. I'll use them to crush you."

Ret and Oren appeared beside him. The two younger men must have taken advantage of the chaos to free themselves.

"Take us away, Ret," Welder said.

Ret hesitated. "If I help you this time, then my sister—"

"Yes, yes, I'll do it. We can't do any good for her if we don't get out of here. Now let's go."

Without another word, Ret towed Welder and Oren away, their blurred forms evading the grasps of the Emberwood soldiers.

Daki shouted, "They're getting away. After them."

He and my guardswomen ran in the direction the three men had gone, but it was a lost cause.

Aiden, Sito, Radi, and I rushed to Carrick's side. I could hear the Emberwood army behind us, arresting Seracedarean soldiers, but the four of us gathered close to Carrick. The rain fell harder, and I sank to my knees into the mud.

"Can you save him, Rilla?" Sito asked. "I can make him calm when I remove the spear, but once it's out, you've got to move fast to seal the wound."

The spear had gone through his stomach and would leave a gaping hole. I didn't know if I had enough power in my wyis to close it fully. But I had to try.

"Do it," I said.

Sito grabbed the spear and pulled it out of Carrick. He howled. Sito chanted, making Carrick calmer.

I sang a refrain.

"Although you've already left me

Although we've said goodbye."

The hole closed slightly, and the blood stopped pouring out.

Carrick's gaze passed between me and Aiden. I could see it in his eyes. The love he still had for us despite everything that had happened.

I continued singing, pouring my wyis into him until sweat drenched my clothes.

"Don't ever forget when you were mine

I will always love you . . ."

The hole disappeared. But it wasn't enough. He had lost so much blood already, and his wyis was quickly fading.

"I'm sorry." He gasped out. "For everything. My child—" Then he was still. His eyes remained open, ghostly and hollow.

I finished singing the rest of the verse. Tears poured down my face.

"I will always love you

'til the last ember of starlight

flickers out in the night sky."

Aiden reverently swept his hand over Carrick's eyes to close them. "We'll find your daughter. I promise, my friend and brother." He turned away and broke into sobs. I hugged him, and we cried together.

Beside me, Radi yelled at the heavens, a piercing, painful wail, then fell over into the mud in a dead faint.

CHAPTER 39

✦ ✦ ✦ ✦ ✦ ✦ ✦ ✦ ✦ ✦

When we returned to Linlang Palace, we raised an alert to catch Welder, Oren, Ret, and anyone else who remained loyal to him. Most of his men and the Emberwood traitors had been at the battle, but Sito and Daki managed to fish out the others. Unfortunately, we knew Welder was long gone with Ret's help, back in Seracedar preparing to fight us again.

That night, I helped Aiden prepare for his address to the people. He had been away for so long without an explanation, and now we were at war with Seracedar for a second time. The people deserved to know Aiden's thoughts and what to expect in the following days.

We made our way onto the balcony. The crowd stood below us, waving Emberwood flags. Sound amplifiers stood on either side of us to make sure everyone could hear clearly.

"My beloved Embers," Aiden started. "First, I owe you an apology. I have been away, distracted by my hope of finding an antidote to cure my parents. Even so, it was no excuse for leaving you and my future queen alone to survive against a traitor bent on destroying our freedom. I left you in a state of chaos and grief, believing I was dead and fearing for your future. My lack of leadership was costly. But I now come to you humbly asking for forgiveness. If you accept my apology and give me the chance to make up for it, I promise never to forsake you again. Along with my future queen, we will lead Emberwood to better days.

Together, with every Emberwood citizen, we will overcome every threat trying to jeopardize our freedom, our happiness, our loved ones."

Aiden paused as the crowd went wild with applause and shouts of approval. After a few minutes, the applause finally subsided. Aiden gestured for me to take a turn speaking.

"Fellow Embers," I said. "For the past few months, my guardswomen and I have struggled to survive against a grave threat. One that no one took seriously despite my warnings. I don't wish to blame anyone for not listening earlier. But I hope everyone now believes me when I say this threat is greater now than ever before. A man I believed was a friend, a man we believed was one of us, Welder has betrayed us and forsaken Old Grandfather Heaven. He is responsible for poisoning King Ashbel and Queen Leonora. He schemed for us to go to war against Carrick even though Carrick was willing to negotiate peace. Welder did all this in the name of his personal revenge. And now he's deceived our brothers and sisters in Seracedar and intends on using them to conquer us. We cannot let him win. Fortunately, he was not able to take the true scepter from us."

I took the scepter, still in the appearance of a flute. I raised it to the crowd. I knew no magic from Welder or my Yao diamond was needed to change it back. The scepter wanted to become its true self again. I could feel its energy. It shook in my hands, elongating and shifting shape. And then I held the Sacred Cedar Scepter in its original form. The body of the scepter seemed to shine under the light of the Lavender Moon. I felt the Will of Heaven pouring down on us.

"Old Grandfather Heaven is still on our side," I said. "He will help us win and heal. And my promise to you is that I will always use the power of the scepter to heal, not to harm. To restore, not to destroy. But in order to bring healing, we must cut out the decay that threatens to kill our land."

Aiden held up his hand, waiting for the noise to calm down.

"Rilla and I can't promise that this fight will be easy or painless. But we do know that we must defeat Welder, or he will take away everything we hold dear. We ask for you to rise up and fight to protect your home, your families, your future."

More shouts of agreement and support.

Aiden spoke again. "In the coming days, we will prepare for battle. But I have a personal request. The former emperor, Carrick, was killed saving my life from Welder. As you know, Carrick and I had a complicated relationship. I served as his bodyguard, but we established a friendship. He was a brother to me before misunderstandings and disagreements turned us into enemies. Carrick made his fair share of mistakes, committed unforgivable sins. He attacked Emberwood, killing many. He kept novelties and took women against their will. I understand that many of you might not want to forgive him or can't. I'm not asking you to. But if not for him, I wouldn't be standing before you today. He sacrificed his life for me, and I have to acknowledge his final act of courage. So I grieve the loss of my brother and friend, and I ask for tomorrow to be a day of mourning. And after the mourning, we will rise again to defeat Welder. Thank you, beloved Embers, for your love and support."

He waved at the crowd, and I followed his cue, waving as well. Then we made our exit from the balcony.

"How do you think we did?" Aiden asked me.

"Sounds like we managed," I said. "I hope public morale will stay high now that you've returned. We need the people to be motivated to fight Welder."

Aiden nodded. His gaze shifted to a guard who had entered the room.

"Your Majesty, we've received word that Welder is back at Cedar Palace and is rallying the Seracedareans against us."

"As expected," Aiden said. "Let's make preparations to attack."

He took my arm, urging me with him, but footsteps sounded on the marble floor and Ponch entered.

"I'm sorry to disturb you," she said. "But can I speak to Rilla?"

Aiden nodded and smiled at me. "Go ahead. You can join me when you're done. I promise I won't leave you out of anything this time."

He made his exit.

I turned to Ponch. "Let's go speak in my chambers for some privacy."

Once we sat down in my sitting room, Ponch lost no time. "It's about Radi."

After the battle, Ponch and I had set up a private room at the clinic for Radi. She hadn't said a word since Carrick's death, and it was worrisome. Prince Sito had worked his tin-chai on her, keeping her calm, but she wasn't responding to anyone or anything.

"She still hasn't spoken to anyone?" I asked.

"Not a word. She isn't eating anything either. She's been sitting in the dark all day. She's barely even taken a sip of water. At this rate, I'm not sure how long her body can take it if we don't intervene."

"I can't believe not even Prince Sito's tin-chai is effective on her," I said. "I don't know what else we can do. Keep monitoring her. I don't want her hurting herself."

"Yes, I'm already on it," Ponch said. "The poor girl. I really wish I could take away her pain."

"Tomorrow is Carrick's burial ceremony," I said. "I know she'll want to say some last words to him, but I don't know how to tell her. She might still be in denial, and I'm afraid of how she might react."

"Leave it to me," Ponch said. "I'll tell her. Better that she knows and has the chance to attend the ceremony than regretting it the rest of her life."

I sent Sito to return to the clinic with Ponch. For the rest of the day, I joined Aiden with his newly appointed general, Daki, to discuss how to attack Welder.

"You need to figure out how to take away his tin-chai," Daki said. "Isn't that part of the power you were granted?"

"I know I'm supposed to have that power through the scepter," I said. "But I don't know how to harness it. I tried to take away Welder's tin-chai before. It was an epic fail. And even if I figure it out, I don't know if I can take away all his power. He's got Faux-blood magic."

"Didn't you say Welder believes I have a part in helping you unlock the power?" Aiden asked.

"Yes, but I don't have a clue as to how. This is part of my amplified tin-chai, not yours."

Aiden sighed. "Let's forget about the scepter for now then. Focus on the battlefront. We have to bring our troops to meet the Seracedarean army. Try to bring the battles outside of our home. Make them stay out of Emberwood."

"We're severely outnumbered," Daki said. "There were only one hundred Seracedarean soldiers that Welder brought into Emberwood, a quarter of a fraction of the whole Seracedarean army. Though we have support from the Ailo, Yao, and Miyu, we're still one man against five. What about Esmeralda and Lymere? Maybe they can reconsider and help us fight if we speak to them again."

Aiden furrowed his brow and crossed his arms. "No, I'm not going down that path again. Esmeralda has had me running in circles, and I won't do it anymore. She'll be sorry if Welder wins. She's next."

I made a face. "Don't say that. *We'll* be sorry if Welder wins."

"And dead," Daki added.

Someone knocked on the door. Alarm bells rang in my head. We'd asked the servants not to disturb us unless there was an emergency. What had happened?

A servant girl opened the door, and Sito and Ponch burst in. They wore expressions of shock and horror. I knew what they were going to say before Sito spoke.

"Radi is dead. She hanged herself."

CHAPTER 40

✦ ✦ ✦ ✦ ✦ ✦ ✦ ✦ ✦ ✦

All talk of politics and war stopped after Ponch's announcement of Radi's suicide. We took the evening to prepare for the next morning's burial ceremony, now not just for Carrick but also Radi.

I went to the clinic with Ponch and watched the servants take away the body for burial preparations. I tried to maintain my composure and gave directions on where to send the body and what to do with the rest of Radi's possessions.

The next morning, Aiden and I dressed for the burial processions. I finished first and waited for him in the courtyard in front of the elevator. The elevator door opened, and Ponch stepped out.

"Rilla, good I caught you before the ceremony starts." She had a note in her hand. "I found this between the bed and the wall. Must have fallen from her things. She left it for you."

I took the folded parchment. On the front, it said: *For Rilla.*

Turning it over, I read the messy scrawl.

Dear Rilla,

You were a good friend, and I wish circumstances had allowed us to stay friends. I can't figure out how to get rid of the anger and the bitterness. The hatred. And now the sadness. Carrick and Cirisa were the only reason I wanted to stay alive. Now that Carrick is dead, I don't want to remain in this world. I want to be with him. I think Cirisa would be better off without me if Welder spares her life. My whole life has only brought darkness and pain, and I don't want my bad luck to spread to Cirisa. I beg of you, find her. Save her from that monster. And if you still have any fondness left for me in your heart, raise her as your own daughter. If there is a next life, I hope we meet again and become friends in a better world.

Radi

I let my tears fall now. They dripped onto the note, blurring the ink. Ponch hugged me, and I sobbed into her shoulder.

"I couldn't help her. I couldn't save her."

Ponch patted my back in a consoling rhythm. "That wasn't your fault. We can't save everyone. Some people's demons are too big to kill. We can only pray that Old Grandfather Heaven lets Radi find her peace in death."

The private ceremony was held in the Gold Song Courtyard with just a few attendees from the palace. The bodies had been cremated, and the ashes had been stored in porcelain urns, which stood on a table in front of us. Aiden and I took turns saying a few words. Though our other friends were there in support of us, we knew we were the only two in the room who had truly known Carrick and Radi and who truly mourned their loss. They had been our best friends before we had each other.

When the ceremony was through, we had a small reception. Aiden mingled with our friends and told funny stories of his time as Carrick's bodyguard. I stood in front of the urns, thoughts running through my head. Welder had Cirisa. How was I going to get the child back from him?

I didn't know how yet, but I was determined. I had to keep her safe.

For her biological mother, Arlyn's sake. And for Carrick and Radi's sake. And I would raise her as my own.

I touched two fingers to my lips and transferred a kiss to Radi's urn. "I promise, my friend."

That night, Aiden and I prepared for bed. I was exhausted. A servant stepped in to deliver a letter.

"This just arrived, Your Majesty."

"Thank you." Aiden took it and closed the door behind the servant. He looked back at me and gave me a sardonic smile. "Well, as expected, Esmeralda sends her apologies, but she's refused my final appeal. Fauxhemia won't be joining us in our fight. But surprise, her excuse has nothing to do with her reputation this time. Turns out their king has finally passed away, and they are going into a time of mourning."

"That's sad for Prince Lymere," I said.

"Everyone knew King Lieka was about to croak," Aiden said. "It's another excuse. Esmeralda also says, regarding the other favor I've asked, she, and I quote, cannot afford to be associated with your project. If you reconsider my offer to find another Fauxhemian who fits our criteria, then perhaps we can talk again. Otherwise, I wish you the best, King Aiden. End quote."

"Well, we knew we couldn't count on them," I said. "We'll find another way without Esmeralda. To win against Welder and to get an antidote for your parents."

Aiden's eyes were sad and tired. "I hope so. But let's focus on Welder first. Any new ideas on how to take away his tin-chai?"

I frowned. "No, but maybe we can brainstorm a bit. Do you remember when we were at the inn at Candlelace on our way back from Seracedar?"

"How could I forget?" He grinned. "That was the first night we slept together. What I consider our real wedding day."

My cheeks flushed. "Yes, but I'm referring to the morning after. When we received the Will of Heaven and tin-chai amplification. Can you remember what you were feeling when you turned into light?"

"Yes, I felt your wyis reach out and come into me. Our combined power was greater than anything I've experienced on my own. Next thing I knew, I was zooming around in light form."

"What if your ability to become light is the key to taking away Welder's tin-chai? The whole concept that Welder was talking about with defensive and offensive tin-chai, yin and yang. Maybe it means I need to focus my wyis onto your light form in order to have enough power to take away tin-chai."

Aiden frowned. "But I can't maintain that form for long."

"Maybe you need my wyis to sustain you," I said. "We should try it."

"Somewhere in this conversation is a double entendre," Aiden said with a snort.

I rolled my eyes. "Please don't make some inappropriate joke. This is serious."

"I'm trying very hard not to. So let's have at it before I do."

I ignored his suggestive smirk. "Stop being dirty and just turn yourself into light."

Aiden transformed into a ray of light reflecting on the wall. I focused my wyis on him.

"Do you feel more power?" I called to him.

There was no answer, but he probably couldn't answer. His ray of light disappeared. Where did he go?

I looked around and found him on the other side of the room. He disappeared again, then reappeared on the ceiling. His light bounced from wall to wall, so fast I couldn't keep up.

Apparently, whether in light or human form, he remained an unfocused ball of energy that couldn't keep still and couldn't decide where to stay.

"Stop moving," I said, feeling my impatience flaring up. "I can't direct my wyis into you if you don't stay in one place."

I didn't know if he'd heard me. If he had, he wasn't listening because he continued leaping around the room.

My frustration overcame my concentration. Aiden reappeared next to me in his normal form.

He gave me a sheepish look. "Sorry, it was a struggle to direct my wyis internally when I was light. It's like I naturally wanted to direct it somewhere else, but I didn't know where to focus. That's why I kept moving. We can try again if you want."

I sighed. "I don't have enough energy to try again. Maybe tomorrow."

"Are you mad at me?"

"No. I just wish I could figure out how to take away tin-chai."

"You will," he said. "I believe in you. But maybe turning me into light isn't the answer. When I was in light form, I didn't feel like I was capable of doing anything. The only thing I felt was restless and unsure what you needed me to do. I think the answer still remains within you. Somehow, Old Grandfather Heaven is going to give you enough power to be able to take away Welder's tin-chai."

I nodded, but Aiden's words didn't make me feel any better. I didn't want him to just believe in me. What I really wanted was his reassurance that he would help me figure it out. That we'd work together to defeat Welder. But I didn't think it would be much use telling him so. We'd only end up arguing, and I was already exhausted.

"I'm tired. Let's just go to bed. I'll be able to think better in the morning."

"Okay." He kissed my forehead, then my stomach. "Good night, baby girl."

His gentle tone appeased me a bit. "Could be a boy," I said.

"This isn't a debate. It's a girl. Good night."

I closed my eyes and tried to sleep. Even though I was tired, my mind kept racing. How was I going to take away Welder's tin-chai? And let's say I did manage to unlock that power. What if I could only remove his tin-chai? His Faux-blood magic was the most dangerous, but never in history had I heard of the scepter's powers affecting other types of magic besides tin-chai.

Yet I believed that Old Grandfather Heaven didn't just exist in the Shyan kingdoms. And he didn't just care about the Shyan people. He had to exist outside of us and protect all nations and tribes. After all, the Ailo prayed to him. So did the Miyu women, though they had their own mythology around Old Grandfather Heaven.

As for the Yao tribes, Sago once said she didn't pray to Old Grandfather Heaven. She believed we were responsible for our own choices, and our destiny couldn't be decided by any deity in the sky. But she also admitted to believing there was a higher power somewhere, reaching into each of us to give us courage and strength if we chose to accept it.

Then there was Fauxhemia, who didn't worship Old Grandfather Heaven at all. They worshiped San, the deity of deities, said to control all nature and magical forces in the universe.

But what if Old Grandfather Heaven and San were the same being, just known by different names?

I said a silent prayer. *Old Grandfather Heaven, you know better than I how dangerous Welder is to the Shyan kingdoms and to the rest of the world. So if you are truly the deity of deities and the protector of all nations and people, then help me. Tell me how to strip Welder of his magic and his power.*

With that, I fell asleep.

In my dreams, I found myself standing in front of my childhood home. The gate was open, and bright purple peonies bloomed around the stone lion sculptures that decorated the entryway of the courtyard. From within, I heard the notes of a zither.

A woman's voice sang.

"United in love, the two shall become one

He shall be fire who bears the flame

And she who sees life's future present

Shall further give or take away."

Her voice sounded so familiar. Mama? It couldn't be.

I walked into the courtyard to investigate. I passed my bedroom on the west side and my brother's room on the east. Then there, sitting on the stone bench in the center of the courtyard were my mama and baba. Baba's friendly grin spread across his face. His kind, gentle eyes watched me. Next to him, Mama sat with a zither in front of her. She was playing it. But as I approached, she stopped and looked up. Her expression was as serious as ever. Rarely had I seen her smile.

I walked closer, in disbelief. "Baba, Mama, is that really you? What are you doing here?"

"It's good to see you, my darling girl," Baba said. "Come sit next to me. We've come here to talk to you."

He patted the space between him and Mama. I sat, looking at him and back at Mama.

"We were sent to speak to you," Mama said.

I gaped, still in shock to see them. "Who sent you? Old Grandfather Heaven?"

"To you and to us, he is known as Old Grandfather Heaven," Baba said. "But he's known by many other names in our world and the worlds beyond our reach. He has heard your cries and your prayers, and he sent us to give you guidance."

"Guidance about Welder," I said. "I don't know how to defeat him."

Mama played the zither again. This time, Baba joined, singing.

"United in love, the two shall become one

He shall be fire who bears the flame

And she who sees life's future present

Shall further give or take away."

They stopped and looked at me again.

"Old Grandfather Heaven has already given you the answers you seek," Baba said.

"You mean it's in the song," I said. "I know that already. But I still don't understand."

"Old Grandfather Heaven has given you the power to give and to take away," Mama said. "You hold the Will of Heaven, and you can strip Welder of his power."

"But I've tried. I failed. I don't have enough power in my wyis to channel through the scepter."

"You aren't the only one who holds the Will of Heaven," Baba said. "The White Moon is powerful on her own. She controls the tide, guides the birds in their migration, and decides the length of a day. However, she still needs the light of the sun to reveal herself in the sky."

Baba always liked to speak in metaphors and stories. Sometimes I didn't get it, but this time, I knew exactly what he meant. "Yin and yang. I've already guessed that I need Aiden's help to use the scepter on Welder. And I know Aiden can become light, which I'm guessing is the key. But how?"

"Old Grandfather Heaven put your baba and me together because we worked better as partners," Mama said. "Your baba was my sun, and he focused his light on his moon to make me feel seen in a way I never had before. Your sun needs to learn how to focus his light on you."

"Focus his light on me? I still don't understand."

"The two of you haven't been working together lately," Mama said. "You've been acting apart, on two separate missions. Learn to connect and work together. When he focuses his light on you, and you on him, your power will increase exponentially."

I still wasn't getting how we were supposed to connect. Were we supposed to combine our wyis to take away Welder's tin-chai? And how was Aiden's light supposed to help us do that? Even if we figured it out, it didn't solve the other problem.

"Let's say we do unlock the power to take away Welder's tin-chai," I said. "He has Faux-blood magic in him. If we can't take that away, too, then he'll still be unstoppable."

Baba pointed at the sky. I looked up and realized all three moons were visible tonight. Something that would be catastrophic if this were not a dream.

"Did you know we only had one moon when the world was created?" Baba asked. "But the White Moon was powerful, and she became prideful, so Old Grandfather Heaven decided to split her into three parts. He set the other two pieces of her closer to our world, and they became the Lavender and Sapphire Moons. When all three moons are high in the sky, there are both devastating and beautiful effects. They create destructive tidal waves and cause winter to come in summer, but they also bring new species of plants and animals into existence. They are all part of the same moon, capable of many things and more that are yet to be discovered. And they all need the sun's light to be visible to us."

"Why are you being so cryptic?" I asked. "Just tell me what you mean."

"I know what your baba is trying to tell you," Mama said. "You've already uncovered so many hidden layers of your tin-chai without the scepter. Now that you've been given the scepter, it only adds to the possibilities of amplified tin-chai yet to be discovered. Who's to say your power doesn't extend beyond what you think is possible? You just have to try."

"So you're saying you believe I have the power to take away Welder's Faux-blood magic?" I asked.

"The important thing isn't that I believe it but that you believe it," Mama said. "I was wrong before about your voice being dangerous and something to fear. Your voice is a gift that should be cherished. You've used it to change the world for the better, and you must believe that it has the power to continue doing so. I'm proud of you."

Never in my childhood had I heard Mama utter those words, *I'm proud of you*. I felt tears in my eyes.

"I believe in you, my girl," Baba said. "You'll be able to figure it out. But I'm afraid our time here has come to an end. We need to go."

"Remember," Mama said. "Your voice is powerful, and that makes you unstoppable."

I opened my eyes, waking in my bed. The sun was fully out, and I realized it was already early afternoon. How had I overslept this late? This pregnancy must be making me more tired than usual.

I looked next to me, but Aiden's spot was empty. Why hadn't he woken me up?

I sat up and saw a note on the dresser beside the bed addressed to me in Aiden's scrawl. My heart pounded. No. He was forming a pattern of leaving, and if this was happening again, I'd kill him.

Rilla,

Welder is drawing close to the border with the Seracedarean army. I left before dawn with Daki, Colonel Beyling, and five hundred Emberwood soldiers. The royal council and Captain Kang will remain at the capital to protect the palace as they see fit. Now that you're with child, I need to be sure you are safe and protected. I can't lose anyone else in my life. I know you're furious right now but try not to take it out on Sito. I put him in charge of watching you.

Aiden

Strike the thought of killing him. I was going to kill Sito first. Then I'd kill Aiden.

CHAPTER 41

✦ ✦ ✦ ✦ ✦ ✦ ✦ ✦ ✦ ✦

I stormed through the palace looking for Sito. I found him in the meeting room with the royal council. Miah was there as well. Also, to my surprise, Sago. Everyone appeared to be in a serious discussion. Without me. This, of course, only added to my aggravation.

Sito looked up, saw me, and blanched. He stood. "Before you say anything, I think you should calm down. We're in front of the whole council."

I felt him try to assert his wyis on me. "Don't you dare use your tin-chai on me. I don't care who's here. I'm furious."

Despite telling him this, I still felt a wave of calmness putting a damper on my anger. Damn Sito.

"Doesn't matter how much you try to calm me down," I said. "I would still punch you if we were in private. Why wasn't I informed of this meeting or that Sago was here?"

"She arrived early this morning," Sito said. "You were still sleeping, and since you're in a delicate condition, I told the servants not to wake you. It's what my cousin told me to do."

"You're this close to me using tin-chai on you," I said, pinching my fingers together.

Sago stood and hugged me. "I'm glad to see you, child. Congratulations are in order."

"Yes, and apparently everyone thinks excluding me from everything is a part of my pregnancy," I said.

Captain Kang cleared his throat, reminding me of the royal advisors' presence. "Rilla, since you're here now, I insist you join us. You didn't miss much. We just started. And by the way, it wasn't the council's idea to exclude you. I told Sito to wake you up. I think I speak for everyone on the council when I say we should have listened to your warnings. We won't make that mistake again."

All the men in the council stood. "Hear, hear." They bowed, a gesture that expressed sincere apology.

My anger dissolved a bit. "Thank you for your apology. Let's just figure out how to defeat Welder now."

Lord Tu smiled at me. "A gracious queen indeed."

The council sat back in their seats, and I did the same.

"We were discussing how the Yao and the Ailo nations have decided to become our allies," Lord Pan said.

I turned to Sago and Miah. "Really?"

Sago nodded. "I convinced the other Yao leaders to defend Emberwood and fight alongside you. We are in agreement that Welder is a threat to all nations and must be stopped."

"My father as well," Miah said. "He and five hundred Ailo are on their way to the border to help the king's army. Brix and Mottle are with them."

"Thank you," I said. "This is great news. But who agreed to letting Aiden leave before deciding how to employ our allies?"

"He left before we received the news," Lord Tu said. "Some of us voiced our concern to him that we might wait a bit and discuss his decision with you rather than being so hasty, but he was adamant."

"He wanted to get to the border before Welder does," Sito added. "And he knew you wouldn't let him leave without you."

I curled my hands into fists, frustration tensing up my whole body. "He can't keep making these decisions without me. We're supposed to be a team. That's why we both received the Will of Heaven together. He could have at least asked for my opinion."

"I told him that as well," Captain Kang said. "I reminded him that leaving you out of the decision-making hasn't ended well in the past. But the king said we can't all be at the same place, fighting the same battle. He asked Sito and me to stay here with the queen's guardswomen and a hundred of the king's army. We're to be the capital's defense. If Welder gets past the border, the palace is the first place he'll come."

A good point. One I hadn't thought of. But I remembered my dream.

"You don't understand." I wrung my hands, desperation coursing through me. "Last night, Old Grandfather Heaven sent my parents to speak to me. My parents said the White Moon needs the sun's light. Aiden's light needs to focus on me. Only then can we defeat Welder."

Sito gave me a wary look. "What does that even mean? Are you sure Old Grandfather Heaven actually sent your parents to give you answers? Sometimes a dream is just a dream."

I wanted to shout at him in frustration, but his tin-chai was still affecting me, and my tone came out even. "You don't have to believe it was really Old Grandfather Heaven or my parents, but the answers I found in my dream do make sense. Aiden and I were given the Will of Heaven together. So to use the scepter to defeat Welder, we need to work together."

Sago stepped forward, placing a hand on my shoulder. "Rilla is right. I might not believe in your deities, but I do trust her intuition and her power to utilize the scepter's magic. If she believes she needs to combine her power with Aiden, then she needs to go find him."

"Thank you," I said. I could always count on Sago to support me.

"We'll have your guardswomen and Sito take you to the battlefield," Captain Kang said.

"But what about the defense here?" Sito asked.

"We have things under control," Lord Pan said. "Captain Kang is here to lead the soldiers, and the council will make decisions in the king and queen's absence."

"The Yao are ready to do whatever you need as well," Sago said. "I will tell the Yao leaders to send our people here. We'll help you keep watch over the palace and this city."

I gave Sito a look that said I was not going to take no for an answer. "Any further questions?"

Sito sighed. "No."

"Good," I said. "Then let's move."

It took two hours for us to drive our coaches to the border and the village of Ashin, where we'd received reports that a battle had already started.

As we entered the city, I could smell the stench of death and destruction. Bodies littered the ground, soldiers and civilians. There were more dead Emberwood soldiers than Seracedareans. A few Ailo as well. Some bodies were twisted up and mangled by vines, others broken and in pieces from flying rocks or wind gusts. All dead from powerful tin-chai. Buildings had tumbled and burned, and debris blocked the roads.

We found the Emberwood army and the Ailo soldiers camped out on a field to the north of the village. Hundreds of feet across the field, lights flickered from where the Seracedarean camp lay. It seemed they had ceased fighting for now.

I went up to a soldier. He looked exhausted but gasped and stood straight when he saw Sito and me.

"Where is the king?" I asked.

"I-I don't know," he stammered. "But General Daki is over in his tent. I can tell him you're here, Your Highnesses."

As he said this, Daki walked out of the tent and spotted us. His gaze widened and he strode over. "What are you doing here?"

"We've come to help." I gestured to the guardswomen behind me. "We need to get to Welder. Aiden and I have to use the scepter together to take away his powers. Where is Aiden?"

I scanned the camp but didn't see him.

"I've been trying to find him," Daki said. "Haven't seen him since the end of the last battle." He rubbed at his temples. "I don't know if we can win this. The Ailo arrived early this morning to help us, but even then, we'd already lost a hundred men."

Blasts and shouts sounded in the distance. Rocks and wind swirled in the air above the Seracedarean camp.

"They're getting ready to attack again," Daki shouted. "Soldiers, on the defense."

"Guardswomen," I said. "You need to help get me close to the enemy camp. Close enough for them to hear me sing."

I signaled to Felicity and Lina. "Felicity, use your tin-chai along with me. We'll do double the damage. Lina, amplify our voices. Both of you, stay close to me."

We charged. The Seracedareans catapulted rocks at us. The ground rumbled, threatening to make us lose our balance. They were using all their tin-chai against us.

Our soldiers incinerated the rocks, helping my guardswomen and me inch further. The wind was strong, trying to force us back. A rock grazed my cheek where Empress Limera had branded me. I felt liquid on my face. Blood. I wiped at it and continued on.

I could see the first line of Seracedarean troops on their horses coming toward us.

I motioned to Felicity and Lina. "Now."

I sang louder than I ever had before. Beside me, Felicity echoed my words.

"You can try to douse my fire

And spit on all my dreams.

My light will grow brighter

For the world to see."

Lina channeled her wyis into our voices and blasted the music toward the Seracedareans. The first line of soldiers cried in anguish and fell off their horses. The skin on some of the men formed rashes and boils. Other men, affected by Felicity's tin-chai, keeled over and writhed in pain on the ground. We kept singing.

Now we were in the heat of battle. The Seracedarean soldiers attacked on foot.

The guardswomen sprang into action. Miah attacked, pummeling a soldier to death with her body. Galai sent her watery arms into two men at the same time, drowning them. Wray fired her blood-filled canister. Sparkling diamond mist traveled through the air.

Several soldiers screamed and cowered on the ground. "Ghosts. Don't let them get me."

Nena fired her canister, and her blood shot into the air. The trees grabbed those soldiers, thrashing them in the air.

Ponch gutted a man with her sword. The other guardswomen continued to attack. Felicity and I kept on singing with Lina amplifying us. We aimed for any Seracedarean in sight.

And then, I heard the sound of a trumpet followed by a shout. "Retreat!"

The Seracedareans backed away, fleeing back to the hills. I couldn't believe it. We had won this battle.

But Daki came to me wearing a grim expression. "Don't celebrate yet. More Seracedareans have been spotted a few miles from here. At least five hundred."

"That means we're outnumbered three to one," Sito said.

"Any sight of Aiden yet?" I asked. That stupid man would kill me with worry.

Daki was interrupted from answering as a soldier stepped forward.

"General, I have bad news."

Daki groaned. "I don't think I can take any more but go ahead."

"Our scouts saw Welder leading three hundred men around the hills into Emberwood."

Daki swore. "All this time, we thought Welder was here, but he must be using this battle to distract us."

"He's leading those men to the capital," Sito said.

"I have more news," the soldier said, looking grim. He handed Daki a note.

Daki scanned it and turned white.

Sito read the note over Daki's shoulder. "Rilla, you need to sit down for this."

"Just tell me," I said. "Is it about Aiden?"

Sito nodded. His hands curled into fists. "It's a ransom note. Welder has taken Aiden hostage along with Cirisa, Carrick's child."

CHAPTER 42

✦ ✦ ✦ ✦ ✦ ✦ ✦ ✦ ✦ ✦

I trembled and took the note from Daki, reading it for myself.

I know you have it. Can't believe I didn't try to change the hair stick back until last night. I shouldn't have underestimated you. I've taken your king and Princess Cirisa with me back to the Emberwood capital. You know what I want. Meet me at Linlang by sundown, or both of them die.

"He wants the scepter in exchange for Aiden and Cirisa," I said. "I need to get back to Linlang Palace."

The ground shook violently. An earthquake. We took cover. Eventually, the shaking stopped.

"The Seracedareans are just sending a message for now," Daki said. "They're getting ready to attack again." He looked up at the hills and pointed. "Look."

In the distance, there were so many Seracedarean soldiers that it looked like the mountain was covered in black. They weren't moving yet, but they could at any moment.

"What do we do now?" Sito asked. "Rilla is one of our most powerful weapons, but if she doesn't leave now, she won't make it back to the capital in time."

"I can stay," Felicity said. "My voice might not be enough, but I'll fight until my dying breath."

"I'll stay, too," Lina said.

Another soldier next to Daki made a sound of alarm as though he'd sensed something. His pupils elongated like binoculars, and he squinted, blinking at what lay ahead. "General, more troops behind us. They're approaching fast."

Daki swore. "Are you telling me we're surrounded?"

"I don't think they're Seracedarean troops. They don't have the same uniform. I think they might be Fauxhemians. One of them is almost here."

"Fauxhemians? Are you sure?" Sito asked.

"They've got gold and white uniforms. They look tall, and most of them have blonde hair."

"What are they doing here?" Daki asked.

"Guess we'll find out." I pointed to a single rider who had just stopped at our camp.

The man got off his horse. His profile seemed familiar though I couldn't see his face.

"It's Prince Lymere," Sito exclaimed.

Sito ran to meet him. Daki and I followed.

Prince Lymere bowed. "We have come to assist you against Welder. I'm sorry it took so long to keep my promise to you, Rilla."

I blinked, astonished, almost forgetting to bow back until Sito nudged me. I gave a hasty bow. "Your Majesty. I thought Queen Esmeralda decided against joining us."

"She did," he said. "But I am about to become king now that my father has passed, and I told Esmeralda that I will make decisions for my kingdom from now on. As much as I love her, I can't sacrifice Fauxhemia simply for public approval of my marriage to Essie. I told her that even if her reputation is destroyed and the priestesses won't acknowledge us as husband and wife, I won't let anyone pressure me into taking another bride. Essie will be with me for the rest of my life, and I know San will forgive her for defending herself and her mother against my father's cruelty. But right now, I can't stand by and allow Welder to grow in power and eventually come for Fauxhemia. Essie has to realize she can't make the decisions anymore. Especially not decisions that are my responsibility to make. So I'm here now with my army, and we've already started fighting. I hope you don't mind."

Daki stared at him. "What do you mean? There are at least five hundred Seracedarean soldiers about to attack, and your army is here."

"Oh, this is only half of my army," Lymere said. "The other half is up there. See for yourself."

We looked up at the mountains. Gold-uniformed soldiers suddenly came behind the Seracedareans, shooting arrows. There were shouts and cries. Fearful cries. The black uniforms were running around in chaos, making it easier for the Fauxhemians to kill.

"We've mastered our blood magic to use as poison that goes into the tips of our arrows and into canisters that spray in the air," Lymere said. "The Seracedareans are having all kinds of hallucinations. I don't imagine they'll be able to fight anytime soon. When more of them come, we'll be ready."

"You're a pure genius, my friend." Sito slapped Lymere's back. "You'll make a great king."

Lymere beamed. "I rather think so, too. So let's go. We've got to take over the rest of Seracedar now. Take over the palace."

"I have to go back to Emberwood first," I said. "Welder is there, and he's taken Aiden and Princess Cirisa hostage."

"And I need to go with her," Sito said. "Aiden asked me to protect Rilla, and I'm not going to abandon my duty."

"Yes, you go and save your king," Lymere said.

"We'll finish the fight here," Daki said. "Then we'll go back to the capital."

I let Lina and Felicity stay to fight with the soldiers, but I took the rest of my guardswomen with me. Along with Sito, we drove back to Linlang Palace, arriving to see the Yao and Emberwood soldiers defending the capital. Fighting had broken out all over the city's streets. Homes had been destroyed, coaches had been overturned, and civilians were huddled away, trying to stay out of sight.

We got out of our coaches and continued toward the palace on foot. But as we approached the front doors, Oren barred our entry with a line of Seracedarean soldiers.

My guardswomen attacked, fighting the soldiers with all that they had.

"No tin-chai," I shouted.

But Oren ignored them, letting the soldiers continue fighting. Instead, he came straight for Sito and me. Ponch and Jun stood by, bracing themselves.

"Finally, I get my revenge," Oren said.

Sito intercepted first. "Sleep," he said. Oren's eyelids fluttered closed, but Ret jumped down from the terrace.

"No, you don't," Ret said.

"Watch out, Sito!" I shouted.

Ret spun a circle around Sito, and before any of us had the chance to help, he had a knife to Sito's neck. "One word out of you, and I'll kill you, Your Highness."

Oren had snapped back to attention. He grinned at the sight of Sito being held captive. "Another hostage."

"Don't do this," I said. "I can help you save your brother and Ret's sister."

Ret looked at me, and I could see his hand loosening its grip on the knife. "You would do that? Really? Why should I trust you? You disfigured my sister in the first place."

"I'm sorry about what I did to your sister, and I wish I hadn't," I said. "I was only thinking of getting away from Terran. But now she's no longer a serving trifle, and with Terran dead, she no longer has to be. I can heal her and make her ten years younger. She'll have the chance to start her life over."

"Don't listen to her, Ret," Oren growled. "She caused your sister pain. Welder promised to save her."

"He hasn't though," Ret said. "All he's done is humiliate us and treat us like godogs. Sometimes I wonder if he'll ever keep his promise."

Oren grabbed Sito away from Ret and held his knife to Sito's neck. "If you're going to get soft, then I'll deal with this."

Ret pulled away. He held his hands up in surrender. "I just want my sister to be healed." He turned to me. "I'll fight on your side as long as you save her."

"I promise," I said.

"Coward," Oren spat.

Ret ignored him, joining my guardswomen in fighting the Seracedareans. He ran at several Seracedarean soldiers, spinning around them. A few of them fell through the loosened dirt, and rocks piled on them.

"I can save your brother, too," I said to Oren. "Just let Prince Sito go."

"My brother's dead," Oren growled. "It's too late. He died last week. Because of the injuries you gave him."

He lifted the knife, about to take the finishing blow. But then Sito disappeared. Oren jolted up. "Where did he go?"

I realized Jun had disappeared, too. And then she and Sito reappeared behind me.

Oren gaped. "How did you get past me?"

"You can't steal my tin-chai unless I'm on the offense," Jun said. "In this case, I was simply trying to defend Prince Sito." She looked at me. "I can learn, too. Sometimes winning requires a softer approach."

"We'll fight him," Ponch said. "He can't steal my tin-chai either, and I'm twice the fighter he is. Go Rilla."

I rushed through the double doors and into the front lobby. Sago, in fox form, was fighting three men in the entryway. Behind her, a daowolf Yao fought two other Seracedarean soldiers. Sago struck her opponents down with her tails and ripped out their hearts. At the same time, the daowolf ripped off one of the soldier's heads. He turned to the other man and clawed him through the chest.

Sago saw me. "They headed to the Water Crystal Courtyard. Welder has five men, and more men infiltrated the palace. They've destroyed everything in sight."

"Welder has the child and Aiden," the daowolf said. "We tried to go after them but got held up here." He swore. "More of them incoming."

From the corridors to my left, a dozen more men stormed in from within the palace. The daowolf sneered through bloodstained teeth as he stood before them. "Leave them to us. I've plenty of room in my stomach for more Shyan hearts."

"Go," Sago said. "Don't worry about us." She turned, her tails whipping through the air as the men attacked.

I wasted no time and ran toward the glass elevator. But the glass had been smashed, and the lift hung askew, dangling from a snared rope. I turned down the hall and headed up the emergency stairs.

One step after another, I climbed. The stairway curved, each flight feeling steeper than the last. Sweat drenched my body. I huffed and puffed, my lungs screaming at me to stop.

Finally, I reached the landing of the Water Crystal Courtyard level. I burst through the door that led into the open corridors. No one was there. Not a guard or a servant. The servants must have been evacuated. At least I hoped they were safe. But the silence was eerie. I kept my sword up in front of me knowing at any moment someone could spring an attack.

But no attack came, and I reached the end of the corridor that brought me to the courtyard and the clear, frozen lake that covered the ground. I looked out across the courtyard at the gazebo that stood in the center of the lake, and there they were. Welder stood with five of his men. Three guards had their swords pointed at Aiden, who had his hands covered and bound behind his back. The other two guards stood next to a bird cage hung from the ceiling of the gazebo. Inside, I could see the one-year-old princess. Thankfully, Cirisa was sleeping for now. I hoped she slept through this until I could rescue her. The guards had their swords pointed at the open bars.

"Hello, Rilla," Welder said. "We've been waiting for you. First of all, put your weapon down."

"Don't listen to him, Rilla," Aiden said.

"Shut your mouth," Welder snapped. "Drop your weapon, or I'll cut out his tongue first."

I hesitated, but seeing as I didn't have much choice, I complied and placed the sword on the ground. I didn't need it anyway. Aiden was here, and I had to trust that Old Grandfather Heaven would help us get the chance to use the scepter on Welder.

One of the guards came forward and grabbed my sword.

"Do you have what I want?" Welder asked.

"Yes. Let them go."

"You can't give it to him, Rilla," Aiden said. He struggled against the bonds. One of the guards struck him in the face. He staggered, falling to the ground. The guards took turns beating him.

"Stop!" I shouted.

Welder motioned for his guards to stop. "That was a warning. If he speaks again, I swear he'll lose an ear or better yet, his tongue."

"Keep quiet, Aiden," I said. "Let me handle this."

The guards pulled Aiden back up. He gave me a sullen look but kept his mouth shut.

Welder smiled. "Good. Now show me the scepter. Move slowly."

I pulled out the scepter from my cloak and waved it.

"You were quite clever," he said. "Stealing my blood to use my tin-chai. I didn't even realize how you did it until last night, when I discovered you stole back the scepter. Must have been when Sago challenged me to a fight just to whiplash me. You're lucky to have her on your side, or you wouldn't have been able to get this far."

"Old Grandfather Heaven allowed me to make the right friends," I said. "But why do you want the scepter so much? I thought you don't believe in the Will of Heaven anymore."

"I don't. I stopped praying to a deity who would allow injustice and tragedy to come to those who worked hard and did their duty all their lives," he said. "He did nothing for me. It was only when I started taking things into my own hands that everything started falling into place for me."

"If that's true, then why are you so scared of letting me keep the scepter?"

"I'm no fool," he said. "The scepter is filled with power. I never said Old Grandfather Heaven is a myth. I know he's real, which is why I need to defeat him and his plan. As long as I have the scepter, Old Grandfather Heaven can't use you or anyone else to stop me." He glared at me. "I don't have to explain myself to you. Hand over the scepter."

"Let them go first."

He paused, tapped his foot with impatience, and pretended to think for a moment. Then he said, "You know what? Since you're being hesitant, I've changed my mind. One hostage dies now. The other will be spared once you give me the scepter, or they will die, too."

"Wait, that wasn't the deal," I said.

"I don't care. Now make your choice. Who gets to live?"

"No. I won't do that. Release both of them."

"Choose now," he snapped. "Or I'll kill both."

The guards moved, one of them putting the tip of the sword to Cirisa's face. The child woke up and started howling. Another guard sliced his sword across Aiden's shoulder. They took turns beating him again.

"Stop!" I cried. "Don't do this."

"Choose Cirisa," Aiden shouted between beatings. "Forget me."

"I can't," I screamed. "I can't do this on my own. Don't abandon me again. Only you can be my light. Do you understand? Be my light and focus on me."

Understanding dawned in his eyes for a second. I felt his wyis reaching out to me, focusing on me. Then he disappeared. The bindings that had been on his hands dropped to the ground. The guards gasped, looking for him.

I saw his form, a beam of light. His light form entered into me, and I could feel his wyis mingling with mine.

Welder roared. "What happened? Where did he go?"

The scepter shook in my hands. With Aiden's wyis melding with mine, our power became one. We directed our wyis into the scepter. I sang the scepter's song.

"United in love, the two shall become one

He shall be fire who bears the flame

And she who sees life's future present

Shall further give or take away."

The power in the scepter grew. It lit up, glowing, then becoming fire in my hands. But it didn't burn me. I felt the power travel from the scepter and move in several directions all at once.

Screams resounded around me. I looked around. The guards dropped their swords, the metal clanging onto the frozen lake beneath us. The koi fish scattered away.

The guards fell on their knees, shaking, their shrieks sounding more of fear and confusion than pain. One of them looked at Welder like he was a helpless child.

"I can't use my tin-chai," he said. "I felt it leave my body." He lifted a palm and looked at a rock. "It won't move. Why won't it move?"

Welder stared at me in wonder and shock. He scanned the ground, looking for something. He found a leaf, touched it. Nothing happened. "Change, damn it. Why aren't you changing?"

Then to my surprise, he laughed. "I can't believe it. You've finally figured it out. My theory was right. It was all in the song. You and Aiden had to combine your power to take away tin-chai."

"Surrender yourself," I said. "This fight is over."

Welder continued laughing. "You may have taken away my tin-chai, but I still have my Faux-blood magic. And my soldiers still outnumber you." He gestured to his men.

"Pick up your weapons, you fools. Maybe she took away your tin-chai, but you should still be able to fight."

One guard picked himself off the ground. He reached down for his sword, but the weapon fell from his hands. "Why can't I remember how to use a sword? Twelve years of training, and I don't even have the strength to lift it."

The other guards picked up their swords, but they also stared at the weapons, their expressions stunned.

"Leave," I said. "Or I'll finish the job and sing you to sleep."

They ran away, leaving Welder alone with me and Aiden's light within me. Our wyis blended together was stronger than anything I'd ever felt.

Welder breathed out. "Impossible. You couldn't possibly take away a soldier's ability to fight."

"It is quite possible," I replied. "The song that the scepter sang spoke of giving and taking away, but it never limited that ability. Looks like Aiden and I can take away more than just tin-chai. Non-magical, learned abilities. And I have a feeling if we try it another time, we can take away Faux-blood magic as well."

"It can't be." Welder roared in anger. He came at me, sword high. I forced the power from the scepter into his body. Sparks of electricity and bursts of light came out of the scepter and entered him. He flew back, hit the gazebo wall, and fell to the ground.

He was still conscious, but a crazed expression took over his face. "What did you do to me? I feel so weak."

The scepter shook again, but this time, its fire burned off, returning to its original form. A burst of light flew out of me, transforming back into Aiden.

Welder stood and shouted at Aiden. "I want to see it with my own eyes. It's not possible that you stole my Faux-blood magic. I still have Oren's blood in me. So attack me. Attack, you coward."

Aiden looked at Welder with pity. He lit up a flame in his palm. Welder stared at it as though trying to will it into himself. But the flame remained in Aiden's control.

"No," Welder screamed. He fell back to the ground, looking like a lost child.

Aiden, still on guard, watched Welder. I went over to the bird cage, broke open the door, and took the child into my arms. She was wailing and looked so scared.

My heart softened. The poor girl had been through so much.

"You're safe now," I whispered to her. "I'll always protect you, I promise."

She looked into my eyes, and her crying faded into sniffles. She cushioned herself more comfortably in my arms. As I cradled her, the Emberwood soldiers poured into the courtyard. Sago was with them.

"We managed to subdue the Seracedareans," Sago said. "The remaining soldiers have surrendered."

"Thank you, Sago," Aiden said. "We couldn't have done this without you and the Yao."

"You're welcome," she said. "We're friends, and we faced a common enemy." She nodded at Welder, who remained on the ground. "I see you were successful."

Welder was hitting another leaf.

"Stop doing that," I said. "Get up."

Welder still didn't look up or give any indication that he'd heard me.

He dropped the leaf and found a different one. "Become the scepter." He hit it. "Why aren't you listening to me?" He tore it up, looked up at the heavens, and laughed.

"Bree, did you see me?" he shouted. "I made the scepter. I'm going to conquer the world and avenge you. Old Grandfather Heaven can't stop me. I made the scepter."

Welder started singing. "United in love, the two shall become one . . ."

I looked away. It was such a sad sight.

"Guards," Aiden called. "Take this man away. He will remain in prison until we determine his punishment."

Sago looked at him with what looked like pity. "Will he be executed for his crimes?"

"I'm not sure," Aiden said. "Taking away all his magic almost seems like enough punishment. Maybe worse. To live a life without power, still obsessed with revenge."

As the guards took Welder away, he continued singing the same phrase on repeat. "And she who sees life's future present shall further give or take away."

"He's been driven to madness," I said. "I hope Old Grandfather Heaven helps him to heal."

"In any case, he will serve as an example to the Seracedareans," Sago said. "They will pledge their loyalty to you, for fear that you will take away their tin-chai."

CHAPTER 43

✦ ✦ ✦ ✦ ✦ ✦ ✦ ✦ ✦ ✦

In the days following, we counted our losses and stayed busy rebuilding the capital and restoring the palace. There was a bit of bad news from Ponch and Jun. They said Oren had managed to escape when more soldiers had come to help them. One of them, forgetting about Oren's tin-chai, had used his fire tin-chai, allowing Oren to steal it and get away. We sent men to find him, but the boy had vanished. I hoped he wouldn't cause trouble in the future. I hoped he decided to find his happiness and wouldn't let revenge fuel his mind as Welder had. But if he did come back one day, I'd have to be on guard.

I had Galai and Miah take care of Cirisa while Aiden and I took care of matters around the kingdom. Cirisa seemed to be healthy, though she cried frequently. She was barely a year old and had gone through so much trauma already. Of course, Aiden and I could never replace her parents, and we wanted to make sure she always knew about Arlyn, Radi, and Carrick. But I hoped we could give her a happier childhood in the coming years and that maybe one day she'd come to regard us as another Mama and Baba.

Aside from caring for Cirisa, I was busy healing as many as I could in the city, including the Seracedarean soldiers, though most of them seemed to fear me and cowered when I sang a single note. Sito helped calm them down. After I sang to a few patients, the soldiers saw I was healing and not killing, and eventually, they began to relax around me without Sito's influence.

As I did this, Aiden met with Daki and Prince Lymere, who had returned from their victory at the border. They had brought back the commanders of the Seracedarean army, Kenbo and Laht, as well as the traitors who sided with Welder. They were willing to negotiate terms and pledge their allegiance to Emberwood or accept whatever fate Aiden decided for them.

One night, Aiden and I returned to our chambers, exhausted. Aiden sighed, getting into bed. He turned to me.

"I don't like being the one administering punishment. For the traitors, I'll gladly do it. But the Seracedareans were just trying to defend their people. Yet they look at me like I'm a monster that might kill them any second."

"We need to address this in our speech tomorrow," I said. "This is a new era. We're to be two kingdoms, united as one, and we have no wish to be like their former emperors."

"The question is how to make them believe it." Aiden sighed, closed his eyes, and two seconds later, a snore emerged from his throat.

I smiled. The man could sleep anywhere at any time and under any kind of stressful condition. Careful not to wake him, I kissed his forehead, then went to sleep.

Early the next morning, we prepared to address the kingdom, which would also be broadcast from Shyan sound amplifiers into Seracedar. I knew this was going to be the most important speech of our lives. No pressure at all.

I took Aiden's hand, and we walked out onto the balcony. Lina stood behind us, acting as the first sound amplifier who would transfer our words to the other sound amplifiers standing amidst the people.

I looked out at the crowd below, which extended into the streets beyond the palace. I'd never seen this kind of turnout. It looked like everyone in the city had come to hear our address.

Aiden cleared his throat and began his part of the speech.

"Fellow Embers, first I'd like to thank all of you for your support and bravery. It's because of you that we have been able to claim victory over Welder. But more importantly, it's because of you that we're now reunited with our brothers, the Seracedareans.

"To the Seracedareans, I want to say that we do not claim victory over you. We claim victory *with* you. For too long, the Seracedarean people have suffered at the hands of one corrupt emperor after another. Emperors who have tainted the power of the scepter and used the belief in the Will of Heaven to do as they pleased and to make their subjects fear them. But Rilla and I don't wish to instill fear into anyone. We wish to build you up, not bring you down. To support you to become stronger, not step on you to make ourselves stronger. We want to become the kind of rulers that listen to the citizens and who work alongside you to create a better future."

Applause sounded, and Aiden gestured to me to continue with my part.

"Our wish is to bring peace to both Shyan kingdoms. Old Grandfather Heaven gave the right to rule to both of us. But for a time, we had to remain separated. Had to learn lessons on our own.

"In my time apart from Aiden, I learned to be capable on my own. The power Old Grandfather Heaven gave me alone was strong enough to do many things. And Aiden was able to accomplish difficult tasks without me as well. But in order to defeat Welder, we had to come together. Our power combined was stronger than anything I could have done on my own. As you already know, I am a Seracedarean, and Aiden is an Ember, and Old Grandfather Heaven brought us together to soon be united in marriage. Likewise, it's through our marriage that we are now able to build a bridge between our kingdoms. Seracedar and Emberwood were once nations divided, each with their own strengths and weaknesses. But my hope for the future is for Seracedar and Emberwood together to make a stronger, greater nation that will bless each other and bless our neighbors. We are all Shyan, and I ask all of us as one people to usher in a new era of change. Because we are truly stronger together."

Aiden and I raised the scepter together. Music played, but it wasn't only in my head. Everyone could hear it coming from the scepter.

Scanning the people, I located a Seracedarean girl, about twelve or thirteen, sitting in a chair. Her parents were behind her. She looked sad, and I saw that she was missing one leg. Maybe the family had decided to flee here after their home was destroyed. Welder had burned down so many villages.

The girl was also a koong, I realized. Reading her wyis, I knew she had no tin-chai.

I'd failed in my attempt before to use the scepter to give a koong a tin-chai. My wyis hadn't been strong enough. I also had never used my normal healing tin-chai to replace someone's missing limb. My wyis wasn't powerful enough to heal what was already dead and gone. It was why I couldn't save everyone who was on the brink of death.

But for this girl, maybe it was possible to restore her leg and give her a tin-chai through the scepter. After all, Old Grandfather Heaven had said that together, Aiden and I had powers through the scepter beyond what we could even imagine. My wyis combined with Aiden's was strong enough to take away Welder's tin-chai and Faux-blood magic. Why not healing and the giving of tin-chai as well?

I turned to Lina. "Amplify my voice to that family with the girl in the chair."

She nodded, and I spoke. "What is your name?"

The girl looked to her left and to her right, then up to me in surprise. She pointed to herself, a question in her eyes.

"Yes, you."

"Kailin," she said. The sound amplifier closest to her directed her voice back to me.

"Kailin, King Aiden and I are glad to meet you and your parents," I said. "We hope we can make you feel welcome in your new home here in Emberwood. Is it all right if I use the scepter's power on you?"

Kailin nodded, her gaze wide. Her parents burst into tears.

I turned to Aiden. "Here's your chance. You can be a healer with me."

He grinned. "Let's do it."

We both focused our wyis on the scepter. Aiden turned into light, and his form entered into me. The scepter became fire.

I pointed the scepter at Kailin, and I sang an old favorite, one Lady Arlyn had loved.

"My love, she is a summer rain,

Renewing this parched soul.

She marks the end to all my pain;

She's the cure to make me whole.

Only she can make me whole."

A light shone through her, and a new leg formed on her body.

She got up from her chair, a look of shock on her face. Her parents cried out in disbelief as well. Kailin tested her leg, wobbled a bit, and found her balance. Shock turned into joy.

But Aiden and I weren't finished yet. Again, I aimed the scepter at Kailin.

"My love, he is a sturdy tree,

A shield on stormy nights.

He gives me strength to be set free;

He's the sun that gives me light.

Only he can be my light."

Her body filled with light once more. This time, she transformed into a bird. She flew high into the sky and came up to me. She landed on the balcony next to me and shifted back into Shyan form.

"I can't believe it. I was flying," she exclaimed. "I thought I'd never walk or dance again. But now I'll be able to travel the entire world like I always dreamed."

She beamed at the crowd as a chorus of awe went through them.

Aiden flew out of me and became his physical form. He took his spot next to me.

"May you always feel safe and loved in Emberwood," I said, and Aiden nodded in agreement.

"Fly as far as you wish," he said. "But don't forget to return home once in a while to see your family." He nodded to her parents, who were crying happy tears. They waved at us, and we waved back.

"Thank you, Your Majesties."

The crowd applauded her. The sound was deafening.

I kissed Kailin's head. She transformed back into a bird and flew down to rejoin her parents in the crowd.

The shouts and applause grew louder. All the Emberwood subjects bowed. "Long live Queen Rilla and King Aiden. May they live a thousand years and a thousand more."

But it wasn't just Emberwood. We could hear the sound amplifiers coming from Seracedar. The Seracedarean crowds were chanting, too.

"Old Grandfather Heaven has spoken. Long live Queen Rilla and King Aiden. May they live a thousand years and a thousand more."

CHAPTER 44

✦ ✦ ✦ ✦ ✦ ✦ ✦ ✦ ✦ ✦

The months flew by. We rebuilt the capital, and Seracedar was on the way to a better future as we helped invest in better technology and equipment for the farming and fishing villages. It was going to be a long road to complete recovery, but we were determined.

We also finally had our wedding. I was about five months pregnant, and Aiden wanted to make sure we were married before the baby came. It was a lot less formal than the first wedding we'd attempted as we decided to invite only close friends. Rell, Nia, and Tristan attended and planned to stay until after I gave birth.

All my guardswomen were my maids in waiting. Cirisa was my flower girl. Ponch guided Cirisa down the aisle. She was supposed to drop flowers from a basket down the aisle, but she dumped the whole basket over her head. It was a disaster, but it was perfect.

However, the wedding was still a bittersweet moment. We still had no cure for Aiden's parents, and they continued to be under forced sleep hypnosis so they wouldn't hurt themselves. All was not lost, though. A few months before, King Lymere had managed to convince Queen Esmeralda to donate a vial of her blood to us. How he did it, I'd never know. I supposed they really did love one another. The two of them were engaged, and no amount of bad publicity would stop Lymere from marrying Esmeralda, not even the priestesses who still wanted Esmeralda to give up her blood before they gave their approval.

I didn't know if Esmeralda would be able to hide her Faux-blood and involvement in Lieka's poisoning forever, but for now King Lymere was still determined to save her from ruin. He made us promise to keep the blood donation private and develop the antidote in our own lab.

We hadn't been able to get an antidote before the wedding, and I knew how disappointed Aiden was. Even more frustrating was that there was no guarantee we could develop an antidote at all. I wished I could take away his sadness and figure out a cure by myself.

But I trusted Sito. He assured us that he was leading a team of the best researchers in the kingdom on the project.

One afternoon at the clinic, I took a break from my morning counseling work with patients. These days, I felt like I was in the body of a wailing wanpo. I was nine months pregnant, and the baby would be coming at any time. I just wanted it to get out of me. I couldn't sleep in any position that was comfortable enough, and my ankles were as thick as sycamore trees. Despite this and all the work I had as queen of two kingdoms, I still kept some of my hours at the clinic, which I found to be the most fulfilling.

I sat on the bench to watch Ponch lead a group of guardswomen-in-training practice their martial arts. Most of the original guards-women had left the clinic and gone on to start new life phases. I was proud of all of them. Some stayed in touch, while others did not. But life continued on. New patients came and went every day. Ponch, Galai, and Miah were still here, working with me as counselors. Our work here would never be done.

An excited cry sounded behind me. Aiden's voice burst through the clinic.

"Rilla, they got it. They finally got it."

He ran across the garden towards me. Sito was close behind him. Both of them wore wide grins on their faces. It could mean only one thing.

"You have the cure?" I stood, feeling the stir of hope in my chest.

"We're 99.8 percent certain," Sito said. "We ran tests in the lab on shurats, and,"—he paused, saw my face—"don't worry, none of them were killed. All that's left to do is try it on the patients, which we're here to do now."

Aiden took my hand, looking hopeful but also hesitant. Like a kid who dared not expect much having been disappointed too many times before. "Will you come with me?"

"Of course." I smoothed my hand across his, trying to offer support and comfort.

We walked over to the other medical building, where Doctor Flamyor worked and where the patients with physical ailments were treated. Ashbel and Leonora had been staying in a suite there, observed by a team of highly skilled doctors and healers with powerful tin-chai to keep them comfortable in their sleeping state all these months.

Sito looked confident. He strode briskly and wore a proud expression. "I'm so happy our hard work has paid off. Well, I shouldn't say it for certain until my uncle and aunt wake up, but if it doesn't work this time, we're definitely close."

His words gave me hope.

Aiden, on the other hand, stayed quiet. He must have had so much on his mind. I rubbed his arm. He looked at me and smiled, though I could see apprehension in his eyes.

We entered the suite where Ashbel and Leonora lay side by side. Whenever we came to visit, they both looked as though they'd been frozen in time. They were completely still, but I could see their chests rise and fall in a steady rhythm.

A window surrounded the suite, and outside were the former king and queen's team of caretakers. I knew several had a similar tin-chai to Sito's, which allowed them to take turns keeping Ashbel and Leonora in their comatose state.

Doctor Flamyor entered the room. She held a tray with two syringes filled with liquid. She set the tray down on the table and looked at us. "Your Majesties, this is a simple process. I'm going to inject the antidote into their blood and then take them out of their sleep induction. We will be able to determine if the cure works when they wake up, which shouldn't take long. Do you want to wait here? We can call you when they wake up."

"We'll wait." Aiden held onto my hand tighter.

Doctor Flamyor inserted the needle into Ashbel first, injecting the antidote. Then she did the same to Leonora. When that was done, she gestured to the team through the window, and a woman nodded. The woman moved her hands and said some words I couldn't hear.

"They've been taken off the sleep induction," Doctor Flamyor said. "Now we wait."

Fifteen minutes passed. Neither Ashbel nor Leonora stirred.

I glanced at Aiden. He was quiet, and tension strained his body.

"I've been waiting for this moment for so long," he said. "Now that it's come, I'm having so many mixed feelings."

"It'll be all right," I said. "If this doesn't work, we'll try again."

"It's not just that. Once they wake up, they'll be king and queen of Emberwood again. I want nothing more than to see them well, but I've also gotten used to making the decisions. What if things go back to the way they were with my ah-fu and ah-mu telling me what to do?"

"We've got the scepter, and we're still king and queen over Seracedar," I said. "That makes us equals with them whether they like it or not. It'll be an adjustment, but you'll have to remain firm and stand your ground even if they use guilt to manipulate you. I don't think it will be easy, but with time, I hope they'll learn to respect both of us as adults and kingdom leaders."

Aiden grinned. "You always know what to say. I feel much calmer now." He nodded in Sito's direction. "Poor guy looks worse than me, though. It's too bad he can't use his tin-chai to calm himself down."

Sito paced the room and wrung his hands. He looked nervous. Like he was waiting for the results of a huge exam that would decide his future career. He looked at Doctor Flamyor. "Shouldn't they be conscious by now?"

"It could take longer than expected," she said. "After all, they've been under sleep induction for a long time."

"Sito, why don't you take a seat and breathe?" I said. "I'm sure—" A sudden sharp pain stopped me from finishing. I'd never experienced this kind of pain before.

I was going into labor.

No, not now. What horrible timing. Maybe I could hold it off.

"Is something wrong?" Aiden asked. "You look pale."

"It's nothing," I said. "I just—I hope for Sito's sake they wake up soon. He's wearing a hole in the floor with all that pacing."

Spasms of pain started again. I bit back a cry. *No, baby, no. Stay in for a little bit longer.*

"My uncle's hand moved," Sito exclaimed. "I saw it."

Aiden jerked up, got out of his seat and rushed forward. I stayed seated. The spasms were coming on closer together. I tried to take my attention off of the pain and focused on Ashbel and Leonora.

"My ah-mu is waking up, too," Aiden said. "Her eyelids fluttered."

Ashbel opened his eyes first. His gaze was filled with confusion at first, but he looked at Aiden, and recognition appeared. He moistened his lips, and when he spoke, his voice was groggy. "Son, what's going on? Aren't we supposed to be at your wedding?"

There was clarity in his gaze, something that hadn't been there when he'd been hallucinating from the effects of Clox's poison.

Sito shouted a joyous cry. "It worked!"

Now Leonora opened her eyes. "Where am I and why do I feel like I've been sleeping for a hundred years?"

I heard Aiden answer, but I couldn't pay attention to what he was saying. The pain was coming on stronger. I gritted my teeth. *Hold on. Just a little longer.*

Doctor Flamyor checked Ashbel's vitals, then Leonora's. "Both Your Majesties appear to be in good health. As far as I can tell, the antidote has done its job."

I felt something wet drench my clothes. Doctor Flamyor turned to me first, and her gaze widened. "Rilla, you're going into labor."

"Yes," I grunted. "Seems that's the case."

Aiden looked at me in shock. "Why didn't you say anything?"

I was taken to another private suite down the hall. Seven hours and a horrible amount of pain later, I carried my baby boy in my arms. But looking at him made me forget the pain.

Aiden had left once while I'd been in labor to check in on his parents, but now he stood next to me, wearing a look of shock and awe as he stared at the baby we'd created.

"How are your parents?" I asked.

"Fine. On their way to full recovery." He reached out his arms. "I want to hold him now."

I transferred our son into Aiden's arms. Aiden made little cooing noises. "I've never seen a baby this beautiful."

A knock sounded, and Sito entered carrying Cirisa. Rell and Nia followed with Tristan. They opened the door wider, and out in the hall, I saw Ponch, Jun, Daki, Galai, Miah, and some of the other guards-women.

"The doctor said it was okay for us to come in," Sito said.

"Come see your baby brother," I said, gesturing to Cirisa.

Sito carried Cirisa closer, and she set her gaze on the baby.

She smiled and stretched out her hands, wanting to touch him. Aiden brought the baby closer to her, and she gently patted the blankets that swaddled him.

"Have you decided what to name him yet?" Rell asked.

Aiden and I looked at each other. We'd discussed a few options, but none of them had really clicked.

"We're going to learn more about our baby's personality first," I said. "That should help us decide."

Our visitors took turns looking at the baby, everyone oohing and aahing. I shifted in the bed, trying to get more comfortable. The pain and exhaustion were getting to me.

Nia patted my shoulder. "You need to get some rest." She gestured to all the visitors. "Everyone except Aiden has to leave now. Let the new mama have some privacy."

She ushered everyone out and closed the door behind her.

Aiden and I stared at our baby.

"I can't believe we made him together," Aiden said.

I shot him a look. "Well, I did most of the hard work."

He kissed my cheek. "I won't dispute that."

"We really should name him soon," I said. "The kingdom is going to want to know what to call their new prince."

Aiden gave me a hesitant look. "Actually, I have something in mind."

"Oh? Well, don't keep me in suspense."

He took a deep breath and exhaled. "Carrick Marseas Ai." He paused. "How do you feel about that?"

I smiled, staring into my baby's face. "It's perfect."

Our baby let out a loud cry.

"Whoa, that's a powerful voice you've got there." Aiden rocked our son in his arms.

My smile grew wider.

GLOSSARY

✦ ✦ ✦

CHARACTERS

AIDEN LANG/PRINCE LANGDON AI—(EY-den LAHNG/LAHNG-den EYE) *The crown prince of Emberwood; holds a fire tin-chai*

AMIKA—(ah-MEE-kah) *The Miyu princess*

ASHBEL—(ASH-bell) *The Emberwood king and Aiden's father*

BEYLING—(BAY-ling) *A colonel and royal advisor in Emberwood*

BREE—(BREE) *A Fauxhemian princess who committed suicide after being forced to become Terran's faela*

BRIX—(BRICKS) *A diplomat from Ailo Kingdom*

CARRICK—(KEER-ick) *The newly crowned emperor of Seracedar*

CIRISA—(suh-REE-sah) *Carrick's daughter and the princess of Seracedar*

DAKI—(DAH-kee) *A shatooth Yao and the admiral of the Seracedarean navy with the tin-chai to create transport vessels*

DRIBIN CLOX—(DRI-been CLOCKS) *An assassin of Fauxhemian descent*

ESMERALDA—(EZ-ma-RAL-dah) *The queen consort of Fauxhemia Kingdom*

FELICITY—(FUH-lih-SUH-tee) *One of Rilla's guardswomen who holds a tin-chai to inflict pain through her singing voice*

FLAMYOR—(FLAME-yore) *A doctor in Emberwood who supervises Rilla during her training*

GALAI—(ga-LIE) *Rilla's childhood friend who holds a tin-chai to transform into water*

JUN—(JOON) *One of Rilla's guardswomen who holds an invisibility tin-chai*

KANG—(KAHNG) *A captain and royal advisor in Emberwood*

KENBO—(KEN-boh) *A lieutenant of the Seracedarean army*

LAHT—(LOT) *A colonel of the Seracedarean army*

LEONORA—(LEE-oh-NOR-ah) *The Emberwood queen and Aiden's mother*

LIEKA—(LIE-kah) *The king of Fauxhemia Kingdom*

LINA—(LEE-nah) *One of Rilla's guardswomen who holds a sound amplifying tin-chai*

LYMERE—(lie-MEER) *The crown prince of Fauxhemia Kingdom*

MIAH—(MY-ahh) *The princess of Ailo Kingdom*

MOTTLE—(MAH-tol) *A diplomat from Ailo Kingdom*

NENA—(NEE-nah) *One of Rilla's guardswomen who is a Fauxhemian with blood magic to communicate with nature*

OREN—(OR-ehn) *A soldier who is also Welder's right-hand man and holds a mysterious tin-chai*

PAN—(PAN) *A nobleman and royal advisor in Emberwood*

PONCH—(PAHNCH) *The leading counselor at Linlang Clinic who becomes Rilla's bodyguard; holds the tin-chai to hear minute sounds*

RADI YING—(REY-dee YEENG) *Carrick's wife and the empress of Seracedar; holds tin-chai to form gold when dancing*

RET—(RHETT) *A soldier who works for Welder; holds a tin-chai to move at fast speeds*

RILLA MARSEAS—(RILL-ah MAR-see-aahs) *The story's protagonist; has a tin-chai to heal and to kill (and more) with her voice*

SAGO—(SAY-go) *A fox Yao and overprotective mother*

SITO—(SEE-toh) *Emberwood prince and Aiden's cousin; holds a tin-chai of persuasion using his voice*

RIFE—(RYFE) *The chief magistrate of Bellflower; holds a tin-chai to move metal*

TRINE—(TRYNN) *Another counselor at Linlang Clinic who is also a maocat Yao*

TU—(TOO) *A nobleman and royal advisor in Emberwood*

VENN—(VEHN) *One of Rilla's guardswomen who has a tin-chai to disguise people into anyone else*

WELDER—(WELL-der) *General of the Emberwood army; holds a camouflage and transformation tin-chai that changes objects into any other object*

WRAY—(RAY) *One of Rilla's guardswomen who is a Fauxhemian with blood magic to summon the dead and talk to spirits*

WYLE—(WHY-el) *A fox Yao kit; Sago's son*

YIN—(YEEN) *One of Rilla's guardswomen with a tin-chai to control electricity*

YISA—(YEE-sah) *The Miyu queen*

ZELDA—(ZEL-dah) *The Fauxhemian Chief of Diplomatic Affairs*

✦ ✦ ✦

SEVEN KINGDOMS OF CALIWYIS

(CAL-uh-WEES)

AILO—(EYE-low) *Kingdom of Ailo, a race of rock dwellers who were conquered by Seracedar and became a tribute kingdom*

EMBERWOOD—(EHM-ber-WUD) *Kingdom of Embers, also of the Shyan race who rebelled and started their own kingdom two hundred years ago*

EXENTRIA—(ex-EHN-tree-ah) *Kingdom of the Exentriks, technologically advanced people who can banish ghosts and demons with their magic*

FAUXHEMIA—(fo-HEE-mee-ah) *Kingdom of the Fauxhemian race, artists and storytellers with magic*

MIYU (MEE-yoo) ISLANDS—*Sea nation of fish-shapeshifting women warriors said to descend from the sea goddess Mi (MEE)*

SERACEDAR—(SEER-ah-SEE-der) *Kingdom of Shyan people, a race born with tin-chai, unique magical abilities controlled through four channels*

YAO—(YOW) *Kingdom of Yao, a race of animal spirit shapeshifters conquered by Seracedar and who became a tribute kingdom*

✦ ✦ ✦

PLACES MENTIONED

BELLFLOWER—(BELL-flower) *A village in Seracedar*

CASCASEA—(KASS-kah-SEE-ah) *Protagonist Rilla's hometown. A fishing village in Province Ca*

CANDLELACE—(CAN-dull-LAYCE) *The main port of Emberwood*

CINDERTRANCE—(SIN-dehr-TRANCE) *A city in Emberwood*

DAWNING—(DAHN-ing) *The capital of Fauxhemia*

ENYI—(EHN-yee) *An ocean in Caliwyis that lies between Emberwood and Fauxhemia*

LINLANG—(LEEN-lahng) *The capital of Emberwood*

MORROW—(MAHR-roh) *A town in Fauxhemia*

SENLIN CITY—(SEHN-leen) *Imperial City*

✦ ✦ ✦

OTHER TERMS

AH-FU—(AHH-FOO) *The Emberwood term for father*

AH-MU—(AHH-MOO) *The Emberwood term for mother*

FAELA—(FAY-lah) *The Shyan term for concubine*

FAUX-BLOOD—(FO-blood) *A Fauxhemian with magic in their blood; type of magic depends on the color of their blood (diamond, sapphire, amethyst, emerald, rainbow)*

KOONG—(KOHNG) *A Shyan born with no magic*

TIN-CHAI—(TIN-chhye) *A Shyan's magical ability*

WYIS—(WEES) *Spiritual energy*

ZHUME—(ZHOO-may) *The Ailo term for princess*

ACKNOWLEDGMENTS

Rilla's adventures may have concluded for now, but there's no such thing as a happily ever after *forever*. New challenges always spring up, threatening to dismantle the safety and comfort we've grown accustomed to living. Whether or not we like it, we're once again required to adapt and grow. I'm sure this will be the case with Rilla, and perhaps one day, I'll return to writing another tale about the girl with the dangerous, powerful voice. Because I'll always be grateful to Rilla, Aiden, Carrick, and Radi, who helped me develop my writing voice and my personal voice.

I also have many real-life people who have been pivotal in helping me find my voice and in encouraging me to actually complete this whole trilogy.

First, of course, I have immense gratitude for my parents, who raised me and taught me that being kind and having good character is far more important than being a doctor or having lots of money and status. I know you worry about me, and you might not agree with all the decisions I make, but I do appreciate the space you've given me to figure out how to be an adult on my own.

A shoutout to my brother, who has a big heart and makes sure to tell me his thoughts on all the latest movies and anime.

My grandparents, both maternal and paternal sides. Your rich life histories give me the inspiration to write more.

The usual suspects. Tiffany Wong, Esther Kim, and Christina Colorina. My book club ladies and friends who have read the earlier drafts of these books. Christina, you saved me when you had a draft of Book 3 that I'd forgotten to transfer from my old to my new computer years ago. I'm so grateful to the entire Colorina family for coming out to my book events no matter how far (thanks to Ron for driving) or out of the way. You make time for your friends.

You make your friends not only feel loved, but know they are loved.

My friends for life, Wing Taketa (shoutout to Cameron), Cindy Shao, and Jean Tseng, I'm so thankful for your encouragement, and I'm blessed to have you in my life. And Rie Takata, who did the art and the map for my books, I'm eternally grateful to you, even through the silence and distance. I'm always here for you, and I hope you're doing well.

Melanie Hooks, thank you for your bright personality and wonderful friendship. I can always count on you to talk about all things writing and life. I love how we've become closer now than when you lived just a few cities away. Your phone calls always make my day better.

Jordan Duncan, thanks for being my foodie and travel buddy, but most of all, thanks for encouraging me to keep writing books when I feel like giving up.

Sonya Stephens, you believed in me from the beginning. Thank you for reading my drafts and being such a loyal friend and supporter.

The Hui family, who I'm so grateful for having met. Thank you for your support and encouragement. First, the SoCal Huis, whose friendship means so much to me, especially Auntie Helen and Uncle Edmund, whose generosity and hospitality have been a light in my life, and Emy and Arthur, who have been so friendly and helpful. Elsie, I'm so thankful for having you in my life. Thanks for your friendship and for being like a big sister to me. Second, the NorCal Huis, who have also been so encouraging. Janelle, Auntie Shirley, and Uncle Edmond, I'm thankful that God let us meet, and you felt like family in the time we were able to have together. And of course, Nate, who will always have a special place in my heart.

I'm always and eternally grateful to Holly Kammier and Jessica Therrien, who loved my story from the beginning and continue to believe in me. I will always remember that conference where we met, and I know God dropped you in my life at the perfect time.

Molly Lewis, the greatest editor ever. Thank you for supporting my voice and helping me make sure my writing executes my power in the best way possible. I love the way you call me out whenever I'm being lazy with the details. I've become a better writer throughout this trilogy because of you.

To the greatest, cutest cats, Lumi and Lucas. Thank you for being my cuddle buddies on the cold, dark nights.

And last but not least, words can't express my appreciation for all the readers and writers who have supported me, whether we've met in person or interacted through social media. I love you all.

AUTHOR BIO

After graduating from UC San Diego, Christina Fong built her career as a food scientist, but she never gave up on her true calling, writing poems and YA fantasy novels based in Asian American culture. She especially loves reading and writing about underestimated good girls who are pushed too far and must embrace their dark side to kick some butt. When Christina isn't writing, you can find her jamming out to her girl crush, Taylor Swift, or playing with her adorable munchkin cats, Lumi and Lucas.

www.ingramcontent.com/pod-product-compliance
Lightning Source LLC
Chambersburg PA
CBHW020601310726
48979CB00008B/1301/J

* 9 7 9 8 8 8 5 2 8 0 8 5 3 *